Desire

Also published by Handheld Press

HANDHELD CLASSICS

1 *What Might Have Been: The Story of a Social War* by Ernest Bramah

2 *The Runagates Club* by John Buchan

4 *Vocations* by Gerald O'Donovan

HANDHELD RESEARCH

1 *The Akeing Heart: Letters between Sylvia Townsend Warner, Valentine Ackland and Elizabeth Wade White* by Peter Haring Judd

2 *The Conscientious Objector's Wife: Letters between Frank and Lucy Sunderland, 1916–1919*, edited by Kate Macdonald

Desire

Una L Silberrad

with an Introduction by Cornelia Wächter

Handheld Classic 3

First published in the UK in 1908 by Hodder & Stoughton, London.
This edition published in 2018 by Handheld Press Ltd.
34 Avenue Heights, Basingstoke Road, Reading RG2 0EP
www.handheldpress.co.uk

ISBN 978-1-9998280-2-8

1 2 3 4 5 6 7 8 9

Series design by Nadja Guggi and typeset in Adobe Caslon Pro and Open Sans.

Printed and bound in Great Britain by TJ International, Padstow

Contents

Cornelia Wächter is Assistant Professor (*Juniorprofessorin*) of British Cultural Studies at the Ruhr University Bochum, Germany. She is the author of *Place-ing the Prison Officer: The 'Warder' in the British Literary and Cultural Imagination* (Brill, 2015) and co-edited *Middlebrow and Gender, 1890–1945* (Brill, 2016) with Christoph Ehland.

ACKNOWLEDGEMENT
The publishers gratefully acknowledge permission to publish this edition of *Desire*, from Hugh Silberrad on behalf of the Una L Silberrad estate.

Introduction

BY CORNELIA WÄCHTER

Una Lucy Silberrad was the author of thirty-six novels, several volumes of short stories and a guide to Dutch gardens, published in a steady stream of productivity between 1899 and 1944, yet she is barely remembered today. In 1903, a reviewer for *The Pittsburgh Press* claimed that Silberrad was 'rapidly coming into prominence as one of the strongest recent English novelists [...]' (1903, 10), and by 1915 she had been declared a 'well established [novelist]' by the *Irish Times* (1915, 3). In *Letters to A P Watt*, the literary agents A P Watt & Son include her in their list of 'well-known' clients alongside G K Chesterton, Winston S Churchill, Wilkie Collins, Sir Arthur Conan Doyle, H Rider Haggard, Thomas Hardy, Rudyard Kipling and W B Yeats (1909, xii). Nevertheless, and unlike many of her, especially male peers, she fell into obscurity in the 1950s (Macdonald 2014, 5). Silberrad shares this fate with numerous other female middlebrow writers – authors who were prolific and successful at the time of their writing but whose impact was overshadowed by attention to their male contemporaries by later critics.

Critical assessment of the modernist period, in which Silberrad was publishing, notoriously privileged avant-garde experimentation over realism, the masculine over the feminine, elitist exclusivity over mass appeal – with obvious consequences for the work of writers who did not meet these selective criteria. Since the 1990s, more female writers have been given critical attention, especially those who worked outside the modernist spectrum. Una Silberrad is one of those whose work has been rediscovered in this way. She wrote about 'the middling people of the middle class, so neglected by the novelist – except for the purposes of caricature' (*The Academy* 1909, 780), and her novels understood and reflected the society of her time.

Silberrad was born in Buckhurst Hill, Essex, on 8 May 1872, the eldest of ten children.[1] Her parents were the horticulturalist and bulb merchant Arthur Pouchin Silberrad and his wife Clarissa Savill. One of her brothers was the renowned industrial chemist Oswald Silberrad, an inventor of explosives. His university education had been funded by an uncle, the famous actor-manager Sir Charles Wyndham, and Oswald was to establish the family fortunes (H Silberrad 2014). Oswald possessed laboratories of his own at Buckhurst Hill, and shared his scientific research with his elder sister Una. Women working in chemistry and science is a recurrent theme in her contemporary novels, as well as in alchemy in her historical fiction (Macdonald 2011a, 221–222). Una Silberrad, though 'a local celebrity, left very few traces of engagement with public life' (Macdonald 2014, 7). She never married and lived with family members all her life. By 1931 she had moved to Burnham-on-Crouch, Essex, with her youngest sister Phyllis, where she continued to be active in the Women's Institute and in her Church of England parish, writing several plays for charitable performances. She died on 1 September 1955 at the age of eighty-three, eleven years after the publication of her final novel, *The Three Men Who Went to Ardath, 1760* (1944).

Silberrad began her writing career at the age of twenty-seven with *The Enchanter* (1899). Her most successful novel was *The Good Comrade* (1907), which was rapidly reprinted several times. She published with Macmillan, Heinemann, Constable (who brought out *Desire* in 1908), Hodder & Stoughton, Thomas Nelson & Sons, and exclusively with Hutchinson from 1915 onwards. In that year, *The Irish Times* claimed that she was one of those writers 'who have only to write and be published to be read' (1915, 3). Her work received a plethora of positive and sometimes even enthusiastic reviews (Macdonald 2014, 5). *Punch*, for instance, asserted that her

1 For the most extensive biographical account of Una L Silberrad to date, see Fox 2009.

novels were 'invariably good' (1914), and *The Buffalo Commercial* opined that 'a certain fine literary distinction [...] marks everything that Miss Silberrad has done' (1905, 9). Upon the publication of *Desire*, Constable advertised the novel in *The Guardian* with a quote from a *Morning Post* review that praises Silberrad as 'one of the few writers whose books become friends at once, appealing to the best in their readers' (1908, 5). The reviewer describes *Desire* as 'a well-written book; it satisfies the intelligence at the same time as it appeals to the emotions, and it sets up a fine romantic standard of life which should not be missed' (1908, 5).

This combination of pleasure and the satisfaction of intellect is not a coincidence. Numerous critics have drawn attention to the fact that any attempt at defining a dividing line between what would be categorised after the war as highbrow and middlebrow writing is futile. Nicola Humble describes both from the perspective of reading and the body. 'Middlebrow' reading is a relaxed and often reclining way of reading, whereas 'highbrow' reading involves a studious leaning forward, with pen or pencil in hand. Most importantly, both are possible with the same text depending on the context and the inclinations of the reader (2011). One can argue that a middlebrow text invites both: relaxed reading simply for pleasure as well as further scrutiny and active cognitive effort – it 'may at the same time be conducive to escapist consumption *and* include challenges to the established order' (Ehland and Wächter 2016, 3). This is certainly true for *Desire*.

Desire, the novel's protagonist, is first seen at a London '*soirée* which the artistic gave to the fashionable' (1). She is being observed by Peter Grimstone, an author whose first novel is about to be published. He is conspicuous in his refusal to even try to gain access to Desire's circle at the event, and this piques her curiosity. Peter is a provincial nobody; Desire is the independent upper-middle class daughter of Sir Joseph Quebell, a financial adviser to the government. Although she was born out of wedlock to a dancer of questionable reputation, her father treats her like a legitimate daughter, the men of her social environment flock around her and the women are (more or less secretly) jealous of her. Like many other of Silberrad's characters, Desire privileges her own value system (Macdonald 2011, 226), which renders her not just indifferent but often oblivious to the social conventions that she defies. This particularly concerns her relationships with men, whom she discards just as readily as she invites their attentions.

After she reads Peter's first novel, *The Dreamer*, Desire is deeply moved and decides to promote the book, thus launching Peter's literary career. Peter, in turn, agrees to pretend to be her new flirtation, to allow her to end her engagement. Desire's fiancé has turned out to have abandoned his long-term lover and child out of physical passion for Desire, which she considers degrading to herself. Before Peter can harness his success as an author and develop his writing, he is called home to assist his ageing father in the family pottery business in Twycross, a fictional town in Staffordshire. Desire's life also takes a decisive turn when her father dies unexpectedly and leaves her destitute. She must leave not just her home, which her unfriendly stepmother now owns, but her entire social circle, which she does with good grace and optimistic resolution. She moves to a boarding house and decides to take lessons in office work to be able to earn her living. Soon, however, it becomes apparent that her social class not only prevents her from making friends with the other students but also prejudices her chances of ever finding a job. Peter, the only person to take the trouble to search for her, finds her on the brink of desperation. Coincidentally, he is in need of help in running the family business after his father has suffered a stroke, and he offers Desire a job. Over the course of the following months, it becomes obvious that the two complement each other ideally – especially in the face of adversity, personified by Peter's brother Alexander. True to the conventions of the romance, the man has to lose the woman again before they are finally united, but eventually both settle into a relationship that is characterised by both passion and mutual respect, and they lead a life of honest labour in a remote rural landscape that contrasts starkly with the urban alienation Desire has left behind.

In their promotion of the novel for the American market, Doubleday made use of the *New York American* review: 'We think so highly of Miss Silberrad's book that we reckon it belongs among the few published this season that are really worth while' (1908a, 41). Not all reviewers were equally enthusiastic, though. *The Spectator*, for instance, gave it a less than favourable review, complaining that '[t]he opening chapters of [Silberrad's] new novel are entirely unconvincing, and the behaviour of the heroine and descriptions of life in London society are such gross caricatures as to make a very firm faith in Miss Silberrad's talent essential to the patience of the reader' (1908a). Even so, this reviewer considers that the novel improves significantly once the action has moved to Twycross, and even more so once Silberrad abstains from descriptions of society. The review ends on a conciliatory note, maintaining that while the book is 'decidedly unequal, [...] the author's charm of writing and sincerity of purpose will reward all readers who have patience and perseverance enough to proceed with the unsatisfactory early chapters' (1908).

In *The World's Work*, Doubleday advertise *Desire* with the words: 'The exquisite character drawing, the broad knowledge of human nature, which made "The Good Comrade" so satisfying a novel, is brilliantly handled in the romance of 'Desire" (1908b, 20). Even *The Spectator* grants that Desire is 'a striking figure, though Miss Silberrad is not so successful with her as with her last heroine, Julia, the "good comrade".' Peter Grimstone is considered to be 'the most attractive figure in the book, and his struggles, aided by Desire as his secretary, with the affairs of Grimstone and Son, and with the machinations of his wicked brother Alexander, are not a little interesting' (1908). At least one reviewer, however, vehemently contests the 'exquisite character drawing' proclaimed in the *World's Work* advert: 'J M', a reviewer for *The Guardian*, argues, like their *Spectator* colleague, that the novel has a two-part structure and that the second part is far superior to the first. The nature of this criticism is very different, though. According to 'J M', the first part of the novel focuses on characters, the second on 'incident or situation' (1908, 5), and it is the characterisation that they regard as deeply flawed. The severest criticism concerns Silberrad's rendering of Peter Grimstone. 'J M' avers that the author is 'ignorant, one supposes, of the ways of men' but grants her 'a sympathetic knowledge of her own – far more interesting – sex' (1908, 5). They go on to assert that 'Peter in many ways is impossible. No such man ever walked this earth in trousers' (1908, 5). Tellingly, Peter – the man who displays sensitivity and creativity, and who regards women as his equal – is discounted as a mere female fantasy. Peter's brother Alexander, on the other hand – the villain of the piece, the calculating, aggressive businessman who treats all women with contempt – is regarded as 'the most life-like man in the book' ('J M' 1908, 5). J M does qualify that '[w]e do not praise him as a portrait. We accept him, rather, as a personification of Miss Silberrad's personal antipathies' (J M 1908, 5). Yet Alexander is considered to be 'life-like' as opposed to 'impossible'. He may be exaggeratedly vicious but he is still more realistic than Peter. These distinctions shed an interesting light on gender stereotypes of the period and indicate the influence of fiction in the imaginative creation of alternative gender roles and gender relations.

Alexander corresponds to the 'bourgeois ideal' of masculinity in so far as it was defined in contrast to 'the feminine', and emphasised 'the combative initiative of the middle-class businessman and professional' in appropriation of earlier warrior ideals (Izenberg 2000, 6). This type of masculinity has often been described as 'in crisis' at this time due to female 'encroachment' upon supposedly masculine spaces of business. Another type of masculinity, that of the artist, came to be even more seriously challenged by the end of the nineteenth century: by falling short of the bourgeois ideal of masculinity and its traces of the warrior ethos, as well as by a separation of spheres which entailed the allocation of the emotional and the aesthetic to the feminine realm (Izenberg 2000, 12). Hence, it comes as no surprise that Silberrad chose a male character representing the latter type of masculinity as the love interest for her New Woman. Silberrad was not alone in this; for instance, Amy Levy in *The Romance of a Shop* (1888), and Victoria Cross in *To-Morrow* (1904) and *Five Nights* (1908), opted for emphatically artistic/writerly male protagonists in their exploration of potential new love relationships. Most notably, for female writers of Utopian New Woman fiction at the *fin-de-siècle*, the vision of the New Man was frequently that of an artist or a writer (Showalter 1999, 49).

Not just *Desire* but most of Silberrad's pre-First World War fiction can be classified as 'New Woman' fiction – an 'ideologically heterogeneous' body of works exploring gender roles and gender relations at the turn of the century and beyond' (Ardis 2004, 72). More generally, Ann Ardis points out that 'the treatment of sexuality in these works is quite diverse: while some New Woman writers celebrated women's 'discovery' of their sexual and/or maternal desires, others were social purity campaigners, valuing chastity within as well as external to marriage' (2004, 72). *Desire* belongs to the former category. Over the course of the novel, the heroine discovers both her maternal instinct and her sexual passion. The discovery of female sexuality in *Desire* is inspired by a reconnection with the protagonists' 'primitive' instincts, sparked by a reconnection with nature in Staffordshire's 'wilderness', and the characters' separation from social boundaries and expectations.

The intersection of primitivism with the exploration of sexuality is another subject that is characteristic of the period, famously represented by D H Lawrence. Unlike Lawrence, Silberrad only hints at the consummation of 'primitive passions' in a tableau of Desire at night in her nightdress, and a violently passionate embrace and a kiss. It seem as though actual sexual contact is deferred until marriage – but this ultimately remains ambiguous. From the moment Peter and Desire confess their love to each other, subsequent to Desire's return to Twycross, Desire considers themselves as 'more than half married already' (348). Thus, based on her own 'somewhat unusual standards', she decides to move in with Peter, unchaperoned and entirely unconcerned with people's opinion. What exactly this premarital cohabitation entails, remains subject to the reader's imagination.

Like Silberrad's oeuvre in general, and like much other middlebrow fiction, *Desire* does not completely reject the Victorian ideal of the 'Angel in the House'. While the novel is subversive in many respects, it remains comparatively conservative, especially in the ultimately safe containment of female sensuality in heterosexual monogamous marriage. In Macdonald's words, 'Silberrad's use of the marriage plot was perhaps the most conventional aspect of her fiction. Romance sold, and romantic novels required a love story with a happy ending, especially if they were to be sold as cheap fiction to the less highly educated' (2011a, 220).

Nevertheless, we can see a challenge contained within the containment. In line with many other writers of her time, Silberrad presents new conditions for marriage, and some of her female protagonists even prefer domestic independence (Macdonald 2011a, 222, 226). *Desire* has a conventional marital ending, but the eponymous heroine does not treat marriage as her ultimate aim in life. On the contrary, it is only under the right conditions and circumstances that she is willing to enter into marriage at all. For a large part of the novel, romance is neither on Desire's nor on Peter's mind. In fact, Desire picks Peter as her fake love interest precisely because he is the only man whom Desire trusts not to misread her intentions. Instead, the novel revolves around both characters' struggle to find their place in the world and fulfilment in occupation. In this context, they develop a business relationship (and friendship) that draws on both their individual strengths and allows them to complement each other. In *Success*, which was published three years later in 1911, Silberrad went a step further and 'allowed her female and male protagonist to conclude their successful working partnership without needing to marry' (Macdonald 2011a, 223).

The late nineteenth century saw increasing access to education and to paid work for women, which brought about a fundamental alteration in the preconditions for renegotiating established gender roles and gender relations. This also destabilised the boundaries that had structured Victorian gender relations. Consequently, it is hardly surprising that many New Woman writers explored the new occupational spaces opening up for women in their fiction. Struggles for financial as well as emotional independence pervaded New Woman fiction from its inception in the 1890s. *Desire* is one of those New Woman novels in which the death of a parent 'impel[s] the heroine towards financial independence' (Liggins 2012, 109). In choosing typewriting for her heroine's career, Silberrad opts for a distinctly 'modern' profession that gave especially lower-class and lower-middle-class women access to clerical positions and independent incomes, and she presents the opportunity of work as a feminist aspiration: 'Many men had offered her many things in the past, love and friendship, luxury and jewels, entertainment, dogs, amusements, homage – some she had accepted, some refused, but no man before had offered her work' (254). Typewriting represents technological progress, as well as monotonous drudgery and alienation – another prominent theme in the Modernist period.[2] But due to Peter's job offer, Desire is spared the mechanical toil of the profession and instead finds meaningful work in the Grimstone family business.

From the outset, a strong sense of alienation pervades the novel.

2 It is noteworthy that in Grant Allen's *The Type-Writer Girl* (1897), the heroine is also left destitute by the death of a parent and, as the title indicates, decides to become a typewriter girl to earn her living.

Desire's 'home' consists of a large hotel-like space in which 'the three members of the family did not have to meet too frequently' (14), and she describes the social circle she moves in as 'a whole lot of marionettes' (3). Although her father apparently likes her, he is detached enough to forget to provide for his daughter in his will. Desire's own search for pleasure and stimulation suggests a *desire* in the psychoanalytical sense, driven by lack and frustration. Peter's family is equally lacking in meaningful relationships. His father despises him for not being a suitable heir to his business, and Peter's mother 'had never felt more for [her first son] Alexander than the parent animal's instinct for its young [...]' (71). The only relationships in the novel deserving of the name are those between Peter and Desire and his mother.

Both homes are characterised by silence – not the comfortable silence of mutual understanding but rather as a marker of estrangement. Peter's mother, for instance, who used to enjoy conversation, is effectively silenced by her husband, and when she dares to speak more than usual, Mr Grimstone is irritated and 'fancied that it might be an indication that he was losing his old grip on things' (117). This also points to the distinctly patriarchal structures of the two families, which correspond to the dominance of father figures and, more generally, the older man in Silberrad's entire oeuvre (Macdonald 2011a, 223). Even in debilitating illness, Mr Grimstone continues to exert an overwhelming influence over his family and employees, and the power of Desire's father is equally crucial in that his wife and daughter depend on him entirely in financial as well as legal terms.

As Macdonald points out, Silberrad's work displays a conspicuous absence of positive mother figures (2011a, 222). In *Desire* too, the heroine's birth mother is dead. All we learn about her is that she was a variety actress with the reputation of being 'more beautiful than virtuous' and that Desire was born out of wedlock (37). Desire's stepmother has only one emotion, and 'that [is] dislike for her step-daughter, Desire' (15). Desire eventually builds up a loving relationship with Peter's mother, but Mrs Grimstone is so starved for attention and cast in such pathetic terms that it is Desire rather than the older woman who assumes a maternal function. *Desire* also reflects the general absence of positive depictions of siblings in Silberrad's fiction (cf. Macdonald 2011a, 222). Desire is an only child, and Peter's brother is the novel's antagonist.

Over the course of the novel, Peter and Desire both learn to overcome the intersubjective alienation that characterised both their families and, even prior to marriage, build up an intimate 'hearth-sharing relationship' (282). Desire herself contrasts it with the Quebells' 'hotel-like life [in which] it was the butler who knew one's tastes, the housekeeper who ordered the household, the sewing-maid who did the mending' (282). The narrative 'solution' Silberrad presents with regard to the more general sense of alienation is inextricably intertwined with her criticisms of capitalism. Desire, who was raised with a silver spoon in her mouth, is nonetheless immune to the lure of wealth and instead bemoans the shallowness of the world she grew up in. She only finds fulfilment and happiness once she has embraced work for its own sake. The narrator repeatedly emphasises that for Peter and Desire work is not about financial gain. The same holds true for Peter's writing. Desire observes that he will never write the kind of sensationalist and racy fiction that sells 'a goodly number of thousands' (306). Instead he is 'one who builds things, not one who does them in a flash of inspiration' (5) – and someone who builds up a strong personal relationship with his work and its final product.

Desire and Peter are contrasted with Alexander, who is the personification of capitalism. Alexander's work bears no connections to process or product since he is solely driven by the pursuit of profit. He stops at nothing to make the family business his own, yet he 'had no more feeling for the little old firm than for his father [...]' (77). Desire, by contrast, maintains that '[i]t's a bore, of course, to be without money sometimes, but one can be very comfortable without much of it' (350). Nonetheless, in order to affirm the satisfaction of the novel's end, Silberrad allows the couple to become, by their own hard work, 'comfortably off as Desire's people count wealth, quite rich as the potters count it' (350). In the end, their success is financial as well as emotional.

This joint financial success partly compensates for the couple's difference in social class – another central theme in the novel. On the one hand, Silberrad acknowledges the power of Desire's upper-middle-class *habitus*. When getting to know Desire and her social circle, even Peter, whom one of his friends describes as 'our Puritan penman, our Nonconformist conscience, our Industrious Apprentice', finds, to his surprise, that 'there's something attractive about the people who don't work, and can't work, and haven't worked for generations [...]' (9). On the other hand, Silberrad undermines any claims to superiority by virtue of that class affiliation. From the outset of the novel, the members of the upper and upper-middle classes are denigrated as superficial. Sometimes this takes an almost Wildean tone, as when Desire remarks about a friend: 'he is not such a fool as he looks; I sometimes suspect he has brains though he would blush to have it known [...]' (4). Desire is aware and makes use of the power lent to her by her status as far as her business endeavours are concerned, but her social status is not generally privileged by the narrative as a whole. On the contrary, Desire has to develop strength of character by shedding most of her privilege and by literally and metaphorically climbing a steep path through unknown and challenging terrain.

Conclusion

In its themes, Silberrad's *Desire* is a distinctly 'modern' work. It is suffused with a sense of alienation deriving from the disintegration of the family, urbanisation, capitalism, and the looming dangers of monotonous, meaningless and disassociated work and society. Silberrad resolves these issues in the novel by her characters' reconnection with nature and the rediscovery of 'primitive instincts'. This serves as an antidote to mechanised urban alienation, and reconnects workers with their work – a work that means more than financial gain. Additionally, this reconnection serves as the basis on which Peter and Desire build a meaningful and intimate relationship on equal terms. Thus, in spite of the rather conservative ending, I argue with Macdonald that 'Silberrad used her fiction to offer a critical commentary on contemporary society in that society's own terms, which marks her as a middlebrow writer before middlebrow had been categorized in the public press' (2011a, 215).

References

Academy. 1909. November 27, 1909, 780.

Ardis, Ann. 2004. 'The Gender of Modernity.' In *The Cambridge History of Twentieth-Century English Literature*, edited by Laura Marcus and Peter Nicholls, 61–79. Cambridge: Cambridge University Press.

The Buffalo Commercial. 1905. Review of 'The Lady of Lovell' by Una L Silberrad. March 4, 1905, 9.

Fox, Tony. 'Una Silberrad, Authoress, 1872–1955.' *Essex Journal* 44, no. 2 (Autumn 2009): 58–63.

Constable & Co. 1908. Advertisement. 'Desire.' *Guardian*, October 8, 1908.

Doubleday, Page & Co. 1908a. Advertisement. 'Desire'. *The New York Times*. December 5, 1908, 41.

—. 1908b. Advertisement. 'New Fiction: Desire, by Una L Silberrad.' *The World's Work* 16, no. 6 (October): 19.

Ehland, Christoph, and Cornelia Wächter. 2016. 'Introduction: '… All Granite, Fog and Female Fiction.' In *Middlebrow and Gender, 1890–1945*, edited by Christoph Ehland and Cornelia Wächter, 1–17. DQR Studies in Literature Volume 62. Leiden, Boston: Brill Rodopi.

Humble, Nicola. 2011. 'Sitting Forward or Sitting Back: Highbrow v. Middlebrow Reading', *Modernist Cultures* 6, no.1, 41–59.

Hyam, Ronald. 2010. *Understanding the British Empire.* Cambridge: Cambridge University Press.

The Irish Times. 1915. October 10, 1915, 3.

Izenberg, Gerald N. 2000. *Modernism and Masculinity: Mann, Wedekind, Kandinsky through World War I.* Chicago: University of Chicago Press.

Lane, Christopher. 1995. *The Ruling Passion: British Colonial Allegory and the Paradox of Homosexual Desire*. Durham and London: Duke University Press.

Liggins, Emma. 2012. 'Having a Good Time Single? The Bachelor Girl in 1890s New Woman Fiction.' In *Writing Women of the Fin de Siècle: Authors of Change*, edited by Adrienne E. Gavin and Carolyn Oulton, 98–110. Houndmills and New York: Palgrave.

Macdonald, Kate. 2011a. 'Edwardian Transitions in the Fiction of Una L Silberrad (1872–1955).' *English Literature in Transition* 54, no.1 (January): 212–233.

—. 2011b. 'The Use of London Lodgings in Middlebrow Fiction, 1900–1930s.' *Literary London: Interdisciplinary Studies in the Representation of London*. 9, no. 1 (March). www.literarylondon.org/london-journal/march2011/macdonald.html.

—. 2014. Introduction. *The Good Comrade* by Una L Silberrad, 5–14. Brighton: Twentieth Century Vox.

M, J 1908. Review of *Desire*, by Una L Silberrad. *The Guardian* October 14, 1908, 5.

Pittsburgh Press. 1903. October 10, 1903, 10.

Punch, or the London Charivari. 1914. Review of *Cuddy Yarborough's Daughter*, by Una L Silberrad. February 11, 1914. www.gutenberg.org/files/22573/22573-8.txt.

Ray, Carina E 2015. *Crossing the Color Line: Race, Sex, and the Contested Politics of Colonialism in Ghana*. Athens: Ohio University Press.

Showalter, Elaine. 1999. *Sexual Anarchy: Gender and Culture at the Fin de Siècle.* Repr., London: Virago.

Silberrad, Hugh. 2014. 'The Silberrad Student Centre: The Story Behind the Name'. Interview. September 9, 2014. www.essex.ac.uk.

Spectator. 1902. Review of *Princess Puck*, by Una L Silberrad. February 8, 1902, 26.

Spectator. 1906. Review of *Curayl*, by Una L Silberrad. April 14, 1906, 24.

Spectator. 1908b. Review of *Desire*, by Una L Silberrad. October 24, 1908.

Watt, A P & Son. 1909. *Letters to A P Watt*. London: A P Watt & Son.

Wächter, Cornelia. 2016. 'Middlebrow Negotiations of Lawrentian Sexuality.' In *Middlebrow and Gender, 1890–1945*, edited by Christoph Ehland and Cornelia Wächter, 259–280. Leiden: Brill.

The works of Una L Silberrad

Novels

The Enchanter (1899), Macmillan.
The Lady of Dreams (1900), Heinemann.
Princess Puck (1902), Macmillan.
The Success of Mark Wyngate (1902), Archibald Constable & Co.
Petronilla Heroven (1903), Archibald Constable & Co.
Curayl (1906), Archibald Constable & Co.
The Good Comrade (1907), Archibald Constable & Co.
Desire (1908), Archibald Constable & Co.
Ordinary People (1909), Archibald Constable & Co.
Sampson Rideout, Quaker (1911), Thomas Nelson & Sons.
The Affairs of John Bolsover (1911), Thomas Nelson & Sons.
Success (1912), Archibald Constable & Co.
The Real Presence (1912), Hodder & Stoughton.
Keren of Lowbole (1913), Archibald Constable & Co.
Cuddy Yarborough's Daughter (1914), Archibald Constable & Co.
Co-Directors (1915), Hodder & Stoughton.
The Mystery of Barnard Hanson (1915), Hutchinson & Co.
The Inheritance (1916), Hutchinson & Co.
The Lyndwood Affair (1918), Hutchinson & Co.
Green Pastures (1919), Hutchinson & Co.
Jim Robinson (1920), Hutchinson & Co.
Rachel and Her Relations (1921), Hutchinson & Co.
The Honest Man (1922), Hutchinson & Co.
The Letters of Jean Armiter (1923), Hutchinson & Co.
Joe, a Simple Soul (1924), Hutchinson & Co.
The Vow of Micah Jordan (1925), Hutchinson & Co.
Blackstones: A Novel (1926), Hutchinson & Co.
The Book of Sanchia Stapleton (1927), Hutchinson & Co.
In the Course of Years (1929), Hutchinson & Co.

The Romance of Peter Waine, Timber Merchant (1931), Hutchinson & Co.
The Will of James Mark Crane (1932), Hutchinson & Co.
The Strange Story in the Falconer Papers (1934), Hutchinson & Co.
Saunders (1935), Hutchinson & Co.
Sun in November (1937), Hutchinson & Co.
The Abundance of Things (1939), Hutchinson & Co.
The Escape of Andrew Cole (1941), Hutchinson & Co.
The Three Men Who Went to Ardath, 1760 (1944), Hutchinson & Co.

Short Stories

'A Romance of the Molehill Country', *Leisure Hour* (July 1896): 778–86.

'The Temptation of Ezekiel', *Everybody's Magazine* 5.28 (December 1901): 651–57.

'The Dower Chest of Ann Ponsford', *Blackwood's Edinburgh Magazine* (February 1903): 1048, 190–221.

'The Winning of Elizabeth Fothergill', *Blackwood's Edinburgh Magazine* 173 (May 1903): 1051, 638–667.

'Mr Smallpage's John', *Pall Mall Magazine* 30 (July 1903): 342–361.

'Priscilla's Maying', *Pall Mall Magazine* 31 (October 1903): 203–218.

'The Witchcraft of Chuma', *Harper's Monthly Magazine* 108 (Feb 1904): 645, 428–37.

'Concerning the Death of James Deering', *Pall Mall Magazine* 245 (February 1904): 156–164.

'In the Course of Business', *The London Magazine* 18 (March 1907): 43–48.

'Monsieur Abraham', *The London Magazine* 18 (August 1907): 681–688.

'The Test', *Harper's Monthly Magazine* 115 (November 1907): 690, 931–35.

'The Great Feversham', *The Cornhill Magazine* 25 (November 1908): 631–48.

'Concerning the Wreck of the Merry Rose', *Gunter's Magazine* 8 (January 1909): 6, 841–61.

'The Burning of Babel', *Harper's Monthly Magazine* 119 (October 1909): 718, 764–73.
'On a Windy Night', 1913, *The Odd Volume. Literary and Artistic*, ed. John G. Wilson, London: Simpkin Marshall Hamilton Kent, 8–23.
'The Soul of Lydia', unpublished.
'The Return', unpublished.

Short Story Collections

The Wedding of the Lady Lovell, and Other Matches of Tobiah's Making (1905), Archibald Constable & Co.
The Second Book of Tobiah (1906), Hodder & Stoughton.
Declined with Thanks, etc (1911), Archibald Constable & Co.

Plays

The Mad Lady Caryll, unpublished.

Non-Fiction

Dutch Bulbs and Gardens (1909) (painted by Mina Nixon, described by Una Silberrad and Sophie Lyall), A & C Black.

Modern editions of Silberrad's novels

The Affairs of John Bolsover, in *Political Future Fictions: Speculative and Counter-Factual Politics in Edwardian Britain*, vol. 2, *Feminist Future Fictions*, ed. Kate Macdonald (London: Pickering & Chatto 2013).
The Good Comrade (Twentieth Century Vox, 2014).

Further reading

Ardis, Ann L. 1990. *New Women, New Novels: Feminism and Early Modernism*. New Brunswick: Rutgers University Press

Ardis, Ann L., and Leslie W. Lewis, eds. 2003. *Women's Experience of Modernity, 1875–1945*. Baltimore, Md.: Johns Hopkins University Press.

Cockburn, Claud. 1972. *Bestseller: The Books that Everyone Read 1900–1939*. London: Sidgwick and Jackson.

Daly, Nicholas. 1999. *Modernism, Romance, and the* Fin de Siècle: *Popular Fiction and British Culture, 1880–1914*. Cambridge: Cambridge University Press.

Hapgood, Lynne, and Nancy L. Paxton, eds. 2000. *Outside Modernism: In Pursuit of the English Novel, 1900–30*. Basingstoke: Macmillan.

Hipsky, Martin. 2011. *Modernism and the Women's Popular Romance in Britain, 1885–1925*. Athens: Ohio University Press.

Macdonald, Kate. 2013. 'Introduction: Feminist Future Fiction' and '*Legions of the Dawn* and *The Affairs of John Bolsover*: Commentary on the texts', in Volume 2. *Fictions of a Feminist Future*, ed. Kate Macdonald, in Kate Macdonald (gen. ed.), *Political Future Fiction. Speculative and Counter-Factual Politics in Edwardian Fiction*, 3 vols (Pickering & Chatto, 2013), ix–xiv, 267–286.

Radway, Janice A. 1987. *Reading the Romance: Women, Patriarchy, and Popular Literature*. London: Verso.

Radway, Janice A. 1997. *A Feeling for Books: The Book-of-the-Month Club, Literary Taste, and Middle-Class Desire*. Chapel Hill: University of North Carolina Press.

Singer, Christoph. 2011. 'Gravitating Away from an Empire's Heart: London in Una Silberrad's *The Good Comrade*'. *Literary London: Interdisciplinary Studies in the Representation of London*. www.literarylondon.org/london-journal/march2011/ singer.html.

Chapter I

Peter Grimstone stood in a doorway looking on. Nature had given him some faculty for that, or at least endowed him with characteristics which made him content without a star part in things. He had reason to be content to-night; the company in which he found himself was in part fashionable, in part artistic, and he was neither the one nor the other; the occasion was a *soirée* which the artistic gave to the fashionable, and he had entrance there by right of a ticket handed on to him by a man who, in turn, had received it from another. He knew no-one present, and—this was stranger—had no wish to know any one. He had frankly said when he accepted the ticket he wanted to see what it was like, and he literally was seeing and nothing more.

There was a great crush; Peter recognized several well-known men. Of the women he did not know any even by sight, but though he knew nothing of the hundred distinctions there were between those present on such an occasion, he did know that some few had the appearance of being much more perfectly finished than the others. There was one not far from his doorway who particularly caught his attention; she was not really beautiful though, like others of the perfect sort, she gave one an impression of it, a more lasting impression too, than greater beauties among them. Her hair and eyes had a curious red shade in them, and she was tall and powerfully built, with a beautiful strong body which followed natural lines in defiance of fashion. Her dress rather defied fashion too, for in spite of a general taste for things which stuck out hers clung about her, winding round her when she walked and revealing the splendid strength and grace of her movements in a way Peter admired—at least he did till he caught the moist eye of a man at his elbow fixed on the beautiful figure. Then he looked away, vaguely ashamed.

At that instant the woman glanced round and caught his look. She said something to her companion, she had a man with her: a succession of men had sought her notice. This one glanced towards Peter, without interest, and Peter was momentarily amused, for his utter insignificance removed him as far from any one present as if he wore a cloak of invisibility.

A stout dowager and a famous artist passed; they paused a moment while the lady made some gracious speech; when they moved she of the red hair was alone, her cavalier dismissed on some errand. Two others quickly took his place, and Peter, himself no longer under observation, watched her again until the dismissed one returned. The kaleidoscopic crowd came between, and Peter lost interest in him; when he next saw him he was approaching Peter himself; almost unavoidably their eyes met, and as they did so a look of recognition came into the stranger's.

'Why!' he exclaimed, 'it is you! I've been puzzling over your face no end. Who'd have expected to see you here?'

'No-one would,' Peter answered, with truth. He was a good deal nonplussed, it was almost as much of a shock to be accosted in this crowd as in solitude. He also knew the stranger was mistaken and he said so.

'What! you've forgotten me?' the other said. 'I'm Bamfield.'

Peter was perfectly sure that he had never seen the man before to-night, he had not even known any one of the name; he said so politely. But the other did not heed, probably did not hear, there was a continuous noise of talk and music going on, also he was speaking himself, apparently quite assured of Peter's identity and the sufficiency of his own explanation.

'Beastly crush,' he said; 'no end of strange animals here. I suppose you don't know any one hardly?—don't know many myself—one or two of our people. D'you know Miss Quebell? I'll introduce you.'

Now Peter Grimstone was an essentially straightforward person, but when the man who had called himself Bamfield mentioned Miss Quebell, and glanced towards her of the reddish hair, Peter hesitated—then went.

He was introduced, but he did not catch by what name though he listened. Miss Quebell said she was glad to meet him, or some other commonplace, which would have sounded nothing in another voice but which in hers had an alluring, almost personal note new to Peter. He wondered who she took him for; she was very gracious and even allowed him the coveted seat beside her, but no word she uttered helped him.

In a little she dismissed the obliging Bamfield. When he had gone she turned to Peter. 'Well,' she said abruptly, 'what do you think of us all?' Peter was surprised alike by the question and the intimacy of the manner. In his limited experience one made acquaintance—if one did it—by slow degrees, and he hardly knew how to answer. 'I don't think I quite understand what you mean,' he said.

'Yes, you do,' she retorted; 'you stood in your doorway and looked on at us, at the whole lot of marionettes, like a man from another planet, till I was inclined to come behind you and demand your thoughts. Perhaps you think I am rather doing that now? So I am. What is your opinion of us?'

'I don't think I have got one,' Peter answered truthfully. 'You see, I am not in a position to have one. I don't know anything about any one here.'

'Don't you really?' she said with mock gravity. 'I thought you looked as if you knew everyone here.'

Peter, who watched her face all the time she spoke with earnest gravity, smiled. Then he made his confession— 'I don't know that man, Bamfield, who introduced me to you; I don't know who he took me for, but I am certainly not he.'

'How can you be sure of that?' she asked. 'If you don't know who he took you for you can't know you are not he. Why shouldn't you have made the mistake and not Mr Bamfield?'

'I never saw him before,' Peter persisted. 'I don't know any one—of his sort.'

'"Of his sort"!' she laughed. 'Poor thing! He's an idler, I grant it, a mere fetcher and carrier, but you need not entirely relegate him to 'a sort'—he is not such a fool as he looks; I sometimes suspect he has brains though he would blush to have it known, and, anyhow, he does know some serious people who work, like my father.'

Peter did not doubt it, still he maintained that he was himself unknown. She listened to his explanation, watching him with the whole-souled attention she seemed to devote to the object of momentary interest, whatever it might be. When he had finished she said—

'Don't you think you might tell me who you really are, since you are not who he said?—though I have not the least idea who that is.'

'I am afraid I am nobody,' Peter confessed; 'my name is Grimstone, and I am a writer of sorts: I suppose a journalist, after a fashion: that is to say, I do a certain amount of writing for papers and magazines and things.'

'And don't like it?'

'I don't know; I do in a way. Why do you ask?'

'Because I'm sure you don't really. You have not the look or the manner one associates with journalists.'

'I am not altogether one,' he explained; 'there is other work which I like much better, and by and by—Well, I don't suppose I shall always be a journalist, though I expect I shall always be a writer.'

The moment the words were spoken Peter was surprised at himself, he had never, except under pressure of dire necessity, given so much confidence to a human being before. It is hard to say what induced him to do it now, unless it was the, to him, astonishingness of her interest.

She, for her part, showed no surprise: perhaps she was used to confidences; she just nodded. 'Novels?' she asked.

'Perhaps,' he answered; he could not go further than that in self-revelation even though the thing was so near fruition that it was less ambition than fact now.

'Do you think I don't look like that either?' he asked.

She considered him thoughtfully. 'Of course you are so young yet,' she said, and then, seeing the frankness was rather a surprise to him, she added, 'You don't mind my saying it, do you? You may grow into a novelist one day, though I don't know. You will never write yellow, or purple, or whatever you call the sort of novel which sells by the hundred thousand. I tell you what you look like, a constructor: one who builds things, not one who does them in a flash of inspiration. Can one build novels?'

'I hope so,' he answered, rising, 'if it is the only way I can do them, for I mean to do it.'

'I have meant to do several things at several times,' she answered, making no sign of dismissal.

'Have you?' he began with interest, then, remembering the nature of his introduction, he stopped and apologized. 'I've no right to ask you about it,' he said; 'no business to be talking to you at all.'

'Why?' she asked. 'Why have you no business to speak of my characteristics and I to speak of yours? Because we have never met before to-night and may never meet again? I see no reason in that. Life's not long enough to bother over making acquaintance; if a person is worth knowing let's come to hand-grips at once. Don't you think so?'

'It sounds a good theory,' he allowed, 'but how are you to know what a person is worth without some preliminaries? He may not really be worth what you think he is.'

'Then you can drop him,' she said; 'but,' she added, 'I always know when a person interests me, that is all any one is worth to me; when they do that I seek them out without any ulterior motives. You interested me when—' she was going to say 'you were abashed for me', but she changed it to—'when I saw you looking on. Of course, I don't flatter myself that I necessarily interest you—very likely I bore you to death, if so the remedy is simple—go. If I don't, take the advice of an old hand, and don't for Heaven's sake throw away a chance of amusement, however slight.'

Peter sat down again.

He was still there when another woman, equally expensive looking but totally unlike the first, and some years older, approached. Miss Quebell presented him to the newcomer, who, to his great surprise, appeared to be her step-mother. The older woman not only did not look nearly old enough, but was so utterly and entirely unlike the younger that there might have been a century of civilization and the whole gamut of womanhood between. Her manners were gracious though just a touch condescending; after a few words she bore her daughter off, saying they had to go on to another party. Peter left directly after.

It was a fine, dry night in early April, and he walked leisurely back to his own part of the town, thinking in a curiously slow and unsuitably logical way of several new things.

It was said by some who knew him that Peter Grimstone did not know what comfort was; certainly the rooms he at that time occupied suggested it. He had been nearly three years in town, but he had done little to soften the appearance of the cheap furnished apartments which were still all the home he boasted. Little, that is, except to clear away what of the superfluous he could.

'There's not a decent chair in the place,' Austin said, when that evening, some half-hour before Peter's return, he invaded the place.

Austin was the man who had given Peter the card of invitation. A card, by the way, which he ought to have used himself since he was an artist with his way to make. But being young, and chockfull of theories of revolt and other of the golden froth of youth, he had passed it on to Peter as the most unsuitable person of his acquaintance. He had known Peter on and off for some time, principally off, for though the two of them at one time had something to do with the same paper, he had never really got to know anything of him; no-one did. Peter was in their world but not of it. This naturally did not diminish Austin's good-natured contempt for him, rather increased it.

'He has gone to-night,' so Austin said, with amusement, 'to see what it looks like.'

He said this to Farmer. He had fallen in with Farmer at the *Circle*, a small and select club of the apostles of the Ugly.

Farmer showed little interest, he thought the card ought to have been passed on to him. It was his opinion that it was a clear waste that the chance to meet those who might be useful should be thrown away on a writer, and one who was not even a member of the *Circle*, and who, so far as any one knew, had no more views on art or literature or aesthetic revolt than a bricklayer.

But Austin only laughed. 'No waste,' he said; 'for he, in going, will achieve what he went for and you wouldn't, my son.'

'Rot!' Farmer returned.

'I tell you he will,' Austin maintained; 'he will stand in a doorway and look round and be satisfied. I bet you he won't speak to a soul there, and won't want to.'

Farmer did not believe in the existence of such a fool—ie a

man so unlike himself. Eventually they made a bet on it, and it was for the settlement of this that, a while later, they and the fox terrier, Paddy, repaired to Grimstone's rooms, there to await his return. Paddy, who liked all that appertained to Peter, accommodated himself on a pile of manuscript. Farmer, still ill-tempered, stretched himself on the knobby horsehair sofa, and Austin filled up the time by executing a couple of rude and rapid sketches to adorn the chimney piece. He had just finished the second, and was putting it in its place, when he heard Peter at the door. 'Ha!' he said, turning, 'here comes our David, back from the camp of the Philistines.'

'Hulloah,' Peter said, without enthusiasm; 'you here?'

'Seems like it,' Farmer answered gruffly.

And Austin explained. 'We've come to see how you enjoyed the party—if you saw all you went forth to see.'

'Oh yes,' Peter said, without attention; his eye had caught a large brown paper parcel, which had not been in the room when he left it some hours earlier. Its shape and size suggested books, but the sight of it sent a thrill through Peter that it is not given to all books to produce. Swiftly he looked away like one who has sighted a treasure and does not want by his own attention to direct others to it, then he glanced furtively at his companions. Neither showed the least interest, if they had observed the parcel at all it was clearly just a parcel to them. Peter breathed a sigh of relief and wondered how soon he could get rid of them.

Not immediately it seemed. Farmer had not moved from the sofa and Austin had taken up a position in the easiest chair in the room.

'Well,' he said filling his pipe as if he were prepared to stay indefinitely, 'and what did you see? All the big Paint Pots, and all the little ones, a-swilling champagne and a-sunning themselves in the condescending eye of any plutocrat that would look that way?'

Peter had not noticed that—'Though,' he said, 'I dare say it was to be seen.'

Austin looked across at Farmer and laughed. 'He didn't notice the leading lights of Art as she is bought by the great BP,' he said, 'and he's been among 'em for two blessed hours! I told you he was a rare, a wonderful creature.'

Farmer did not answer, and Peter moved restlessly to the chimney piece and took up the sketches.

'These yours?' he said, and stood looking at them without seeing them.

Austin took them from him. 'Go on,' he said; 'what did you see, since you overlooked all our distinguished confrères?'

'Oh, you know—lots of people, all sorts, not all painting ones.'

He crossed the room, he wanted to be nearer the parcel, to be sure that he had made no mistake about it, but he was afraid to go right up to it for fear of arousing their attention, so he stopped by Paddy and turned him off the manuscript. The dog, who loved him for some dog hero qualities unknown to men, appreciated the act as an attention.

'It's odd,' Peter said—it seemed he had got to make conversation of some sort or they would see the matter in his mind—'it's odd, but it never struck me till to-night there's something attractive about the people who don't work, and can't work, and haven't worked for generations—don't you think so?'

He stooped to Paddy who lay on his back with his feet in the air to court further attention. 'You look better right way up,' he said, while Austin laughed.

'Hear, my Farmer!' he said; 'hear him! Our Puritan penman, our Nonconformist conscience, our Industrious Apprentice, has been caught by the glamour of the Idle Rich! What, think you, would have become of you if I had not saved your artistic soul by not putting temptation in your way?'

Farmer apparently did not think favourably. 'Oh, dry up!' was his answer. At the same time he brought his legs to the ground and took up a sitting posture on the uneasy sofa.

'Did you see any one there you knew, Grimstone?' he asked.

Peter had not.

'And you did not make the acquaintance of any one either?' Austin suggested. 'You didn't speak to any one?'

'A man spoke to me—' Peter began, when he was interrupted by an exclamation of—'Pay up!' from Farmer, and an eager disclaimer from Austin.

'Doesn't count!' the latter said,' Ruled out—speaking and spoken to are not the same—one can't help being spoken to, you know, if one is young and charming.'

'What on earth are you talking about?' Peter asked.

'Oh, it's just a bet,' Austin answered, while Farmer said—

'We want to know what you did, whether any one spoke to you or you spoke to any one, or what.'

Peter, seeing that it was his only hope of getting rid of them, told them what had occurred, down to and including his introduction to Miss Quebell. This last Farmer held to decide the case in his favour, and Austin could not contend it; indeed, he did not try, he was too much taken up with the occurrence itself.

'Who was she?' he inquired; 'one of the admired Idle Rich? By Jove! The daughter of Sir Joseph Quebell, Financial Adviser to the Government! But no, it couldn't be, you couldn't have got in with that lot!'

Peter did not know, and it is to be feared he did not care. 'She spoke of her father,' he said, 'as if he were some one well known, and she introduced me to a Lady Quebell, her mother.'

'She did, did she?' said Farmer, and grinned sardonically. He knew that Austin would be regretting the waste of the ticket now as heartily as ever he could.

But Austin did not heed him or his grins, he was absorbed in astonishment at Peter's fortune. 'How the devil you managed it—' he began.

'I told you once,' Peter returned impatiently.

And he had told all he knew. It did not even now occur to him that Bamfield, having been notified of Miss Quebell's momentary interest in the stranger by the door had hit on this simple, though unauthorized way of gratifying her passing desire to know him. Such an explanation occurred neither to Peter nor yet to the others.

'Did she find you out?' Farmer asked.

'I told her, of course,' Peter answered.

And Austin was again astonished though this time at Peter's folly in thus throwing away such an opportunity.

He was even more astonished when it appeared that Peter had not by the confession succeeded in throwing anything away. He had, it seemed, in spite of it received an invitation of sorts.

'She asked me to go there next Sunday,' he said; 'she, they, her mother or somebody, has a kind of at home thing then, I think.'

'What!' Austin exclaimed.

Farmer grinned more sardonically than ever. 'Serves you right,' he said, rising. 'Good-night, Grimstone; hope you'll enjoy the other party as much as you did this one.'

'Good-night'—Peter spoke with more enthusiasm than he had shown yet—'The party? Oh, I don't think it is one, anyhow, I don't suppose I shall go.'

He turned away as he spoke. Farmer stopped to laugh, not at him but at Austin.

'Not go!' Austin exclaimed, and words to express an opinion on such folly failing him, he swore at his own ill-luck.

Farmer, in perfectly restored good-humour, took him by the arm. 'Adjourned till next session,' he said; 'save the rest of the parliamentary flow till then,' and he drew him out, pulling the door to after him.

Peter stood a moment listening to their departing footsteps, he wanted to be quite sure they were not coming back. He even went downstairs after them and secured the bolts of the front door in the way his landlady approved. Then he went up again and shut himself in. Carefully he took up the parcel, turning it over so that the address side, on which it had been standing, showed. It was addressed to him on a white, stuck-on label where there was printed 'Books with care' and the name of a respectable though unimportant firm of publishers. Books, yes it was books, in a moment they were unfastened—six copies of the same thing; six thickish, lightly-weighing volumes with the publishers' wrappers still on. Beneath the wrappers were ugly ginger-green covers, and printed thereon in staring white and unnecessarily distorted type—*The Dreamer*, by Peter Grimstone.

His first book, and he held it in his hand at last—a tangible thing. For long, very long, years even, it had been a thing in his mind only; then, afterwards, for long too, a mass of manuscript, to him, perhaps, the manuscript would always most truly stand for the concrete form of the idea. But now, tonight, it had passed out of the nebulous form, and out of his own personal, private form, into the domain of other men. It was a book, a small but substantial something; a thing which would be bought and sold (perhaps), would be abused and spoken of (perhaps)—and perhaps forgotten.

But he did not think of that to-night. To-night it contented him to have written it, to have got it published, to see it there before him, to turn the pages gently, the contents of which he almost knew by heart. He would not, if he could, have shared it with the general public that night any more than he would have shared it with Austin and Farmer. Other people had not entered into his thoughts in the making of it; he had been alone in its conception, alone in its slow creation, alone in the wearisome and repeated efforts to secure its publication, he was alone now and it satisfied him, he was quite, quite happy.

So he sat for a half-hour, unconscious of himself and the world and time, in a quiet, incommunicable happiness not quite like anything he had known before or perhaps ever knew afterwards. But at the end of the half-hour he separated one book from the rest, wrote in it, and then wrapping it up to go by post, addressed it to his mother. He had begun to take other people into account. His mother would like to have that book, she would feel vaguely proud of it, though books and book-making were not much in the line of her people. It is possible she would not altogether understand the contents if she read it, but he did not think of that, it never occurred to him to send it to her to read, rather to have. She would like to have it because she was fond of him, though she knew nothing really about him and his work. And he would like her to have it though he had never dreamed of seeking her sympathy in the long birth struggle; had they been together now he would hardly have spoken of it. They were a singularly undemonstrative family, the Grimstones.

Chapter II

The Quebell household was carried on the lines of the greatest possible liberty consistent with three people living on good terms under the same roof, and maintained on the same income. The three members of the family each went his or her way almost as much unhampered by interference from or consideration of the other two as if living in an hotel. Some tact was necessary, of course, in the matter of inviting guests, and occasionally arranging not to clash with each other's entertainments and engagements. A certain amount of sense, too, was demanded in keeping within stipulated bounds in money matters; but all three possessed tact and sense in good store, and the incomes were large. The house also was large: there was no need for people to rub elbows in it uncomfortably; the three members of the family did not have to meet too frequently.

Sir Joseph, of course, was immensely busy; his official capacity and private tastes, which lay in the direction of astronomy and higher mathematics, occupied most of his time. He had his own circle of interests and friends; the last were not entirely confined to the learned or the official, for he had curious traces of some small taste for the world, the flesh and the devil, though they were not identical with those of his wife and daughter. It was seldom considered necessary that either of them should accompany him, or he them, to a function, except on the rare occasions when their invitations lay the same way.

Lady Quebell, on the other hand, was essentially and entirely of the polite world: she went where she ought to go, did what she ought to do, and said what she ought to say, according to the canons thereof; she was perhaps one of the most perfect and emotionless supers that was ever put on the human stage. Though it would be doing her an injustice to say she was entirely without emotions, she had at least one, though she never spoke of it, and seldom gave it scope—that was dislike for her step-daughter, Desire.

Her step-daughter did not dislike her. Desire Quebell did not dislike people, either she liked them or she was indifferent to them, she never thought of condemning their actions or taking offence at their proceedings, she merely said she 'couldn't do with them' and dismissed them from her mind. She could not do with her step-mother as a friend, so she dismissed her from her mind, except where it was necessary to consult her wishes for their mutual benefit; and she never dreamed that she herself raised any other feelings. They got on well together, seeing just enough and not too much of each other, and having each their own life; their interests and friends were almost as separate from each other as both were from those of Parker, the immaculate butler. Desire had no idea that this very separateness, though it was partly of her step-mother's tacit arranging, was one cause of annoyance. Lady Quebell, in some way, felt her prestige impaired by the younger woman holding a position so nearly equal to, and quite detached from, her own in the same house.

Desire was engaged to be married, the wedding was to be in the summer, the chosen man, a brilliant barrister of unimpeachable connections. A few people thought Lady Quebell had had a good deal to do with the engagement, but the opposite was the more general opinion, founded on the fact that Desire usually did what she pleased without opposition. If married she must be—and it was obvious to the most casual observer that she must, the only wonder being that she had contrived to evade the fate so long—if it must be, Edward Gore, the selected man was as suitable as any, and for once Desire and Lady Quebell would seem to have been of the same mind about a person.

He was at present abroad; a severe breakdown consequent upon overwork had necessitated the rest and change of sea-voyaging. He was not expected back till well on in the summer, and the wedding, for the convenience of fitting in with other plans, was to be soon after his return. In the meantime Desire enjoyed life as she always had done, and the fact that she was engaged to one man did not prevent her from making friends with others. It did not occur to her to question the advisability of plunging into intimacies, interests and friendships as they presented themselves—in this matter, as in most others, she had always done as she pleased without so much as thinking about appearances or side issues. There is no doubt there was permitted to her a somewhat wider margin than is permitted to most, for she had—Lady Quebell perceived it though she herself did not—the gift of success. No matter how she outraged accepted standards, how old-fashioned, new-fashioned, odd, bizarre, or even middle-class her proceedings might be, they always passed. If she elected to wear a dress a year behind date it was a success, not because of her beauty, which after all was a debatable thing, but because of her personality. If she elected to go to a not usually frequented place of entertainment with an unheard of man, even though she were affianced to Gore, no-one found fault with it; it was not merely condoned, it was thought no more of by her world than by herself. She had assumed to herself most of the liberties and privileges of a married woman, and a good many not accorded to all such—this with a total unawareness of it, or of anything but her own momentary object, which Lady Quebell at least found irritating.

But among her step-daughter's proceedings the most annoying of all to Lady Quebell was her faculty for making friends, or rather, perhaps, it was the friends themselves. Her circle undeniably did number some people, notably men, who were not to be met with at the houses frequented by her ladyship. She called them 'utterly impossible', but they continued to exist all the same and not unfrequently to exist in her company and to be found under her husband's roof. It was because' of these people that Lady Quebell instituted the arrangement which had done something towards dividing the sovereignty of the household. On one Sunday, so she had decreed, she was at home to her friends; on the next, Desire was at home to hers, who were not, except under special circumstances, to be otherwise invited to the drawing-room to outrage the sensibilities of the more select. And it was not without secret annoyance that Lady Quebell found that the select showed a marked tendency to brave the outrage and present themselves at the mixed assemblage on Desire's afternoons quite as often as they did at the more exclusive gatherings on her own. She herself was often driven to being present on Desire's afternoons because she found it advantageous that the compliment should be returned.

It was, of course, to Desire's afternoon that Peter Grimstone was bidden, and to which, in spite of what he had said to Austin, he went. Desire expected him to come, people usually did when she gave them the chance, though she never troubled herself to ask why. To tell the truth, she did not trouble herself much in any way; she greeted them when they arrived but did not otherwise concern herself with them during the visit unless she wanted to at the minute. It was Lady Quebell who arranged bridge-tables, broke up groups and introduced people—all of which well-meant proceedings could have been dispensed with by the company that assembled to see Desire. Every one there felt at liberty to do what he liked, and most of them would have willingly bartered the rest of the afternoon's entertainment for a few minutes of the exclusive and complete attention Desire bestowed on those she was pleased to be interested in for the moment.

On the afternoon when Peter came she was pleased to bestow this attention on him, an unusually large share of it, for she had heard something about him.

'So,' she said, without preliminaries, 'when, the other night, you allowed me to hold forth on the chances of your developing into a novelist, you did not think it necessary to tell me you already were one.'

Peter flushed. 'I was not one then, exactly,' he said.

'But I have heard of your book this afternoon.'

He wondered how, and still more, what she had heard. 'But,' he explained, 'it was not published then when I met you, at least I thought not; I found my copies when I got back that night.'

'Oh!' she said. 'And it is your first book?'

Ready sympathy, deceptively easily aroused in her, shone in her eyes as he acknowledged that it was the first. 'How splendid,' she said, 'to see it for the first time!'

It had been splendid with a quiet, inward radiance, but it was astonishing to Peter that anyone else should know.

'How did you hear of the book?' he asked.

'Mr Evans told me; he was here this afternoon but left early—before you came—rather a pity. Do you know him?'

Peter did not, and she went on to explain that Evans had the book to review but had not done so yet.

'Your name turned up in talk,' she said, 'and he remembered it in connection with a book, and as soon as he said so I knew I had been giving myself away when I talked to you about writing and so on the other night.'

Peter assured her she had not done anything of the sort; he had recovered from the first pleasure and surprise at her ready sympathy, it was, he saw, what she had for every passing interest: he was extraordinarily ignorant to have momentarily felt it personal. Nevertheless there was something very pleasant in talking and having her talk about the book; he had never spoken of it to any one before, and he had never wanted to, but he liked it now. Not that he said much, nothing about the tale or the struggle of production and publication, nothing really of the inside of things, just a few words such as might have been said to any one—though he had never said them.

'Are you satisfied with it?' she asked. He was not, few artists, whether their medium is wood, iron, paint or ink, are satisfied with their creations.

'I expect you are not the best judge,' she said. 'Are the people who matter, whose opinion is worth having, satisfied?'

'I don't know,' he answered; 'I have not seen many reviews yet.'

'Oh, reviews!' she said. 'I did not mean that, that is only an outside judgment, important, of course, but different; I mean the people you care about—what do they think?'

The people Peter cared about were an extremely small band and totally unlikely to be satisfied or dissatisfied with a novel of his composition.

He did not say this but Miss Quebell probably divined some part of it.

'Your own people are not literary?' she suggested. 'Though after all I don't know that that is what matters, one's own people would hardly judge one's work by literary standards: one would not want them too, exactly; one would want them to like it, to care.'

Peter nodded. 'My mother is very pleased,' he said simply; 'I don't know that she will even read the book, but she is pleased that I have written it. She takes great care of it; she carries it up to her room every night for fear that any harm should happen to it.'

Miss Quebell looked down a moment; there may have been mirth in her eyes but there was also softness too. 'How sweet of her!' she said. 'I think your mother must be a dear.'

She had been wearing two large round bunches of carnations that afternoon, as she spoke one tumbled out; it had been tumbling out and being replaced all the afternoon; there really was not room for both bunches, but no doubt both had been given her and she was anxious to be fair to both donors. Carnations, it would seem, were her favourite flower; when Peter saw her before she had them, and there was besides about her and her hair and clothes a subtle fragrance of the flowers which to the initiated suggested the possession of a fine essence or oil of them. For Peter the scent had pleasant memories, some of the few idle, sunny memories of his somewhat hard youth. Inevitably it made him think of a quiet, sunny place, and a feeling of having escaped and being alone, at leisure and secure. It seemed odd to meet with the fragrance here in this London drawing-room, yet in a way it was attractive, perhaps made part of the woman's attraction.

When the flowers fell out of her breast as she talked to him he stooped to pick them up, they had become unfastened this time and some fell on her knee and some on the floor. As he gathered up the one or two on the floor their bruised sweetness brought the garden of his recollection, and the afternoon when he escaped there, very vividly before him.

'Do you like them?' Desire's voice inquiring almost startled him.

'Very much,' he answered.

Her keen, changing eyes were on his face, with something of pity in them, she had suddenly divined that here was a bareness and loneliness very unlike her own lot. 'Keep them,' she said; 'keep those. I don't want them.'

She spoke as impulsively as she would have spoken to any child in the street who had covetously admired her flowers, and Peter accepted the gift in the same spirit; without any other thought about it. But there was one looking on who could not view it in precisely that light; that one was Lady Quebell.

Usually she did not interfere in her step-daughter's friends and acquaintances, and offered no comments on her proceedings, however she might disapprove of them. That day she made an exception, and when the last visitor was gone, and she and Desire were alone for half-an-hour, she asked who Peter was.

'His name is Grimstone,' Desire answered, 'he is a novelist.'

Lady Quebell did not feel herself enlightened. 'Who introduced him?' she asked.

'Mr Bamfield,' Desire answered.

She did not, under the circumstances, feel it necessary to explain the mistake there had been, and Lady Quebell did not push the point further, contenting herself with asking the extent of Desire's acquaintance with him.

Desire did not reckon acquaintanceship by hours; with some people, she held, one might pass half a life and get no more forward, with others ten minutes' chance interview made a friendship. Peter, no doubt, came somewhere between these two.

But Lady Quebell did not hold these views, and she took the trouble on this occasion to tell Desire how the gift of flowers to an almost stranger might strike the ordinary observer.

Desire, far from being annoyed or disconcerted, listened with attention. 'How interesting!' she said. 'Does it really strike you like that?'

'Yes,' her step-mother answered; 'and in all probability it struck him in the same "interesting" way. Really, one could hardly blame him, whoever he is, if he presumed to think you meant something by it.'

'I did,' Desire answered cheerfully: 'I meant that I wanted him to have the flowers because he wanted them, and I haven't the least doubt he grasped that meaning.'

'I have considerable doubt,' Lady Quebell retorted; 'it is about the last interpretation he would be likely to put on the act, seeing what other ones are open to him.'

'That is where you are so clever,' Desire said, with admiration; 'you always know all the interpretations and intentions, and so on; I never see any but my own.'

'It might perhaps be better if you did sometimes,' the elder woman observed.

The younger one nodded. 'But I'm afraid it would bore me rather,' she said. 'I should never be able to decide what to do if I had to think all that way round first.'

Apparently this did not seem to Lady Quebell an entirely undesirable result, but it was useless to say it, so she refrained, and merely remarked, 'Of course you have no idea who the person is?'

'Mr Grimstone,' Desire said, moving to pick up some gloves left by a visitor; 'I told you. Oh, you mean, who his people are? No, I don't know, but I'll ask him if you like, or you can if you prefer it, some time when he is here; he will be coming again soon, I expect.'

'So do I.'

Lady Quebell's accurately inflected voice had an unusual note of meaning, and as she watched the younger woman's unconscious back the one emotion of her life showed for a moment in her eyes and in her compressed lips.

'I have no doubt,' she said, 'that he will come—come continually—that you will go with him to all manner of impossible places and do all manner of impossible things and generally make yourself conspicuous, until you meet some other man who "interests" you. Then this one will be dropped, and the other, whoever he is, will be treated to the same process.'

Desire turned round. 'What do you mean?' she asked.

The expression which might have interpreted Lady Quebell's words was gone from her face. 'Nothing,' she said, 'except that I am quite well aware that this Mr Grimstone is your latest "interest", or one of them. Of course I have nothing to say against it, only I think it is rather a pity you should give him flowers quite so publicly.'

She moved towards the door as she spoke, but Desire stood looking at her with surprised eyes: 'Is that how I look to you—to other people?' she asked in a somewhat shocked voice.

Lady Quebell stopped. 'Yes,' she said; 'I think it is how most people regard your somewhat peculiar friendships and proceedings.'

'But it is not true!' Desire protested. 'It is not correct. I like men that interest me, that's true, and I don't care who their fathers are. What on earth does that matter? It is they, not their fathers, I want to know. And of course if I like them I see as much of them as I can, it would be idiotic not to. But as for dropping people—I have never done such a thing. Sometimes I am a little disappointed in them, perhaps, though even then they usually turn out to be nice in other ways; certainly I have never dropped any one.'

'No,' Lady Quebell admitted, and for an instant there was a flicker of the emotion again in her tone, 'that is true, for they will not be dropped. Men continue to come about you long after they have ceased to have a shadow of interest for you; they have not the pride—or the sense—to go when their time is up—but what better are they for that? For the rest—what you say is only another way of stating what I say. No doubt you can manage to see it like that yourself, but you must not be surprised that no-one else does, including the people you are "interested" in.'

'Oh!' Desire said; and then, 'Do you really think so?' The idea was evidently both new and painful. There are distinct disadvantages in being so engrossed in living as to be completely unable to see even a glimpse of your life and actions as others see them. It is such a shock when chance gives you a passing revelation, though it cannot be expected that the revelation, unless it is very carefully handled, will make a lasting impression on such a nature. Lady Quebell did not comprehend the nature; and she did not know how to handle her opportunity.

'You know,' she said more pleasantly, 'I never interfere in any of your proceedings, or with any of your friends, no matter what my private judgment may be. I certainly have no wish to do so now, I only wanted to point out that you do yourself a good deal of harm by these things.'

A look of immense relief swept over Desire's face. 'Is that all?' she said. 'I thought you meant I did the other people harm—you don't think I do? I'm a sort of education, perhaps, for the men I like? I really think I may be. I'm so glad!'

A faint flush, that owed nothing to art, dyed Lady Quebell's wonderful complexion for a moment. 'I think,' she said rather tartly, 'you are making a fool of yourself, and that you have been doing it a good many years. Your reputation, I don't know if you are aware of it, is decidedly peculiar. You are asked everywhere, I know, and accepted by all men and most women—for the sake of the men; but for all that people shrug their shoulders at your doings, and don't forget them. There are several persons waiting to see what will happen when Edward comes home.'

'What'll happen? Why, they'll dance at my wedding. Wouldn't it be delicious to see some of the dear creatures doing it?'

Desire laughed her rich, full laugh at the vision she conjured up, but Lady Quebell opened the door sharply. 'I think,' she said as she went out, 'it is possible Edward may have something to say.'

'About my friends? What business is it of his?'

Desire put the question, but the door was shut before she could get an answer. Not that it mattered, she was quite sure Gore would not say anything on so absurd a subject; her friends were no more his business, in her eyes, than her clothes were. Poor little step-mother, she had lots of quaint ideas! Some uncomfortable ones to possess, as, for instance, an inability to go anywhere east of a given point, or make acquaintance with anyone without a given number of quarterings in their coat of arms—or figures in their income. Desire dismissed her with a tolerant sigh.

But though she was quite happy again about her own proceedings, there came back to her a momentary uneasiness. That sudden vision of herself as she appeared to her step-mother, and, presumably, some other people, was not pleasant; if they really thought like that they must have some grounds, no matter how inadequate, for their opinion. She meditated on the subject while her maid arranged her hair that evening. Mentally she passed in review the people in whom she had been interested, a long list, principally men, and what few women there were could be left out, they were not in her step-mother's charge. Some of the men, it is true, had made the mistake of falling in love with her; some, in spite of her skill, had precipitately proposed, this, of course, before she had fixed the guard of her engagement; but it had come all right, they were still her friends, the incident, in most cases, practically forgotten. A few of them had married other women; she had been very interested in the event always, and was still as good friends with them as ever. With their wives, too, when they would allow it, though she was obliged to own to herself the wives had a tendency to keep her on rather distant terms.

She looked up at this juncture, and saw her maid's face reflected above her own. 'Barton,' she said, 'do you think I flirt?'

The terms on which she was with servants and shop people was one of the things her step-mother resented, and as she carefully refrained from mentioning it the offender was quite ignorant that she gave offence, or, indeed, that she was on terms at all different from the usual. Barton, of course, was quite used to her, though she could still be a little startled on occasions. To the present question, however, she was able to answer at once.

'Why, no, miss; certainly not.'

'You think not?' Desire took a hand-mirror and examined her back hair. 'I wonder if you know,' she said.

'There isn't much that goes on, miss, that we don't hear,' Barton observed.

Desire thought it possible. 'Some people seem to think I do,' she remarked, still looking in the mirror.

'Of course,' Barton said, with satisfaction, 'some ladies always will be jealous.'

'Jealous of me?' Desire put down the glass. 'That's absurd, Barton! Now you are talking of what you don't understand. No-one's jealous of me; why should they be?'

Barton hesitated, she knew her mistress, whatever her faults, was sincere. 'Well, you see, miss,' she said apologetically, 'it's not your fault, you can't help the gentlemen preferring you.'

'They don't,' Desire said; 'you think they do? Then that's where you are mistaken. They may like me; one may like fifty people and still have room to like the fifty-first. That's not what you mean, I suppose? You think I take other women's men? Well, I don't, and I never would.'

'No, miss,' Barton answered submissively, and took up a fluffy petticoat.

A little later, her toilet being finished, Desire dismissed the girl, and, having a few minutes to spare, sat down to think out this new aspect. Barton, of course, was a fool and had a fool's estimate of the value of admiration, but still she possibly reflected some other people's point of view. At all events, one thing at least was clear, she herself obviously ought to be more careful what she did and how she did it. With that thought came also the thought of the carnations she had given to Peter Grimstone; and quickly after came impatience with the whole thing and the nonsensical view taken of the trivial affair. It would never occur to him—she laughed at the bare idea, and at the recollection of his grave, almost absurdly young face. He admired the flowers because they reminded him of something pleasant—perhaps his mother. Her eyes grew half soft, half mirthful again at the thought. Surely no-one could be jealous of her with him! And no-one could accuse her of flirting with any one so completely unresponsive, so reserved and uncommunicative. That was one of the reasons why he interested her; another was that she felt him sincere, and also found him unlike any one else she had come across. But perhaps she had better have no more to do with him, her step-mother's judgment might be other people's; perhaps, too, he would not understand, he did not know her and her ways, he might—It was not in the least likely, but she did not want to hurt him.

But on Monday, Evans, the critic, who by chance had *The Dreamer* to review, sent his copy of that book for Miss Quebell's acceptance.

'It may amuse you if you know the author,' he wrote. 'It isn't bad, a bit amateurish, but rather out of the ruck.'

She found book and note when she came in from a dinner-party on Monday evening. Being tired, she had declined to go on to another party (which she expected to be dull) with Lady Quebell, and so was in comparatively early. She took the book up to her room with her, and, when she was undressed, curled herself up on the bed with it.

None of the reviewers seemed to have found *The Dreamer* a remarkable book, but to Desire it was remarkable. It must, of course, be remembered that she read books as she made acquaintance with people, enthusiastically, almost gluttonously, losing herself completely for the time being, and wringing out the uttermost. To her *The Dreamer* was wonderful. The date and setting of the story was the end of the Middle Ages, the environment largely monastic; it dealt almost entirely with simple primitive things and emotions, and its outlook was somehow the pure, remote, idealizing outlook of solitary youth. There were some adventures in it, of course, and they were vividly depicted, but for all that they were remote, as if subsisting in an atmosphere of their own. There was romance in it, delicate romance, shyly hinted rather than plainly expressed, and that, too, was seen clearly, yet in this pellucid dream atmosphere. And underlying all was a substructure of truth, not a moral purpose, but an unconscious according with the laws of eternal rectitude, such as one finds in the simple tales of simple people and in much of the work of the great masters. Desire knew nothing about this; nor yet whether the details of the book were accurate to date, or whether the curious, remote, youthful outlook reproduced the far-off time or not. She only knew that a whole new aspect of life, a new world, swam before her in a translucent dawn haze; perfectly real, and yet perfectly remote from the world of lunch and dinner, bridge and race and ball, movement and amusement which was hers.

The last late wayfarer passed, the last belated carriage rolled home; the pulsing silence, the nearest London can do to quiet, fell. And before it had fairly fallen the early grey of dawn had come. Still Desire read, among her lace-edged pillows. The dawn light spread. It had spread wide and been streaked with gold from the rising sun before she finished, and, looking out, saw the distant spires and housetops, remote and glorified in the pure light—as was the world of which this writer spoke. She went to the window, a yearning, that was almost tears, in her eyes, an unformed yearning, though it is impossible to say for what, in her soul. For a minute she stood looking out, then she turned away, and sitting down at the writing-table, wrote—

> I have read your book. I cannot tell you what it has been to me. Words are poor things—to me—though clearly not to you.
>
> I feel as though my soul had been washed in the dawn.
>
> It is just wonderful, a revelation.

So she wrote, and, signing her name, slipped the paper in an envelope and addressed it to Peter at the publishers'—she knew no other address. She left the letter lying on the writing-table and got into bed, tucked *The Dreamer* under the bolster, and went to sleep. She slept till a late hour in the morning, in fact, till Barton woke her to remind her of an appointment with the dressmaker.

'Telephone to her that I can't come,' she murmured sleepily.

But Barton did not go to carry out the order, instead she said something about a near function for which the dress was ordered.

'Oh, bother!' Desire said, then, with relaxing energy, 'I can wear something else.'

'Not very well, miss, if you remember.'

Desire sat up, laughing. 'Barton,' she said, 'The County Council ought to engage you as public conscience. I'd give you a certificate. If it were at all possible to inspire me with a glimmering sense of obligation and the necessity of keeping engagements you would do it.'

She leaned one elbow on the bolster as she spoke, and felt the hardness of *The Dreamer* through.

'Oh, the book!' she said, feeling to find what it was. She glanced towards the writing-table, suddenly remembering the letter written in the dawn. It was gone, Barton had taken it, and another written last night, some time ago by now it was posted. For a moment there crossed Desire's mind a doubt, almost a regret—a very unusual thing to trouble her in connection with any of her actions. It perhaps would have been better if the letter had not gone; she had meant to leave the man alone and not follow up the interest she had felt in him. How well-founded, too, that interest had been! She felt pleased to find how right she was, very pleased that he, unlike some of her previous ventures, had surprised her on the right side and not the wrong. Next moment she put the whole thing from her; the letter could not be recalled, regretting it would not undo it, and after all—

'If one meets anything astonishing, wonderful, why should not one mention the fact?' She put the question, a propos of nothing, to Barton, who answered—

'I'm sure I don't know, miss.'

Chapter III

'The ways of fortune are past my following! It isn't as if the fellow had anything to commend himself; there's no more reason for it in him than in his book, which hasn't even the recommendation of indecency.'

Thus Austin holding forth one Saturday in the room he was pleased to call his studio. Farmer, his only listener, grunted in reply, for the subject of remark was Peter Grimstone and the fortune which had befallen him—a subject on which, seeing that it could practically be dated from the *soirée*, Farmer was a little sore.

Farmer and Austin had been puzzled by the measure of success which had attended *The Dreamer*, now published some little time. They were, it must be admitted, inclined to rate the success a good deal higher than did Peter, who had no erroneous ideas about the value of newspaper paragraphs, and who knew that there was a good deal of difference between the commendation of the initiated and the approval of (and purchase by) the hundred thousand others. He thought that some people liked *The Dreamer*, and he was pleased. They considered that he had achieved fame. The book had been received very moderately at first, there was nothing in it to create a stir and it had created none, being reviewed with moderation and praised and blamed with moderation. One exuberant young critic had spoken of it as a work of genius, and referred to the remote setting as a master stroke. Another had condemned that same remoteness, advising the author to confine himself to dramas of today and a strenuous present which alone was worthy to interest the modern mind. It was this last man who really did Peter a service, for it was he who sent him to the Quebells' that Sunday afternoon. Not that

Peter expected to find those, to him, unknown quantities 'dramas of today' or 'the strenuous present' there; but he thought that at least he might see the outside of a phase of life otherwise beyond his reach. So he went—and learnt nothing, which is not surprising seeing that he had already lived and worked three years in London and neither gained nor lost a real point thereby. But by going he did one thing well worthwhile, he secured Desire Quebell as a friend for *The Dreamer*.

It was Desire who gave the book what vogue it had. She admired it enthusiastically, and she spoke of it enthusiastically, making it the fashion in the circles she touched, securing for it a public of sorts—not a very big one, of course, but one that made a good deal of noise for its size. She spoke of it to what editors and writing-men she knew, and they—like most men acquainted with her—being anxious to please her, pushed it to the best of their ability. She also herself did what she could to push Peter, introducing him to useful people and taking him to suitable places. This in her headlong way, for having once broken through her new resolution by writing to him about *The Dreamer* she did the rest as thoroughly and completely as the peculiarities of Peter would allow.

It was some time before Austin found out how it was that *The Dreamer* came to such fame as it had, and when he did he found the explanation more astonishing than the original puzzle. It was only very recently that he had learned of Miss Quebell's share in it, and now he was passing on his information to Farmer and declaiming about the capriciousness of fortune, and still more of women who will at times take an interest in the most unsuitable men and unlikely things. And Farmer merely grunted.

'Serves you right,' he said, 'for wasting that ticket on him; just chucked away your own chance.'

'Rot!' Austin replied. 'Where's the chance? Because she was

pleased to notice him is there any reason why she should have done the same by us? I tell you there's no reason in these things or in the sex either, and she's got plenty of sex. Have you seen her?'

Farmer had not.

'I saw her the other night at the play,' Austin said. 'Somebody pointed her out. I made a sketch of her afterwards. I've got it somewhere.'

He began to turn over loose sheets of paper.

'Handsome?' Farmer asked casually.

'I'll show you if I can find the thing.' Austin smiled a little as he unsuccessfully hunted for the missing sketch. 'A fellow wouldn't bother himself much asking if she were a beauty when he was with her, he'd have enough to do to keep from kissing her before the time was ripe.'

Farmer laughed. 'I'd like to see Grimstone taken that way,' he said.

'Oh, he'll come a mucker sooner or later,' Austin answered. 'He's going at it fresh, mind you, he doesn't know anything about women, and he's getting his initiation in a remarkable school. He'll lose his head before long. Some excuse, too, she must be a bit champagney for a temperate man. I don't seem as if I were going to find that sketch.'

Farmer having an appointment elsewhere, took his departure, leaving Austin still searching for the portrait. He had found it and put it aside and gone back to work when a little later Peter came in.

Peter, of course, came on business, nothing else was likely to bring him to Austin. He stated his errand and waited while the artist looked for some required paper. While he did so Peter's eyes chanced to light on the portrait of Desire, which now lay with other sketches.

It was one of those daring, almost caricature-like portraits for which Austin afterwards became known; a flashlight effect in which one single characteristic was seized, exaggerated and insisted upon almost to the exclusion of everything else, yet without destroying an uncanny likeness to the original. The hair in the sketch was redder than in life, a blurred background which suggested a dull but glowing heat; the eyes were browner than they usually looked in life, and held in them an invitation which was not so distinct in reality, possibly, even, not existent at all except in the roused emotions of the man who looked at them. The lace draperies that had lightly veiled the shoulders of the original at the theatre were gone in the sketch, arms and breast were as bare as the full, round throat—bare as a Venus. In some way the thing suggested the head and shoulders of a Venus, not Venus, type of beauty, but Venus, goddess of love, the quintessence of woman, the lure.

For a moment Peter stood looking at the thing, very still, very tense; so much so that Austin suddenly became aware of it and looked up.

'Hullo!' he said, seeing what he looked at. 'You've found Desire?'

It cannot be said that Peter stiffened, he was already perfectly stiff. 'Why do you call her that?' he said in tones deceptively slow and cold.

'It's her name, I was told,' Austin answered; 'an excellent name, too—the Desirable, the Desired, the Desirous—in short, Desire. Our godfathers and our godmothers in our baptism do not usually show so much sense.'

'Will you let me have this?' Peter nodded towards the portrait but did not touch it. It was noticeable that he had not touched it all along. 'What do you want for it?'

'Nothing,' Austin said, coming round and looking at it. 'As a work of art it is worth nothing. I don't mind admitting it to you, because you can't see it for yourself. It is waste paper—see here.'

He had a pencil in his hand, and with it would have pointed out the technical blemishes, but Peter cut him short.

'Then you will give it to me?'

Austin shook his head. 'If,' he said, 'you haven't the courage to ask the lady to give you a big panel portrait of herself, or a little wee trifle to wear next your heart, I won't help you.'

'You won't?' There was a new ring in Peter's voice.

'No,' Austin said; 'I won't. Charming as it would be for you to have such a replica always before your eyes I'll not pander to you. By the way, I suppose it is for yourself you want it?'

Then Peter looked up and Austin saw there was a faint flush on his face and a steely glitter in his eyes. 'I want it to burn,' he said. 'It is the most abominable, damnable insult that was ever offered to a woman!'

Austin burst out laughing, the criticism delighted as much as it surprised him. He had not the faintest idea that his picture with its suggestion shocked, almost shamed, something in Peter, who, not only had never seen the original thus, but never could so see her. He took up the sketch. 'Not good enough of her?' he asked grinning. 'We can't all see her with the eyes of love, my boy. Now I call this quite a pretty thing—in fact, I rather think of pinning it up on the wall.'

'I should not advise you to,' Peter said.

Austin immediately proceeded to fasten it up.

'I warn you,' Peter went on quietly, 'since you won't sell it or give it I shall take it.'

Austin looked round, for the first time becoming aware that Peter, who plainly was not fooling, was also not taking his fooling the right way.

'No, you won't,' he said shortly. 'You won't take it.' Peter leaned across and pulled the half-fastened sketch from the wall.

The suddenness and unexpectedness of the movement, so unlike the Peter he knew, astonished Austin so much that for a second he did nothing. Then he snatched at the picture angrily.

Peter deliberately tore it across.

Then Austin lost his temper. He flung himself upon the offender and for a minute they struggled, the sketch getting badly torn between them; but the end was easy to see. Peter was the heavier and stronger man, moreover, all he aimed at, the destruction of the picture, was easy to attain. Before Paddy, who barked and jumped round joyously, had realized that they were in earnest, not fun, it was all over and the offending sketch reduced to unrecognizable fragments.

Austin, of course, was furiously angry, and he told Peter what he thought of him, in no measured terms. And Peter, it is to be feared, did not care at all. Public opinion, and personal opinion too, entered very little into his solitary life; it did not matter in the least to him what Austin thought, the only thing which mattered was that the picture was destroyed. That done, the affair was ended for him, and though he saw Desire that afternoon he did not so much as look for any points of resemblance between her and the portrait; he certainly would never have dreamed of mentioning it to her.

His appointment with Desire that afternoon was to have tea with her and meet an important editor to whom she wanted to introduce him. As it happened, however, the great man telephoned at the last minute to say he could not come, so Peter was alone with his hostess. He had been that before; since the writing of the letter about *The Dreamer* he had seen more of her than he had ever seen of any one, that is to say, he had seen her more intimately, and after a time talked to her of things he had never spoken of to anyone else (other men before him had done that).

That afternoon they talked for a time of his affairs and the progress of the novel he was now writing, in which Desire took a warm and enthusiastic interest; afterwards they spoke of her concerns. It was on this occasion that she told him something of her family history.

'My mother was a variety actress,' she said. 'You didn't know that? She was more beautiful than virtuous it is reported.'

Peter did not know and he was surprised to hear it, she gathered as much from his tone, and for some reason resented it.

'You are surprised that I speak of it?' she asked. 'Do you think I ought to be ashamed of it? I'm not. Everyone knows I am not Lady Quebell's daughter; a good many know that I am not my father's legitimate daughter—What difference does it make?'

'None,' Peter said.

And he was right, for, from early childhood, she had had the position and advantages of a legal daughter, and even if she had not her own personality and characteristics would be likely to have carried off a more difficult situation, and successfully stood up against greater disadvantages.

But she was not quite satisfied with Peter's answer. 'It is a shock to you?' she asked. 'Why?'

Peter could not tell her.

But she persisted. 'What do you object to? Is it my mother's profession or her want of virtue? Are you one of those people who think everyone ought to marry no matter what their circumstances? Or is it that you think these things ought not to be mentioned?'

'I don't think things strike you and me in quite the same way,' was all Peter said.

'How do they strike you?' she asked. 'I'll tell you how they strike me, as a good deal of utter humbug. We don't make more than a stereotyped and very transparent pretence about our acquaintances' *chers amis*; we say quite frankly we must ask the Captain if we ask Mrs So and So, and it's no good having What's-his-name if we don't have the Thingummy woman. Why, in the name of all that's rotten, make such a fuss over the name of a poor woman who was not quite so straight as she ought to have been or nearly so crooked as she might have been?'

Peter could not answer her; it was no use, he was aware, as he had been before, that her world and his were miles apart, and that things were openly spoken of and only less openly done in hers that were still regarded as disgraceful and a breaking of Divine commands in the humbler circle to which he belonged. He knew that difference but he could not explain it, he had so long been silent about his thoughts that he found it very difficult at times to give them utterance.

But Desire wanted an answer. 'Why is one so much worse and unspeakable than the other?' she insisted.

'It isn't,' he said.

She repeated the words after him in surprise, and then, as for once the glimmering of a point of view quite other than her own began to dawn on her—'Wouldn't you speak of either?' she asked, with puzzled interest. 'Then I have shocked you? But still I don't see why. No, I don't I'm afraid you must continue to think me shocking. I am quite unable to see why it is worse to speak than to do.'

'It isn't,' he said again; then, as she continued to look at him for enlightenment, he added, 'It isn't worse to speak. But if one thought a thing wrong one might be ashamed—one wouldn't speak—' he broke off. 'I did not mean to say that exactly. Your people are—Things are just different to them. It is no good trying to explain.'

She nodded without entirely comprehending; but she repeated one of his words. 'Wrong?' she said. 'Do you think about things being right or wrong? How wonderful!'

It did not seem to him wonderful, rather an obvious and ordinary way of thinking, but to her it was clearly different. 'Do you know,' she said after a little pause, 'I don't believe I have ever before heard it spoken of—except in a fashionable pulpit where it doesn't exactly count. Oh, of course, I have heard of the wearing of the wrong thing and saying the wrong thing and doing the wrong thing, but that doesn't mean the same, they all belong to the category of the wrong side of the park. But you think about a thing being really wrong? You do? And I have lived all the years of my life without once, even in my childhood, being told, to my knowledge, that a thing was wrong that way. I suppose,' she spoke almost wistfully, 'you were often told it?'

He nodded. 'Very often,' he answered.

'Too often?—I wonder! Your childhood and youth were hard, I suppose?—yes, I think I have always known they were. Yet it must be worth something, that training of right and wrong. I don't think you could have written *The Dreamer* if you had not had it and did not still think that way underneath. I was not trained at all, you know, except in the wearing of clothes and the conforming to conventions. And in both, as you perceive, I'm afraid I rather follow my own inclinations. I believe I have all my life done precisely what I pleased without regard for any rule that I know of, except convenience; I expect I always shall.'

'You would always regard other people,' Peter told her. 'I am certain you never have and never will do what you please if it hurts anybody else.'

'No; because it would not please me to do it. I don't like seeing a hurt. If I can overlook that, as no doubt I often do, there's nothing to prevent me from being a beast to anyone.'

Peter thought otherwise, she saw it in his face when he rose to go, and was pleased.

'I'm glad that you, in spite of your convictions, can continue to think well of me,' she said; 'and yet, do you know, I have a feeling I shouldn't mind if you found me out—isn't that odd?'

It did not strike Peter as odd: no-one thing about her

seemed more strange to him than another, she was altogether outside his range of experience; he did not attempt to judge or measure her.

But to her it was odd, for she liked the man and valued his good opinion surprisingly, seeing he was nothing; yet she was not afraid of losing it. For a while the anomaly of it arrested her attention; she stood thinking about it for quite two minutes after he had gone, and was only recalled to other things when a servant came to· tell her that someone wanted to see her.

'Who?' she asked.

'A lady, miss; she gave no name.'

It was easier to see Desire than many people of her set; as almost everything amused or interested her she went open-handed to meet any happenings that came her way. Today she did not refuse herself to the lady who gave no name, but ordered that she should be shown up.

She came, a woman of seven-or eight-and-twenty perhaps, quietly but well dressed, with an appearance which suggested to Desire that she gained her living by some more or less intellectual pursuit. A lady undoubtedly, and a good looking one, who just missed beauty; without knowing why Desire mentally took her measure, and, considering she rarely troubled about such things, she did not do it badly. A strong woman, but emotional, sympathetic in some ways, good for a sacrifice, introspective, able to suffer, superior to some conventions—her hair was done as it became her, without regard for fashion—but probably sensitive to the criticism that may arise—she had conformed to the usual standards in her costume though it did not quite become her.

The stranger did not introduce herself but plunged straight into the business: which had brought her, after the briefest apology for her coming.

'I wanted to ask you a question,' she said.

And Desire acquiesced graciously.

'I saw in the paper,' she went on, 'that before long you are to be married to a Mr Edward Gore, a barrister, now abroad for his health—is that true?'

'Quite true.'

'Have you—' the visitor appeared to swallow with difficulty but she spoke steadily and with indifference—'have you been engaged long? '

'Since just before Mr Gore was taken ill.'

'The engagement was announced in the papers?'

'I believe so.'

'I didn't see it,' the woman seemed to speak more to herself than to Desire, but directly after she turned to her again; her voice and manner were very calm and self-possessed, indeed almost expressionless, but a close observer might have seen that the muscles about her mouth were curiously tense and the pupils of her eyes contracted under the stress of some hidden emotion.

'Will you tell me how long you have known Mr Gore?' she asked. 'Four or five months before the engagement? You know him well, of course? You—you—care for him?'

Her voice faltered a moment but Desire showed no perception of the fact, she had evinced no surprise whatever at the enquiries, nothing but polite and commonplace interest. 'Isn't that rather a personal question?' she asked pleasantly. 'Won't you tell me something now? For instance, what is your interest in this? You are, of course, a friend of Mr Gore's—one to whom I have not been introduced—Yes?'

'You never would have been introduced to me. I—I am the woman he ought to marry.'

Desire did not wince or start. 'Are you sure of that?' she said gently.

'Sure?' there was a bitter little laugh; 'it is not a question on which there is room for much doubt. I left his child and mine to come to you; I shall find her waiting when I go back. We have been—he and I—'

Desire nodded, and the other controlled her rising passion. 'Perhaps—' she said, and the bitterness had increased, 'perhaps you do not consider that a claim—a man's amusement—'

'I never concern myself about a man's amusements,' Desire said. 'What men tell me I hear, what they do not I do not. But,' and she leaned forward with a sudden concentration of voice and manner, 'you are not a man's amusement and you never have been.'

The other flushed faintly then went white again.

'What I meant, when I asked you if you were sure you were the woman this man ought to marry, was—are you sure you are the woman who can help him—in himself, his career, everything? Are you sure, not whether you have a moral, a legal, an honourable claim on one another, but whether you would fit one another always, not weary one another, not regret? '

A faint surprise stole into the visitor's grey eyes, this clearly was an interpretation of the question which had not occurred to her; she had to think before she answered then she said, rather brokenly, 'I am sure that he loved me—sure that in the past I helped him. Before he came into money, before he was recognized much, when he had his way to make, my sympathy and help were much to him. We ought to have been content with that—being friends, you will say, seeing he could not afford to marry me and I was just a woman of no position, only one of gentle birth who had to make her own way. No doubt you would be right, for a time we thought so too, afterwards—not. We were both lonely, it did not seem to concern anyone but ourselves if we took what of happiness and companionship was to be had. Perhaps you will say it does not concern any one now—if one does wrong—'

But Desire waved that aside. 'I am no judge of right and wrong,' she said. 'Go on, tell me the rest.'

'There is no more,' the other answered; 'he unexpectedly inherited money, as you know; it was just before you met him, he had been ill and went south for the cold weather, you must have met him then. I saw little of him; I thought it was owing to his health, to his being so busy and being away, and then finally breaking down again and having to go for the voyage. I had no idea of—of anything until I chanced to see this paragraph.'

Desire nodded and for a moment there was silence. The woman sat with set face, the haggard tragedy of her eyes at terrible variance with the studied calm of her manner.

Desire's face revealed nothing. 'And then you came to me?' she said at last.

'Yes; I could not understand—it was incredible—I could not believe it was for position, money, influence; if it had been for that it would have happened, when he needed that help. Besides, I know him; he would never, never do it for that. I could not believe—or think why; so I came and—' her eyes for a second passed burningly over the splendid figure—'and saw.'

For a moment Desire shrank in spirit under the glance, a sudden feeling of shame came over her, a feeling as if she were a courtesan, a beguiler of men, and this greyeyed woman was the wife she had robbed. Harder than any charge of cruelty or selfishness or appeal for pity or restitution, the unconscious shaft hit home.

But the other went on unaware. 'I did not know,' she said, her voice breaking a little; 'I did not realize men were—that they could—they did—'

'That they responded to the lure of the flesh as well as the world and the devil? '

Desire's tone was light; custom and common sense always demanded of the people among whom she lived to tread lightly among the deeps of emotions if by any chance they had to be touched; one should always laugh at things even if it were sometimes for fear one should cry. Desire had assimilated the lesson more completely than most, also she had pride of sorts to help her.

'You did not know,' she asked, ' that idols could fall? That women could topple each other's idols down by just existing, or revealing their existence? It seems they can, doesn't it? And "all the king's horses and all the king's men can't put the idol together again!" But sometimes the woman can—that is wonderful, the wonderfullest thing in the world.'

For a moment her voice softened wistfully and the other looked up. 'This will make no difference to you?' she said.

'I was thinking of you,' Desire answered.

'Of me? Of me! Do you think it makes so little difference to me? '

'You cannot forgive him?' Desire inquired curiously. 'You can never forgive a man of flesh for surrendering to the promptings of the flesh? I take it you regard me as the choice of the flesh, and yourself and your union with him as the choice and outcome of the higher part?'

The other woman flushed; she had hardly definitely thought this though it was on these grounds that she had originally justified herself to herself. Somehow it startled her to hear Desire, who stood on the other side, utter it.

'I don't know,' she hesitated, 'I can't explain; I know that he and I—What we have been to one another is not wrong, whatever the world may say, it is the best, the truest thing in his life. But then you came—you are the most beautiful woman I have ever seen—though it is not that only, there is something about you, your voice, your movements, everything.

I can understand that it—that he might not exactly be able to help himself; perhaps even he was not altogether false to me while he loved you.'

Desire nodded. 'That is what I say,' she said; 'there are the two halves to the man, one half is yours, and the other it seems mine. I am not really a beautiful woman, there you are wrong; but for the rest, the effect on him—maybe in part you are right. He completely lost his head about me; I did not know how completely at the time though of course I knew he was what used to be called very much in love. I did not realize till now how little else he lost beside his head and his self-control. I did not know that the rest, the best part, was already given to you.' She laughed, a little short laugh. 'Not exactly flattering to me is it?' she said. 'But it is true, I can see it now; it explains a good deal.'

Her eyes grew brown in thought as she recalled incidents of the past. The other woman watched puzzled; but soon her own tragedy reabsorbed her interest. 'What does it matter? what does any of it matter?' she said wearily 'Nothing can be altered now.'

'It matters a good deal,' Desire answered; 'I do not choose to be any man's mistress. Oh yes! I should be the mistress, you are the wife. The woman with whom a man has been united, as he was with you, with whom he has shared his work and ambition, his hopes and disappointments, his struggle—she is the wife. The woman who temporarily blinds him, so that he seeks to possess her because of some momentary madness of the senses which neither looks before nor after—she is the mistress. As a rule, of course, it is the first kind of woman who has the ring, the second is usually a temporary impulse and a temporary union. With us the case is reversed, but that makes no difference. For myself, I do not accept all the superstitions about the difference between ring and no ring.

In this matter it certainly makes no difference; if what you say of yourself is true, you are his wife; if what I now have reason to believe of myself is true, I should be his mistress.'

She spoke as if the view and conclusion, which meant so much to both, had been arrived at by pure reason quite free from emotion. The other woman for a moment could only look and wonder.

' You will not marry him?' she said.

'No,' Desire answered; and it must be admitted that though she undoubtedly did sometimes arrive at conclusions by reason and a fearless facing of facts, she had a tendency to act upon them with a headlong impulsiveness which was nothing less than precipitous. 'No,' she said; 'I will give him back to you.'

'You can't,' the other said bitterly. 'Do you think he would come back to me when he knew that it was I who deprived him of you? Do you think he would forgive that while he is still—'

'Infatuated?' Desire concluded for her. 'No, I do not. But if the infatuation was over, and he came to himself, I think well enough of him to believe he would come and ask you to forgive him. As to whether or not you would forgive—well, you know best about that—there seems always to be a lot of forgiveness wanted in all contracts between men and women. But I am pretty certain he would come. I do not think I can have been altogether mistaken in the opinion I had of him.'

Again there was a faint wistfulness in the voice, and the other woman wondered what that opinion was. Through her mind there shot a thought of her rival—had she cared? Did she care? Did she suffer, too? What was the cost of it all to her? She leaned impulsively forward, but before she could say anything Desire spoke again, and in the equable tone of kindly justice.

'You must tell me everything about yourself and him,'

she said. 'You will understand that I must prove this and investigate it all. I can't ask him to justify himself, or it would then be impossible to send him back to you—if that should turn out to be the thing to do. So, you see, I myself must do what I can to clear him, and you must help me in fairness to us all.'

'I will help you,' the other said humbly, 'though I don't see what you or anyone can do.'

'Don't you?' Desire said, with a swift and disconcerting return to lightness again; 'most likely you will have to do nothing and say nothing, and I shall have to do a great deal. In the meantime we must talk, and don't you think cognac would help us? Or would you rather have tea at this belated hour?'

'William,' she said to the manservant who answered the ring, 'some tea, please, and some cognac. And, oh, William, I'm not at home to anybody.'

'Her ladyship—' the man began.

But—

'No, not her ladyship, either,' Desire said.

And her orders being obeyed, she was undisturbed from without till it was time to dress for dinner. For, even after her visitor had gone, no-one came to her; and she sat alone, her chin propped on her hand, looking straight before her. When at last the hour was growing late, Barton, who knew her mistress had an engagement to dine out, ventured to knock and enter. She found her sitting very still, but her face was in shadow, and so revealed nothing. She rose, on the maid's hesitating reminder of the time, and stretched herself, frankly, as a boy or a dog, but also as one who throws a burden down.

'It is an extraordinary world,' she said, 'an extraordinary world, so extraordinary that it hurts sometimes. Don't you think so, Barton?'

Barton did not think.

Chapter IV

Desire Quebell undoubtedly had the faculty for surprising even those who knew her well; two people were astonished by her during that June—one was Lady Quebell who, by her own showing, should have been prepared for anything of a distressing nature to occur in connection with her step-daughter.

It was a generally understood thing that Desire would be married at the beginning of August, just before every one left town. Gore was expected home in July, the wedding was to be within a reasonable time after that. Not much in the way of preparation had been made yet, Desire being one who objected to lengthy getting ready, preferring rather to enjoy the present moment and leave the preparations for the next to be rushed triumphantly and excitingly through at high speed. Lady Quebell's tastes were of a totally different order, and through her instrumentality some certain trousseau orders had been placed in reasonable time, not so many as she wished because all had, more or less, to pass through Desire. But by the beginning of June she felt that it was time things were fully in train, and she said so to Desire, and repeated it so many times and with such a manifest intention of seeing to the matter herself that Desire was roused to take action.

'The wedding?' she said. 'You want to order the cake and fix the date and all the rest?' 'It ought to have been done some time ago,' Lady Quebell said, 'seeing how full those last few days always are.'

'Don't you think it is a pity to fill them any fuller?' Desire suggested; then, observing an impatient look, she added, 'Really I mean it; at all events I think it would be a pity to fix the wedding for then because I am not at all sure it is going to take place.'

Lady Quebell put down the pencil with which she was making notes and stared at her step-daughter in blank amazement.

'What do you mean?' she asked.

'Just that,' Desire answered calmly; 'I am not sure that I am going to be married. I can't tell you for certain till Ted comes home, but I don't think you had better fix dates and order cakes and so on before I've seen him.'

'You are going to jilt him?' Lady Quebell, still under the influence of the first shock, seemed hardly able to grasp what was said. 'You mean that—you can mean nothing else—if you break off the engagement now it is nothing less. It is preposterous! Impossible! You cannot mean this—even you.'

'Well,' Desire said, 'of course it may not occur, but I thought I ought to warn you.'

Lady Quebell set her lips. 'I see,' she said freezingly; 'do not trouble to explain yourself, you have of course practically made up your mind to do it already.'

'Have I?' Desire asked. 'I wonder?' and she seemed to be quite as interested in the question as ever her stepmother could be.

Lady Quebell did not perceive that, or at all events did not believe in it, for which perhaps one cannot altogether blame her. 'What are your reasons?' she demanded, forgetting that a moment before she had intimated no wish for explanation.

'My reasons for not being sure what I am going to do?' Desire said. 'Or for what I do—if I do it? They are rather mixed just at present; I really don't think I could explain them. Indeed, if it had not been for your quite natural anxiety about ordering the cake and so on, I would not have troubled you now with what may never come to anything at all.'

But Lady Quebell was neither mollified nor relieved by this and she continued to trouble both herself and Desire; she even took the unusual step of troubling Sir Joseph. So much so did she do the last that he made time to speak to Desire himself.

In the interview that Sir Joseph had with his daughter he did not of course demand information or insist on any line of conduct; the terms of liberty, equality and dispassionate amiability of the household did not admit of that. He no more thought of it with Desire than he would with any friend or acquaintance in whom he was interested. He only asked her what it was she talked of doing about her marriage, and afterwards gave her a little advice on the subject.

'Marriage is a serious affair for any woman,' he said a trifle awkwardly; he had an uncomfortable feeling that the parental position, which he had consistently forgotten, demanded some such remarks of him. Unfortunately the actual presence of Desire had rather the effect of reducing the newly remembered position to something of an absurdity and making the saying things even more uncomfortable than the feeling they ought to be said.

She agreed with him, of course, but added an addendum—'Serious for any woman, and more serious still for some men. Don't you think marriage with me would be a serious undertaking? Some people do.'

'Gore is perfectly satisfied, more than satisfied,' Sir Joseph said, remembering the rather unlooked for eagerness of that serious and ambitious man—an eagerness he had only seen paralleled in his own passion for Desire's mother. That passion, by the way, would certainly have resulted in marriage had it not been for the wisdom and generosity of the woman. It had resulted in the position of the daughter of the union, who did not altogether resemble the mother. Sir Joseph, looking at her now, could trace small resemblance though, so he concluded there must be some, for men seemed to lose their judgment about her as he had about the other woman.

'There is no doubt whatever about Gore's inclination,' he

said; 'and as to yours—you seemed satisfied, you made the engagement for no other reason that I know of than to please yourself; you believed, I understood, that you would be happy married to Gore?'

'Yes,' Desire assented; 'I did, I'm not at all sure I shouldn't be happier married to him than any other way, but, in spite of that, it may not be able to be managed. We'll do it if we can, but if we can't—it is no good crying over spilt milk. Certainly very little good beginning to cry before the milk is spilt and before we know that it is going over.'

'I should be rather glad to learn what your motives are,' Sir Joseph said.

Desire glanced at the clock. 'They would take rather long to explain,' she said; 'and you haven't much time just now.'

Sir Joseph glanced at the clock too. 'That is true,' he admitted: 'still, I should like to learn them at some future date; I might reasonably ask for them, I think?'

'I suppose you might,' Desire said; 'I'm afraid I sometimes forget that you or anyone else has such rights over my affairs. I get into the way of thinking it does not matter to anyone what I decide or how, it is really rather terrible of me.'

'Well, well,' Sir Joseph said hastily, 'I'm not sure it is not the best way after all; your concerns are really more your own than anyone's, you are no doubt quite capable of managing them for yourself, more capable than I who have little time to spare. As for this business, it really seems yours and Gore's more than anybody's; I should advise you to settle it with him.'

'You think that would be the best plan?' Desire said. 'Perhaps you are right.'

But it is to be feared that in spite of her words she settled it without waiting for Gore; at all events, a few days later she took a step that rather indicated something of the sort. This step was the other surprise she gave at this time.

It was given to Peter Grimstone and came to him in a letter. This was the letter—

> I believe I can rely on you—at all events, I am going to do it. I want help, and you are the only one I know who can give it—for a variety of reasons you are the only one, but principally because you are you.

(He had no idea how Desire had reviewed the many men of her acquaintance in the new light lately cast on herself and her doubtful powers before she selected him.)

> This is what I want you to do—I want you to let me pretend to be in love with you. You need not pretend back, if you agree you will only have to put up with my pretence and give me the opportunities of letting it be seen. I cannot tell you why I ask this, I can only ask you to believe my reason is a strong one and one which I think you would not disapprove though it is concerned with people and events of which you know nothing. Perhaps I am asking too much? It is like me to do so. If so just refuse, I shall quite understand and I know I can trust you in that case, or any other, to forget what I have asked.

This was the letter which surprised Peter Grimstone—as it might have another. But Peter, unlike some others, did not feel himself concerned with the whys and wherefores of it; the question which concerned him was not why she asked, only whether he should do it. He considered the matter awhile then he wrote—

> 'I will do as you ask so far as it is in my power.'

He did not, it must be admitted, think it was altogether in his power. He did not see how he could ever loom sufficiently important in the eyes of Desire's world for it to be imagined for a moment that she thought of him, seriously or otherwise. That, however, was her part of the business, as also was the histrionic love-making—which, no doubt, was just as well if it was to be successful, for he had not only never been in love, but, before he met Desire, had had few dealings of any sort with women, or thought of them as more than a necessary, though rather remote, part of the world machinery. But he gave the promise unconditionally, and unconditionally put himself under her orders. In his opinion he owed it to her since it was the service she required, seeing how much she had done for *The Dreamer*.

Thereafter there began for Peter Grimstone a somewhat wonderful time; a time which made Austin, who, owing to Peter's incurable reticence, never heard anything worth hearing, nearly frantic with envy and curiosity and bewilderment. Peter Grimstone, Peter Nobody, Peter the Unsociable, the Unteachable, the Puritan suddenly entered into society—after a fashion. Such an opportunity was given to him as fell to the lot of few of his position, such a chance as would have turned the head of some of them and served as an education to most. Miss Quebell, the light of a bigger sphere, chose him for her *cavalier servant*, a post he was ill-equipped to fill. She took him everywhere possible, and some places not possible to anyone else; he was seen with her in well-known places and little-known; he devoted to her all his spare time—and some he could ill spare, for she was exacting and requisitioned a great deal. He won the dislike and envy and sometimes the contempt of people who in the ordinary way would have been totally indifferent to his unimportant existence. He was severely and frequently snubbed by Lady Quebell—that was an inevitable accompaniment of the role, and might, perhaps, have been part of the education to a man who could have been educated that way. He—it seemed incredible—he actually got himself talked about! Austin was completely at a loss to understand it and he got little help from Peter.

Indeed it was difficult to see Peter at all at that time, except in working hours, for Desire was a hard task-mistress. She seemed bent on rushing the thing through breathlessly, without giving him time to breathe or herself time to think. Peter saw more of life in her company in a week than he had in the whole previous three years he had been in London: more of some things than he would if he had lived there thirty-three years. For besides seeing the gorgeousness and glamour of the world that plays, from the inside, he also saw a woman of considerable experience play love and the love-stricken part. He saw a fascinating woman deliberately showing the wiles of fascination, a beautiful woman showing the charms of beauty, and, in appearance at least, paying him the compliment of her sole favour and interest. It was acting, of course, but first-class acting, for it had got to deceive an audience that rubbed elbows with the actors.

Desire did it very well; she had been made love to many times, and half-way responded, as the much-loved cannot by nature help doing; she knew all about it. Her full voice softened and thrilled for Peter, her brilliant eyes brightened for him and spoke as if he and she had a language of their own; the scent of her clung about him, her carnation was often in his coat. As an exhibition it was really clever, though some people said really ridiculous, by which of course they meant that she was making herself ridiculous.

Besides these public appearances there were also more or less private ones, obvious semi-private *tête-a-têtes* that could be talked about. What was discussed on those occasions did not concern the world, and though, no doubt, the assumed parts were then dropped there was necessarily an intimacy in the position and a great opportunity for talk which must have been new to Peter's experience. He, on his side, had not much to do but follow her lead; indeed, it was the only thing he could do and he did not always do that very well. Once or twice Desire rather wondered that he was not found out. He did his best, following her with attention and sometimes with a rather surprising quickness—the quickness, though, of concentrated attention; he never for a moment lost himself in the part, or forgot that it was a part.

Desire was not slow to perceive this and she was just a little disconcerted by it—although an intuitive perception of its likelihood had a good deal to do with her selection of him. He would not lose his head however she placed him or tried him; he not only would not take advantage of any position, but also he would not want to, the idea would not enter his head. He would regard the risky bargain as a bargain purely, and to the letter carry out his part of it as a business order. Once or twice she wondered what he, with the training and standards she believed him to have, thought of it and of her. He never sought any explanation of the affair, and she, with a shyness rare with her, kept silent about it. He knew nothing and sought to know nothing, but he must think some way. Did he think her that shameless thing she had for a moment looked to herself on the day when the other woman talked to her? She asked herself the question once when she was half-way through with the affair, but flung it from her contemptuously, it mattered nothing to her at all what he thought. He was nothing, a mere pawn in the game which had got to be played—and should be well played in spite of him, in spite of Lady Quebell and everyone else who held and expressed—or suppressed—opinions. And she threw herself into her part with a new zeal and a recklessness which suggested heart and mind at little ease. And still to whatever length her recklessness led her, Peter followed, gravely, with his best attention but sometimes with an ineptitude which showed he missed the meaning of some points of her behaviour. And the misses irritated her jangled nerves, not because of their stupidity but because, for some unexplained reason, they made her shrink from meeting the grave grey eyes which sought direction from hers.

But she held on her way to the end, and not until near the end betrayed herself at all to him. Then one night, when, after a somewhat public exhibition, they had secured a temporary, though quite obvious, solitude, she said sharply—

'I wish you would not look at me like that! If you think I ought not do it, say so and have done with it!'

'I don't think so,' he answered; 'you said you had a reason and of course you have.'

'Yes—,' she began, but stopped on the approach of a third person—which no doubt gave that person an entirely erroneous idea of the nature of the conversation. By the time they were alone again she had largely recovered her equilibrium.

'I'm afraid you have found it all dreadfully boring,' she said; 'and some of them have behaved disgracefully to you. It's abominable—it's made me furious at times, I did not think I was letting you in for quite that.'

'Oh, that's nothing,' he answered her; 'I should have deserved it if this had been real—it shows they think it real, so it's applause, you know.'

She looked at him rather curiously. 'It's generous of you to say so,' she said, 'and to think it. Do you know you are the only one of my friends I could have asked to do this? I thought so, I am sure of it now.'

'Then I am glad you did ask me,' he said simply.

'I wonder if you are?' For a moment the question of what he really thought occurred to her again; but she did not ask it, she could not consider such things to-night, she had got to be gay, she was gay in fact.

'Let us go,' she said; 'we shall become improperly solemn if we stop here any longer.' He rose obediently. 'I'm afraid you are very tired,' he said.

'I? I'm not a bit; I'm going on to another party. I could go on to two; I could dance all night—I never felt more fit.'

'Yes,' he said, 'I know; I don't mean that kind of tired.'

'What kind do you mean? Tired in mind? Please don't distress yourself about that; I haven't got a mind or any other obscure inside thing. There's nothing the matter with me.'

'Of course not,' he said, and looked away.

For a moment a wave of emotion swept over her so that unbidden tears were near her eyes. She felt grateful to him for the acquiescence and the avoidance of her eyes even though it showed he understood somewhat. She had a momentary inclination to thank him but she did not, she only let her touch on his arm tighten a little and said nothing at all.

In July Gore came home. Desire had definite knowledge when he would come, she had it on the evening when she told Peter she could dance all night. Sundry of her friends and sundry more of her enemies speculated a little as to what would happen when Gore returned, and they watched events, when he did come, with interest—no doubt much regretting their inability to know quite all the details of what took place.

The first thing which took place—and that was one of the details generally unknown—was that Desire postponed the meeting between herself and Gore by twenty-four hours. The result of which was that he heard of Peter Grimstone before he saw Desire, and the hearing was not favourable to the parties concerned. The next thing that occurred, also unknown to most, was that at the appointed time of meeting Desire was three-quarters of an hour late. Now Desire was frequently late for things—not inevitably, she was sometimes minutely punctual, there was an uncertainty about her uncertainty which made it quite impossible to allow for it.

But on this occasion, when the man she was to marry in a few weeks returned to her after absence and ill-health, she might reasonably have been expected to be punctual, or even waiting to receive him. She was not, and for three-quarters of an hour he waited for her in her boudoir in the Quebell house; and his eager impatience to see her fought not unnaturally with his growing anger with what he had recently heard. The latter was not decreased by the sight of a book lying on the seat of her favourite chair—*The Dreamer*, by Peter Grimstone.

But at last Desire came; she was in walking-dress, wearing one of the preposterous hats she sometimes affected, and either haste or uneven weight, or the difficulty of steering anything so big out of a hansom in safety had tilted it unbecomingly aslant. Gore noticed it, it was very emphatically obvious, he never before remembered having seen anything the matter with Desire's appearance, wind did not disarrange her, she never came to pieces anywhere, nor found the most unhandy garments any impediment to graceful movement. But to-day she trod on her own superabundant draperies as she came in encumbered with small things—sunshade, gloves, glittering purse, cigarette case. She tumbled them out of her hands and filled the room with her presence.

'Oh, Ted!' she cried, 'I am so sorry! I quite forgot you were coming! How are you?' Taking both his hands into what was to spare of hers. 'Very fit? Yes, you look it; you have done wonders in the way of improving: I don't know how you can have done it in the time, it seems only the other day you went away.'

She dropped his hands, not because of the look in his eyes, but to secure her sunshade which was slipping from under her arm.

'I am glad you found the time pass so quickly,' he said stiffly. 'I hope pleasantly, too?'

'Of course, I always enjoy everything and every minute, but

you know that.' She bent to the bell—'You are dying for tea or whisky or something, I know—I am.'

As she bent, the seductive lines of her splendid figure were brought into sight; the perfect curves, the free movement, struck the eye with their old appeal, the deep, full vibrant voice—though saying things hard to forgive—struck the ear with its appeal too, the appeal to primitive man. Desire, whatever she said or did, was still Desire, and half of Gore for a moment forgot that the other half was justly angry with her. Out of the tail of her eye she saw the look which came into his. He made a step towards her, which she discreetly did not see, being, it would seem, busy disentangling her long chin from a projecting ornament.

'Desire!'

The chain was disentangled and she turned. 'Well,' she said, with the discriminating bravado which goes forward to meet that which must come, 'aren't you going to kiss me?'

For answer he took her in his arms.

But the minute was ill-chosen—or well-chosen—for William, after a knock which one of the two did not hear, had just got the door open, and, being laden with a tea-tray and followed by an excited poodle, found retreat more than difficult. William was an excellent servant and so of course understood all about hearing nothing, seeing nothing and being surprised at nothing. But he was also an Englishman and consequently found his present situation so embarrassing as to make him forget to hide the fact. Gore likewise was an Englishman and had an intense dislike to looking ridiculous. Men in love do not always think how they look, usually they take care there is no disinterested person to look; but only part of Gore was in love, also he was placed with a mirror on one side and the embarrassed William on the other. And Desire wore a hat of vast dimensions, secured with so many and large pins that no trifle would shift its position from her face—though some mystery seemed to have moved it earlier. Also she had put her arms about his neck, with a fervour highly flattering as an expression of affection, but extremely detrimental to his collar.

That embrace was a failure as no previous one in his intercourse with Desire had been, and he freed himself as soon as he could.

Desire looked over her shoulder and called to William, who had effected a bad retreat. 'Come in, William, come in!'

Then she sat down with the utmost unconcern. Her serene disregard for appearances could be curiously irritating, Gore thought.

'Now,' she said, 'tell me all about yourself and everything.'

'I think,' Gore returned a little stiffly, 'it would be better if you were to tell me.'

'It isn't half so interesting,' she said, carelessly sugaring the tea which he always took unsweetened, 'but I'll tell you. What would you like to hear and who would you like to hear about?'

Gore did not say Grimstone, though no doubt he thought it; however, as he soon found, all roads led to that Rome. 'Tell me what you were doing this afternoon,' he said.

'I was with Mr Grimstone; we went—'

'Indeed?' Gore's irritation would not let her finish the sentence. 'You did not think it worthwhile waiting in for me, then?'

'Well,' Desire said truthfully, 'no; I'm afraid I didn't. I knew I should be in in heaps of time, I mean I knew I could have been in if I had remembered. I'm awfully sorry I didn't. You don't think, do you, that I ought to have stopped in in case I forgot? You wouldn't think it if I hadn't forgotten, you know.'

'I really can't say what I might have thought under different circumstances,' Gore said.

'Shall I tell you what you think under these?' Desire asked. 'That I am a most irritating person, and no doubt I am.'

She put a hand lightly on his as she spoke, and her touch he, like some others, found curiously magnetic, almost thrilling. But as she stretched out her hand the hanging laces of her sleeve caught the handle of a tea-cup, so the usual effect was lost.

'Who is this Grimstone?' Gore asked when the tea had been wiped up.

'A friend of mine,' Desire answered. 'He's not usually free of an afternoon, except Saturdays, that's why it seemed such a pity to waste to-day. He's a writer, you know.'

'I have heard of him.'

'His book?' There was a note of eagerness in the tone, as of one who has unexpectedly struck a subject of mutual interest. For a person of Desire's perceptions both tone and question sounded singularly foolish.

'No,' Gore answered shortly; 'not his book.'

After that the conversation progressed unsatisfactorily, as unsatisfactorily as any of the interested friends or enemies could have wished.

Gore dined with the Quebells that evening; that was Lady Quebell's doing. He would have refused if he could. Even when he went home to dress he had thoughts of not returning, but sending some excuse instead; the only thing which prevented him was a suspicion that it might suit Desire's arrangements too well if he did.

Lady Quebell was ignorant of what had occurred in the afternoon, but she guessed from his manner that all was not well. She concluded that he had already heard some of the gossip that was going round. And so far, it seemed, the spell of Desire's personality had not entirely erased the impression, but let him have some more of it and, so she believed, all might still be well; so she insisted on his dining with them. But in counting on Desire's fascination she counted on what did not exist that night. Desire was most unbecomingly dressed, she had unnecessarily and inartistically powdered her face; she seemed tired, too, almost listless, her usual exuberant vitality eclipsed into commonplaceness, and her conversation dull in the extreme. She did not even take an intelligent interest in what Gore said; her mind was apparently elsewhere, and she did not trouble to conceal that fact. She did not actually mention Grimstone more than once, but it was clear to an observer that a good deal of her conversation might have reference to him, and her thoughts plainly were not with her present company. Lady Quebell having the performances of the past weeks in her mind, felt very uneasy and very angry. However, she had one comfort, whatever Gore's justifiable feelings, he could do little. Even if his outraged sensibilities or pride or vanity provoked him so far as to wish, in a moment of irritation, to break the engagement, he could not well do it. She herself could make it well nigh impossible for him to do it creditably; the break, if break there was to be, must come from Desire. So far, in spite of her recent egregious and foolish conduct, she had shown no signs of intending to make it. It is one thing for an impulsive woman to make a fool of herself over a penniless and entirely ineligible man, and quite another to throw over an entirely eligible and recognized lover for him and to face the public talk of breaking an engagement within a few weeks of marriage.

Lady Quebell, thinking over these things, went to bed comparatively happy, recollecting, with satisfaction, an arrangement she had made that Gore should go to Hurlingham with them on Monday. Also of the further arrangement she had privately made that she herself should lunch with friends and join their party to Hurlingham, leaving Gore and Desire to come on alone. 'Give him enough of Desire,' was her opinion, 'and the thing is done, and let him be seen publicly with her again, and the thing cannot be undone.'

But her satisfaction might have been lessened had she seen a letter Desire wrote soon after the Hurlingham arrangement was made. It was to the other woman, of whose very existence Lady Quebell did not know, and would have reckoned of small importance if she had. It ran—

> Be somewhere near this house on Monday afternoon. You may have to wait some while, but have no appearance of watching. When the time arrives, and he comes, you should have the look of being there by chance, and, if possible, not seeing which house he comes from. There is no visible break yet, but our relationship is strained and his patience near snapping point. There has been no mention of you between us; I don't advise there should be any mention of me between you, unless, of course, he tells you of his impending marriage. But I leave you to cope with your situation; you will be playing for a big stake and doubtless will know how best to play.

Desire signed her name to this, and also gave an approximate time for Monday. Then she posted it herself, not because she distrusted Barton, had she done so the posting would have been highly unwise, as likely to give rise to suspicion, but because she somehow felt ashamed for herself and for Gore, and would not admit the maid even to the outskirts of this dethronement.

On Monday Lady Quebell betook herself to her luncheon-party, and afterwards to Hurlingham, in peace of mind. Desire, who had kept her room that morning, on a reputed headache, took her lunch alone. Gore had pleaded another engagement, and said he would come afterwards.

He came, and found Desire in morning dress, her head too bad for Hurlingham. Too bad also, it would seem, for conversation, for anything but the quintessence of aggravation, or at least, so he found it. She, when his irritation became a little apparent, suggested he should go to Hurlingham alone. He refused rather curtly, and in his turn suggested she should give him some sort of explanation of what he had heard.

'An explanation?' she said, with a little weary movement. 'I'll try, if you like, but I warn you, I'm feeling terribly stupid to-day. What am I to explain? Something unpleasant, I suppose, since you seem so—no, I won't say bad-tempered, though it's a fact.'

Gore frowned. 'I should like to know the meaning of the talk I have heard—the talk about you.'

'My dear man,' the flippancy of her tone jarred with the gravity of his, 'what a preposterous request! You seem to have forgotten in your voyaging on the high seas that we never talk when we have anything to say, and always talk when we have nothing. I couldn't possibly tell you what I meant by what I said, and as for what other people do—' she spread out her hands helplessly.

The frown deepened on Gore's face. 'This is mere quibbling,' he said. 'You must know to what I refer; you must be aware of what is being said about you.'

'According to my step-mother,' Desire returned, 'hundreds of things are said about me every day; I must be, according to her, the most thought of, talked of, considered person in town. But I'm not, you know; I don't suppose what I do interests any one: it interests her, of course, when it displeases her, it is then that I bulk largely in her mind, and then, poor dear, she makes the mistake of thinking I must in other people's too. Perhaps that is what has occurred to you?'

'I am naturally interested in what you do,' he said, 'and not unnaturally displeased with what I have heard.'

'Oh dear!' Desire exclaimed with impatience. 'What have you heard? Do for goodness' sake say what you want to say and have done with it! What have I been doing? Cheating, stealing, committing adultery?'

Gore had never before seen Desire's good-humour and imperturbable calm shaken. He did not appreciate it now. 'Grimstone—' he began, but, with a whirl of passion, she cut him short.

'Grimstone, is it? A man who has got brain, who has got character, who is above the common ruck and not understood by them! Well, he's my friend, if that is what you want to know, and I hope he always will be. Will that satisfy you?'

'No.'

She pushed the smelling bottle, ostentatiously placed at her elbow, from her, as if seeking more room. 'Oh, Lord!' she exclaimed, with concentrated irritation, 'what does the man want? I can't explain him away, if that's what you want—and I wouldn't if I could. But go on, ask me questions, I'll answer you if I can; I should think a catechism would best meet your requirements.'

Gore rose. 'I think it would perhaps be better if I were to go,' he said stiffly.

Desire rose with alacrity. 'Well, if you really must,' she said, with a disconcertingly sudden cheerfulness of tone. 'See you to-night, perhaps,' she said carelessly; 'I go to the St Justs' for bridge, do you? And on to the Beauforts' afterwards—if my head's better; I think I shall lie down and take care of it for a while; I must go to the Beauforts' anyhow—I—'

She did not say she had promised to meet, or agreed to take, Peter Grimstone there, but Gore was perfectly convinced that was the case. His manner became stiffer and more distant than ever, also more dignified as he remembered the social unimportance—a matter which weighed much with him—which gossip ascribed to this man. 'I am to understand,' he said, 'that you would rather rest now, in preparation for the'—he wanted to say meeting, but did just say—'entertainment—this evening than give me any sort of explanation of your proceedings?'

It was very clear that he might understand this; Desire let him do so in no propitiatory way. In a short time he took his departure, he had not been invited to sit down again, though during the few minutes he stood Desire contrived to be supremely irritating and unpleasant before she finally dismissed him.

'Good-bye,' she said at last, with a touch of the flippancy; 'and when you come out to-night do let me advise you to leave the grand seigneur manner at home, such wonderful seriousness is quite out of fashion now; no-one has time to do anything but eat, drink, and be merry now, you know.'

He bowed stiffly. 'Good-bye,' he said, and shut the door after him.

She glanced at the clock; she had glanced covertly once before now, as he left her she glanced openly; it was not much after the hour she had appointed. He went downstairs, she listened till her straining ears caught the quiet closing of the hall door. He had gone now. She leaned back and shut her eyes; very much as if she were in the stress of the neuralgic pain she had earlier claimed. They would be meeting soon, somewhere near; she, the other woman, would not miss him, her whole soul, her life almost was in the matter, she would not miss. Desire did not know where they would meet, she had no wish to know or see, had she by an impossible accident been by when they met she would have turned away, she would have gone into a shop, a public-house, a hovel, anywhere to hide herself. Even here, alone, a glow of shame spread over her, not shame for herself exactly, certainly not for the other woman, rather for Gore, and for human nature through him.

'Edith,' that was her name, he would say 'Edith!' in complete astonishment and perhaps at the moment almost fear. He would glance round, and then, in the face of her apparent ignorance, recover and draw her to some less conspicuous spot. He would excuse himself perhaps and be awkward; but she would be gentle and unconscious, not regretful or resentful or anything but glad to see him. He would be relieved; he would find relief and comfort in her company; her sympathy would be balm to him; her gentleness rouse his shamed chivalry. Before they were aware of it they would begin to walk together; they would speak of his health, his journey, his long absence—safe things, soothing things for one who had been jarred on as he had. She would know how to soothe, this Edith who loved; she would be tactful, sympathetic, she would humble herself in heart and soul, hiding her knowledge and her hurt, striving only to win him back. He would say nothing of his impending marriage, he had not the courage before, he would not have now; he would not have the mental courage, either, to repulse the woman he had loved—did love still? The better of him might protest against the duplicity, but the better would also crave for her company in rebound from the company he had just left. For a little he might waver but in the end he would go with her; he would argue that there was no reason why he should not recapture one hour of their old restful happiness. They would drive away together. Where? Perhaps to her home—his home—the child's home!

A spasm of pam contracted Desire's face, and for a little she lay back quite still, her strong fingers crushing a fold of her dress.

After a little she opened her eyes and, though her mouth still twitched a little, they held again the half-whimsical, half-amused look with which she fronted most of the happenings of her life.

'You are a fool, my friend,' so she told herself; 'he isn't worth it, and she isn't worth it, and you aren't worth it, nothing is. A fool, a fool, a fool!'

She took up *The Dreamer*, which had been lying ostentatiously open at her elbow when Gore came in. 'Let us retire to the world of Never Was and Never Will Be, with one who has nothing to do with Things-as-they-are.'

Chapter V

Alexander Grimstone came home in March. He had apparently been expected for some days before he came, quite how many Mrs Grimstone did not know, she only knew what her husband told her—briefly, that he was coming. She was much astonished by the news, but, taught by past experience, did not ask any useless questions. It was enough for her that he was coming, that she should see him again, and probably soon see the wife over whom the quarrel had been begun eight years ago, and the two children, her grandchildren, who were strangers to her. She was happy in the thought, and made what preparations she could. She could not kill the fatted calf, for she did not know for which meal to have it dressed, but she put fine linen sheets upon the best spare bed, and pictured to herself over and over again the manner of Alexander's return. She did not, of course, know what was bringing him, whether the initial move was made by him or by her husband; but her pictures of his return all had reference to repentant sons and forgiving fathers and misunderstandings cleared away. They overlooked such characteristics as mutual obstinacy and mutual cold-heartedness; and also overlooked the fact that Alexander, who at the time of the quarrel had been turned out to shift for himself, had succeeded in shifting very well—a thing liable to make a difference to repentance in some people.

For two days Mrs Grimstone wove her pictures; but nothing happened, there was no sign of Alexander and no word about him. She was rather puzzled, for, from what her husband said, she had concluded that he would come at once, any time; she kept hot bottles in the spare bed and wondered to herself; then, on the morning of the third day, she asked her husband when he expected Alexander. He told her that he had not the slightest idea. Yet, from his manner, she felt sure that he, like herself, had expected him earlier. Wisely, however, she did not say so.

The day wore through, a cold grey day it was, with occasional squalls of rain on a high wind—too wet and windy for any one, like Mrs Grimstone, bronchially inclined, to go out. It was rather a long day, but the old lady, with patient briskness, went about small household tasks. Towards night the wind dropped and it became very quiet, so quiet that one could hear steps a good way off; Mrs Grimstone found herself listening for steps as she sat by the fire mending. It was very absurd, of course, but she found herself doing it, though the very few that came along never stopped there.

Supper was at nine at the Grimstones', and probably always would be so long as Ezra Grirnstone lived; the household being ordered on the lines which found favour with the Medes and Persians, where the laws alter not. On this particular night Ezra and his wife sat down as usual, one at each end of the table, and as usual sat in silence. People who have been married thirty odd years and started without an interest in common seldom have much to say to each other, unless they belong to a class who practise polite conversation in private. Once, as Mrs Grimstone glanced across at the stern face opposite, she wondered if her husband were thinking of the son who had not returned; but there was nothing to indicate it, and the thought was soon banished from her mind by momentary annoyance with Mary, who had brought in the wrong dish.

It was just at that minute, almost the only one in the past three days when he was not uppermost in her thoughts, that Alexander came.

He walked in much as if he had been in the habit of doing so every day, and as if he had walked out not longer ago than this morning. There was no surprise, no emotion; even in

Mrs Grimstone's mind—so strong was the influence about her—there was no emotion, her dominant feeling was regret that she had not prepared a finer supper.

She did rise impulsively and exclaim, 'Oh, Alexander!'

But he only replied, 'Well mother,' and kissed her lightly before she was fairly out of her chair and long before she could put her arms about his neck—if she had any thought of doing so.

Then he shook hands with his father. 'Sorry I'm late,' he said; 'I had to see a man in the town on business, and it took longer than I expected.'

The father merely nodded, and Alexander sat down in the place that used to be his. Mrs Grimstone plied him with food, and did her best to make him welcome. He told her not to trouble, and helped himself, much as if his usual place were at that table. He had a good appetite, but in spite of that and the start his father and mother had had, he was easily done first; he ate as he talked, fast, faster than the average, and as one who thought anything more leisurely a waste of time.

Mrs Grimstone longed to ask after her little-known daughter-in-law, and even more after the children, but she was afraid in her husband's company. She had to content herself with inquiries after Alexander's health, which was obviously very good, and remarks concerning her own which did not greatly interest him. The father and son spoke a little together on impersonal topics, rather as might two unsociable strangers who are thrown together at an hotel table. Mrs Grimstone, listening, glanced from one to the other, and noticed, without understanding, the changes time had made in Alexander. He was a little like his father in some ways, but with several marked differences, the most striking being the eyes, which in him were over-near together and of the opaque hardness of stone. He was a good deal fairer than his father, too, having the greyish-yellow colouring of some animal. There was nothing in his appearance to suggest the repentant son; and nothing, it must be admitted, in the elder man's to suggest the forgiving father.

At last supper was finished, and Mary, the elderly servant, accompanied by Robert her husband, came in for prayers. The old man fetched a Bible, and let it, perhaps by chance, fall open at the parable of the Prodigal Son, as he put it before his master. Mr Grimstone turned back the leaves till he came to the place where he left off reading last night. It was the prophet Jeremiah's reproof to an unrepentant and backsliding generation. He read a passage in a level voice, and afterwards they all knelt down, and from another book he read a prayer. It was a formal prayer, and he read it formally; only once did a trace of feeling creep for a moment into his voice—when the text contained a supplication that all present might be brought to right courses and kept therein. But no-one observed him, Mrs Grimstone was surreptitiously wiping her eyes, moved less by the occasion than by her own previous pictures of it—and Alexander was thoughtfully picking his teeth.

When the prayer was concluded they all rose, and Mr Grimstone asked his son to come with him to his office. Mrs Grimstone hesitated a moment; but no-one invited her to come—evidently no-one thought of her—so she remained where she was, rather wistfully looking after them.

Would the reconciliation, the real reconciliation, take place now? She wondered—was sure—was doubtful—and sure again. She wished so she could help, not so much for Alexander's sake. She had never felt much more for Alexander than the parent animal's instinct for its young—it is doubtful if any woman could have done—and though the eight years' absence had obliterated the memory of some of his unlovable ways, it had not really increased her affection, whatever she might for the moment think. But for the sake of the children, her grandchildren whom she had never held in her arms, she could have forgiven him anything. If only Ezra felt the same! For a little after the two left her she stood listening; once she was almost inclined to follow uninvited, in the hope of helping to ratify the peace which might or might not be made. But she did not, the habit of submission kept her where she was; and common sense warned her, too, that though there was a chance that father and son might not come to terms, there was no chance at all of her being able to help them. So she sat down again and took up her mending, while Mary cleared the table and commented, with the familiarity of long service, on Alexander and the changes she observed in him.

But in the small room at the back the father and son were not talking of reconciliation, such a thing, in the emotional sense of the word, was not in the power of either of them. What they spoke of was a commercial understanding, a species of business treaty which, it is true, some might mistake for a form of reconciliation. Ezra Grimstone had sent for his son to make him an offer: to take him into the little old firm of Grimstone & Son; to ignore the eight years' absence, and the quarrel which had preceded it, and the accumulated differences which had preceded that; not to forgive or to forget them, but to ignore them in the commercial relationship.

That was the offer; not magnificent pecuniarily, perhaps, for the firm of Grimstone & Son was very small. Ezra Grimstone was a potter, as his father and grandfather had been before him, though he was not of what is considered the true potter breed. The first Ezra was not a native born, and the family, in spite of the work, had never really amalgamated with the potter caste, but kept much to itself, mixing little. In the far-off time of the first Ezra, which had been the time of small concerns and working masters, the firm had counted for something. In these days of large concerns, with their eight or ten ovens, rotary kilns, and several hundred hands, it counted for little more than a curious survival.

It paid still, even though it was situated some way from a railway—it had been built in the days when water was the highway—but it was in no way important. To Ezra, however, it was everything; he had worked in it and lived with it as his father and grandfather had; it was all his life, as it had been all theirs. To him the continuity of the pottery was as the continuity of the name to a great family, perhaps more, for he had nothing else besides. For its sake he had made this overture to Alexander, a thing he would not have brought himself to do for his own sake or his wife's, or Alexander's, or the grandchildren's, or anything in the world. For the sake of Grimstone & Son he had sent for him, for, whatever else Alexander was, he was the man to carry on the business. He had sent for him, and to-night he made him the offer.

And Alexander said nothing. Even when the offer was made he sat quite still a moment, a thing rare with him, for he was a curiously restless person. Whether the proposal surprised him or not did not appear, like all the Grimstones his face masked his feelings well; but he eyed his father once or twice as if seeking to find if he had any ulterior motive. He passed his hand over his long chin, a habit he had when he was approaching anything warily. 'How do you stand?' he asked. 'The books—have you got them handy?'

The elder man nodded. 'You are cautious of accepting a gift,' he said, 'but you never were great at either giving or receiving.'

'No,' Alexander said carelessly, and did not add, as he perhaps might, that the characteristic was inherited. He stretched his legs before the cold grate. 'I take it,' he said, 'the proposal is in the way of business?'

Ezra did not answer, he was unlocking a safe in the corner; from it he took books, which he carried to the high desk.

Alexander rose and came to examine them, and his father drew away.

For a little there was silence except for the turning of leaves.

Ezra had taken his son's place in the black leather chair now; unlike him it was natural to him to sit very still, he sat so now, watching the long back of the younger man as he stooped to examine the entries.

At last Alexander closed the books and pushed them from him. 'You seem to be holding your own still,' he said, almost as if he thought it rather strange.

The elder Grimstone put the books away without speaking; when that was done he turned to his son. 'Well?' he said curtly. 'You are satisfied as to the position, and you hear what I offer; what's your answer?'

'I'm considering,' Alexander said, leaning back against the mantelpiece and picking his teeth again.

'Considering!' Ezra's voice for a moment lost its distant coldness and rang sharp. 'It's a new thing for a son of Grimstones'—and such a son—to consider whether he shall come into the pottery or not. One would think I was asking you a favour!'

'Not they! No-one who knew us would think it, we don't deal in favours, this is business pure and simple.'

'Poor business on your part,' the father said, 'if it takes you so long to decide if you'll have something for nothing.'

'One's got to make sure just what the something is,' Alexander told him. 'Oh, I know your opinion of the firm of Grimstone —it's natural, of course, though not necessarily right on that account. But outside this house—I don't want to hurt your feelings—but outside the opinion's not the same. What is Grimstones' to the average man? A two-man-and-a-boy affair, a one-kiln curiosity where they can turn out five crates a week. It makes a profit, I know, a small one, just enough to keep going. It has a good name, too, and a decent connection of sorts, something might be done with it, but at present—Why, my own show's much bigger, my turnover's a lot more.'

The elder Grimstone's eyes gleamed, but he kept himself in hand. 'You are a tradesman,' he said, 'and if all that is reported is true, not too honest a one in all your dealings.'

'We're all in trade,' his son answered carelessly. 'I buy and sell pots, you make 'em, there isn't much difference, and we all make what profit we can. By the way, I'm trying a new line, something more in your way: we do a bit of decorating at my place now. There is something in that—buy pots cheap and decorate 'em yourself—don't you think so?'

'I don't know anything about it,' Ezra said coldly.

'And don't want to?' Alexander inquired with a little amusement. 'But you will—that is, if we amalgamate.'

'We are not going to amalgamate.'

'Not?'

'Certainly not. That is not what I offer. My offer is that you join me as I joined my father, and he joined his. That Grimstone & Son is Grimstone & Son, as it always has been, and always will be.'

This interpretation of the offer had never occurred to Alexander, and for a moment he could hardly realize it, it was so altogether absurd.

'You don't mean that?' he said. 'Why, it's madness! What about the business I have built up? If it is not to be amalgamated, what do you propose I should do with it?'

'Anything you choose—sell it, wind it up—do what you please, but get rid of it before you come to me.'

'Get rid of it? Get rid of it?'

'Certainly; get rid of it, and hope that you may get rid of the name you have begun to get in it. I don't say anything about your ways of doing business. I have heard of them, of course, and I may regret them as I may regret your choice of a wife and your want of religion; but I can't undo what's done. This is all I have to say—I am ready to overlook that, and have you here in a son's place, but on the understanding that you wind up your present concern, dispose of your capital how you like—I won't have it—and come to me with empty hands and an intention of keeping them clean.'

Alexander drew in his breath in almost a whistle; the folly of his father's words was such to him that it made him for a moment forget to notice the slight on his integrity that they held. To refuse to amalgamate, to refuse the new young business, to refuse even the capital it might represent. It was incredible! To imagine for an instant that he, Alexander, would think of acquiescing in such an arrangement was an insult to his intelligence—as big an insult as the comments on his ways of doing business (which certainly had been near the wind, but had always come off safely). He was for a moment really roused; nevertheless, when he spoke it was with no contemptuous or angry expression of outraged dignity, for, above all things, he loved money, and he seldom lost his head or his temper where it was concerned. He saw advantages to himself in a treaty—on rational terms, of course—with his father, advantages greater than the elder man could. He believed that the union once made and himself fairly in power at the little old pottery, as well as in his own business, the way to fortune would be comparatively cleared to him and his pace along it accelerated. Therefore, having no wish to refuse his father's offer entirely, and no intention of giving up his own concern, he spoke cautiously and with moderation. He argued for the amalgamation, pointing out such advantages as he deemed wise; without, however, showing undue anxiety for it, or letting it be seen that he had all along meant to accept his father's offer—on his own terms.

But in the years that had passed since he and his father had discussed any affair he had forgotten two things—the immovableness of his father's prejudices, and the fact that they two had never been able to get on the dark side of each other. In vain did he put his case speciously, and explain his own past proceedings and condemned methods with ingenuity and a fine frankness. He might just as well have made his statement baldly, the older man followed the working of his mind perfectly and did not alter his own a hair's-breadth.

With complete obstinacy Ezra held to his original offer. 'Either,' he said, 'you come on my terms or you don't come at all. You are surprised? You always thought money everything, you think so now, I suppose? Thought you would come to me on your own terms with your capital and I should be glad to have it? But I tell you, such capital is dross to me, husks—yes, husks, as if when the prodigal son arose and went to his father he took a bushel of the swine's husks with him.'

Alexander bit his lip, nothing but his keen eye for pecuniary advantage kept his tongue under any sort of control. 'We'd better stick to trade,' he said curtly, 'if you start in with Bible parables we shall get no further. Though, let me tell you while you are on the parable tack, that, even if you do believe you feel like the biblical father, I don't pretend to feel like the repentant son. Also, you might bear in mind, that it was you who said "come", not I who said "I will go", in this case.'

'I know I did,' Ezra returned. 'I did it for the pottery—I want nothing of you myself, seeing the way you think and act and have acted, you can be no son to me. It was not for that I sent for you, and it was not for that you came. But there is the pottery, you are wanted there; Ezra is dead, Peter is no use; you are of use, you are the one who must come after me if Grimstone & Son is to go on and not die out when I die.'

There was a subdued passion in his voice which, plainer than words, showed Alexander the strength of his position. He himself had no more feeling for the little old firm than for his father; but he saw, probably for the first time, the depth of his father's feeling for it, and seeing determined to profit and to hold out for his own terms.

'As father,' the elder man was saying, 'I have nothing for you;

you married against my wish—a shallow, shiftless fool with a little money to her name, and it was the money which took you, not the fool. You thwarted me at every turn, you scoffed at what I hold to, you ran counter to me where you could. You are a stranger to me, neither you nor I wish anything else, we do not pretend about it. But as Ezra Grimstone, the third Grimstone, I have this for you—you can come back and join me as I joined my father. As I joined him, mind—not otherwise. Those are my terms.'

Alexander laughed, a short loud laugh, not infectious. 'Your terms are too high,' he said, and felt for a cigarette. Ezra eyed him over, and his eyes were very cold. 'You refuse?' he asked quietly. 'To bind myself to make pots with old Robert and a boy for the rest of my life? Yes, I do.'

He held the cigarette-case for a moment, but did not open it, the old stringent rules against promiscuous smoking still had an unconscious influence. 'Is it likely,' he asked, 'that a man of my age, and one who you say yourself has some capacity, is going to be content with that sort of job, little better than the job of a labourer at thirty bob a week, in a little pot-bank in his own backyard, all because his grandfather and great-grandfather did before him? It's not good enough. I'm going to make money, I am making it now, but I'd make it quicker if I joined up with you, we'd make it together. We'd run the old place more or less on the old lines—if you liked, you could run it if it's your hobby, but we'd couple it, at all events—couple the name up with several new things, and you may bet they'd pay.'

'Then you refuse?' Ezra repeated the question in the same level, emotionless voice.

'I've told you so, but—'

'Then no more need be said. Good-night.'

The voice, though still emotionless, somehow cut off what Alexander had to say, and with a sharp finality. For a moment the younger man looked at the elder uncertainly, as if in the years which had elapsed since they last did battle he had forgotten. Then he turned away with his short laugh; he remembered, but he did not repent; he, too, had learnt nothing of giving way. Moreover, he lay this comfort to his mind, if he lost by refusal, the father lost still more—so much more that he must at some future time be driven to make the offer again.

'Good-night,' he said, and went to the door.

Mrs Grimstone, sitting by the parlour fire, heard the office door open, heard steps in the hall, heard the front door open and close again, and then the dull rasping sound as the bolts on the inner side were shot home when it was made fast for the night.

'Alexander!' she called.

There was no answer, and, made bold by anxiety, she went to look down the hall. 'Alexander!' she said. Ezra Grimstone rose from stooping to the lower bolt.

'Alexander has gone,' he said.

'Gone! Isn't he going to stay the night?'

'No.'

'When is he coming back?'

'Never.'

And Ezra went slowly down the hall, back to the office, where he went in and shut the door.

Neither then nor later did he tell his wife any detail of what had happened, or indeed make any reference to it. It might as well have never occurred. Alexander might never have come home for all that was said between them about it. Alexander himself did not write to his mother, he sent no line of farewell or regret at not seeing her again. He was busy, and it did not occur to him; he felt no regret himself, and never thought of her in the matter. Demonstrative affection, like the social amenities, had been entirely absent from the boyhood and youth of the Grimstones, a lack which cold natures and strong and energetic ones cannot always afford. The habit of considering others, even when there is no heart in it, is worth something. Alexander had neither the heart nor the habit, so he wrote no word to his mother, and she had to guess as much as she could of what had happened.

As for Ezra, he grew even more silent; each day seemed to make him grimmer and graver and greyer; she saw it vaguely as Mary and Robert did, and was as far from any spoken confidence as they. Daily he worked as before, longer hours rather than shorter; but it was as if a frost was on him and on everything he touched.

Thus through the spring and early summer, and on till the end of July, when he was taken ill.

It was not a serious illness, though it kept him from work a little while, and would have kept him longer had the work been further away than his own house, and his workman and chief factotum any other than Robert. But the illness did two things. In the first place it gave Mrs Grimstone the opportunity for which she was hungering, of feeding and caring for some one. Her husband was not a good subject, still he bore her ministrations with patience—more could hardly be expected of him. And in the second it decided Ezra to make some definite provision for Grimstone & Son. If he died, and of course he must die some time, or if he was long incapacitated by illness, or in any way forced to lose his grip on things—and he realized with a bitterness that was almost humiliation that this was as likely to befall him as another—if any of these things happened Alexander would take for himself and on his own terms that which he had refused on his father's. There was only one way of preventing it, someone else must be put in to hold what Ezra prized when he no longer could. But who? As he lay ill he thought about this, and about very little else. He was a man practically without friends, and possessed of few relations, none of whom he thought anything. He had no-one to put in his place in the pottery but Robert, a man almost as old as he was, and not equal to dealing with Alexander—and Peter, who he himself had described as no use.

Peter was no use, his father had never thought him so; for this reason it had not seemed to him important what profession Peter followed so long as it was honest. The one chosen was one of which he had no opinion—it belonged to the realm of play, not work, in his estimation. He had not interfered with Peter's choice of it, because he thought him useless for anything better, but the choice was only a further proof of the uselessness and Peter's recognition of it. Yet it seemed that on this useless one Grimstones' must now fall back. It was bitterly hard, he had no business ability, no potter's instinct, none of the required characteristics; but there was no-one else. One only quality useful to the position did Ezra recognize, Peter would make a fight to hold his own against Alexander; he might or might not do it, but he would make a stubborn fight for it. For the rest, he must himself try to teach him, and endure how he could the incompetency and ineptitude.

He rang for his wife, and ordered her to bring writing materials.

She brought them, the ink with some reluctance. Some of her fine linen sheets were on the bed, and she was afraid for them in the neighbourhood of the ink-pot.

'Wouldn't it be easier for you to write with a pencil?' she said.

'Eh?' Ezra said. He was looking to see if she had brought him the paper he wanted.

'You will be careful of the ink, won't you, dear?' she ventured.

'The ink? Oh yes. You have not brought me an envelope.

Ah, here's one. Well, address it yourself if you like, and I can write the letter in pencil. Address it to Peter; then you can go downstairs again. I shall be some time writing. Peter never had much sense, still he is all there is—'

The last was hardly spoken to Mrs Grimstone, and she did not answer it, but it caught her attention. That her husband should write to Peter at all caught her attention, she could not think what it could be about. She went downstairs wondering much; she was not clever, and she had no very good clue, but like many another simple woman she sometimes divined things where her heart was concerned. Instinctively she felt that much hung on this letter of her husband's, and when she felt that it came to her, though she trembled at the boldness of the idea, that she too must write. She had done nothing when Alexander came; she stood aside, as it seemed she ought—and he had come and gone. Perhaps she ought to do nothing now; perhaps this matter was not the same, perhaps even it was not really important. Yet she would try. Peter was different from Alexander, Peter would not laugh or mind if she wrote or if she seemed silly. Writing was not easy to her, at most times a letter was a matter of composition needing thought and care, and expressing little of what she felt. Now there was no time for this, she must pen a few hasty lines before she was called upstairs. She felt, almost guiltily, that she must get her letter written and out of the house before she saw her husband again. And she did it, thus happening to catch an earlier post than he did.

Chapter VI

A firm of publishers, old-fashioned and of repute, had written to Peter Grimstone, saying in the impersonal way used in English houses, that they would be glad to see a novel by him. If he had written, was writing, or was contemplating writing a second work of fiction of not less than seventy-two thousand words they would be pleased if he would give them the opportunity of considering it.

To Peter the letter meant a great deal; it was, after Desire's appreciation of *The Dreamer*, the most important thing which had happened since the publication of the book. He still ranked Desire's appreciation first, not only on account of its results, but because to him it was a wonderful and beautiful thing—as all human sympathy really is. But the publisher's letter was important; it meant that outside opinion was justifying his choice of a profession (which mattered little to him), and also that by and by perhaps he would be able to give up the side he did not like, and confine himself to the side he did—which mattered a great deal.

On the same day that he received this letter something else happened, he had a semi-business interview with the important editor to whom Desire had made efforts to introduce him. He had by now seen the great man once or twice socially, but on that particular evening he had a semi-official interview, and one of a most satisfactory order. He was told to come to the office tomorrow in working hours, but in the meantime he had to consider an offer, verbal certainly, but really formal too, such as was the ambition of most men in his position. No wonder, then, as he walked back to his rooms that night he felt the world was opening before him. He was not one much given to exuberance or excitement, but just for once he felt a stir in his blood, the thrill of hope and power. His first book was a success, his second well begun—not being written easily, still, being written with a certain mastery of the tools which made even difficulties not all bad. Life itself was widening to him, there were new powers, new sights, new things. Desire Quebell had done more for him than push *The Dreamer*. To serve herself, truly, she had done a good deal for him; she had shown him a bigger and a fuller world, and not least she had admitted him into an intimacy with herself which was educational after a sort. Life held promise that night when Peter walked back to his rooms along streets, somewhat in need of the washing of the rain, which were to him as the streets of the dream city known only to youth.

He did not exactly build air-castles for the future, he was too cautious and diffident for that; he did not exactly exult in the share of success that had come to him, he had too just an estimate of its actual value, too low an opinion of his own ability; he certainly did not fancy himself in love with Desire Quebell, or make any mistake about her interest in him. But in some way he appreciated and enjoyed all the promise of the future, the fulness of the present, the stirring power within himself. It was to him that night as when one has walked up a steep way in a grey, rugged country, and, coming suddenly out of the shadow at the top, feels the risen sun and sees spread all before the world below. Tardily awakened youth stirred in his blood, and he, teetotaller in such things by necessity as well as by choice, tasted for the first time of the wine of life.

By the time he reached the door of his lodgings he wanted to share what he could of this good thing, wanted to tell someone. Not Desire, she had never climbed the steep grey way, she had started with the sunshine and the spread world at the top, she did not occur to him as a confidante now, only one person did, his mother. She, of course, would not completely understand, he never imagined she would. But many mothers have the divine attribute of understanding by sympathy their children's feelings even when they cannot by reason understand the cause of them. It was this attribute of mothers which Peter unconsciously thought to draw on when he determined to write to his mother that night.

But when he reached his rooms he found, rather to his surprise, a letter from her waiting for him. He also found the fox-terrier Paddy, who had been out on some expedition of his own, and gone home to Peter instead of to his master, a thing he not infrequently did. On these occasions he usually managed to creep unobserved into the house some time when the door was open, and, as now, lay in wait in a dark place till he could make himself known to Peter, apologize for his appearance, and demand congratulations on his ingenuity. Peter told the dog he was a scoundrel, and at the same time made him welcome; then he took up the letter. It was not his mother's day for writing, she wrote once a fortnight; never otherwise, except once when he sent her his book, it must be something very exceptional which made her write now. For a moment it flashed into his mind that perhaps she had read the book now and wrote to tell him her opinion of it, even that hardly seemed too impossible a thing tonight. But the idea went almost as it came, for it really was impossible, also the first glance at the letter assured him that was not its subject.

'My dear Peter,' it ran, 'Your father is writing to you—'

Peter looked round, but there was no other letter, doubtless it would come tomorrow—

> Your father is writing to you, I don't quite know what for, except that I am sure it is about the works; but pray do not come and go away for good and all as Alexander did in the

spring. I do not know what your father asked Alexander or said to him, but I am sure he is never coming again. If he says anything to you, please do try to do it.

Your loving Mother,
Susan Grimstone

PS Your father, who as you know has been ill, is recovering now. I hope you are quite well.

So Peter read, and stood so long with the paper in his hand that Paddy jumped up at it to create a diversion. Peter put the dog aside and returned to the letter. What did it mean? What could it mean? It was written apparently without his father's knowledge, perhaps even in defiance of his implied will; certainly in haste and perturbation of mind, the style and writing betrayed that. Peter could not understand it. He had heard, of course, long ago of Alexander's coming and going away again, but he had heard nothing of importance in connection with it—Mrs Grimstone knew little and could explain less. What had it to do with him? And why was his father writing? What was he going to ask?

A shadow had begun to spread over Peter's exultation. He could not see how he could be robbed of what had so lately come to him; yet he had an intuitive perception of the possibility. He sat down and went over the letter again, trying to read the worst meaning into each phrase and to answer it to himself. At the end a sudden emotion, half anger, half defiance, shook him. He was a fool, and this was folly, and whatever it meant or threatened, it could not and should not hurt. The future to-day had offered him something, the future should fulfil it! He put the letter aside and went to bed. It did not matter what the writer meant, or what the other writer would unfold tomorrow—nothing mattered, nothing could and nothing should. And yet—The exultation was gone, the sun was gone again, and all within was grey and rugged as the hill landscape of his childhood.

Paddy liked staying the night with Peter; apart from his inordinate affection for his adopted master, which would have reconciled him to any discomfort, there was no discomfort to be endured. He spent the night on the foot of Peter's bed, and he always had twice as much breakfast as he did at home. On this, which also proved to be almost the last of his unauthorized visits, something went wrong. He spent a peaceful night, and there was a plenteous breakfast, but he did not enjoy it. Peter did not give it to him at first, he had a letter, newly come, which absorbed his attention, and when at last, reminded by the dog, he remembered to put the food down, there was that in his face which spoiled Paddy's appetite. The dog put his nose in the bowl, then he looked up doubtfully. Peter was sitting down to the table, but he was not eating, he was looking at a pencil letter, which was short enough for him to have already read it once or twice. The dog looked at him curiously, wistfully, face and attitude told something to the half-developed mind, something which vaguely roused fear and sympathy. He left the bowl and moved uneasily, finally he came close, nuzzling against the man. And the man replied by an automatic touch of the hand, the touch of one who by instinct will not hurt a creature's feelings, but who has just now no thought or attention to spare.

Paddy lay down at his feet, nose on paws, mute anguish of dumb and patient sympathy in his eyes. The morning sun streamed in on them and on the neglected bowl of food, a fly buzzed on it, but the dog gave no heed. And the man gave no heed to the sunlight. The sun had gone down on his world, the sun that had only risen clear of the mists yesterday. It was the old grey prospect again, the steep rough climb, the mountainous way which wound always up and up, and never reached the open spaces where there were pauses of rest and margins of pleasure and the far-off view of golden promise.

Why?

He threw up his head with an unconscious movement. Why should he accept it? Why throw away what he had and what he might have for this—this less than nothing, this which must end in failure, this cramping of mind and life, and doing ill what if done well was almost nothing at all? The grey way, the hopeless, ineffectual way was before him; but the other was too. He was not compelled to either, the choice was his own to make.

There was a step on the stairs; Peter heard it, and, with an animal's instinct to hide suffering, turned so that his back was towards the light.

Austin burst cheerfully into the room. 'Congratulations, old chap!' was his greeting. 'Congratulations, and a bespeak of the first good thing you have to give away! Of all the lucky devils in the world you are the luckiest! Not content with casting spells over great ladies for you, fortune must needs cast 'em over great editors too!'

Peter looked up, his face, even if it could have been seen, betraying him very little. 'Congratulations?' he said. 'Oh, you have heard of last night?'

'Yes, I heard. Mason was there, you know. He didn't exactly hear what was said, but he pretty well guessed, and he came along and told us.'

'More than there was to tell, I think,' Peter said, and rising, went to the window and threw it wider. 'It was only an offer,' he said, his back that way, 'and I am not sure that I shall accept it.'

'What!' Austin sat down in astonishment. 'Have you come into a fortune, or achieved fame in a musical comedy, and modestly withheld your name?'

'No,' Peter answered, still looking out of the window; 'but

I'm not sure I shan't throw the whole thing up and go back to my people.'

Austin stared at his back. 'Well, I'll be damned!' he said. Next moment he added inquisitively, 'When did she refuse you?'

'She?—who?'

There was no mistaking the genuineness of Peter's tone. He had for the minute completely forgotten the existence of Desire. Austin saw that, though he answered, 'Queen of hearts, Miss Quebell—though I suppose you will say she has nothing to do with it. Well, well, well, all I can say is your people must be an extremely fascinating lot—wish mine were.'

He rose as he spoke, and turned Paddy over with his foot. 'Ugh! Brute!' he said to the depressed dog; 'is this the way you greet your master?'

The dog took no notice of him, only moved nearer to Peter. 'What's the matter with the beast? He looks as if he had had the thrashing he deserves for desertion.'

'I think he wants to stay with me,' Peter said. 'You might leave him for the present.'

Austin left him, it suited his arrangements. 'Bye-bye,' he said, 'and don't forget I've bespoke the first good thing, Mr Editor.'

From which it is clear he did not now believe in Peter's doubt about taking the offer; in his opinion it was bluff, show-off, youth's vanity pretending to hesitate about accepting what it was in reality ready to jump at. He was very far from realizing that the words held less than the truth, rather than more, and that the battle was more than half over. Peter hardly knew it himself when he spoke; afterwards he did. Afterwards he felt as if he had subconsciously known all along that this would be the end, no matter how he struggled. Whatever the reasons for his not going, in the end he would go. Why?

It was useless to ask why, the thing would not defend itself, did not defend itself, but like most of the motives that really matter, it was as imperative as it was unanswering. A man may struggle with it even though he foresees the end, but the end is the same. Peter struggled all day; not giving way from a sense of duty, from any motive high or low that he knew of, but all along knowing quite well that he would give way, and yet struggling in spite of the knowledge. Throughout his work the thing haunted him, filling in pauses, making itself an accompaniment, everything going to the tune of struggle, the struggle incessant, the end inevitable.

At the end of the day he went to see Desire. He had no appointment with her, but in his assumed role he often went when he could spare time without that. He would probably have gone anyhow that day to tell her of last night's interview and offer; it was necessary he should go now to hear when he could get his discharge.

But when he was shown into Desire's boudoir, where she sat alone, he quickly became aware that she had affairs of her own on her mind. Instinctively his affairs shrank away before them; they could wait, they mattered nothing to her, to anyone but himself. He had lived so solitary and starved a life that he never dreamed of demanding a hearing, let alone sympathy.

'Are you busy?' he said. 'Shall I go?'

She turned a curiously hard face, with eyes glitteringly bright. 'No,' she said, 'better stay. Have you come to talk of wages?'

'Wages? What for?'

'For playing the part of Romeo, a distasteful part well played, to the much wasting of your time.'

'That was paid for beforehand. You have done more for me and my book than can ever be wiped off that way.'

Some of the hard lines on Desire's face smoothed a little, perhaps because she was glad that he had not learnt any of the language of compliment.

'That's nothing, and cost me nothing,' she said, then announced abruptly, 'My engagement's broken off; have you heard?'

He had not, and he knew it must be a very recent doing for him not to have done so, seeing that he had seen her or Gore or both almost every day since the latter's return.

'You've not heard? Well, I tell you now, it's a fact accomplished.'

'I am glad,' he said.

'Why?'

'It is what you wanted, I imagine.'

She laughed, rather a mirthless laugh. 'I told you I always got what I wanted, didn't I?' she said. 'So I do. Of course the breaking of the engagement was what I wanted, I contracted with you to play Romeo for that purpose.'

He nodded. 'I see,' he said, avoiding her eyes. Desire moved uneasily. 'What do you see?' she asked. She would have no avoidance.

He hesitated, then answered truthfully, 'That you thought for some reason your engagement ought to be broken, though it,'—he paused for a word, then concluded—'though it hurt to do it.'

Desire flushed. Even to herself she had not admitted so much. 'What a complicated person you make me!' she commented lightly.

'I am sorry,' he said. 'I ought not to have said that.'

She turned round on him with one of her sudden transformations. 'Why not?' she demanded almost fiercely. 'Why should you not say what you think true? You at least can deal in what you take to be truth, even though it is miles away from other people's idea of it. You are one of the few, too, to whom one can tell the truth—I will tell you the truth of this matter.'

'Don't,' he said. 'I mean, don't if you don't want to. There isn't a bit of need to explain anything to me. I knew all along that you had some sufficient reason which was no concern of mine; it does not matter to me, it never did.'

Desire's curious red-brown eyes softened for a moment. 'What a strange creature you are,' she said. 'All the same, I think I'll tell you.'

And straightway she told him the whole thing, from the first coming of the other woman to her. She told it, of course, with lightness and almost flippancy, anything else would have been impossible in her state of mind.

'There, my friend,' she concluded, 'you have the episode; and the moral is—vanity. "Vanity of vanities, all is vanity". I was so vain a fool that I thought, having pleased a man's eye—that, I am told, is what I did—I had the whole of him. She was so vain a fool that she thought, having pleased a man's brain and helped him in need, she was enough for the whole of him. And he was such a vain fool that he thought half of him was enough for any woman. But my vanity was the biggest and the one which came out top, for I declined to understudy any woman or be understudied by her—and, thanks to you, I have won.'

Peter looked up, but before he could speak she said quickly, 'How does the incident strike your literary soul? Your literary soul, mind; don't tell me about anything else.'

He answered her obediently, and she was grateful to him.

'To my literary soul the end is wrong: the one who did the wrong is the only one who has got off free.'

'And who is that?'

'Gore.'

She laughed, but with a little shiver. 'How rude of you!' she said. 'He has been jilted by me, isn't that misfortune? Besides, how can you know what retribution will be eventually appointed to him? If he marries Edith he may be fool enough to regret it as a mésalliance. If he does not he will certainly regret it sooner or later as an actual loss. A thousand things may happen—undoubtedly will happen. In this kind of farce we don't leave off at the dénouement, we get up next morning.'

Peter accepted the correction. 'But so far as you and I are concerned,' she went on, 'the thing's concluded; there's no more to be said.'

'You don't want me any more?' Peter said. 'The play is done?'

She nodded. 'The curtain's down on the act,' she said, 'and I leave town almost immediately. But as for wanting you,'—she spoke almost wistfully—' I should like you to be my friend, if you can, in spite of this. Perhaps that's too much to ask?'

It was not, Peter said so simply and meant it more literally than she knew; but at the same time he saw little likelihood of ever seeing much of her again, as he himself would have left London before she returned for the winter. He told her so, and of his going away.

'Going?' she said in astonishment, 'for good and all?—why? Do you mean to throw up your work here just as you are beginning to succeed and be recognized? You are beginning to be recognized, too; do you know it?'

'I know,' he said; 'it is largely thanks to you. I had an offer last night which was really through you. I am very grateful, but I am afraid I have got to go—my father wants me.'

Desire for the first time began to be aware that he, too, had come to some sort of crisis in his affairs. No idea of it had crossed her mind until her own concerns were talked out, and even now his manner deceived her into thinking that he himself did not realize the importance and full meaning of what he said, or at least that he did not care much one way or the other for it.

'Explain,' she said; 'tell me what you mean, what are you going to do, and why?'

He obeyed her briefly; he even showed her the two letters, but without succeeding in making his decision plain and reasonable to her—which was not entirely surprising, seeing that he did not know why he had decided himself.

'It is sheer folly!' she exclaimed at last. 'Sheer, utter imbecility!'

'Do you think so?' he said. 'I'm sorry; I'm afraid you must think me ungrateful too.'

'Oh, gratitude's nothing,' she returned impatiently; 'there's nothing to be grateful for. What I do think is that it is folly. I have no patience with your ridiculous duty worshipping people who devote all your time to doing—and making others do if you can—all the hard and unpleasant things to the exclusion of everything else. Oh yes, it is extremely bad to be like me, no doubt, and have no sense of duty at all, but it is no better to be like you and have such a sense of it as to refuse, on principle, to do everything agreeable and pleasant. A lot too much has been made of sacrifice, I consider. I haven't such an opinion of the self-sacrificing saints; I prefer a cheerfully selfish sinner. I thought, too, there was something in the Bible—on which, no doubt, you were brought up—about people who hid their talents and wasted them. What do you think you will be doing with yours?'

'My talent isn't worth much to anybody,' Peter said. 'I don't think anyone would be the better or worse if I wrote or did not write a book or two.'

'There you are wrong, there is one person at least who is the better for you having written a book—that is myself; I don't mean to suggest that matters—it doesn't; only if *The Dreamer* has affected me you may be sure it has affected other people better worth affecting. To me it is a book apart, a sort of human thing impossible of course, but good to have known. Do you think it is no loss if there are no more such human things?'

'Was it that to you?' he asked. 'Did it really seem that?' He was glad, though it made his sense of what he was losing greater; yet it did not shake his determination. Far down in his mind even there was a vague, almost superstitious feeling that, did he stay in the present circumstances some illusive thing which belonged to his craft would leave him.

'Very likely I could not write another such book,' he told Desire. 'That book grew after a fashion; I am not sure I should keep on growing them, the present one isn't growing, it's being made, it isn't really so good—besides,' —he saw from her look that she either could not or would not understand—'I expect I shall have some little time to write at home, not a great deal, but I probably should do it better for having to do it slowly. And anyhow, it doesn't really matter, there are plenty of people to write books but no-one to go home in my place.'

She was entirely unconvinced. 'That is absurd,' she said; 'another man can no more write your books than he can go home in your place; your books are you, and if you don't write them, or if you take fifteen years writing one when you might take one we are that much poorer. You have no business to make the sacrifice and your parents have no business to ask it of you.'

'They are not asking a sacrifice,' Peter said, 'at least they don't think so.'

'That adds to the preposterousness of it,' Desire returned, taking up Ezra Grimstone's letter which clearly demonstrated the fact. 'Your father,' she said, 'evidently thinks he is giving you a great chance, at which you will jump even while you feel yourself as unworthy as he thinks you. It's absurd, of course, but it makes it easier for you; you can refuse without hurting him; you can say you appreciate his kindness and all the rest of it, but know you can't deserve it or do justice to the opportunity, so will just stay where you are. You need not mention that you are earning more and doing better, that his offer is penal servitude, and accepting it would be an egregious waste of time, talents and opportunities. You would not have to hurt his feelings at all.'

Peter knew the Grimstone feelings, wherein they lay and what affected them. 'It is his pottery he thinks of, not himself,' he said.

'With all due deference to you,' Desire retorted, 'I should imagine the pottery would be quite as well without you.'

'It would be all right while he lives,' Peter told her, ' afterwards—'

'It and you would be a failure.'

Peter thought it more than probable, but it did not alter his decision. Desire perceived this and perceived for the first time the real immovableness of the man she had heretofore always found diffident and ready to follow her suggestions. This time it dawned on her that her words made no impression.

'It amounts to this, I suppose,' she said, 'your mother wants you to come home for yourself because she is lonely and "Alexander"—who apparently is an unpleasant person—has behaved unpleasantly. Your father wants you for his business, of the value and success of which he has as erroneous an idea as a country squire, with three hundred years of pedigree and three hundred pence of credit, has of his family. He wants a "Son" for the firm, and someone to supplant or circumvent the unpleasant Alexander. And you think these reasons are good enough to justify you in giving up work, career, friends and duty to yourself.'

'I don't know what I think,' Peter said.

'But you know what you are going to do.'

He smiled. 'I think I do.'

'Then go and do it,' she said angrily; ' there is no good in wasting further words.'

He rose. 'Good-bye,' he said, 'and thank you very much for all you have done for me. If there is ever anything I can do for you will you let me know?'

'No,' she answered, 'I will not. Our account is balanced, or if there is any debt at all it is on my side. Good bye. Sometimes I am ready to hate every man in the world, generally for their want of virtue—sometimes for their possession of one of an aggressive and uncomfortable kind.'

So Peter was dismissed, and so it would seem was to end cloudily his curious intimacy with Desire. But two days later, on the day she left town, the post brought him a letter from her.

> 'Forgive me,' it began, 'for being a beast to you when you came. I don't think I was quite myself that afternoon, and I do think I was so personally disappointed at the loss both of the future books and the writer of them that I did not judge fairly of anything else.
>
> I have no doubt you have decided wisely; I should hate to have you degenerate into a successful author, a handy corner man at a dinner-table and all the rest. In going, however, quixotic as you are, you are at least true to yourself and I like you for it. Also I am not going to believe that we shall be eventual losers, I expect there will in time be a successor to *The Dreamer*, another "real" book of sorts. When there is you may be sure its warmest welcome will be from
>
> Your friend,
> Desire Quebell'

This letter was one of the two good things Peter took with him when he left London. The other was Paddy. Austin gave him the dog, partly because he found him rather a nuisance, partly because he showed such a strong objection to being parted from Peter.

Chapter VII

The little old town of Twycross lay rather off the track. It was not far from several pottery towns—noted for dirt and bankruptcy, not very far from some much larger towns, noted for all manner of things of commercial interest, but it itself had no claim to fame. The folk who lived there were mostly either retired, and they, not thinking an enormous fortune necessary to happiness, retired while they were still able to enjoy, or else engaged in some one of the towns to be reached (in time) by an inconsequent railway. Comfortable, substantial folk they were for the most part, a little like their town in that they seemed to have rather dropped behind the times and to have small wish to catch up. In the main they were dissenters in religion, liberals in politics, good men of business, or good housekeeperly women. They dined early and went to bed early, read little besides the daily papers on week-days and the Sunday papers on Sundays, and concerned themselves not much with things beyond a twenty-mile radius.

The Grimstones lived on the outskirts of Twycross, some way from the town and close to where the canal crossed the valley on an aqueduct. Theirs was a grey, flat-faced house, built by the first Ezra, close on to the pottery. The requirements both of the work and the family were greater then than at the present time; there were rooms in the house which were never used now and buildings abutting it where empty benches and idle wheels spoke of work and times which were gone. Not that the place looked decayed or falling to ruin; everything was in very fair repair but very quiet and still.

Beyond the house the hills rose, and it was towards the hills not towards the town that most of the long, many-paned windows looked. Sharp-edged hills they were, cutting clearly against the sky; boulder strewn and bare for the most part, though here and there patched now with the brown of dead heather and bracken, and, more rarely, the black of wind-twisted pines in winter dress. These were the grey hills of Peter's vision, up the nearest one went the long, steep road of which he had thought.

Up that road he went on a November Sunday afternoon—as he had often gone that autumn when he came home, Paddy went with him; it was a fascinating country to Paddy; it abounded with wild, no man's rabbits, and mysterious holes and little gaps between great stones which led no-one knew where. The only thing to be regretted was that when he and his master went this wonderful walk up the hills he could not wander and investigate with an easy mind. He had an uneasy feeling that he must keep coming to and from to see that all was well with the man, for so often he bore with him on these walks—or found and took up on the way—that evil thing which had first come that sunny morning in town. Paddy did not know what it was, something that gave him a pain and made even rabbits to be disregarded, and kept him close to his master's side as silently they went up the lonely path together. A long path it was; at first widish and fairly good though rising fast, soon narrower and rougher with bare bones of rock breaking through the surface, then rising more steeply, winding sometimes, sometimes going straight, or from boulder to boulder, like ill-made stairs. Then, quite suddenly, when one had climbed the big boulder with the black gap beneath it, the track dropped again and ran for a while quiet and secret, in a curved hollow full of dark pines. The ground was loose and sandy, no sound of steps was here. It was a good dog's paradise, the very haunt of rabbits where the loose soil smelt of them, a mysterious place where in the dark shadow of the trees one fancied cotton tails innumerable bobbing. But other shadows would seem to dwell here too, at all events the man did not linger, he walked on with bent head and clouded eyes fixed on the silent sand and the hand which did not hold his stick was clenched hard. But when the hollow was passed and the path rose again, the pines ceased or only grew, one here and there, a gnarled tree, all aslant, clinging to the boulders by horny roots or lying overthrown by some past gale. Even these had ceased before one came to the last steep piece, over the grey boulder with the hollowed crown where the rain collected in wet weather, and so to the top.

This way did Peter and Paddy go that November afternoon, not pausing until they reached the top. At the top was brown heather and grey sky and a curlew crying as it circled and wheeled, and beyond, an edge like the edge of the world. Peter walked to the edge and stood where the last tuft of heather overhung the brow, like matted hair on a shelving forehead, and looked out over the wide land spread below. Fields and trees and streams, isolated villages dotted in the distance, and in the greater distance towns dim seen in their cowls of smoke, and the shining line of the canal threading the whole as it pursued its course through high country and low. A great wide land, somewhat bare in this autumn-time, grey and brown rather than green, except once when a gleam from the low sun, hidden here, struck a far-off spot and turned it to silver.

The world which he had left, that it represented to Peter—and for a while he stood looking out over it. Left, not lost—a man can in his mind carry some part of what he will, especially a man who writes. Peter still wrote; all the autumn he had been doggedly going on with the second novel in such scraps of time as he could give. But it did not progress as he wished, it in no way satisfied him, and the cloud which came to him on Sundays often owed some part of its origin to the book and to his consciousness that it was falling below his own standard. The long hours spent at the mechanical and technical toil of the pottery, and the effort given to grasping the business details, seemed to take all there was of his brain, and though it made no demands on the best of him still it left no margin. He was, it appeared, a person who could only do one thing at a time. Possibly he was aware of this characteristic but he fought with it all the same. He fought this November Sunday, reviewing the book's difficulties on the silent hillside, making them declare themselves, going over in his head the points that did not satisfy him till he thought he saw some light or at least some hope. At that time it was usually hope he brought back with him from the hills, literary hope; later, he was content with resignation which had nothing to do with literature.

But whatever it was he brought back Paddy was always aware that the homeward walk was not as the walk out. It was one glorious hunt for him, his responsibilities were over, and, in joyous abandonment, he chased rabbits, real and imaginary, and those ghost beasts, twilight quarry, unrecognized by men. Once or twice he came back to see what his master did, but though he did not hunt and proclaim joy aloud the dog felt it was well with him. He came from boulder to boulder, from soft patch to hard, from the dark group of pines to the grey where the stones showed pale in the fading light—with sure step, with shoulders square, and raised head and eyes which looked fearlessly before. So till the end of the path was reached and the twilight was all fallen and the hill behind reared a black shoulder against the dark sky. Below was the wide white road and across it the grey-faced house with one lighted window which showed a solitary gleam in the gloom.

Sunday evenings Peter usually spent in the kiln-house, a place dear to Paddy, who much appreciated the warmth and the mysterious dark centres of heat where there were little doors and glowing cracks not good to sniff at. Here, after tea on Sundays, Peter came with a lantern and the manuscript. Here he thought to come this Sunday, reinforced by the walk on the hill and ready to go once again to the fashioning and refashioning of the book; but that evening while they sat at tea Mrs Grimstone said something which intervened. They sat soberly in the dining-room to tea as they had done evening after evening for long. Mrs Grimstone, at the head of the table, fitted the wool-work kettle holder to the handle of the old-fashioned tea-pot and poured out tea on the same system that she had always followed, and her mother had always followed—so much water to warm the cups, so much milk to break the tea, so much tea in every cup—water the pot, tea again, then cream. A lengthy business, interrupted to-night by dropping the holder as she transferred it from the handle of the tea-pot to that of the kettle; Peter, watching as he had often watched before, picked up the holder and gave it to her.

Mrs Grimstone, perhaps emboldened by this break in the usual routine, volunteered a remark. 'Our old minister is going to preach to-night,' she said; 'it was not given out this morning, but Mrs Harvey told me after chapel.'

'Is he?' Peter said, he had no idea who the old minister was.

'You remember him?' his mother went on—'oh no, of course you don't! He used to be here before Mr Williams, long ago, when I was first married. You remember him, Ezra?'

Ezra nodded without answering. He had grown, if possible, more taciturn of late, Peter's home-coming had made no difference to that, nor to the frost which as it were locked him in a silence like to the silence of winter.

But Peter in his intercourse with Desire Quebell had learnt something of those courtesies which had been left out of his earlier life. It hurt something in him to hear his mother's conversation ended thus.

'Did you like the old minister?' he asked.

'Very much,' she answered; 'he was such a nice man and a good preacher too. He has not been here for many years. I should like to have heard him to-night. I did say something to Mary about coming with me.'

'Will she go?' Peter inquired.

She would not; she and Robert belonged to a lonely sect that had its meeting-room somewhere among the hills; all other sects were avoided by her with severity. Mrs Grimstone knew this and was not surprised by the refusal, only sorry. 'For I should have liked to have heard him,' she said. 'Mrs Harvey did say, why not go and sit with them? but it's a long, dark walk home afterwards all alone.'

She spoke with some regret, but still clearly accepted her disappointment as a matter of course. But to Peter there seemed for the first time something pathetic in her patience, and her cheerful acquiescence in going without the small things she wanted. She had probably not wanted any but small things all her life, her taste had been for little homely things, always simple, often perhaps trivial, and she had nearly always been denied them. The little matters for which she cared had always been—almost unconsciously—sacrificed to the seemingly greater ones of other people. He himself was as guilty as another—was he not now unhesitatingly prepared to sacrifice her pleasure to his work?

'I should rather like to hear this preacher,' he said; 'I remember you used to speak of him. Perhaps you and I could go—if you don't think the walk would be too much for you.'

Mrs Grimstone smiled with pleasure. 'Should you like to hear him?' she said. She never doubted him, why should she? The men of her household had never to her knowledge said or done a thing purely to please her. 'He always was such a good preacher, I am sure you would like him. We'll start in good time; I shan't be tired.'

They started in good time. Paddy waited in vain near the kiln-house door that night and the manuscript lay untouched upstairs.

It lay untouched most of the week that followed, they were unusually busy just then at Grimstone's. They worked long hours there—an hour before breakfast at eight, from directly after breakfast till the midday dinner when, reluctantly on the part of Ezra, a halt a trifle longer than was absolutely necessary for the silent meal was made. Then on again in the afternoon till tea, and often on again till supper at nine. There was little waste of time there, no hour spent in journeying, few minutes used in going to and fro. The office was in the house itself; the sheds and buildings, where the small manufacture was carried on, practically adjoined the house and bordered the yard which lay parallel with the garden. Beyond the kiln at the bottom of the yard was the canal, but that long and almost deserted highway was not more a point of contact with the outside world than the old, wide road which ran by the house front, and where often an hour went by without a single wayfarer except mornings and evenings, when men from some quarry in the hills passed that way.

Of workmen on the little pottery there were practically none but Robert, who lived in the house as his master did and had worked always in the same place and under the same conditions. There was also an oafish young man who had started as boy and still continued to be a 'boy' though he was approaching five-and-twenty. At one time there had been two men besides Robert, but they were both dead now. Ezra had not replaced them, it was not easy to find workmen up to his exacting standard, especially in district from whence work was all gone. Also, the employment he had to give was lessening, and though he would not allow this even to himself he did allow that the profits he made were lessening and so it behoved him to save. The men died singly and as each went his work was portioned out, Ezra himself taking the lion's share. He was a man of great energy and extraordinary physical strength, and the work, in the cause of his heart, had not been beyond him. When Peter came home there was not left for him more than an ordinary man could do.

Alexander, in the spring, had believed the little old pottery was holding its own; he knew it to be small and old fashioned, but he had seen that its position was secure. Ezra himself believed the same against all odds, but with Peter it was different; he had very little business faculty, but a keen intuitive perception for the atmosphere of things, and he saw not only what was, but also what was likely to be. To him, the end, whatever the present position, was plain; not very near but inevitable, and the recognition of it was almost a consolation to him for his own unavoidable failure. It mattered less that he eventually failed as a potter since the pottery was failing too. That recognition, however, made no difference to his method of working or his endeavour to master the ways of the failing industry. He could only do things one way, slowly and methodically with the whole of himself. So he did this, applying himself somewhat as he did to the fashioning of *The Dreamer*, laborious and quiet, finding the right way very slowly, often going the wrong and pursuing it a long time before he found it out—quite unable to learn by precept or example, compelled to make everything his own by rediscovery. His extreme slowness and ineptitude did not surprise Ezra; sometimes, though rarely, it goaded him to angry irritability, more often he bore it with the stoical silence of one who expects no better.

Silence was the keynote of the house, the inmates seldom talked unnecessarily; Mrs Grimstone, perhaps, originally conversationally inclined, had long since ceased to speak unless she had some necessary fact to communicate or unavoidable question to ask. Strangers and visitors hardly ever came there. Ezra, though he had lived all his life in the one place, had made no friends, he had nothing in common with the people he met, so from choice he met them as little as possible. Mrs Grimstone, of course, was more genial by nature, or she had been once, though she seldom saw her neighbours now except in chapel on Sunday, or when she made an expedition to the town for shopping. If Peter missed the intercourse with his fellow-creatures which he had had during the time he was in Desire's service, he did not show it. Nor did he show that he missed the, to him, far more valuable intimacy with herself. He had had it, that was unexpected—he had lost it in fact, that was inevitable sooner or later—but in memory and imagination he still had it, and he always would, what had been was always part of himself. He accepted the return to the solitude of his youth philosophically, and certainly made no attempts to supply what he had lost by making new acquaintances or renewing old. He had been home a good many weeks before he exchanged a couple of sentences, except on business, with any but his own people, and it was with considerable reluctance that he accepted the first invitation he did.

That invitation was given on the Sunday evening when he accompanied his mother to chapel. It was the Harveys who gave it, those same kind-hearted people who had suggested Mrs Grimstone should sit with them if she came alone to evening service. Mr Harvey, a genial old man who had retired on a small sufficiency while he was still vigorous, stopped to shake hands after service and pressed Peter to come and see them.

'Why don't you come down to us sometimes?' he said. 'Why, I don't believe you've so much as spoken to the boys all this while you've been back! Young reprobates, they're always off after something on a Sunday instead of coming to chapel, and you never come down our way in the week. Why don't you come one night this week? Fix a night and come to tea.'

A refusal was on Peter's tongue but it was not uttered. Mrs Harvey, who was talking to Mrs Grimstone, caught her husband's words and warmly seconded the invitation.

'Yes, do come,' she said. 'You come, too,' she added, turning to Mrs Grimstone. 'Which day will suit you? Thursday?—Friday? Let's make it Friday. I'm sure you can come; you don't often go out of an evening.'

By the light of the gas-lamp above the chapel door Peter saw his mother's face. He saw her momentary pleasure in the invitation, but after a timid glance at him she began a refusal. 'I'm not sure, thank you; I'm afraid—'

'Don't you think you could manage it?' he asked.

Again transparent pleasure lightened her face. 'Oh yes,' she said. 'Of course I can come; I should like to so much, but I was not sure if you—about you—'

And again Peter came to the rescue. 'We shall be busy all the week,' he said, 'but I think I ought to be able to get away by Friday evening. I shall be very pleased.'

So the Harveys' invitation was accepted, with fluttered pleasure on Mrs Grimstone's part, and an unconsciously formal politeness on Peter's, which amused the two Miss Harveys a good deal. And on Friday at six, the first time that week there had been any leisure, Peter accompanied Mrs Grimstone to the Harveys'. And the manuscript still lay untouched upstairs, and would still lie tomorrow, for tomorrow was no half-holiday at Grimstone's, there was still work to be done.

Chapter VIII

In the early spring one of the things Ezra Grimstone had foreseen as possible happened. He was not prepared for it; though he had foreseen the chance of it, it was only as men foresee the inevitableness of death. He was alone when the blow fell, and alone when he came to the full realization of it. How long there was between the two he did not know, but there was an appreciable time when, in spite of his iron constitution and will, he did not clearly know what had happened. When he did know he sat quite still with his one living hand clenched and his half-numb jaw set grimly. There was no-one to give him the counsel of Job's wife—'Curse God, and die', nor did he want it, there is an emotion beyond curses, a dumb fury of the impotent who have been left only the power and the pride not to cry out.

Mrs Grimstone was waiting for supper. She wondered at the lateness of her husband's coming; regularly at five minutes to nine it was his habit to come in, and Robert, hearing him, then went to tell Peter, who was usually either finishing some work or writing in the kiln-house. Tonight Ezra was late, very late; such a thing had hardly occurred before within her memory. It was nine; it was ten minutes past; it was twenty minutes past. He must be very busy, some letters had come by the evening's post, they must be keeping him. She took up her darning again. Five minutes, ten minutes passed, then the clock struck the half-hour. In the silent house it sounded loud, and though she was used to silence broken only by the clock it startled her a little. She rose, perhaps Ezra had gone out without her knowing, she would go to the office door and try to hear if he were there. She went down the hall and standing close to the door, listened. Her hearing was not very quick and at first she heard nothing, then gradually she became aware of a sound, an odd sort of noisy breathing—he was there and he must have fallen asleep. It was incredible; she could hardly believe it; she opened the door quietly and looked in.

Ezra was not asleep. He was sitting, or rather lying propped, as if he had risen and fallen back, in a chair. With his left hand he gripped the edge of the desk before him, while his right hung limply beside him; his mouth was drawn a little aslant, but his eyes were open, conscious, very fierce, and if anything more brilliant than usual.

'Ezra!' Mrs Grimstone began, but the name died on her lips, frightened by the strange attitude and the loud, difficult breathing. 'What is the matter?' she cried. 'What is it?'

He raised his left hand imperiously, he would have no outcry made for him by her any more than by himself; he tried to speak but the words trod on one another, they were incomprehensible to her.

'Oh!' she cried. 'Oh, Mary! Peter!'

She would have given way to her fear and run for help, but he stopped her with a gesture. He made a second and greater effort to express himself, and though she did not as yet distinguish the words this time she understood his meaning.

'Yes, yes,' she said, gathering self-control; 'I won't make a noise. You gave me such a turn, dear. I'll, I'll fetch Peter.'

She backed towards the door as she spoke, and he making no sign one way or the other, she hurried away.

Peter was in the kiln-house, writing, she could see the glow of his light through the chink of the door. Quickly she crossed the yard and burst in upon him.

'Peter!' she cried, the momentary restraint she had been obliged to put upon herself gone. 'Oh, Peter! Your father's ill! He's had a fit or something. Come, come at once!'

But Ezra Grimstone had not had a fit, it was a stroke of paralysis that had fallen upon him, the doctor who attended him last summer had warned him that such a thing might befall him and had given him some advice, which he had not followed. The same doctor, hastily fetched, attended now and did not ask if his advice had been followed, it was pointless to trouble Mrs Grimstone with such useless questions. He allayed her fears, prescribed the usual things and went away. On one thing only did he insist emphatically, there must be perfect quiet, no excitement, no movement, nothing disturbing even to the mind: an order one might reasonably expect to be carried out here. The doctor was satisfied that it would be when he left his patient; but Peter was not so sure, he was not deceived by the outside stoical calm, also he was partly able to understand his father's halting speech.

In obedience to the command of that halting tongue he went down to the office late that night to look for the letters which had come by the evening post. There were only two; both lay open on the desk; the top one, judging by its date, had been delayed in transit and should have arrived in the morning. It was an order of unusual magnitude, one which required immediate execution and which, even under the best circumstances, would have taxed the resources of the little pottery to the uttermost and scarcely then be done within the stipulated time. The thought of it would not materially add to the peace of mind of the man who lay helpless upstairs. The other was a letter, typewritten, expressed in business terms on business paper headed with telephone number and telegraphic address and similar modern things with which Grimstone's had nothing to do. Peter read it to the signature at the end—Alexander's signature. It would seem that Alexander had got to know of the order contained in the other letter. He also knew the difficulty, or perhaps the impossibility, of the little pottery executing it in time. He wrote to offer help. He said he could let the parent firm have a certain amount of stuff—on moderate terms—to supplement their own and so enable them to execute this order.

Alexander was not a potter, he did not manufacture, he bought 'seconds', slightly faulty products of other manufacturers, and sold them again. It would be possible for him, no doubt, to find among his purchases plenty good enough to pass muster with the cheapest of Grimstone's making—the order was but for the cheapest—this was what his offer meant. And Peter, reading it, perceived what the glitter in his father's eyes meant—it was an anger very near to hate. Peter did not know whether the anger was for the standard of ethics of the writer or for the insidious effort to couple himself with the parent firm, or for the covert insult carefully conveyed in the offer of help, and he did not stop to think. Though as a novelist the motives of men and the mainspring of their actions should have interested him. But he was no novelist now, he was for the first time really identified with the poor little dwindling firm and with the stricken man upstairs. He folded the letters and put them in his pocket, and according to his orderly nature set in its place the chair which had been overturned when they carried Ezra Grimstone away. Then he went out to the kiln-house. Paddy, who was not supposed to come indoors, had been once to investigate matters, and gone back again to lie on the manuscript as he used to like to in the old days in town. Peter found him there and turned him off, then gathered the loose sheets and carried them into the house. He might have put them into the furnace for all the good they seemed likely ever to be.

Two things Peter had inherited from his father, a magnificent physique, and a capacity for work, which Austin and Farmer and various of his London acquaintance had regarded with a mixture of surprise and amusement. Both these qualities were called into play in the days which followed Ezra's seizure. They worked double time at Grimstone's then; possibly, if it was a factory within the meaning of the Act, they laid themselves open to several penalties. But it concerned no-one what they did. Robert worked for the old master's sake, and willingly would have worked ten times harder if he could when he knew the reason; he was a tough man, taciturn as his master, cross grained but flawlessly loyal, of few sympathies and no interests outside the pottery which was his world, as it was Ezra's. Bolt, to Peter's surprise, proved of value at this pinch. He had not counted on his doing more than his usual allotted task, throwing down his tools and slouching away when six struck; but as it happened he did much more; he worked longer hours than Robert could, he came a good second to Peter. He developed capabilities before unsuspected; it seemed when he chose he could do other and better work than that which was usually his. It was he who mended the brickwork of the long-disused second oven when the only bricklayer in Twycross declared himself unable to attend to it for a week. It was he, too, who could do without sleep for long stretches of time, and who did do it. But it was not for the sake of the old master, or the firm, nor yet liking for Peter, or pride, or a sense of duty, or emulation, or any of the younger qualities of the soul. By accident he overheard some words which passed between Robert and Peter relative to Alexander; not many, Peter was not communicative, and had not the listening Bolt had his wits sharpened by the single emotion he could strongly feel he would hardly have understood.

'Is 'e trying to cut us out?' he asked. He spoke the dialect of the hills which few born far from their shadow can easily understand and which Peter had had to relearn.

'Who do you mean?' Peter inquired. 'Alexander,' Bolt answered, he had no use for titles of respect, few of his people had.

'No,' Peter said; then, his instinctive love of exactitude getting the better of his reserve, he added, 'not exactly, he would be glad for us not to be able to take this order.'

'Ho, would 'e!' Bolt said. 'It'd be a good turn for'm if we didn't?'

'He thinks so.'

Bolt nodded. 'All right, maister,' he said, with a momentary gleam in his dull eyes, 'you can count on me.' Peter believed him, and found the belief justified in the days of breathless work which followed.

And Ezra lay helpless upstairs; nursed and waited upon by Mrs Grimstone, and to a certain extent following out the doctor's orders with regard to keeping quiet. He was quiet, very quiet in the main, certainly he seemed to have little wish to use his injured powers of speech. In a little he began to improve; he was a man of fine constitution and temperate life; he showed signs of a partial and comparatively rapid recovery sooner than the doctor anticipated. There was every hope, he said, that eventually the patient would be able to speak almost plainly again, also a likelihood that he would partially regain the use of his limbs, even be able to walk again in time, though probably never have much power in his right hand and arm. Mrs Grimstone was much cheered when she heard this. She had herself already noticed an improvement in her husband's speech which made it easier to understand and wait on him—though to her it would never have been hard to wait, for she loved to give the small personal services for which there had been little demand or room in her life before.

As for Ezra, he received the hopeful news much as he had received unhopeful; to neither had he much to say. For the most part he lay through the long, light March afternoon in silence, eyes on the door and ears acutely sharpened for any sound which might indicate word from the office or yard. No word came and no sound from the outer world till Mary, tapping at the door, called Mrs Grimstone out. Ezra moved slightly, but the woman would be charged with no message from the yard or office, and nothing else mattered. Ezra lay looking before him again, listening as before.

'Wants me?' Mrs Grimstone was saying by the door. 'Very well, I'll come. I won't be a minute, dear.'

Ezra did not answer, it was of no importance whether she was one minute or twenty; her coming and going were as the coming and going of the night and the day to him, inevitable, necessary no doubt, but making no impression of taste or distaste. She was not long gone this time, in a little she returned bringing word that Mr Williams, the minister, was below.

Mr Williams had been several times to inquire after the invalid, and had had one or two sympathetic talks with Mrs Grimstone. Today, hearing of the great improvement and the good hope for the future, he suggested that perhaps the sick man would like a few words with his pastor. Mrs Grimstone came to ask if the invalid thought it would be too much for him.

He did not think so—it would make no difference; it was one of the necessary things that must happen sooner or later to him as a chapel member. It might as well be now as not. Mrs Grimstone led the pastor upstairs and left him there.

A well-meaning man, Mr Williams, perhaps a little given to the use of the set expressions of his office, but not to be accused of cant on that account, for most of them had become as natural to him as the lurid language of a bargee is to him. With Ezra Grimstone Mr Williams was not intimately acquainted, he had supped at the grey house once and talked of edification and schism and similar things, but beyond that his acquaintance did not go. Mr Grimstone, of course, he knew a little better, and he had that day been talking to her of the hand of the Lord and of mercies and blessings. She had listened with appreciation and wiped her eyes afterwards; but when he spoke in the same strain to Ezra there was no answer.

He put that down to the invalid's weak state, and went on to say a little more, concluding fervently, 'How much, how very much we have to be thankful for!'

'Glad—you—have,' the unsteady tongue answered.

'Glad?' Mr Williams, not yet used to the speech, hardly understood. 'You are glad, dear friend, that your tongue is given to you again to praise the Lord, that your feet by and by shall bear you again to His house.'

Ezra made no answer, but the expression of his face was grim. Mr Williams did not see it.

'Your hands,' he went on, warming to his topic, 'your hands will rest awhile—what a blessing He can make these resting-times! A quiet resting-time, a pause in these your latter days in which to think and to gather together the harvest of a busy life. Truly there is much to be thankful for!'

'There is not!'

The words were emphatic, the clearest Ezra had spoken since his seizure; they seemed to have been jerked up from some inner depths.

Mr Williams was startled by them. 'You are not thankful? No; I misunderstand you. You are sensible of the great mercies that have been shown you in your affliction.'

'I am not!' the same emphasis and the same unmistakable clearness.

Mr Williams, having seen Ezra Grimstone Sunday after Sunday in chapel, knowing him for a member of the congregation and an austere and upright man, could hardly believe his ears.

'A professing Christian,' he said; 'a chapel member! My dear friend I fear your affliction has for a moment turned your heart; you do not see the hand of the Lord.'

'I do,' Ezra retorted; 'the Lord can do as He pleases—but there is no reason why I should be pleased—'

He hesitated as he spoke, and stumbled in spite of his efforts, but the words lost nothing of point, they were unmistakably clear to Mr Williams although the speaker's attitude was not.

'I believed that you had found grace—' he began but Ezra cut him short. 'That has nothing to do with it,' he said. 'This is my matter; I have nothing to say of it—but neither has another—I can hold my tongue, but I cannot lie—I don't want another to lie for me to or of my Maker. Will you offer a prayer?'

Mr Williams clasped and unclasped his hands in real distress. He had often spoken of the Old Adam in his sermons, but he did not know him when he met him, nor did he realize that it was possible that an upright and God-fearing man might still be a primal creature with the pride of Lucifer and the anger of a trapped beast. There was another thing he did not realize—when the shutter was dropped again on a momentarily exposed soul. He addressed himself to this soul now, but the shutter was down and the glimpse of the turmoil within gone, the words slid by as the singing of Psalms on Sunday. When he ceased Ezra repeated his request for prayer, as he would have repeated a request for any other customary thing, grace before dinner, receipt for payment. And Williams, good man, regarding the repetition as an indication of softening, fulfilled it and went away, not satisfied perhaps, but hopeful.

And Ezra addressed himself again to his watch of the door and his listening for sounds he did not hear.

The afternoon waned, the light lingering long, at last grew dim, he could hardly see the face of the clock when from time to time his eyes turned to it. Mrs Grimstone had come back some while ago; she talked sometimes and sometimes read aloud scraps from the paper, but as she asked for neither answer nor comment it made no appreciable difference what she did.

At last Ezra roused himself to speak. 'Has Peter come in?' he asked.

'No,' she answered; 'he said he would not have any tea today. I wish he would; I don't like his missing meals like this. You know he can hardly be said to have had a proper dinner to-day, or yesterday either, or a good many other days. He says he's too busy. He must be very busy; he goes back to work after supper every night. I do hope he won't work too hard and make himself ill.'

'He won't,' Ezra said shortly. There was a line between his brows; he, like Alexander, disliked long sentences; experience had taught this to Mrs Grimstone, and she usually so little indulged her natural tendency this way that she had almost lost the habit. It irritated him that she should speak so now, he even fancied that it might be an indication that he was losing his old grip on things.

The hours drew slowly on, the lamp was lighted and the curtains drawn, still Peter did not come. Mrs Grimstone seeing the watch kept on the door, suggested that she should fetch him.

'Certainly not,' Ezra said; 'I don't want to see him.'

Mrs Grimstone said no more and they settled to a silent evening. When she came up after supper she announced that Peter had been in to that meal though he had not stayed long. 'He's gone back to work,' she said; 'they have all gone back. Bolt is still here; they have sent some supper out to him.'

Ezra grunted as if that was as it should be. His wife, however, did not think so. 'I believe they are going to work all night,' she ventured.

It was not entirely Ezra's fancy; his illness, and the

new importance it had given her, did sometimes, quite unconsciously, lead Mrs Grimstone to say more perhaps than she would have done before.

'I told Peter to come to you,' she said. 'I told him to come so soon as he left off work, and he said he was afraid that would not be till too late—or too early! And Ezra, do you know, I believe he has done it before! When I told him he mustn't work so late he laughed and said he was quite used to it!'

Again Ezra muttered an acquiescence, he did not seem distressed by the news. Indeed, it seemed to satisfy him somewhat for soon after he gave up his listening and watching and submitted to being settled for the night with that curious forced patience which characterized him.

He slept lightly and fitfully at times, very lightly that night; in the grey of the morning someone crossing the landing woke him. He knew the step, it was Robert's. Robert, ordinarily, had no business to be there, the kitchen, back stairs and servants' quarters were all quite separate from the front part of the house.

'Robert!' Ezra said.

The old man opened the door; his face looked haggard in the light of the night-light and the struggling grey dawn, and the rims of his eyes were red as from want of sleep, but there was a certain grudging satisfaction about him.

'I was just listening to hear if you was awake, maister,' he said in his emotionless sing-song. 'I thought maybe if you was, I'd give you a call to say we're done.'

'Ah!' Ezra said, his voice, too, was motionless but his eyes glittered. 'Packed?'

''N ready to go,' Robert answered; 'they're takin' the crates to the cut side now.'

'Why?' Ezra asked sharply. 'They must not be left there, they might be tampered with.'

'They won't,' Robert said; 'the barge'll be up in less'n an hour.'

But Ezra was insistent, the crates must be kept under lock and key till the barge came; Robert, unconvinced, and still muttering his want of conviction, undertook to see to it.

He did not, however, go out again, he went up to his room which looked out at the back, and opening the window called the order to Peter, who was still in the yard.

'All right,' Peter said, and the old man closed the window, drew down the blind and went to bed. Peter stood a moment looking at the crates ranged on the canal bank.

'We won't move them again,' he said to Bolt who had helped to bring them out; 'the barge will be here in half-an-hour or so; I will stay with them, that will do just as well, you had better go. Good-night, or rather good-morning.'

Bolt did not go. 'I'll stop here, maister,' he said. 'What's the good o' goin' home now?'

'You need not come back to-day,' Peter said; he knew the lonely cottage among the bleak hills where Bolt lived with his old grandmother, it was a long way from here.

'I'd soonest stop,' Bolt answered.

'As you like,' Peter said, supposing he was too tired to care for the long, rough walk. 'Better go into one of the sheds, you can sleep there.'

Bolt hesitated. 'I s'pose I'd hear if any one came—if anythink happened?'

'Of course,' Peter said, and Bolt slouched away.

Peter sat down by the crates wondering a little what Alexander had done to rouse animosity in this mind of few emotions. Of course it was Alexander who Bolt thought might come or send for some nefarious purpose; and Alexander that the sick man in the house thought of. Peter knew that it was not in the least likely Alexander would do any such foolish thing, or even think of it, or know it possible: but that they should have thought of it showed the kind of opinion held here and the kind of hate hated. But Peter did not concern himself greatly with the matter, he did not concern himself with anything, he was too tired. In a few minutes he was nodding to sleep as he sat, though he woke again directly, stiff and chilly. The morning air was rawly cold, he rubbed his hands together and felt the skin gritty from the work he had been doing—the work that was done. He looked at the crates with a sense of ownership faintly related to the feeling he had had when he first handled the bound copies of *The Dreamer*. It was something done, not very well done, perhaps, but still something, a tangible presentation of an idea. The idea! What was it?—he was getting very drowsy again. It was not pot-making, earthenware, china clay, firing, dipping and packing. They were the medium? Yes, of course, the medium, just as ink and paper and words were a medium—the idea was something different. It was—what was it? Was it Alexander—or Grimstones', perhaps? Or a fight?—he had a vague feeling of having fought a long time, though it did not seem at all clear with or for what. But it was interesting—perhaps someday, in a book—a long book—or another life perhaps—it would be possible to work it out—the concreting of an idea—in different forms—or chapters.

His head nodded and he woke with a jerk. He rose and, stretching, walked down to the water's edge to wake and warm himself.

The light was coming fast now, all the low, open land beyond the canal was silver pale; a small hoar frost lay on the ground and a thin mist hung in the air, though things were very clear in spite of it. There were some bushes on the other side of the canal, the lower branches seemed more distant than the upper by reason of the mist which was thickest close on the water. There was never a hint of bud or sign of life in the bushes, never a gleam of green or gold in the pale landscape, yet there was a feeling of spring even in the cold air. The birds were singing, they had been singing a long time, before it was fairly light, only he had not heard them before. He heard them now and wondered at the extraordinary penetrating liquidness of the notes in the thin air; in some way it intensified the silence and made him feel very far away from the world, as one feels on a mountain top.

The mist, lying on the water, began to rise, like some ghost thing that gathers its skirts and flees at the coming of the working day. Far off, carried up on the water, came a human voice, a man speaking to a horse, then silence again, but not the same aloofness, the world was becoming man's world, the mist was gone and the hoar frost was thinning, showing the green of grass here and there. By and by came the sound of a horse plodding along the towpath, and afterwards, in due time, the animal came into sight, his breath streaming out into the cold air as the smoke from the little stove on the barge streamed out, tarnishing for a minute the clearness.

It was a small matter, though to Peter unnecessarily lengthy in the doing—the loading of the crates, the exchange of some few words and the getting under way.

At last the barge moved again, the man by the towing horse cracked his whip and called something to the man by the little stove, who not troubling to answer, he began to whistle. The whistle grew fainter and fainter in the distance, until the quiet swallowed it up, and the ripples left by the barge on the canal grew less and less till the water was still again. Peter turned and went into the house.

Chapter IX

Ezra Grimstone progressed on the lines indicated by the doctor as likely. By the middle of April he had to a great extent recovered his speech, and spoke no more seldom and little less plainly than of old; by that time, too, he had begun to get about a little. He had not been brought downstairs, but he moved about in his own room with assistance, and, in spite of his helplessness, was to a certain extent restored to his old position. He could not go down to the yard or office, it is true, but he could and did know everything that was done there, and practically direct affairs. Daily minute accounts had to be rendered by Peter, checked usually by Robert, who, with the reinstating and partial recovery of the master, was also back in his former position. During the earlier days of Ezra's illness, and in the time when there was so much to do, Peter had assumed command, and the old man had sourly but unquestioningly let him. That was over now, and Peter was once more entirely subordinate. Bolt had also returned to his original position—or his original lethargy—what he was paid for, that he did grudgingly, and extra pay for extra work had small charm for one who had few opportunities and fewer tastes for spending; there was not much to be got out of him.

The whole arrangement was unsatisfactory; Peter knew it; the division of a director who cannot even look at the work, and a lieutenant with small experience and no authority, is bad and bound to work badly. There was small satisfaction for anyone; it would have been impossible to satisfy Ezra anyhow, and impossible for Peter to satisfy himself, seeing that he was trying to work on his father's plan, although he was one essentially suited to work out his own way only. There was little doing now at the pottery, so the great waste of time entailed by the present arrangement did not so much matter. By all being occupied all the time they just got through, and the afternoon quiet of slow decay settled down on the place more firmly than ever.

And the novel was untouched. Sometimes, when he was doing purely mechanical work, Peter thought about it and planned to alter this or that. But it wanted more than altering, more than he could give it now; it had got into two or three different keys; he had lost the original theme, the primary inspiring idea had become confused, he was not himself any longer sure what he had to say. Once or twice he took the manuscript out and looked at it, but he never had any length of time to devote to it, and, besides, the thing itself seemed to be gone from him. His present life, it is true, did not make large demands on his intellect, but it made very large ones on his patience, his energy and his slowworking mind; it seemed to leave him very little margin. No doubt there was a loose screw in his intellectual constitution, seeing that he was unable to do two things, certainly he was not one of those who storm the world's heights, only a plodder on an uphill path.

On a Sunday at the end of April Peter took out the manuscript for what proved to be the last time for long. He looked at it a little, making a correction here and there from force of habit, then he looked up and out of window. He was at the time in his own room and the window was towards the hills, towards a gap in them, so that one saw not only the grey rampart but also a glimpse of the open land beyond. For a moment he sat thinking of the patched book, of its incoherency and his own incompetency. Then by chance his eye was arrested by a fluff of gold over the road, a palm bush in blossom in the swampy ground at the foot of the steep path. Suddenly there came to his mind the smell of the tufted branches as they grew here and there in the soft spots on the hillsides. It was imagination purely, but it was so plain that for a minute he almost seemed to hear the humming of the bees busy about the flowers. He rose and, putting the manuscript into a drawer, went out. Whatever else had gone these at least were left—the sun and the wind and the good days which befall the earth in times of man's fortune and his misfortune.

Far on in the afternoon, but before Peter was back, someone came to the grey house. Mrs Grimstone, dozing over a sermon in her husband's room, did not hear the knock, and was quite startled when Mary came up to tell her she was wanted.

'What is it?' she asked. Mary beckoned her out and carefully shut the door. 'Mr Alexander,' she said shortly.

'Alexander!' Mrs Grimstone exclaimed, and then looked behind her as if fearful the shut door should have heard. 'Is he here? Did he—did he ask for the master? He is here?'

'In the parlour, waiting,' Mary said, and Mrs Grimstone went hastily downstairs.

Alexander was standing by the window when she went in, looking precisely as he had looked when he last came more than a year ago, and now, as then, as much at home as if he had but walked out that morning.

'Alexander!' Mrs Grimstone exclaimed.

And—' Well, Mother,' he said, just as he had said the last time. 'How's the old man?' he asked, when he had kissed her perfunctorily.

'Your father? He's better. He's been very ill, you know. Did you hear about it?'

'I heard, that's why I came; I was over in this part of the world, so I thought I'd look in and hear about him.'

Mrs Grimstone smiled with pleasure. 'I'm so glad,' she

said, 'so glad you thought of it—you're so busy, too, I was afraid at one time you and he had perhaps—didn't agree quite last year.'

'We didn't, but I don't bear malice—never do, for the matter of that.'

Mrs Grimstone appreciated this magnanimity. 'I'll go and tell your father you are here,' she said. She was not quite sure how Ezra would receive the news or the visitor, but she felt she must go and tell him at once, she had no right to have her son's society clandestinely.

But Alexander was not in such a hurry. 'There's plenty of time,' he said. 'I've got a bit of time to put in here; you and I may as well have a talk first. Tell me about the old man's illness, how it happened and all the rest.'

Mrs Grimstone therefore told him, explaining fully and freely all that had occurred. Peter's name, of course, came in more than once in her narrative. Finally Alexander, who had rather the air of listening more or less, specially less, picked it out. 'Peter?' he said, 'I heard he was here.'

'Such a good thing,' his mother said. 'Of course he's not so clever as you, but he's quite your father's right hand now. I don't know what he'd do without him.'

'H'm,' was Alexander's comment. 'I thought Peter was by way of being a poet, or something of that sort.'

'Oh, yes, he wrote a book, not poetry but a beautiful book' (Mrs Grimstone may have been thinking of the outside, as it is not certain she had read all the in); 'but of course when your father offered him to come here he was glad to come, and, as I say, it is a very good thing he did.'

'I shouldn't have thought he'd make much of a potter,' Alexander said. 'Are they busy now? I suppose not. Peter ought to do all right if there wasn't too much on hand.'

'Peter works very well,' Mrs Grimstone said, and afterwards, with a little questioning from Alexander, she told what she could of the doing of Grimstones' in the weeks of the master's illness. It was not very much, and Alexander's interest soon ceased; when it ceased he did not scruple to stop his mother by another question.

'Who works here now?' he asked.

'Robert and Bolt.'

'Bolt? Don't remember him. Oh, the boy, of course, there used to be a fuddle-headed lout of some sort, I remember. And old Robert—how's he? At home to-day? I must have a talk with him by and by.'

'He is out,' Mrs Grimstone said; ' he has gone to afternoon chapel—the Ark, you know, where he and Mary always go. It's a long way from here; she can't manage to go for the afternoon class meeting if she goes in the morning, but he always does.'

It did not occur to Mrs Grimstone to doubt if Alexander were quite sincere in his wish to talk with Robert, his father's loyal adherent, nor did it occur to her to think it strange that Alexander should have forgotten this invariable Sunday habit of the old man. Her interest was not centred in these things just now, but in the grandchildren, about whom there seemed so little opportunity to ask.

'The kids?' Alexander said, when at last she managed to put the question 'Oh, they're all right. One of 'em's got the whooping cough.'

'The whooping cough! Oh, my dear!'

'Beastly nuisance, can't go to school, nor can the other. I say she had much better look sharp and get it and have it over. Florence is a fool, she makes no end of a fuss, she cockers the children up. Peter's not in, is he? When do you expect him?'

Mrs Grimstone did not know, but she thought soon, as it was nearly tea-time.

It was not such a great while before Peter did come in. If he was surprised to see Alexander he did not show it, and if the real purpose of Alexander's visit had been to see him that was not shown either. The brothers presented something of a contrast to one another. Alexander was the taller though Peter the more powerfully built. Alexander spoke and moved quickly, for one of his family he talked a good deal at times, and in his movements there was an energy and restlessness which was very noticeable. Peter spoke much more slowly, using few words and seeming to choose them; and for his movements, he was so still and sometimes so almost unready that one was liable to be unprepared for the swift precision his actions occasionally showed. In type of head they were opposed too, Alexander the long and narrow, Peter the short and flattened. Alexander had a curiously slit-like mouth, given to unbeautiful smiling; Peter's fuller and more mobile lips smiled little. Alexander's eyes were light and particularly bright; Peter's intensely grey, very direct and serious. Both had inherited the father's square jaw, and each seemed to possess the true Grimstone capacity for keeping his own counsel. As they sat at tea and talked on a variety of topics, mostly of the elder's introduction, Alexander did not fail to observe how little Peter said. He put it down to caution and a fear of betraying himself.

After tea, Mrs Grimstone was dismissed by Alexander, who had a somewhat cavalier fashion of dismissing his womenfolk when he wanted to be rid of them. He told her now to go and tell his father that he had come, and when she was gone on the errand he turned to Peter with the air of one coming to business.

'Well,' he said, 'what are you doing?'

'Doing?'

'Yes, what's Grimstones' doing?'

'Much as usual,' Peter said, with the polite indifference of one speaking of an indifferent subject.

'Is the old man directing?' Alexander asked. 'I suppose he is.

How long's he going to keep it on?'

'So long as he lives, I imagine.'

'Game old cock. Still, he won't live for ever; what's going to happen when he dies?'

'I don't know.'

Alexander laughed, his short laugh which somehow suggested a bark.

'You're a bit of a fool, you know, Peter,' he said good-naturedly; 'I suppose you think I'm trying to pump you, come to see what you're up to. I've not, it's not to you I'd come for that, you can make yourself easy on that score; I know all I want to about Grimstones'. I know you all tore your guts out to worry through with that order, and I know, though I own I didn't last year, that you aren't so flourishing here as most think you; I know precisely how you stand.'

Peter saw no reason to doubt it, and, not doubting, he equally saw no reason to remark on it.

'What I'm here for,' Alexander went on, leaning his back against the mantelpiece, 'is to give you a leg up if you want it. I've got some money idle, I should rather like to have it in the old firm; I don't go in for sentiment, but, other things even, I'd sooner have it in the old concern than anything. I've a notion the other things might be made even, so there it is when you want it.'

'Thank you,' Peter said in the same entirely polite and indifferent way, 'but I'm afraid it's no use speaking of it to me.'

'You've got no say in things?' Alexander asked, then laughed; 'I suppose you wouldn't have,' he said. It amused him, even though it temporarily upset his plans, to see how poorly Ezra thought of the son who for spite he had taken to be with him; it pleased him, too, to think that, after experience, the old man saw no reason to alter his opinion.

'Do you know what we fell out about, he and I?' he asked, biting his thumb nail.

'I've not heard much about it,' Peter answered.

'Oh? You don't know? Well, as he hasn't told you I won't. But I'll tell you this much, the old man's no more likely to have any of my money in the business on his own account than he is to fly. I came over to propose it because I thought you'd be likely to have some sort of say in things by this time, especially as the old chap's doubled up. I reckoned that if you had you'd have the sense to see the advantage of my offer and either to persuade or compel him to take it.'

'I see,' said Peter.

'Of course, you'll come to that some day,' Alexander went on. 'He'll get more and more dotty by degrees, and though he'll hang on to every scrap of power he can to the last, you'll soon have to run things on your own more or less, and shut your mouth about it. When you do, and when you want help, you'd better come to me. It'd pay you best to do it—pay me too, of course; I'm not a philanthropist, but you'll have to go to someone, and it had better be me.' He shot a glance at Peter, from which one might have fancied he was not so sure of his facts as he sounded, wishful rather of getting a hint as to how far they were well founded. 'And look here,' he went on more genially, 'any time you get into a howling muddle—and being a poet and not a potter, of course you will sooner or later—you'd better let me know, and I'll pull you out of it if I can, or at all events advise you.'

'Thank you,' Peter said.

Alexander looked at him with the unbeautiful smile twisting the corners of his mouth and showing his yellow teeth. 'Does that mean you will or you won't?' he asked, with the amusement of one contemptuous of a caution he can see through.

'The opportunity is not likely to occur,' Peter answered.

'It is dead sure to,' Alexander retorted. 'And you're dead sure to make a muck of it for fear of being done! I suppose you think if I once got a foot in here I'd collar the lot?'

'I have not thought about it.'

'Rot!'

'But now that you mention it,' Peter went on politely, 'I should think such a thing very probable—if you did get a foot in.'

Alexander laughed. 'If!' he scoffed. 'If! Don't you know I can have the whole concern for nothing by and by? In case you don't know it I'll tell you. When the old man's gone I shall inevitably be Grimstones', the only Grimstones'. The most of the old concern will naturally come over to me. The name and reputation, which is all I really want, will come without my agreement or purchase money or anything. I shall call myself Grimstones', and right away I shall be it. As for the connection, I can have that before if I want it.'

'You think so?' Peter said indifferently. Whether or not he thought so, or even if he thought at all, did not appear. Alexander, partly irritated and partly contemptuous of so stolid an antagonist, went on further to explain how he would become Grimstones'.

'I make you a present of the information,' he concluded. 'I don't mind playing with you with the cards down. I don't mind telling you, either, why I was willing to give something for what I can have for nothing later on: it's because it is later on, and I should be glad to have it, at a moderate price, now. Oh, I can do without it, don't excite yourself on that point. But to have it now and without trouble's worth something to me. If you weren't a fool you'd see it was worth a good deal more to you. As you are there's an end—'

He turned as he spoke, for Mrs Grimstone had entered, her face troubled and a little pale.

'What? Won't the old man see me?' Alexander said carelessly. 'Well, I'm not surprised, and anyhow I must cut in a minute.'

'It isn't that,' Mrs Grimstone said. 'Oh, Alexander, he is

so angry! He wants to see you—he insists on it, and he is so dreadfully upset, I have never seen him like it. I ought never to have let you stay. When he heard you were downstairs talking to Peter he was terrible!'

Alexander looked across at Peter and laughed. 'He doesn't seem to have much opinion of you and your discretion,' he said.

Peter did not answer, but turned to his mother urging her strongly not to take Alexander upstairs. 'Oh, but I must!' Mrs Grimstone said, aghast at the idea of disobedience. 'He said he was to come at once.'

'That can't be helped,' Peter told her; 'he will be angry of course if Alexander does not come, but nothing like so angry as if he does, that will be far worse for him. You know what the doctor said about excitement.'

Mrs Grimstone did know, and Peter, seeing his advantage, followed it up with further persuasions, which might have brought her to the point of disobeying her husband, for about the first time in her life, had not Alexander interfered. To him the fact that Peter did not want him to see his father was suspicious. From it he argued that the illness had weakened the iron will as well as the iron constitution, and Peter was afraid that the father, though angry now, would be worked upon by him (Alexander) to his advantage. There was something to be gained by going, or at all events Peter fancied so, so Alexander would go.

'Bosh!' he said, when he saw his mother wavering at the thought of the danger of excitement. 'I shan't do him any harm, not half so much as the fury he would get into when he found he was disobeyed. He'd never know a minute's peace after, or give you one either, when once he had discovered that you didn't do as he told you now he can't get about to see after things himself.'

'Yes—' Mrs Grimstone said doubtfully, 'yes, I'm afraid that

is so. Perhaps'—this with shamefaced hesitation, for she was transparently honest—'perhaps we ought to tell him you had to catch a train.'

'And perhaps he'd believe you,' Alexander said contemptuously. 'No, I'm not going to have that gammon; I came over here to see him and as he's willing to see me I'm not going away without.'

He went to the door as he spoke and Peter followed him with his eyes. There was something unnaturally rigid about Peter, and a curious little ripple seemed to pass through his whole powerful frame; the knuckles of his clenched hands stood out—for half a second Alexander was in great danger of a broken head. Then the tension relaxed, it was not the time or place to try conclusions with the weapons Peter best understood; there might come a day, perhaps, when the raw, natural thing in him spoke out plainly to Alexander and bade him stand up to it; but it was not now, and fortunately man's wisdom checked boy's impulse. Alexander, quite unconscious of his momentary danger, went out, Mrs Grimstone accompanying him as far as the door of her husband's room.

'You won't upset him, will you?' she pleaded rather anxiously.

'All right,' he said, and went in, shutting the door after him.

The house was well built, the doors and windows, with the exception of one or two altered in more recent times, fitted very well. It would have been almost impossible for Mrs Grimstone to have heard anything which passed inside the room even if she had tried, and she was far from any thought of trying. Indeed, she only lingered upstairs from the vague instinct which keeps people near the scene of their anxiety, even when the affair is quite beyond their control or reach. She observed that the white dimity curtain by the landing window was crooked, she went and set it straight with the neat precision dear to her soul. The window looked west, and the sloping beams of the evening sun fell on the sober matting on the floor. She did not notice the sun but she did notice a thin place in the matting, and mentally decided the length must be shifted tomorrow so as to bring the worn part further along. As she stooped to see how much there was to shift she heard a sound—Alexander laughing his short, loud laugh. It made her jump, but only for a second, the father and son must be getting on well if there was laughing. Experience had not succeeded in teaching her that when Alexander laughed it was more often at than with any one, and that other people then seldom had much reason for merriment or pleasure.

She went to the other end of the strip of matting to see how much was turned under there, a little new piece at that end would be a help in rearranging the strips. While she looked she heard Peter come into the hall below.

'Is that you, Peter?' she asked.

He looked up to answer, coming a little way up the stairs, so that the sloping sunbeams fell on him.

'I think it is a good thing Alexander went—' she began, and suddenly stopped. There came a strange sound from behind the closed door, inarticulate, yet loud, for they heard it plainly here, and in some way horrible—rage, pain and impotency blended in its inhuman note.

Peter sprang up the stairs and passed her; but before he had reached his father's door it was opened by Alexander who came out rather hastily.

'Alexander! What is it?' Mrs Grimstone cried.

'The old man's had a fit or something,' Alexander said. 'Here, you'd better not go in,' he caught her by the arm as he spoke, and pulled her aside so that Peter could pass, 'he looks a bit bad.'

She tried to free herself. 'I must go!' she said.

'Nonsense,' he answered; 'Peter's there, that's all sufficient. Come downstairs and see about sending for a doctor.'

She hesitated, but the habit of obedience, and the necessity of sending for the doctor carried the day, and she came. 'Is it a bad fit?' she asked. 'Is he faint?'

'He'll be all right after a bit,' Alexander said; 'you know he's likely to get this sort of thing.'

'Faintness?' Mrs Grimstone queried.

'He's not faint,' Alexander said shortly.

'Another stroke? Oh, Alexander, did you excite him? You must have excited him!'

'No I didn't—he excited himself. Choked himself with a curse.'

The last was scarcely addressed to Mrs Grimstone, who was busy giving directions to Mary about fetching the doctor.

'Here, where does he live? I'd better go,' Alexander said impatiently; 'you won't have him in a month of Sundays at this rate.'

And he went and brought the doctor back with what speed he could.

Not that it was much use, no doctor could do much for Ezra Grimstone now. Another stroke, such as he, even in his most clear-sighted moments had not foreseen, had fallen upon him. Speechless, motionless he lay, with distorted face and fierce fixed eyes that appeared to recognize no-one. Everything but just the bare breath of life was gone. The mind was gone, gone never to return the doctor thought, though in such a case, he said, one cannot absolutely foretell. And Peter, to whom this was said, acquiesced, saying little. He did not know if there was any passion of revolt left in the shrouded brain, but he did suddenly know, as he had not before, what there had been beneath the outside calm. He also knew now, as if he had been there, the fury of rage and hate which had boiled up to bring about the last overwhelming catastrophe. And he found it hard to believe that this was all gone, all dead. The passion, a moment ago so terribly, so astonishingly hot, must, it seemed to him, be slumbering and latent if not still actually there; to think otherwise was in some way horrible, almost like the denying of the existence of soul and the reducing of humanity to mere carrion. Whatever Ezra Grimstone was to others to Peter he was not and never would be just an inanimate heap of barely breathing flesh. Whether it was for days or for months or for years, to Peter he would always be an impotent, prisoned soul; speechless, powerless to communicate, locked away from his kind, as in the heart of an iceberg, but there, and supremely pitiful.

Chapter X

There were disagreeables in the Quebell household; not exactly outspoken ones, certainly not quarrels—there were insurmountable difficulties in the way of quarrelling with a person like Desire—but there was a frigidity in the atmosphere and a strainedness in the relations between the two women, which even the younger of the two could not fail to perceive. Nearly a year had elapsed since the breaking of Desire's engagement with Edward Gore, but Lady Quebell had neither forgiven or forgotten the affair. It had outraged her sense of propriety, it had greatly upset her arrangements, and it left Desire still on hand. The circumstances had never been explained to her, they had never really been explained to Gore or to any one else except one totally insignificant man, who had since dropped out of the Quebell circle. Lady Quebell naturally put her own interpretation on the break and the interpretation was not favourable to Desire—who took no more trouble to palliate the blow to her step-mother than she had to soften it to the victim, seeing which one cannot say that the lady's feelings were altogether unreasonable.

During the autumn the two women had seen little of each other, they had as much as possible visited separately; in the early months indeed Desire had seen few of her own set, spending her time travelling with her father. When, after Christmas, she came to town again the affair of the engagement was largely forgotten by a people who were too busy amusing themselves to remember much. Desire herself, to all appearances, had forgotten it too, at all events she seemed prepared to take up her life and circumstances as before. Lady Quebell was not prepared and had not forgotten, and through the winter and spring the position grew more and more strained. Everything Desire did aggravated it, all in her proceedings which in the past annoyed her step-mother did a thousand times more so now, and her previously condemned faculty for becoming absorbedly interested in people—principally men—appeared an even more heinous thing in her step-mother's eyes, though she seldom said anything about it. She seldom did speak plainly to Desire at that time; it was not till Julian Lee came to the fore that she gave any idea of the nature and extent of her feelings.

Julian Lee was an extremely rich and quite unattached American, an agreeable person in every way, who that spring had come into the Quebell circle. He had interested Desire, not because of his wealth or eligibility, but in spite of them, and for some quality of originality she found in him. The consequence was the not unprecedented one that he fell in love with her and proposed marriage. This in itself, though distressing, did not matter tremendously; he was what Desire called a sensible person, and took his refusal well. Apparently he had not much expected anything else yet, and, though he announced his intention of waiting indefinitely for the more favourable answer, which Desire did not encourage him to expect, he did not let the incident make any difference to his present unembarrassing friendliness. But unfortunately Lady Quebell discovered what had occurred, and she felt it her duty to speak to Desire on the subject.

She spoke very plainly indeed and after having denounced Desire and her doing—not without some justice—in the old terms, she demanded sharply if she realized her age.

'You do?' she said, when Desire readily owned to her twenty-six years. 'Do you realize that your chances of a satisfactory settlement in life are diminishing rapidly?'

'Do you think they are?' Desire asked. 'Well, now, I don't; I don't believe there ever was a chance of my settling satisfactorily. I can't conceive of any walk in life now open to me where Satan would not "find some mischief still for my hands to do".'

Lady Quebell did not mean that. 'I meant, make a satisfactory marriage,' she said, 'and you know I did. In your circumstances I really cannot understand your present conduct; it is worse than folly.'

'Is it?' Desire said, with the interest of one discussing a general topic. 'You think so? I expect you are right.'

'Of course I am,' Lady Quebell said shortly; she knew what Desire's easy acquiescence was worth. 'Why did you refuse that man?' she asked; 'you like him personally, he interests and amuses you, and, what is of more importance, he understands you and would not expect too much. He is rich enough even for your extravagance; he appears to have no relations whom you could shock, and he is not likely to be in any way exacting. I can't think of a match more suitable to you in every way.'

And she proceeded to enlarge on the suitability, without, it is to be feared, producing much effect, although Desire, with justice, agreed with most of what she said.

'Are you going to reconsider your refusal?' she asked half deceived by the agreement.

'I'm afraid not.'

'Then why is the man still coming here?'

'I don't know, unless it is because he likes to; perhaps because he likes me and I like him.'

'Like him! You mean because you like men dangling round you! It must have been a disappointment to you'—she spoke spitefully now—'that the impossible person, Grimstone, with whom you played so disastrously last summer, gave you up so completely when he got his *congé*.'

Desire did not explain that the man in question had received no *congé* and courted none. She never felt inclined to discuss Peter Grimstone in the pleasant superficial manner she was ready to speak of most other people introduced into conversation by her step-mother. In some way he stood to her for a thing separate and apart, a ridiculous thing, perhaps, but one she could not replace, and regretted with an intermittent but persistent sense of loss.

Lady Quebell knew nothing of this, but she felt that her remark concerning the man had touched somewhere, and she went on with a maliciousness which was nearly ill-bred.

'I suppose,' she said, 'you rather expected Edward Gore to return to you after a time?'

Desire was aware of the bad manners and the bad feeling, and together they rather jarred on her. 'No,' she said briefly, 'I expected him to marry someone else; by this time no doubt he is married.'

'He is nothing of the kind. Who should he marry?'

Desire looked up, her attention arrested. 'Are you sure he is not married?' she asked quickly. 'How do you know?'

'I heard about him the other day from the Russels,' Lady Quebell answered; 'he is certainly not married; he has not got over your treatment of him.'

Desire was sure he must have. 'People don't break their hearts over me,' she said; 'he did not really care much, not that way anyhow.'

'Oh,' Lady Quebell retorted, 'is that how you explain his non-return?'

But the shaft missed, for Desire was thinking of something else; what it was soon appeared. 'I shall go and see the Russels,' she announced, 'and ask about him—'

'Ask about him!' Lady Quebell exclaimed; 'you can't!'

'Why not? They can tell me all I want to know.' That to Desire was a more than sufficient reason.

She knew pretty well what Gore's movements had been since her jilting of him last summer. He had first left London for some considerable time; then, when work compelled his return, he had applied himself to it with an attention which banished him from society of most sorts, and in the early spring ended in another breakdown. He was not very strong nervously. For that reason, if for no other, it was perhaps a good thing he was not tied to Desire, whose too exciting personality would undoubtedly have worn him even more than the work it would have stimulated him to do. These facts Desire knew; the thing she did not know was what had happened on his recovery, whether or no he was yet married to the woman of the grey eyes—one who, unlike herself, would have supplemented and soothed him alike in struggle and success.

But she very soon found this out, at all events all that was known to his friends the Russels. They, whatever their opinion of her inquiries and the motive of them, gave her the information she wanted. She learnt that up to the present they at least believed him to be unmarried. So if any ceremony had taken place they—and presumably other people—did not know of it. If it existed it must be of a private nature, which was surely not quite what justice demanded.

There was a smoulder of anger in Desire's eyes when she went upstairs after her visit to the Russels. Gore had had time enough, even allowing for the difference between his nature and her own headlong one; he had had time to get over the blow of her dealing; he had lost himself in work since, been ill and was better, and he had not yet married the woman. He was a little afraid to take the step doubtless; afraid about his position, perhaps. Who and what she was before marriage might not leak out, possibly never would, but, on the other hand, it might. Desire realized now, as she had not during her engagement, that he set store by these things—which did not count at all to her—that, whatever his convictions, he had a tendency to rule his life by that thing unrecognized by herself, the usual standard. He was just a little bit of a coward; a brilliantly clever man, but just a little lacking in physical stamina, moral stamina too, perhaps—at any rate lacking the fearless robustness with which she had endowed him at one time, probably solely because she possessed it herself. And so he had not yet married this Edith. And she, poor soul had doubtless feared to put fortune to the touch—she, too, lacked the headlong decisiveness. What she must have suffered during these months, this woman who, in spite of her brave words, never really lost sight of the world's estimate of her position! Desire, in her place, would not have given a thought to the world, but she dimly realized that this other one did, and realized, too, that the nervous nature, which fears to miss the opportunity and fears to take it, suffers a martyrdom in waiting, watching, doubting itself and others, and making a thousand abortive starts unknown to those who leap without looking and usually land safe on the other side.

Desire rang the bell. Months ago now she had almost forcibly discarded the whole affair, she had compelled herself to set it aside as something which could not be bettered by thinking, and she had come instinctively to shrink from thought of it. But now, it seemed, she had got to reopen this incident. She had, it seemed, assumed a responsibility of sorts, when she played the part she did; and now she had to see it through to the end. When the man answered her summons she told him to call her a cab.

Soon she was driving away, and it was as well Lady Quebell knew nothing about it, for her destination was Gore's chambers in the Temple.

No doubt it was someone's business to ask a visitor's errand at the Temple chambers, or at least his name, before he was permitted to penetrate to the room where Gore sat at work. But this did not befall Desire. When, as now, her whole mind was bent on her object, to the exclusion of everything else, other people were either, quite unconsciously, swept aside by her, or swept along with her, or too surprised to recollect the thing they normally did until she was gone. So it happened now, and she passed through to Gore unquestioned and unannounced. When he looked up on the opening of the door she was already there, a completely surprising and scene-filling presence.

'I am sorry to interrupt you,' she said, without any greeting or excuse; 'but I want ten minutes' talk with you; can I have it?'

It was the same curiously thrilling voice, the same oddly, frankly intimate manner which made one feel as if one had never parted from her; the same seductive figure, standing, glowing-haired, in a shaft of sunlight. Gore recognized it, as he recognized the irresistible, all-pervadingness of her, with a sense of shock.

'Anything I can do for you?' he said formally, placing a chair for her as he spoke.

She sat down without noticing the stiffness of his tone or the way it strove to indicate disapproval of one who, having behaved to him as she had, came to him on any pretext whatever.

'It is about your marriage I want to talk to you,' she said without preamble. 'You are not married, I suppose?'

She flashed a searching look as she spoke, and there was a momentary hope in her eyes. He saw it in some astonishment, and perhaps he is not to be blamed for misinterpreting it.

'No,' he said briefly.

She nodded as if it was what she expected. She did not say she was sorry, but Gore could not help perceiving it; and he was at once nonplussed and irritated.

'I was not aware that you took so much interest in my affairs,' he said stiffly.

'No,' she answered, 'l suppose not—' she broke off as if

uncertain, then went on again : 'I thought you would have been married by this time; I expected you would.'

He could not conceal his surprise and annoyance, the annoyance of one who resents an unwarranted intrusion.

'I fear I do not understand you or your interest in me,' he said.

'No,' she answered; she was finding it embarrassing, though not, perhaps, from quite the causes which would have embarrassed most women. 'The fact is, you ought to be married, you know; you have kept her waiting a long time.'

Gore's face suddenly froze. 'What do you mean?' he demanded. Desire looked away; she was intensely sorry for him, so sorry that she felt it was impossible she could ever have been anything else.

'I know about it,' she said, with the awkward shamefacedness of one who is herself discovered in what is discreditable; 'I knew before you came back. I chanced upon it by accident, and then went into it and found out everything, and made her promise not to tell you. You must not blame her for not telling you. I made her promise. I thought we could manage without a scene. I hate a scene.'

'You knew?' He repeated the words in a stupefied fashion.

'Will you please tell me with what you are charging me?' he said. 'Perhaps also you will tell me why, if you consider you had reason for breaking off our engagement, you did not tell me of it at the time, and give me an opportunity of explanation, or, at least, confession?'

'Because I hate a scene,' Desire answered; she, too, had recovered, and spoke easily now as one dealing with impersonal topics. 'Besides, really it would have done no good; there was that woman, Edith, there was you, and I, the three of us; we couldn't make ourselves into two, could we?'

The thing was literally sprung upon Gore, at a time, too, when it would have seemed madness to dream of it. It was not wonderful that he was completely taken aback and mentally disorganized. Desire's method of doing it, too, and her very manner, giving no clue to her motives and emotions, was further calculated to produce disorder in the mind of a highly strung person.

'Am I to understand,' he said, 'that you knew of and resented my—my—er—connection with—'

'Not resented it,' Desire said quickly, coming to his rescue; 'it wasn't exactly any business of mine to resent. She had first claim on you, it was for her to resent.'

'I don't understand,' he said helplessly. 'You don't resent—you—What is it then? You think I should have told you? '

'Good Lord! What difference would that have made?'

He looked at her bewildered for a second, utterly at a loss to understand her attitude. He rose and went to the window; to him it was impossible they should discuss such things facing one another across the writing-table. He was also both embarrassed and ashamed.

'I know I did wrong,' he confessed with his back turned. 'I was a cad, I know it; I hadn't the courage quite to break with her even after I knew you, she—she was a great comfort—besides, she cared—but I did break, you know—I would have if we had—'

'I know.' Desire spoke rather breathlessly, with a quickness begotten of a desire to prevent him from unconsciously making further rents in the character with which she had endowed him. 'I know just what happened, I can understand. People have cared for me like that before. It's my fault, there's something queer about me. I can quite see how it was that you really cared for her all the time, and just got momentarily fascinated by me.'

He turned sharply. 'You think,' he said, 'that I cared more for her than for you?'

Desire straightened suddenly and the pity left her eyes. 'If I did not think it,' she said, and her voice thrilled with anger, 'if I did not know it, I should move heaven and earth to prevent you marrying her or marrying any other decent woman.'

She rose in her turn and went and stood with her back to the mantelpiece. 'Look here,' she said, and though she spoke pleasantly and easily again, she had lost the manner of the one who pleads, 'we understand all about it, there isn't any need to go into how it happened or why it happened and all that, it's all quite simple and straightforward and no real harm done; you and I found out our mistake and you and she will marry.'

A light at last broke on Gore, the object of the visit was at last explained. It was, then, to bring about his marriage with Edith, the other woman. He found it a very surprising reason.

'Of course,' Desire went on, turning to the mantelpiece as she did so, 'marriage means a good deal to her. I don't suppose I should bother in her place, though there's the child, that might make a difference—but she's a proper kind of woman, a good woman, a real, true, good woman, just the wife for you, though—' and she looked round and spoke half jestingly, her mercurial temperament rising, 'she's rather too good for you, my friend.'

Gore was essentially a person of codes and traditions. Right and wrong, moral and immoral, were things of accumulated precedent, not private notions to be arrived at by individual thinking. He may therefore be excused for not understanding Desire, even, perhaps, for being a little shocked by her.

'Am I to understand,' he said, 'that the object of this visit is to point out to me what you consider my duty?'

The light died out of Desire's eyes and her lips drooped, but she did not deny it, and irritation arose in his overstrung nerves.

'Thank you,' he said, 'I am obliged to you, but I assure you I am able both to see my duty and to do it.'

'Oh, Teddy I' she cried, almost wailed; 'oh, Teddy, don't!' For a moment she hid her face—he might have left her something, some shadow of her old estimate!

He stared in blank astonishment; 'What am I to understand, then?' he asked.

'Understand anything you like!' She flashed round on him in sudden anger. 'You can never understand the facts, it seems! Your duty! Why, man, it is your fortune, your happiness, your high honour to win for your life companion the best woman you have met! To give the gift she wants to her—one who has stood by you in bad times, waited your good pleasure in good—who is worth a thousand of you!'

She went to the door. 'But, of course, you were going to marry her all along,' she said, with a sudden drop to conventional tones—'I know that. But if I were you I should let it be soon, the facts are so likely to become known. Things do leak out so, don't they? I shouldn't be a bit surprised if these did—'

Her eyes met his for a moment with an uncompromising directness. He could not mistake the threat, and his pale face crimsoned. But she went out looking neither to right nor left, nor able to meet any one's glance for very shame, and scarcely seeing the door for a mist of tears.

Chapter XI

It was in early June that Sir Joseph Quebell died, so suddenly as to be inconvenient to those whose business is the writing of obituary notices. The suddenness of Sir Joseph's death was inconvenient to others besides newspaper men, indeed it left what his lawyer characterized as 'a very much to be regretted state of affairs'. Sir Joseph was the sort of man whose affairs are expected to be in the most perfect order, and the main block of his personality justified such expectations, but there were a few curious stars and flaws in his character. It was one such, of course, which had brought Desire into existence. The condition of his affairs was exactly on a level with his character. In the main they were in good order, everything touching his official capacity perfect; but in his private matters there was one glaring lack; it was this which really made the lawyer speak of the suddenness of his death as so much to be regretted.

Desire mourned her father's death with a depth of affection and reality which might have surprised some, seeing the semi-detached nature of the family life and feelings. She was grieved for the loss to the world of a very clever man still in his prime, and for the loss to herself of an indulgent parent whom she sincerely liked. But there was more in it to her than that, for Sir Joseph's death occurred within a week of her visit to Gore, at a time when she was scarcely ready for another blow. She felt somehow as if she were losing things rather fast, as if the pillars which propped her pleasant house of life were being shaken, and as if her agreeable world-fabric—which her innermost self realized was only a woven dream fabric—was in danger of being pulled down, and leaving her face to face with unknown real things outside.

To Lady Quebell her husband's death came as a shock; she was very sincerely shocked by the ill-timed intrusion of death into her crowded engagements. Concerning her personal feelings it was impossible to judge; so far as anyone could perceive she had none to speak of except dislike for Desire, and that, one might almost say, had become the single paramount emotion of her life. How strong it was Desire had an opportunity of judging soon after her father's death.

The funeral was over, the time in which convention demanded that the widow and daughter should not be troubled with mundane considerations—other than millinery—was fulfilled. Mr Whitehead, Sir Joseph's solicitor, had an interview with Lady Quebell. What transpired Desire did not know—she was not told and she did not ask. The next day he had another interview with Lady Quebell and afterwards sought one with Desire. She was always easily accessible and she readily received him in her boudoir. He came to her, a polite, formal person, so formal that Desire quickly perceived that the interview with Lady Quebell had been unpleasant and had left unpleasant things to be said or done or thought. Consequently she strove to make it up to him, and to make him welcome in her genial way.

But he would not be made welcome, would not smoke her cigarettes or allow her or himself to forget that he was come on business solely. It was as if he felt that to do so would only make this unpleasant task yet more unpleasant still.

'I must trouble you with a few words about your father's affairs,' he said stiffly.

'They are in a muddle?' she suggested. 'That's not very surprising; the dear old man, for all his wonderful ability, had some weaknesses—that's why one could love him, I expect.'

The lawyer bowed, then made his first statement with brevity. 'He made no will subsequent to his marriage with Lady Quebell,' he said.

'Indeed?'

She raised her eyebrows slightly; they were finely pencilled brows, dark-coloured, like the long lashes which gave part of their charm to her glowing eyes. The lawyer observed them, though he was chiefly interested in the fact that she showed no other sign of surprise, no sign at all of consternation. Plainly, he thought, she did not understand what his news entailed.

'There is a will made prior to the marriage,' he explained, 'by which you are amply provided for. But the marriage, I must tell you, cancels that, it cancels any previous testamentary document; the estate of a deceased person who has made no will subsequent to marriage is administered precisely as if he had died intestate.'

'I see,' Desire said.

But he was not at all sure that she did really see. 'Under these circumstances,' he went on, 'you are very unpleasantly situated. You are not now legally entitled to the sum your father originally bequeathed to you. Indeed, you are—your position—'

He hesitated, and she came to his rescue, and also at the same time cleared up any doubts he had as to the understanding of the situation. 'As I am illegitimate,' she said, 'I am in the present circumstances entitled to nothing. Is that it? How tiresome, isn't it?'

'The bulk of the property goes to Lady Quebell,' Mr Whitehead said. 'There is very little real estate, land and so on; what there is goes to the male heir-at-law, a poor man; but, as I say, it amounts almost to nothing, Lady Quebell practically takes everything.'

Desire nodded. 'She'll be really very comfortably off,' she said in a conversational tone, which once again made the lawyer doubt her ability to understand the situation.

'I have been urging on her the necessity of making some

suitable provision for you,' he went on; 'some separate provision such as it is evident, from Sir Joseph's early will, he wished and intended.'

The red-brown eyes shot a swift, keen look, which was gone again before Desire asked quite lightly—'And she won't?'

'No.'

The lawyer cleared his throat. 'Of course,' he observed, 'I do not know anything of a difference between you.'

'A difference?' Desire smiled. 'A hundred! Bless you, it was all difference nearly—didn't she tell you so?'

'No.' His tone was very grave. 'But I advise you, for your own sake, to try and sink those differences. Believe me'—there was meaning in the gravity now—'it is most advisable, most necessary that you do your best to sink those differences.'

Desire stretched out her hand and took a cigarette. It was a large, strong, well-shaped hand, and the lawyer found himself looking at it and at her as she watched the match flame with which she lighted the cigarette. The flame did not waver at all. Neither spoke till she threw the match away, then she said—'D'ye know, I believe there are two differences people can't sink—a difference in their sense of humour and in their sense of decency—propriety, whatever you call it.'

She rose and stood with her back to the mantelpiece, and the lawyer, who before had been aware of her alluring femininity, was suddenly struck with something curiously masculine in her.

'It's awfully good of you to come and tell me about this,' she said. 'I am no end obliged to you. I am afraid it has worried you quite a good deal—more than it does me, I have no doubt; things don't worry me, you know; I always come through somehow right side up. I have no doubt I shall this time. Must you go?' He had risen when she did. 'Won't you have anything, whisky, tea, something? Do!'

He would not, and as it was clear she did not intend to

discuss the matter further now he shortly took his leave, wondering much what she really thought and what she would do.

What she did was to stand where she was and smoke her cigarette out slowly, and without moving at all. When it was done she threw the end away with a curious little shrug, and the only definite thought which accompanied the shrug was—'What a mercy I saw after that affair of the Edith woman when I did!' Then she went downstairs to Lady Quebell.

Lady Quebell was seated at an open secretaire writing, she glanced round as Desire entered but did not speak. Desire shut the door, and sitting down in an easy-chair propped her head against a cushion comfortably. 'Mr Whitehead has been talking to me,' she said.

'Oh!'

Lady Quebell did not leave off her writing to give the answer; Desire watched her a moment, turning her eyes but not her head.

'Wasn't it rather an unnecessary formality to make him the bringer of the news?' she asked. 'He found it so unpleasant—didn't like it at all.'

Lady Quebell re-read the last sentence of her letter. 'It was necessary you should be told the state of affairs,' she said.

'Oh, of course,' Desire agreed. Lady Quebell returned to her writing, and Desire watched her; under the watch the pen moved more and more slowly and with more frequent pauses for erasion.

'What are you going to do?' Desire asked at last.

'Leave London as soon as possible. After all that has occurred I feel the need of rest and retirement at first, and afterwards change. I don't suppose I shall come back to town till well on in next year, but my plans are very unsettled.'

Desire acquiesced and again dropped into silence. The

writing, which had ceased for the answer to be given, was resumed and progressed much as before until she interrupted by asking—

'And I? What do you advise that I do?'

'I do not advise,' Lady Quebell answered coldly; 'you are at liberty to go or to remain here if you choose, until I give the house up, which, of course, I shall do so soon as it can be arranged.'

'Yes. And afterwards?'

'Afterwards you will please yourself.'

'Don't I always do that?' Desire interpolated. 'I think I remember to have heard you say so.'

Lady Quebell compressed her lips. 'In the future you will be able to do so quite uncriticized by me.'

'Thank you.' Desire turned a little in her chair so as more directly to face the writing-table. 'I am afraid I am a very stupid person,' she said, 'but I really never can understand what is meant unless it is put plainly; won't you tell me in so many words what you propose to do?'

'About you?' Lady Quebell was driven into saying. 'I do not see that I or anyone else is in a position to do anything—you have always chosen to follow your own course. You have had every chance—education, surroundings, introductions, opportunities of the best sort, and—forgive me—quite other than those to which you have an actual claim. If you have chosen to do nothing with them and make nothing of them I do not feel that I, or anyone but yourself, is to blame. Nor do I feel called upon to provide you with further opportunities, which you, if you had them, would, no doubt, treat in a precisely similar way.'

She paused, and Desire politely asked her to go on. 'Won't you tell me what you do intend to do?' she said. 'That is what you don't, please tell me what you do.'

'Nothing,' Lady Quebell answered sharply, a faint colour

mounting under her skin as she spoke; she lacked the courage to enjoy the doing of what both in thought and retrospect she thoroughly enjoyed. 'You have no claim on me,' she said, her voice rising a little with annoyance at the way she had been forced into the answer. 'I am not compelled to do anything, and, as I say, your past conduct is not of the sort to incline me to give you a further chance of wasting opportunities.'

'Thank you,' Desire said; 'now I understand.'

She rose, and Lady Quebell turned round with the cautious inclination of persons of her sort, to palliate in words what they have no thought of softening in action.

'Of course,' she said, 'I have no wish to inconvenience you, you can remain here a month or two if you find it necessary. Indeed, I should rather advise you to do so; it will give you some chance of arranging something, of seeing your friends, and so on. Mr Lee called today—'

'Thanks so much,' Desire interrupted; 'I quite understand.'

'And are quite determined not to be advised,' Lady Quebell said shortly. 'You must please yourself, fortunately I am not concerned with your marrying or not marrying. You are entirely your own mistress now; I do not pretend to have even a nominal interest in your proceedings.'

Desire nodded. 'Thanks for explaining,' she said; 'so much better to speak plainly about things, isn't it? We know where we are then.'

And undoubtedly Lady Quebell did feel that she knew where she was. She did not know where Desire was nor what she would do; but she felt that did not matter, she was about to be quit of that irritating surprise for good and all. She was a woman of very little imagination, and seldom realized more than her own immediate concern in an affair, and only a limited part of that. In this she realized scarcely anything besides her own interest; what became of Desire bulked little if any more in her mind than did what might become of a servant she dismissed for incompetency. The opportunity had come to be rid of an unsatisfactory, a more than unpleasing person, she had availed herself of it as it was within her right as well as her power to do. The very real personal dislike she had for the individual made her quite impervious to anything the lawyer or another might urge in favour of generosity. The dead man's daughter could claim nothing and she would have nothing but her personal effects.

And the daughter realized it perfectly as she went upstairs; she had had more than a suspicion when she went down, but now she realized it plainly. And the strongest feeling in her was a sense of shame—for herself, curiously enough, as well as for the older woman. Her uppermost instinct—and it was a most rare one with her—was to pretend, even to herself, that it was all quite right. She would not for the world have admitted that there was anything amiss with Lady Quebell's attitude or conduct. It hurt something in her to find another woman behaving so, to find this standard of conduct among her own people; it hurt her joyous estimate of humanity and other things—so much so that she was too great a coward to face it. It was a shock, too, to find she was so disliked. She, so she would have reasoned, no doubt deserved dislike, only she herself did not dislike thus, and under no circumstances would ever have acted thus. The revelation of this thing in her own immediate surroundings, in the person of her entirely cool and well-bred step-mother was rather stunning to her. She carried up to her room a sense of loss and shame; but the loss was more of agreeable illusions than of property and income; and the shame had nothing whatever to do with her own birth and position but entirely with the discovery of a code of honour which did not at all jump with her previous ideas. No-one must know it, that was her predominant feeling, curious, perhaps, for one who before had troubled so little, known so little even, about public opinion. None of her friends or acquaintances must know it; she could not stand the thought of its being canvassed and discussed, kindly or unkindly, the hurt was too near and personal, she would always be ashamed for it to be dragged into the light of day. And her secondary feeling—it arose probably out of the first—was that she must end well. She could at least do that, she would leave a gay impression behind and not add one to the world's objects of pity. With the child's instinct to hide her hurt she also had the brave braggart's instinct for a good retreat. No-one should know anything, not her step-mother, not even herself.

Thus it came about that in the days which followed she was in the cheerfullest mood; she and Lady Quebell continued on terms as polite as could be desired, almost more polite, perhaps, than the older lady liked. Practically nothing more was said on either side about the end which was approaching. It is doubtful if Lady Quebell wished to re-open the subject, but even if she did she had no opportunity for doing so. She was, of course, well occupied with her own concerns during these days; she had a business-like mind in small matters and reduced her affairs to wonderful order, settling details down to the proportion of wages due to a discharged kitchen-maid. Desire did not, to her stepmother's knowledge, make any arrangements at all, or do anything different from usual, except attend when requested to receive what of her books and properties were collected when an inventory was made of the contents of the house. She smoked a good deal, more than was wholesome though it was not likely to affect one of her strong constitution much; and she did not sleep very much, though that again produced little visible effect on her, nature having given her an outside well calculated to stand such liberties.

At length the last day of Lady Quebell's present residence in town came: the last of her affairs was disposed of, the last of her things packed. The two women met at breakfast for the last time, Lady Quebell exactly punctual, Desire late, but bringing with her into the room when she did come, a pleasant gust of gaiety rare at morning meals. A few remarks were made about Lady Quebell's journey, the chances of the train keeping time, and her catching a connection at a junction, but nothing whatever to indicate that her going was different from an ordinary going. Desire was very pleasant and bright with just that small touch of eagerness in her manner which she would have shown to one who was in an awkward position and who she wanted to set at case and persuade that the awkwardness was not observed. That was rather how she did feel towards her step-mother; seeing how the elder woman's action impressed her, she almost unconsciously assumed that it must embarrass and humiliate its perpetrator even more. In Desire's parlance, 'to do a rotten thing made one feel such a bounder—and so badly dressed'—and as she always did her best to set at ease those who were badly dressed, and to hide the deficiencies of those who were not equal to their company, she now strove to show her step-mother that her deficiencies were concealed. And Lady Quebell, though she did not in the least comprehend the attitude, and never could have comprehended the feeling which prompted it, had to submit to the power of the stronger and warmer personality.

At last the hour of final departure came, Lady Quebell, dressed for her journey, came downstairs. At the bottom of the stairs she turned, her suspicious eyes looking for Desire: 'Do you know where Miss Quebell is?' she began to ask the butler. But Desire herself was there before the question was fairly put.

'What! going already?' she said. 'You will have plenty of time. Thomas is rather early, I think. I hope you'll have a lovely time and get really rested and set up.'

'Thank you,' Lady Quebell said coldly, then added, 'Parker

is in charge here until September; most of the servants will be leaving at the end of the week, but he stays on and will no doubt do what he can to make you comfortable while you stay.'

'Thanks,' Desire answered; 'I didn't think of staying after to-morrow.' Lady Quebell raised her eyebrows slightly, it was the first she had heard of any of Desire's future movements. 'Good-bye,' Desire said. 'Parker, I believe it would be better if you put the dressing-bag on the opposite seat.'

'Thank you,' Lady Quebell returned; 'it is quite satisfactory as it is. Good-bye; I suppose I shall not see you again?'

The vindictive spark showed for a moment in her eyes as she leaned forward to the window to say this, but Desire answered lightly—'Oh, I don't know, it's a small world, you know; we are sure to run up against one another some time.'

Then the carriage drove away.

When the hall door was shut Desire stopped a moment to speak to the butler.

'I am expecting some people to-night, Parker,' she said.

'Yes, miss.'

'About twenty or thirty.'

'Yes, miss.'

The number was rather surprising seeing the deep mourning of the family and the departure of the mistress of the house, but the doings of Desire were always incalculable, and had long ceased much to surprise the servants. Parker was not even surprised that she had not mentioned the fact before and left him now to make what arrangements he could. She had probably forgotten, he thought.

She had not, but she had not chosen to mention it before, for though she had asked her step-mother's permission to receive people at the house while she remained there, she had not explained that she contemplated receiving them all at once. She had all along intended to do it; some days ago now she had written notes to certain of her friends and acquaintances, the people she liked, who interested or amused her, and asked them to come and see her on that evening.

'I am in mourning, I know,' she wrote, 'but that is no reason why I should be shut up in solitary woe.'

And most of them came.

A somewhat mixed assemblage they were that were: collected for the last time in the big drawing-room. They did not know it was the last time; the invitations did not say so, and there was nothing whatever in the entertainment to indicate it. Desire herself was as usual, even more: brilliant perhaps. She certainly looked very well in the eyes of at least some present, in her mourning gown, and the long string of pearls she wore, in defiance of the convention for bereaved daughters, became her marvellously.

Lee, the man who Lady Quebell had mentioned as a possible solution of the problem of how to live without an income, was among those that thought thus. He had been invited with the rest; Desire, however much she might dislike her step-mother's insinuation concerning him, would not let it prevent her from including him in the company which assembled at her invitation that night. She did not bestow any large share of her favours on him, it is true; he had no more of her society than anyone else. She divided her favours that evening as never before, singling each out in turn, giving him such undivided attention for the time being, that the few minutes were cut sharp and distinct as a cameo on his mind and hers; but she was always careful that none should have so much as to cut short the rest.

Either because of this or because of some spirit which was abroad, the gathering was a singularly successful one. It was odd in several ways. There were no magnificent decorations, only the ordinary summer flowers in the ordinary places; no professional entertainers, no hired musicians. There was some little music, for there were among those present one or two who could only really express themselves that way. And since Desire would have each and all of her friends express themselves to her that night, these must do it this way, to her and for her—the rest listening to what is usually reserved for the elect to hear. But the thing which made the gathering different from most others was that everyone present was here because he was really wanted, and because he wanted to come, pleasure not duty had dictated every invitation and every acceptance. All who came, came as early as they could and stayed as late as they could; it was no social function sandwiched in between others to serve some purpose, it was a seeking enjoyment where it was expected to be found. It must be admitted men largely predominated in the gathering, and the haze of smoke was blue in an atmosphere where formality was not greatly regarded. Desire herself was brilliant with a brilliancy which was rather meteoric and which had something of recklessness in its whole-hearted abandonment to the moment. Not that anyone noticed it, unless perhaps Julian Lee did, and he, besides still being in love, had the advantage of being the only person to whom she gave the slightest hint of the possibility of there being aught amiss.

It was to him she expounded her theory of happiness. 'The whole art of happiness,' she told him, 'lies in the possession of water-tight compartments. If you are properly fitted up with them you can shut away what is not necessary for the moment and enjoy the time being, if so be the time being is enjoyable. Don't you think so?'

'Don't know,' he answered; 'I should think it depends rather what it is you've got to shut away. Some things,' his eyes were upon her, 'are rather big.'

'No, they are not,' she assured him. 'Nothing's too big or too bad, though sometimes we think it so: that's our mistake. I—' she pointed a fan at her own breast, 'I who tell you, know it.'

'No you don't,' he said bluntly; 'you don't know anything about a thing which is too big and not to be cleared out by a pleasant pastime—but I can tell you something.'

He made a movement forward, and she held out her hand. 'Must you really be going?' she said sweetly.

He looked a moment, then he laughed, there was always so much of jest in Desire's rudeness that people seldom resented it.

'No,' he said; 'I must not, and unless you order me to, I will not yet.'

'Better,' she advised him, 'better go while the glamour is still on, glamour does not last.'

There was an underlying earnestness in her light tone, he observed it but he did not take the advice, he stayed to the very end. Indeed, he was one of the two guests who left last of all.

The hour by then was very late, or rather early, for the summer dawn was beginning to filter in through the drawn blinds, no-one seeming in any hurry to cut short the present good moment. But at last they went; someone who had an early train to catch made the first move; others followed, and at length the big drawing-room was left empty. Desire went to the stairhead with her last but one guest, an elderly politician with a hard day's work before him. Lee, the last of all, perforce followed them when she paused in the doorway for him to do so. She shook hands with him as well as the other when they came to the stairs, and reluctantly he accompanied the elder man down, she standing alone looking after them a moment—somehow a gorgeous figure in spite of her black dress and the merciless dawn light.

'Good-night!' she called, leaning on the balustrade. 'Good-bye!' The white carnations in her breast tumbled to the rail and were crushed against her body till she pulled them out.

'Give them to me,' Lee said, looking up, and he made a movement as if he would come back for them.

'Catch!' she said, and threw them past him into the hall, far down towards the doorway. 'For farewell,' she said, leaning down to see him pick them up. Then she turned away.

As she turned, the hair on which her pearls were threaded gave way. She caught the string as it slipped so that only three fell to the floor and these she found at once, but she had a feeling that this too was for farewell. Like Cinderella's slipper the pearls had fallen now that the hour was passed. She gathered them all and went slowly upstairs.

In her bedroom she found her maid, contrary to orders, waiting up for her; for a moment the woman's presence, anyone's presence, jarred on her.

'Barton,' she said, 'did I forget to tell you to go to bed?'

'No, miss,' Barton answered apologetically, 'but I thought perhaps you might want me after all; I'll go if you don't, but I thought you might be tired, sleeping badly as you have been of late.'

'How do you know I have slept badly?'

'By the pillows, miss,' Barton said, with a touch of superiority; 'they are so tumbled, and then there is the cigarette ash.'

Desire smiled, the woman's watchful thought for her touched her, pleased her too, for at that moment it seemed to indicate that after all the world was a good world and the people in it more kindly disposed to one another in the main than she at least deserved.

'I'm glad you have waited. Yes, I think I am tired.'

But in spite of the admission, when she had her dressing-gown on and her hair brushed, she changed her mind about going to bed. She had suddenly come to a decision—somebody must be told something about affairs, and Barton was perhaps the most suitable person, especially as she was always liable to find out a certain amount on her own account. If she was to be told there was no time like the present.

'Are you sleepy?' she inquired of the woman.

'No, miss.'

'Sure? Could you do without going to bed at all—if you could sleep for a week afterwards to make up? All right then, draw up the blinds; I have got crowds of things to do, and I should be glad if you would help me. First of all I must tell you I am leaving here to-morrow—no, to-day it is, leaving for good and all, I mean.'

And forthwith she proceeded to tell what she thought it necessary Barton should know. It was more than she wanted to tell, but not so much as the woman and the other servants would be likely to discover or invent for themselves if they were left completely uninformed unofficially. Needless to state Lady Quebell and her action did not figure in the information at all, it concerned Desire alone—that at her father's death her income ceased, that she was not going to keep a maid or live with her step-mother in future, that she was, in fact, going to strike out a line for herself.

Barton, helped as she was by sundry rumours which had reached the servants' hall, could not at once realize or accept all this; it took time for her to grasp a situation so terrible in her estimation. When she did, she did not at all see it in the light in which Desire put it; she only saw it as an overwhelming catastrophe which had overtaken her mistress. And when she grasped the news of the doing without a maid she burst into tears, to the great discomfiture of Desire.

'Now, Barton,' Desire said, 'don't! What on earth are you crying for? I'm sorry to give you such short notice, it's mean of me, I know, but I'll get you another situation, a good one; there are plenty of women I know who'd be glad to have you. What, crying because you are going to leave me, or rather I you! You shouldn't do that, you'll never get another mistress who's half the plague I am. It's awfully nice of you to mind leaving me. I mind, too, but it can't be helped, you know.'

Barton thought it could, she did not want any wages for a long time, she said, she had plenty of savings, she only wanted to stay on. Desire had to make plain to her that she could not do that; that, much as she herself appreciated the devotion, she could not accept the service, the loan of savings, or any of the other things which were offered in succession.

At this Barton wept afresh, and Desire had to become severe. 'You know,' she said, 'it really is rather selfish of you to go on like this, just because I'm going to have the time of my life and going to set out to seek my fortune. There's nothing in the world half so fine as seeking your fortune.'

'If you'd let me stay with you, miss—' Barton began.

'It'd be lovely, of course, but I can't,' Desire said hastily; 'besides, you'd get demoralized; there'd be nothing for you to do. I shan't have any jewelry to lock up, or any engagements to keep, or any clothes to put away. Brush my hair? I'll brush that myself, or if that's too much bother cut it off and give up brushing except on Sundays.'

Barton gasped at the idea of such sacrilege.

'If you don't stop crying,' Desire threatened, 'I'll cut it off right away and give it to you to wipe your eyes on. Now, let's leave off talking nonsense and get to work. First of all I want all the jewelry I have got collected together and packed in a box. You have got my keys, I think?'

Barton produced the keys and obediently began to collect the jewels, sniffing a little at intervals.

'If it isn't a liberty, miss,' she said when she was composed, 'I should like to inquire what her ladyship says to this.'

Her respectful manner was quite colourless again. She knew better than her mistress how to hide the antagonism which she felt, far more strongly than Desire, for Lady Quebell.

Desire was stripping the rings from her fingers. 'I'm not

sure it is not rather a liberty,' she said without looking round; 'still, I'll tell you—her ladyship has nothing to say; she never does to anything on which I have set my mind.'

Barton did not answer but busied herself with the jewels; however, after a minute she ventured in the same respectful way. 'Her ladyship has the money, I suppose, miss? Mr Parker said she had.'

'Of course,' Desire said; 'what else is there for the poor soul to have? I have all the games.'

Barton sniffed, but it was not altogether tearfully. 'I'd be ashamed,' she muttered to herself as she went to a wardrobe for a gold belt for which Desire had asked.

'What did you say?' Desire thought it wise to inquire. 'That it is an unfair division and uncomfortable for her ladyship? So it is; it places her in a very awkward position, but it can't be helped. Is that the belt? Thank you; now pack everything together. As soon as you can I want you to find out how I can best sell these things.'

'Sell them?' Barton queried.

'Yes; I'm not going hungry while I am seeking my fortune, and, great as is my belief in myself, I don't expect to find it tomorrow morning.'

Barton set her lips and began to pack the jewelry in a wooden box, she was as nearly shocked as it was possible for one who had long attended on Desire to be. Desire herself was quite unaware of it, and set to getting out her clothes—dresses, petticoats, coats and cloaks and hats, a great quantity: Barton had packed the jewels long before she had done.

'What a heap they look!' she exclaimed when at last everything was out and every article of furniture and most of the floor space piled with things. 'I had no idea one had so many clothes; it'll take for ever to sort them. But we must do it, the greater part won't be a particle of use to me and will have to be sold.'

Barton began to help with the sorting; she offered no remonstrances; it was clear she felt the case beyond words. Desire on her part was quite cheerful, and discarded without a pang lace ball dresses, embroidered opera cloaks, and other fragile sartorial triumphs.

'I shall keep a good lot of the most serviceable things,' she said; 'there's no telling when I shall get any more. It's as well I never followed the fashions too closely for, as I shall have to wear them as they are for the next four or five years, my clothes will all be of one date. Barton, I ought to have learned to sew; it has never struck me before; I shall have to darn my stockings, you know.'

'I could do that, miss,' Barton said almost cheerfully; 'you can't do without someone, miss, and I—'

'Am not coming,' Desire said, with a sudden drop to gravity. 'I appreciate your still wanting to come much, but it can't be done. That is already settled; you understand it, don't you?'

Barton did now, at least she understood that when Desire spoke like that she was the mistress and as unapproachable as the most haughty lady in the land.

The sorting took long and the necessary packing longer. Breakfast-time had come before they had finished, lunch before Desire was ready to go. It was not till the afternoon that she took her final departure and then her destination was of Barton's suggesting.

'My eldest sister lets rooms, miss,' the woman ventured; 'you'd be as comfortable there as anywhere for a night or two, till you have made your plans.' Making plans had not heretofore been much in Desire's line; she had usually rather taken things as they happened and let the next happening take care of itself. However, it was necessary to have a temporary address and a place for things to be sent, somewhere to tell the cabman to drive to. As it evidently pleased Barton to be able to do this much she thanked her and agreed to go to the sister's, on condition that she went unheralded, and also that Barton kept the secret of her whereabouts from unsuitable persons.

A cab was fetched, the luggage loaded on the roof and Desire, after a painful parting with Barton, went out.

'Good-bye,' Desire said to Parker, who was superintending the placing of the luggage; 'I'm afraid I shan't see you again for a good while.'

'Good-bye, miss,' Parker replied, with a solemnity befitting his position.

But there was that in Desire that upset position, sometimes actually a person's notion of his own, and reduced even a first-class butler to mere man. Desire, with outstretched hand and full, deep voice bidding farewell, got at the man in Parker. He put her into the cab, he said good-bye to her as if he were human and she were human, and he minded that she was going.

'Good-bye,' she cried; 'you'll find it blissfully peaceful without me,' and she leaned forward to nod to him with her expressive smile.

Then the cab started, and she leaned back, the smile fading from her lips, but lingering bravely in her eyes. She did not look back, she would not indulge even herself in any effective or affecting scenes, possibly she was less ready to indulge herself than anyone else. She felt for her cigarette case and lighted a cigarette with a curious concentration of attention. Then slowly she smoked it, a thing she rarely did in so public a place as a cab. Perhaps it was as much with a view to the cigarette as the quantity of luggage that she had ordered a four-wheeler and not a hansom.

Chapter XII

Miss Barton was a somewhat dreary person; interested in nothing, not even her lodgers' business, and enthusiastic about nothing, not even her own. Life had been hard on her; in her early days she had had a large family of stepbrothers and sisters to bring up—the Barton who attended on Desire Quebell was one of them. In her later days she let lodgings to superior people, generally the poor superior who knew something about the other side of the self-same struggle that was hers, but in whom, as in herself, it had begotten drabness and dreariness rather than sympathy. This, possibly, was small deprivation to Miss Barton, for she wanted to hear nothing from them but what they required to eat, to tell nothing to them but whether they could or could not have it, to receive nothing from them but the money which was her due, and to give nothing to them but the service she was paid for. It is doubtful whether among her own kin even she was more expressive and reciprocal, certainly she did not feel the slightest interest that Desire Quebell was recommended to her rooms by her half-sister Barton, the maid; nor yet in the fact that her lodger's surname was the same as that of the family where her sister served. Probably she did not remember that, certainly she did not think about it if she did.

Desire found herself established in the apartments with very little talk and commotion. It had taken a wonderfully short time to transfer her from her old life to this new one, or this sort of waiting-room of the new one. In some ways Miss Barton's was like a waiting-room, too, the same featurelessness, the same sense of temporary accommodation only. Before tea Desire was established; she had even unpacked everything she wanted unpacked and put most of it away—a less congenial task to her, but one she did conscientiously to-day. After that she had tea, and after that—there was a whole long evening before her with nothing to do and no-one to speak to! When she suddenly realized that there was nothing more to happen it rather startled her. Next minute she laughed, possibly at herself for finding it startling.

She rose and began minutely to examine the sitting-room, its furniture and ornaments. She had almost always found things interesting, even the things other people ordinarily found dull; this room was one of the few exceptions. It was a little shabby, eminently respectable, quite featureless; the furniture was neither new nor old, it had never been beautiful or very good; or gaudy or very bad, it was merely sufficient. The ornaments, which did not ornament, were much what a small furniture dealer would have set forth on a cabinet in his show-room; there were no family groups, no portraits, no presents from anywhere, not a human touch. Desire turned to the window. The outlook was respectable; a quiet, rather narrow street, shabby genteel houses in need of paint opposite; a few, a very few, genteel people, some shabby, some even without that characteristic, passing occasionally, nothing more. A long, light summer evening, entirely without sun, the street was too narrow for the sun to get there—and nothing further to happen. Desire sat down in the saddle-bag armchair near the window, and in her mind she began to be aware that the rock on which her ship of fortune was most likely to wreck was monotonous respectability. A horrible unnamed fear shook her. Supposing she was not able to stand it?

The next morning she set out to try and find out the best way of selling her jewels. To do this she went eastward, which was both new and amusing. She did not find out very much about the selling of jewels that day, but that did not matter, there was no immediate hurry, she still having some balance at the bank. But she enjoyed the expedition, it brought her in contact with people and things, people and things, too, with which she had had heretofore little dealing. The afternoon, a long afternoon, she spent within doors trying to teach herself to darn stockings. In this she was not very successful, and after a while she threw the stocking aside and smoked, and considered her position and future, and she found it grimly amusing—she never saw things as desperate.

The next day, a Saturday, a niece came to see Miss Barton. She was a girl of nineteen or twenty, wearing a smart blouse and a flowery hat. She also wore a long string of beads, which broke as she was coming upstairs. Desire, who was passing, saw it, and helped pick them up, reminded inevitably of the breaking of her own string of pearls. Of course, she became acquainted with the owner during the picking up. She had not held intercourse with a human being since she parted from Barton, unless one could count as intercourse her interviews on the subject of jewel selling. Also she had never before met a young lady of this sort, and was consequently interested in her. The girl returned the sentiment, though in a different form. Desire, something both new and strange to her, aroused her curiosity, and also a subconscious antagonism, half disapproval, half jealousy.

The girl, Desire learnt, was a typist in a city office; she had a satisfactory situation and a sufficient salary, and was pleased with herself, her work, her liberty and everything else. Desire was much struck with the happiness of this frame of mind, and became greatly interested in the way it was arrived at and the circumstances of its fortunate possessor and her work.

'It sounds quite delightful,' she said, 'I think I'd better become a typist.'

'You!'

Miss Barton's niece looked at her in unfeigned astonishment. She admitted to few superiors and had no recognition of the old-fashioned prejudice of class distinction, but she felt that

Desire was 'different'.

'You couldn't,' she said shortly.

'Why not?' Desire inquired. She had not thought of the matter in a serious light, but the curtness and decision of the girl's tone at once inspired it with an additional interest. 'How did you become one?' she asked.

'I learnt,' was the answer.

Desire of course wanted to know how; she invited the girl to come into her sitting-room and tell her about it. And the girl accepted the invitation because she was curious to see the photographs and ornaments and other personal effects which she expected to find added to the furnishing of the room.

In this, however, she was destined to disappointment; Desire kept few of these feminine appurtenances, and had unpacked none. The visitor was sorry she had come, more especially as Desire in her own room had the same manner that she had when she was 'at home' on Sundays, or at any other time and place when she received company—a manner the very easiness of which embarrassed the typist and made her feel unsure of herself. But since she had come she did not see how immediately to go away again, so she stayed and told Desire what she wanted to know. How she herself had attended classes in the city for book-keeping, typewriting, shorthand and kindred things. How, when she was certified proficient, she had secured her present situation by answering advertisements. She told where the classes were held, how much, or rather, how little they cost, and the beautifully simple system on which the term was arranged, so that a pupil could begin when she liked, leave off when she liked, and learn what she liked. She also gave further details of her present work, its advantages and disadvantages.

Desire's interest was fully aroused; this, so she decided in her headlong way, was the kind of thing for her; if she had any ability at all it would be for this sort of work; and if she had any chance whatever of getting on it would be in some such work as this, which was not cast among women, whom she never understood, and by whom she was seldom liked. She would attend the classes, become proficient, and secure a situation. She had still a part of the last instalment of the liberal allowance her father used to make her, there were her clothes and jewels, too, still to be sold; she could easily afford to try the experiment, it would be better than doing nothing, and would not, of course, interfere with any future plans if she made them. No thought of unsuitability or incongruity troubled Desire, nor any notion of other people's opinions; nothing did when once she had caught hold of an idea except that which would help or hinder it. Let her once get a thread, no matter from what unlikely place, and she would follow it with enthusiasm: it was, no doubt, to this faculty that she had heretofore owed much of her enjoyment and some of her success.

So it fell out that as soon as might be she entered herself as a student at some of the classes described to her. It was an easy thing to do, as easy as establishing oneself at Miss Barton's rooms, requiring no more talk and little more notice. There were always classes for beginners there, and always beginners for the classes; it was all coming and going and no being, no more pause or stay in the pupils and no more importance in individuals than in the crowd at a railway station. It was a novelty to Desire, not altogether an attractive one, but very convenient.

She began as soon as possible to attend the classes with great regularity, applying herself to learning with all her might. At first, it must be confessed, she found it difficult; the whole thing, the very speech and habit of mind, was new to her, to learn this sort of thing and in this sort of way was very troublesome to her for a little. But pretty soon she grew used to it and, the difficulty of novelty once overcome, she began to get on fast. There were some things, of course, which she never learned. They were not among the subjects which she had undertaken, but had more to do with conforming to accepted standards and similar things. She never learnt to conform, nor did she ever really become aware that there was anything to conform to or that she did not do it. She was in these new circumstances just herself, as she had been in her former life; and, as in her former life, the people with whom she came in contact had to accept it as it was, she always remaining unconscious that there was any difference between it and others.

What they thought of the new student at the Commercial College is not recorded. They must have found her somewhat astonishing; it is worthy of notice that, though she was usually a friendly person, and certainly in her present circumstances a lonely one, no-one became intimate with her during the time she attended the classes. The students held aloof from her, not because she was proud or they stand-offish, or either side generally disinclined for acquaintance, but simply because she was herself and utterly alien to them and their experience. Some of the girls distrusted her on sight without knowing why, some were unconsciously jealous of her, some genuinely shocked by ways and sayings and outlook which, entirely unknown to her, failed to conform to their standard; one and all knew her for a stranger. With the men she got on better, though she never really established her usual friendly footing with any of them. For them all she had one manner, from the superintendent to the doorkeeper and the youngest embryo office-boy, she treated them with the frank camaraderie she had for all men, from peers to porters. A few took unpleasant advantage of it—such are to be met with in all classes—but they did not transgress twice. She knew how to treat that mistake, no matter by whom made. For the most part, however, though they were dazzled they were also puzzled by her, and felt that she did not belong, that she or they were out of the right element. The door-keeper, an old soldier, was the man with whom she got on best, the only person completely at ease with her. She talked to him always as a man and a brother, and he saluted as she passed as if it had been the general under whom he used to serve, opened her umbrella for her on rainy days as if he had been her butler, and once by accident addressed her as 'my lady.' The girls said he was an old fool and she spoilt him; they did not perceive that he had done what they had failed to do, in a measure succeeded in placing her in his scale of things.

The Commercial Classes were not an unmixed success so far as Desire was concerned. She learnt what she went to learn, it is true, but they depressed her, they were one of the few experiences of her life out of which she extracted little amusement and no enjoyment. Also they—or her loneliness or something else, or all combined—made her almost for the first time conscious of herself. Her pleasant house of life was tumbling and crumbling under the shocks of the past year; several of the old agreeable illusions were gone, and herself was beginning to show plainer and more real, at times to be the only real thing left. Nevertheless, she went on with the classes; she had undertaken to master several subjects and she would do so even though they were small use to her afterwards. Some of the girl students had assured her they would be no use at all; one, in an unusual burst of friendliness, warned her that she would never succeed in the city.

'Why not?' Desire asked.

'Because you wouldn't,' was the unenlightening answer. 'But you never thought really of it, did you? Why, we never thought of you and city work! You couldn't do it anyhow.'

'Why not?' Desire repeated. 'Of course I came here with the idea of preparing for it; what else should I come for? What does anyone come for?'

The girl did not tell her that none of them had been able to imagine why she had come, and that none of them in the wildest flights of fancy ever dreamed she was so absurd as to think she was going to enter a city office as a clerk or typist. But when she persisted in her inquiry as to why the work was impossible to her, the girl was obliged to give some sort of an answer.

'You're not the sort,' she explained; 'you'd never do. Oh, I know you've learnt typing and the rest all right, but you don't look—Appearances are against you.'

'Appearances?' Desire said. 'Face? Too plain, or too pretty?'

'Neither,' the girl answered shortly. She did not feel at ease discussing appearances with Desire; she even had a suspicion that she was being made fun of, or perhaps condescended to, or something equally unpleasant. 'It's the whole thing,' she said; 'you're altogether wrong for it, dress and all.'

Desire glanced at her own dress, then at her companion's; then she looked away quickly for the girl coloured a little.

'A skirt's a skirt for a' that,' she said lightly. 'It must be the blouse which is wrong. Won't you tell me about blouses? Mine is wrong and yours is right. I might get one something like yours perhaps. Where did you get it? Will you give me the address of your dressmaker? Women hate to be asked for that, I know, but the circumstances are exceptional aren't they? And I'll promise not to steal her. I'll get just one blouse as a pattern—.'

'I made this myself.'

The girl's voice marked several hundred leagues of difference between them, and Desire perceived she had made a mistake of the worst sort. How silly of her not to have remembered that the blouse was likely to have been home-made! All girl students made blouses, she heard them talk among themselves of gauged yokes and val. insertion and bias fronts and other technicalities which were as Greek to her. She complimented the ingenuity of the home dressmaker now and quitted the delicate subject to return to her original question.

'Why do you imagine I shall not succeed as a clerk? Appearance is a thing which is easy to alter, you know; if I set that right I suppose there is no reason why I should not do as well as anyone else?'

'Yes, there is,' her informant answered bluntly; 'no man in his senses would take you on; for one thing he'd feel all the time you were a woman, not a machine, and that you were—oh, I don't know—and, anyhow, he couldn't give you orders.'

Desire frowned. 'That's rather nonsense, you know,' she said; 'I think I could take orders as well as any one.'

'No-one's ever given 'em to you, I bet; no man, anyway. Why, look at the men here!'

The conversation was getting to an unprofitable channel; Desire did not pursue it further, she only announced her intention of proving the matter for herself, and trying, when she was qualified, to get a situation. After that she went home to her rooms.

It was a Saturday, a very wet Saturday towards the end of July: there had been a lot of wet Saturdays that month. It rained all the afternoon; she stayed indoors and spent the time at her typewriter. She had bought a second-hand machine from a student who was in some trouble; she had paid what would have been considered at the college a perfectly reckless price for it, and had conducted the transaction with a briefness and privacy unusual there. Since she had had it she had spent much time practising, and by now she was quite proficient—so much so as to make the copying of the newspaper, and the inditing of letters to no-one, ridiculous. Nevertheless that afternoon she went on with it persistently; it was the best thing to do; whenever she paused to choose a word or insert a fresh sheet of paper she heard the rain pattering on the window pane; there was not very much else to be heard, hardly anyone passed along the street except a milkman, and once a coal cart. Sometimes one heard distant sounds from the less genteel side street not far off. In the side street there was a shop which sold sweets and tinned things inside and vegetables out, and which did nearly as much trade in bad weather as in good.

In that street, too, people sometimes exchanged opinions in shrill voices from doorsteps. Desire had more than once found herself wishing her window looked that way. She would not have minded the talking from the doorsteps, she would have liked it, even possibly joined in; she would have been interested in the trouble the talkers appeared to have with their husbands, the rent collector and the children; and have sympathized with the satisfaction they seemed to find in an occasional glass in the public-house at the corner.

The wish came to her again that wet afternoon. It came as it nearly always did, with the accompaniment of a humiliating fear that she would not be able to hold out, would not be able to keep on enduring the colourless monotony of the present. She had been so used to movement, variety, vivid interests, that she found the monotony and narrowness and lack of human outlet in her present life almost terrible. She missed the luxury, and money spending she had lost very little; she missed the change and interest and eager human spending acutely. She fought the feeling and would not give way to it; she was vaguely conscious though without actual recognition, that monotony is necessary discipline, that nothing is achieved without it. She was very fully aware that it is the lot of at least nine-tenths of the human race, and that she, who had had many years of sunshine and champagne, had small right to complain at receiving a share of grey weather and wholesome but unexciting milk and water. She was also aware that it was of her own choosing; but that last was not a good thing to be aware of for it entailed the other fact that she could also choose to throw it up if it became unendurable, a humiliating remedy. That wet afternoon these thoughts, all familiar company by this time, passed through her mind in some shape or another; her fingers were busy with the typewriter but her attention was elsewhere, and in a little she was brought up with a jerk by running beyond the line. She stopped in some self-contempt; she was like a young servant whose head is too full of the holiday she has had for her to be able to attend to what she is doing. Desire had always felt sympathetic with such young servants, but she was rather ashamed to find herself like them. And yet—

Oh, for just ten minutes with someone from the old world! Even ten minutes' talk about the old things! Not better things or a better world, but the ones she knew. To speak again to one who meant what she meant by what he said, to hear again of what she used to hear, to strike something which would respond at once! She would not wish for the entertainments of the past, to tell the truth, they had lost something of their savour, and, anyhow, they matched ill with a working life. But for the talk! Ten minutes, just ten minutes with someone or other of the men she used almost daily to meet! She clasped her hands behind her head and gave herself up to recollections.

But in a little a question forced itself upon her notice. Supposing one such were here? Supposing Bamfield, obliging, useful Bamfield whom she had known for years, who had served her for years—supposing he were here, brought by her thought as he easily could be by her written word—what then? It would be quite unendurable. Neither he nor any of the others would understand her position or the real inside of what had befallen. And she certainly did not want them to try: it was the last thing she wanted. She had gone out from among them cheerfully and left them with a gay recollection. Rather a theatrical ending, perhaps, but her mother was of the theatres—she was not of the sort to commit an anti-climax and appear after 'positively the last appearance'. For a moment she recalled that last appearance, and Julian Lee, the persistent, who would stay to the end, who even then tried to come back. Now possibly he was looking forward to the winter when he would expect her to re-appear in town. He would certainly come at her bidding, come to this genteel little room and probably ask her to marry him. There was always the alternative of marriage if this was unendurable—she shivered just a little for, inevitably, the thought of marriage recalled another man from the old life, Edward Gore. He was married now: she had taken pains to keep herself informed on that point; at last he had married Edith—and she, poor soul, was she happy? Did she know how it had come about? He would never tell her that; his pride would keep it back, and so spare her. Desire shivered again, there were things in the old life not good to recall. But one thing she saw plainly, it was not only her step-mother's act and her father's want of forethought that had ended the old life, Gore had done his part, perhaps the biggest part of all. A wonderful loneliness in which her soul felt for a moment like one naked and alone, had come pressing upon her at times before ever she was banished from the old world. A feeling as of one not filled and satisfied had entered once or twice into the play while she still played. Yes, the thing was ended—she dropped her arms from behind her head—ended. Peace be to its ashes! And prosperity to the somewhat ashy prospect which was all that at present came to hand!

She lighted a cigarette and afterwards applied herself to inditing a correspondence between firms of Rockefellerian magnitude for the purchase and consignment of fifteen million tons of ashes.

Chapter XIII

'A gentleman to see you, miss.'

When Vera, the maid of all work, brought this information to Desire, the clock marked only ten minutes past four; the wet afternoon was not nearly spent, though the fictitious correspondence on the subject of ashes had become as voluminous as if the War Office were a party to it.

Desire looked up from her typewriter. 'To see me?' she said. 'Are you sure? I think you must be mistaken.'

Vera was quite sure, she said so decidedly.

'Who is he?' Desire asked. 'What name?'

'I didn't ast,' Vera answered. 'Do you want to know? '

'Oh, no; it doesn't matter. Ask him to come up, please.'

After all, Desire reflected, she might as well see him since he had found her, whoever it was. She wondered who it could be. Her father's lawer? Parker? Vera would not discriminate. Either of the two might want to see her on some matter of business, and Barton would have given the address if applied to for that purpose; she would not be applied to for any other. Desire had told some few people on the night of her entertainment that she was leaving town soon; so she was, their part of it. They had accepted it, and would not be surprised to see no more of her before the winter; and when the winter came they would not be very surprised not to see her; they were all busy living, they had not so very much time for feeling. They might miss her perhaps; a few might ask one another where she had gone, and when she was coming back, but in a little while the gap she had left would close as does a gap in water. Some would remember her—as they remembered a fashion for big sleeves or an operatic star who had been the rage. They would be pleased to see her back when or if she came; for the rest, she had gone, and no-one is indispensable. She knew that quite well, she herself in similar circumstances would likely have done not dissimilarly; she did not feel in the least bitter about it, but she understood.

Vera opened the door, and, having by now satisfied her curiosity on the point of name, announced, 'Mr Grimstone'.

Desire sprang to her feet. 'Oh!' she said, 'I am glad to see you!'

'I'm glad I came,' Peter answered. He did not in the least know why she was so glad, but he did not mistake her sincerity. 'What is the matter?' he asked simply.

'Nothing,' she answered.

In the time which had elapsed since she last saw him she had forgotten his embarrassing direct way of looking. It came upon her with almost a little shock now, it took away some of her self-possession and made her feel that she would soon be telling him her affairs, as she had not told any one else. Accordingly, from perversity probably, she began to talk of his, asking about himself and his work with her usual eagerness.

'What have you been doing?' she said. 'How's *The Dreamer*'s younger brother. It's more than a year since I have heard of him. A whole year!'

Peter did not remind her that had she been interested to hear she could have written to ask. He had not expected her to write, in spite of the curious closeness of their intimacy at one time. He did not expect much of people, so he, unlike most who knew Desire well, was never hurt or disappointed by any of her rather conspicuous shortcomings.

'*The Dreamer* has no younger brother,' he told her.

'No?—Is the second book not finished yet?'

'It never will be. I have given up writing.'

'But—,' she began and stopped, conscious anew of the difference in him, conscious, too, that he arrived at his conclusions a different way from what she arrived at hers;

impressed now, as she had not been a year ago, that there might perhaps be more in his way than hers; 'Why,' she asked, 'why have you given up?'

'Because it's no good,' he said. 'I tried on and off for a year, or nearly a year, and it came to nothing; it was no use.'

'And so you gave up?'

'Not exactly because of that,' he admitted. 'My father is ill and I have his work as well as my own to do, so I could not do anything else if I would. But it does not make much difference. I did little real good before when I had the opportunity—or, at least, as much opportunity as many men. So, you see, either way the thing has come to an end.'

She nodded. 'I see,' she said, but she was not really sure of it. It was hard to realize that the peculiar ability, which had fought its slow, persistent way out before, was gone now, killed by adverse circumstances. Rather one would think it in abeyance, working unseen in the dark, throttled, perhaps temporarily, by duty, but still there, as life is there in the trees that die outwardly in the winter and wait to be recalled by the spring. For the first time Desire felt that there was something about Peter which reminded her of the slow inevitableness and ununderstandableness of the ways of nature.

'I'm afraid I'm a failure,' he was saying, with more apology than regret. 'I wonder if you are?' she speculated; 'I doubt if you are in a position to judge, and I am sure I am not.'

She regarded him curiously, chin propped on hands and eyes studying him in undisguised fashion; she found him much harder to place than before.

'Do you know,' she said, 'I used to consider that you belonged to the-world-of-things-as-they-never-were, but I am not sure now that I was right, I'm not sure it isn't—Oh, well, never mind, anyhow it is not the old world I used to know, or the new one I am trying to. That is why I am glad it is you and not anyone else who came this afternoon—why, you are about the only person who could have come. By the way, why did you come?'

'I heard you were in trouble.'

'How did you hear?' she put the question quickly.

'From Austin, a man I used to know. When I left London last year he gave me his dog, so last night, after I had done the business I came up about, I went to see him and tell him the dog was all right. He told me of your father's death.'

'Did he tell you anything else?'

'No, he didn't know you or Lady Quebell, or anything about you, more than just that—which I might have seen in the papers myself, by the way, only I didn't; I don't read them much.'

Desire nodded. 'Tell me,' she inquired with some interest, 'how did you find me?'

'I went to the house where you used to live, and they told me you were gone, but that Barton, your maid, would know your address. So I found Barton.'

It sounded simple, but Desire knew it really would not have been so easy. Barton, at last convinced that her mistress would not have her services, had fulfilled an off-and-on engagement of long standing, and was married. The ceremony had taken place about a week ago, and Desire herself did not know where the bride and bridegroom were at present to be found. Parker, to whom Peter must have applied in the first instance, was not very likely to be quite sure either. However, Peter had traced them quickly, persuaded the woman that he was not one of those to whom she was forbidden to give her mistress' address, and here he was.

'Did Barton tell you anything besides my address?' Desire asked.

She had not—Peter was not the kind to seek information from a third party. 'She said a letter sent here would find you,' he said; 'but I thought I would come myself, perhaps if you were here you would not mind me coming. You remember we made a pact once, that you could say what you liked, and be what you liked, and so on to me, and if there was anything I could do I would do it without bothering you to explain why. I thought perhaps there might be something for me to do now. If there isn't—'

'There is—'

She spoke abruptly, then broke off. This that she had called the-world-of-things-as-they-never-were was a strange world, a literal, simple world; at least this man would seem literally to mean and simply do what he said.

'There is something. You can listen to me. You can let me tell you what has happened. I think you will understand.'

And she told, as once before she had told him, what she had not told another. She did not mind his knowing of her step-mother's act and her own position, it was possible and natural to tell him. In the-world-of-things-as-they-never-were, the world from whence *The Dreamer* came, one could, curiously enough, state truths and acknowledge bare facts. Of course, long before she had done the telling she had got back her usual composure and her old way, and laughed at that for which she would not weep. But Peter understood, and because he did he made no obvious comments, expressed no condemnatory opinions and showed no surprise.

Once he did ask, 'Does no-one know that you are here?'

And she answered, 'No-one but Barton, and she promised not to betray me, and, in spite of your evidence to the contrary, I believe she will keep her word, even if she should be asked for my address, which, I think, is very unlikely to happen.'

'What about your people?' Peter inquired.

'I haven't any. My father's people are not my people, and such as they are I don't know much of them, nor they of me, except they don't approve of me; they are not likely to be concerned about me. There is an elderly cousin, a Miss

Phoebe Quebell, whose sense of duty may some day give Lady Quebell a bad quarter-of-an-hour; I shouldn't be surprised if it did, otherwise nothing will happen. Of my mother's people, if she had any and was not placed similarly to myself, I know nothing.'

'Your friends will want to know where you are,' Peter said.

She shook her head. 'You don't know people,' she said. 'But they must want to know where you are,' he persisted; 'they will want to know what has become of you.'

'They think I have left town early, and later they will think I am coming back late, and then they will forget; a few, with a thirst for information and a taste for being disagreeable, may ask Lady Quebell about me when she reappears next spring; what she will say I do not know, but I do know that it won't in the least matter to any one.'

Peter found it hard to believe that she would so soon be forgotten. 'Did you say good-bye to no-one?' he asked.

'I had a little party,' she answered. 'I made each one show me himself at the best, and I tried to show myself at the best to them all, and then I "slipit awa". I hope I left a pleasant memory, I know I left no gap. The world's so busy with amusing live people, it can't be bothered with the dead—I'm a deader now. If you were a real live ordinary man you would not have bothered about me, and I would not let you, but being as you are'—her voice deepened suddenly—'you are here.'

'What are you going to do?' Peter asked. 'I mean, do you mind telling me?'

'Of course not,' she answered; 'I should have been disappointed in you if you had not asked. Oh, cautious man! The future would naturally interest you as much as the past; you shall have it.'

And forthwith she told him of her more recent doings and immediate plans.

'Behold me,' so she concluded, 'an embryo clerk, an expert typist, a master, or at least on the way to being one, of the mystery of book-keeping by double entry. In September I get me a situation—if I can. I am told on unimpeachable authority that nothing can be done before, for in August the city fathers sun themselves by the sad sea waves, or follow the giddy golf ball for the furtherance of their figures.'

'What made you think of this?' Peter asked.

'What? The devil "Needs must", to be sure; I can't do anything else. Listen to my list of "can'ts": I can't teach, I know nothing to teach that I'm aware of; I can't paint, I can't draw, sing, write, or follow any other art, if there be any; I can act a bit, it is true, dance and sing, and that sort of thing, but I'm not going on the stage even if I could get there, which is unlikely. One sees there too much of the wrong side of the life I used to know on the right; besides, I always had such a gluttonous appetite for amusement, I should hate to have to work at making it. What other professions are there?—ah! domestic service. I can't cook, so I can't be a cook; I can't be a maid, I'm too untidy; besides, I should have conscientious objections to lacing fat women into tight corsets, and helping nice old grandmothers to turn their silver locks gold. Dressmaking and millinery?—my friend, I can't sew. It's humiliating to confess it, but I can't even mend my own stockings; I've tried since I've been here, but I'd be ashamed to show the result. I called Vera in for advice once; I thought, as she had been educated at the board school, she'd be sure to know; she didn't, she was worse than I. I am seriously thinking of walking down the side street—there's a nice one here—and spotting some hopeful-looking woman and asking for instructions. I simply dare not ask the girls at the classes I attend, though I'm sure some of them know; they petrify me somehow, especially when they talk chiffons. I never before realized how appallingly ignorant I am.'

'There certainly does not seem much left for you to choose from,' Peter admitted.

'There isn't,' she answered. 'Matrimony, of course. At desperate times I have thought of that desperate remedy, and if I could marry half-a-dozen men at once I might perhaps be tempted to it. But one alone!—to put up with one for the rest of one's natural life! It would be too boring.'

At that moment Vera bumped against the door with the tea-tray, and followed up the bump with a noisy entry. She set the table with great care, covertly glancing at Peter as she did so. She did not think highly of his appearance, but he was the first visitor this unusual lady lodger had had, so he deserved some attention.

'I got you a pot of bloater paste,' she informed Desire in a loud whisper; 'I thought you'd like something with your tea as you'd got comp'ny.'

'Thank you,' Desire answered in the same confidential tone. She would not for the world have destroyed the girl's illusion of gentility. 'Thanks awfully, that's capital.'

'Mr Grimstone,' she said, when Vera had withdrawn, 'I hope you like bloater paste; you have got to eat a great deal.'

After tea the fire was lit, the evening had turned chilly, and Desire's economy could not hold out against the temptation of its cheering company. For a while they sat in silence, watching the damp wood catch and the sparks fly up. Suddenly Desire asked—

'Do you think I shall do any good with this sort of thing? Do you see any reason why I should fail?'

Peter considered a moment before he answered, then—'No,' he said, 'I see no sufficient reason.'

'The students at the classes think there is,' Desire told him; 'it's their opinion no city man would employ me, I believe, because I am not the right sort, whatever that is.'

'You are not the usual sort,' Peter admitted, 'but then you could hardly be usual anywhere; I don't see that that matters.'

'It can't," she said emphatically; 'it stands to reason that the only thing which matters is whether you can do what you undertake, type and book-keep and so on, and I'm not an utter fool at that; you can examine me if you like.' Peter declined. He had no doubt she knew more than he did.

For a little Desire sat looking at the slow smoke curling up; the fire was but feebly burning, making a poor attempt to brighten the gloomy little room. The shadow in her eyes and on her face deepened; for once it seemed that her exuberant vitality had dropped low, for a minute she let slip even a pretence of her usual gay pluck.

'I'm a poor thing,' she said, with self-contempt; 'do you know, I feel sometimes as if I shouldn't be able to stand it! It's a mercy I'm a woman, and have got enough sense to know I must stick to the respectable! If I were a man I should not stop here two days. I should sell what I have and go off somewhere, the high seas or the high road—probably the high road, with a barrow. I believe I have got a taste for the less reputable side of life. Once or twice, when I have got very desperate, I have been down to the side street after dark, and stood among the people there, and listened to them bargaining and talking. I have had the greatest ado in the world not to get mixed up in things. I expect I shall if I go often. It is the awful respectable monotony that I can't stand. Week in, week out, the same thing; the future the same, the way the same, the goal the same; the more successful the more respectable, the more monotonous the more successful. Why, respectable monotony is what I am aiming at! It's ghastly!—' She broke off, then laughed : 'I'm a weak fool, am I not? A couple of months' work, and I am sick of it!'

'It isn't that,' Peter said. 'What is it, then?' she asked. 'You ought not to know anything about it, yet I feel as if you did.

I wonder why? You can endure monotony—look at the long, slow work you put into *The Dreamer*, look at your throwing up your life and interests in town, and going home. Is it respectable monotony there? Do you sometimes find it pretty awful?'

'Sometimes,' Peter admitted, then added, 'But there are always the hills. On Sundays I go to the hills.'

In *The Dreamer* nature had played a curious part, not descriptive or exactly obvious, but unconsciously interwoven with the emotions of the primitive human beings of the tale. It suddenly occurred to Desire now, and for the first time she began to understand it.

'Tell me,' she said, 'about the hills.'

He hesitated. There did not seem anything exactly that could be told, and yet, because she asked him, and because he was so intensely sorry for her, he tried to describe to her the lonely upward path, the brown hill-top, and the refreshment that was there. He did not speak well, yet better than he knew; she saw it plainly as she listened, and saw, more dimly, what it was to him, might be to a lonely soul, and her eyes grew misty. 'If only I had hills,' she said at last. 'Oh, Peter, if we could go right away into a large, lonely place!'

She had never called him by his Christian name before. It came naturally now, without her noticing or thinking. If Peter noticed it, which is possible, he did not reveal the fact.

'There are several things which make my life easier than yours,' he said. 'The work is really a bit interesting; at first, I own, I couldn't find it so, but now I do. It begins, too, to matter to me to make good jugs, as it used to matter to choose the right words. I shouldn't be surprised if after a time it got to be the only thing· that did matter, that and similar things.'

A year ago she would have enthusiastically condemned such a thing as waste, now she only asked, 'Is that a pity?'

'It makes it easier,' he answered, 'though in a way I

suppose it is a pity because, when it has gone, there will be nothing left.'

'Do you expect it to go?'

He shrugged his shoulders. 'It is a fight between my brother Alexander and me,' he said. 'I shall make a fight, of course, but I am afraid the end is sure.'

She looked up with interest, momentarily forgetting her affairs in his. 'You like a fight,' she observed. 'Oh, you don't know that you do, perhaps, even, you think you don't, but you do; it's that which really gave you interest in the work, I believe. I should like to be there when you and Alexander close for the last grip! '

'I'm not sure there will be any last grip,' Peter told her. 'I'm not sure; indeed, I'm beginning to be afraid the thing will just melt away. Maybe Alexander has something to do with the melting, I don't know; I don't understand how these things happen, but I know our position is not what it used to be.'

Desire's interest increased.—'Tell me about it,' she said; 'and tell me about Alexander. Have you seen him often since you have been back?'

Peter had only seen him once. 'But he is coming to live at Twycross this autumn,' he said.

'Is he? Have he and your father made it up, then?'

'No; my father is ill, as I told you; he can do nothing either way now.'

'He can do nothing? Now I understand! Of course you cannot write. Tell me, are you trying to do his work as well as your own?'

It was then that the idea came to Peter. He had felt all along that there must be an idea somewhere, though he did not know where or what. Arriving at mental things was to him like climbing hills; he got at the end so slowly, and by such winding and unhandy ways, and often without being able to see, that, when it was reached, it seemed almost sudden. He had not quite reached this yet, but by the time Desire had finished giving her opinion he had.

'You ought to have help,' she declared. 'It is perfectly ridiculous for you to try to do two men's work, and work with which you are not very familiar, too. It must handicap you in the fight with Alexander.'

'It does,' he said; 'it makes it very difficult. I do want help of some sort; I believe we might do better, at least for a little time, if I had someone to do the business part, so that I was free to manage and improve the mechanical. My father did both before I came, but he was a cleverer man than I, also the circumstances were not quite the same. If I had someone to do the business—someone like—like you.'

'Like me? '

Peter hesitated a second; it was a difficult thing to suggest. The idea had come to him at the last with such suddenness that he had spoken before he was fully aware of it; but it still was the idea.

'Yes,' he said rather awkwardly. 'It is not much of a job certainly, though not worse, I suppose, than some city ones. It might not last very long, but of course if it was only for a month or two it might be some use as a reference if you thought of going on with this sort of thing.'

It was not very clear whether he was making an offer or merely explaining a hypothetical idea. Desire did not know; she was completely astonished, and for some reason moved.

'Of course, if you don't think—' he began diffidently.

'I think you are the most extraordinary person alive,' she said. 'Do you know, since you have been here you have not given me one word of advice? You have not told me I have made a great mistake, committed rank folly, or done everything else stupid; you have not suggested any panaceas of your own; you have just listened to my plans as if you thought me sane, and now you speak as if you thought them sensible, and I well qualified to carry them out. I almost believe you would help me with them!'

'Anyone would, anyone who knew you wanted help; you must remember you have not let anyone else know that.'

Desire laughed. 'I know them and you don't,' she assured him; 'some of them, had I told them before I left, would have offered me help of sorts, as well as condolences; some women would have asked me to stay with them awhile—"till things blew over"; some men would have offered to marry me, or lend me money, or something of that sort. Not one of them, had they come to me here and heard what you have, would have seriously entered into things, considering the plan as if it were their own, and offered to help me in my way, not theirs. Without doubt you do belong to the world of things-as-they-never-were.'

'I don't,' Peter said; 'you are quite wrong. But perhaps you consider this idea belongs to that world. You think it impossible?'

Then it was a real suggestion, a real offer, not a hypothetical idea. She might have known Peter better than to have ever thought of that.

'I don't think I ought to let you do it,' she said.

'Why not?'

'Because you must have enough on your hands already.'

'Too much; I want help,' he told her.

And when she laughed he asked, 'Do you think you could not do what is wanted? You must have a very erroneous idea of Grimstones', I'm afraid; even if you were just an ordinary woman clerk you would be too good for the job. The only thing which might make it tolerable to you is that it would not be quite the usual routine, and it would be away, near the hills. As to the work—quantity and quality, too—why,

I could do it myself if I were not a fool at business details. I am that, you know; the technical part I am beginning to understand, it interests me, too; the other—'

'Does not,' she concluded for him; 'but it would me. And if I were to come and bring the typewriter—business letters should always be typed, and I'm sure your father never had one, he wrote the letters himself as the Merchant Princes did—I'd manage all the business part as soon as I could get the hang of it. I really believe I could in time do that, for though I'm an idiot my father was a genius: I've inherited a few of his characteristics. You'd be free to give all your time to the other part, and then we'd see where Alexander came in.'

Her spirits had risen under the stimulus of her imagination, she was once more the virile creature that never dreamed of failure and never failed. But Peter, reluctant though he was to do it, felt bound to chill her anticipations.

'I ought to tell you,' he said, 'that we may go to pieces rather soon—I mean, even in spite of your efforts. You see, there has not for some time been much capital in the firm, there is very little indeed now, but our credit has always been good, until lately. Lately, for some reason, it has been shaken; various people, who in the ordinary way would have been prepared to wait, are talking about their accounts and pressing for settlements. We can't meet them, not all at once, we shall have to arrange something, I don't know what, but whatever it is it can't but be to our disadvantage, and we can't stand much of that. It is the chance Alexander could make good use of.'

'Then,' Desire said, 'I suppose, one may guess he helped to bring it about?'

Peter did not know. 'He might have done it, of course,' he said; 'but it equally might have arisen from my father's disablement, and the fact, which must be known, that I'm not much good. Certainly Alexander told me in the spring that I should want his help.'

'That's the last thing you want,' Desire said emphatically; 'my help would be better than that. I believe I must come—that is if your mother won't mind. Do you think she'll mind me mixing myself up in affairs?'

'Of course not.' Peter was surprised at the idea.

'Oh, well, some women would,' Desire told him; 'but if you think she won't—I wonder if she would? I wonder if I ought to come?—if the help I might be would outweigh the nuisance I should certainly be. You haven't got to go just yet, have you? What time does your train leave Euston? Oh, you can spare a while longer then. Tell me all you can about your business and let me see if I can really be any good.'

He obeyed her, and told what he could, and she listened and asked questions, showing him almost entirely the man side of her versatile self. There was very decidedly a man side to her, a man with some of the great financial adviser's characteristics, shrewd, far-seeing, accurate in perception of essentials, with a judgment for mass rather than detail: a person who brought the ways of the big world to the problems of Grimstones', and saw them in quite another light from what Peter did.

'Yes,' she said at last; 'I really do believe I could do some good—any person, forgive me, but it's true—any person with average common-sense could.'

'I told you I was a fool,' Peter reminded her.

'You are awkwardly placed,' she said, 'though I own it does not appear that your genius lies this way. Well, will you have me to help you? If you will, as it seems I might be a teeny wee bit of use, I'll come—till your mother insists on me being turned out.'

'She will never do that—but—'

'But? Another but? Do you retract?'

'No, only I am not sure you will like it, the life, I mean; it is very different from anything you are used to.'

'Bless the man! Isn't that the best reason in the world for my liking it?'

'It will strike you as monotonous and narrow,' he warned her.

'How do you know that?' she demanded. 'I don't know what would strike me that way, and I certainly don't believe you do. Look here, if you are sorry you asked me, and think I'll interfere too much, and all the rest, I won't come. It'll be all right; I'll just say "no thanks".'

'I am not sorry,' he said; 'for myself nothing could be better, but for you—'

'Well, what about me?'

'I suppose while it lasted it might be better than this,' Peter said doubtfully, looking round the gloomy little room.

'I think it might, too,' she answered.

He rose to go, for it was growing late: she rose, too.

'Do you think,' she said, with a sudden earnest deepening of her voice, 'that I don't know it is because of that you asked me? It was for me you thought, you and your business are just an accident, an afterthought. I know that; I have known it all along, though I have behaved rather hatefully to you. I have to behave rather hatefully sometimes or else—or else I believe I should cry. You'd be sorry if I was to do that.'

'I should,' Peter said hastily; 'please don't. There isn't any reason; I don't see why on earth you should.'

'Of course you don't,' Desire returned; 'there isn't any reason; people don't cry for reasons. You'll miss your train if you don't go, and then your mother will begin to find out the tryingness of having anything to do with what my step-mother called "the most impossible person in London".'

Chapter XIV

Desire was enthroned in the office at Grimstones'—that small room at the back of the house where the last Ezra had fallen beneath the stroke, and the first Ezra, in portrait, looked down with fierce dark eyes and fuller and more sensitive lips than any other Grimstone had shown till Peter, the inefficient, came upon the scene. It was the painted lips which prevented Desire from feeling she was intruding here, she believed in her heart she would have got on with the first Ezra. She did not feel she was intruding, nor had she any thought of being incongruous. She was rather, of course, though she had already partly fitted the place to herself. She had not been there quite a week yet, but already the old precise appearance was gone from the high desk; the right to smoke here had also been conceded, and a rule of having the window open at the bottom so that the person inside could, if desirous, call to the person in the yard, had been established. In the sunless room, where the routine of years had settled like dust, there blew a breath from outside; and a vivid woman, with the scent of carnations exhaling from her silk shirt, plied a typewriter with capable hands where Ezra Grimstone had worked in silence and solitary bitterness.

No wonder old Robert, who felt himself as much part of the house and works as if he were the stones the one was built of, or the name the other was known by—no wonder he combated the idea of such an intrusion. All thought of innovation was painful to him, typewriters and outside help especially; as for women clerks, the which he knew were employed in plenty in the pottery towns lying near, such were clean against all tradition. Therefore his opposition at the outset was fierce. But when the idea became a fact, and Desire was here, his feelings underwent something of a change. He was a servant, and he came of generations of servants, and, with the odd survival of the feudal spirit still now and then to be found in England, he recognized Desire as one who belonged by divine right to the ruling class; one who, no matter how far fate or choice might remove her from that estate, still is served as a matter of course and a matter of choice by the other half of the world. Of course she had no business in Grimstones'; still, since she had chosen to come, Robert accepted her and put up with her, as stokers might a princess who chose to visit their stokehole and ask about the work they did there. He never for a moment regarded her as a woman clerk; he never, even after experience of her capacity, exactly regarded her as a woman of business. At first he looked upon her as a sort of visitor whose questions he answered and to whom he gave information because of the afore-mentioned right. Later he discovered her ability, and also, it must be admitted, rather fell under the spell she not all unconsciously cast. She flattered him by asking information of him, not Peter, of whose ability he not unnaturally shared his old master's somewhat low opinion. She also pleased him by her interest in the little firm and the old ways of doing business, and by asking his advice on all sorts of subjects on which she did not want it. By the end of the first week he was already half her ally. Seeing that this was now Saturday and she had only arrived on Monday night, she should have been satisfied with her progress. Possibly she was; but if so she was celebrating the fact by having a difference of opinion with Peter, who had begun by giving her the freest of free hands.

She sat now at the high desk, a bundle of papers in her hands, watching, while Peter to satisfy himself, not her, looked up some entries in a big book.

'I don't see what's the good of hunting up the details,' she said; 'the fact remains, the account is substantially correct, and it's got to be met if we are to keep our end up, I mean, keep our credit, or whatever you call it.'

Peter was only too well aware of this, for the subject under discussion was the demands for payment he had mentioned to her when he first suggested she should come here. But he was also only too well aware of the obstacles in the way of payment.

'I'm afraid we shall have to find some other solution of the difficulty,' he said; 'at all events, we can't meet them all, not all at once.'

'We've got to,' she repeated, 'to steady our position, also to show off to Alexander.'

Peter's eyes darkened at the mention of Alexander. His feeling here was something quite different from what Desire had encountered before, it interested her and chilled her too, it was so cold, such a quiet, inside, unalterable thing, it gave her a new and rather painful idea of the permanency of human feeling. Peter did not know for certain whether he was indebted to Alexander for this recent shaking of the firm's credit, but he believed it. Desire was ready to believe with him, and to her it was a dishonest and dirty action, she could not understand or accept it as he did.

'Of course we could borrow from Alexander,' Peter said, 'at a high rate, and on the security of an interest in the concern—but I'm not going to do it.'

'Certainly not!'

'In any other way money is not very easily raised. Of ready money I have myself about £70, I got it from my publishers when I was in town, fortunately I got nothing in advance when *The Dreamer* was published, so there was some to come to me; but that's all I have, and we want at least £500 more than I can touch to see us through. As for borrowing of someone else—'

'It can be borrowed from me!' Desire cried. 'If it's only £500 I'm the man!'

She pulled a cheque-book from one of the two capacious

pockets which had been recently added to the front of her skirt.

'You!' Peter exclaimed. 'That is impossible!'

'Don't be rude,' she retorted, 'it's nothing of the kind. I have a balance at the bank at the present. Oh, I hadn't when you saw me in town, that's quite true, I was reduced to counting the change for a shilling—so wholesome and so unpleasant. But I've sold my string of pearls since then—'

'Your pearls?' Peter's voice expressed something near consternation.

'Bless the man!' Desire said, 'one would think I'd sold my skin! What do I want with pearls? What chance have I of wearing them while my complexion's good enough to justify it? If I ever do have the chance, and am in circumstances to want them, I haven't the least doubt I shall be—in circumstances to get more; they are not the only ones in the world, you know.'

'You ought not to have sold them,' Peter said gravely.

'I most decidedly ought,' she returned, 'it's extremely bad business to keep all that capital locked up. I knew I should want money to invest in something if I came down here and got interested in money-making. Besides, I did enjoy selling them, it was worth it for that alone—the one decent interlude in that mouldy exile. I had quite a good time selling those pearls, and one of the best glasses of old cognac I have ever tasted.'

Peter gave it up, he knew that she was speaking no more than the truth. 'I expect you know your own business best,' he said. 'I suppose it was better to sell them, no doubt the money is more use to you than the pearls. But you can't lend it to me.'

'Certainly not. I'm going to invest it in Grimstones'. Five per cent. interest, your note of hand, and all that sort of thing. Security—an unlimited capacity to interfere with the show.'

'You can't do anything of the sort,' Peter said. 'Invest your money in something sensible if you like, but as for this—'

'It's the most sensible thing I know. Oh, it wouldn't be if you were running it, I grant you that. But, my friend, I am! I am here to look after my own interests. Now do you observe the beauty of it?'

Peter did not, and he said so emphatically.

'I'm sorry for that,' Desire said, 'because it would make you easier if you saw the beauty, and it would be nicer if you were easy, as I'm going to do it anyhow. If I can't do it any other way I can pay the people with my cheque instead of yours; of course they would think they had found out you were being backed, and who it was, which is rather a pity, otherwise there is no inconvenience in it. I can help myself to my interest when the time comes without troubling you.'

'It is altogether impossible,' Peter said. 'You must not do it.'

'I must, and I shall,' she replied, 'and you can't prevent me. Didn't I tell you you'd be sorry you let me in before long?'

'I'm not sorry. It's for your own sake—'

'Poof! My sake! What's £500 to make all this fuss about? Why, if I lost it, what is it? Also, I'm not going to lose it, I'm going to make a coup—I and Robert,' the old man had entered at that moment, and she greeted him with a radiant smile. 'It's just as well you've come,' she said, 'Mr Peter really does not understand business. I want to clear up these accounts, and we can't agree as to how it is to be done. Tell me, am I at liberty to play the unjust steward a bit? Clearly these good people don't much expect to get their money, which is very rude of them—don't you think by way of punishment we might knock a little off each bill? They'll be so frightfully pleased to get anything they won't fuss about not getting all. And when afterwards they find out every one's been paid they will observe our credit has been good all the time, better than ever, and feel awfully sold.'

Thus Desire addressed herself to work, and Peter, not convinced but unable to help himself, gave way. The £500 was invested in Grimstones', and Peter inly registered the interest on it as the debt the firm must pay before all others and under all conditions, until such time as it was possible to refund the principal.

But though in the office Desire was an independent and somewhat turbulent element, not readily conforming to all old ways, outside she conformed in a surprising manner to the totally new life and ways; more, she liked them, almost hungrily and eagerly liked them. She lived in the house at present. She had thought of rooms in the town at first; but the town was a long way off, and rooms not easy to get. Also, she quickly realized that to deal properly with Grimstones' you needed to live with it, as the founder and his successors had; she was anxious enough to do so on her own account, but she was not sure of the other members of the household. But it seemed no other idea had ever entered their heads, to both Peter and Mrs Grimstone it was a matter of course that she should live with them. So it came about that she did so, telling herself the while that if it did not answer she could always go; but at the same time curiously grateful to them for expecting her, for making her one with themselves—a thing she somehow felt to be rare with them.

It was only last Monday she came, in a wet August twilight when the grey house looked curiously, yet restfully, lonely among the grey hills. A silent house, she found it, with the reposeful silence of deep water; reserved too, it felt to her, yet not gloomy, in spite of the prisoned life of the disabled master. Essentially a place where men lived and died, not merely ate and slept; where they worked at their allotted task, where things befell with the slow precision, the inevitableness of nature. She had dreaded respectable monotony, it never once occurred to her to think of this as such; to her there seemed a spirit informing this, a feeling of a past behind, a future—not necessarily a good one, but a real one—before. It was alive, in a still, shut-in, yet intense way new to her, alive and something that mattered. The very routine of the life appealed to her in some odd fashion. The orderly way in which things befell, as they had befallen for many years, pleased her in spite of her not very orderly characteristics, and she at once unconsciously fell into line with it as much as she could, disliking her own unpunctuality as she would have disliked picnic papers in a wood. As, on the night of her arrival, she stood in the large white room allotted to her, she had felt it must always be tidy. And throughout the week it had been so tidy—and with comparatively little effort on her part, too—that Barton would hardly have known it for hers.

It is questionable if before she came any one had speculated at all as to what position she was to occupy in the house. She herself seldom thought about such things, and unconsciously and at once she slipped into a position which had long wanted filling—the position of a species of daughter to Mrs Grimstone. Rather an unusual daughter, perhaps, but then she was rather an unusual person. Not that Mr Grimstone found it out, she put down all the surprisingness she found in Desire to her own ignorance.

From the very beginning Desire's heart went out to Mrs Grimstone. There was something in the simple old lady which touched her hitherto-undeveloped sense of veneration; something in the welcome to herself and quiet acceptance of her which roused her sense of gratitude curiously. Desire, not readily given to loving her own sex, felt at once that she could love Mrs Grimstone with a love part maternal, part filial, entirely willing to serve. So, from almost the outset, she had taken her position, a daughter who gave a deference that sat quaintly yet becomingly on a woman of her size and distinction; one who paid a hundred small attentions and services, such as are not always rendered by daughters nowadays, and which Mrs Grimstone found new and pleasant, but very surprising. Desire, who had always had almost more of the service, attention and dues of womanhood than she wanted, found the surprise and gratitude pathetic and almost humiliating. To her it suggested a somewhat bare and hard life when so little could be counted for so much; few people in the past could have been attentive to Mrs Grimstone if she thought so much of this. Peter was good to her. Desire, sharply critical on the point, admitted it, but it was with a different kind of goodness, a sacrifice so complete that the old lady never recognized it as such. The things which she lacked, and presumably had always lacked, were the thousand small amenities which had been to Desire as matter of course and unobserved as the air she breathed, and the man in her was roused to pay them, as the woman in her was roused by something else in Mrs Grimstone.

On the first Sunday after Desire arrived she accompanied Mrs Grimstone to chapel. It was rather a bare chapel and not very large, but too large now for the congregation. The Dissenters of Twycross were not so numerous as they used to be, less because of any increase in the church following than because religion was not the important factor it used to be, especially with the young people. Those who attended the chapel now were mostly elderly, the heads of families or the remains of them, old men or widows or the unmarried daughters left at home. Desire was quickly conscious of the decay which had come upon the place and felt sorry for it, and moved to a sympathetic attention and support. Mr Williams, not used to the glowing and obvious attention that day bestowed on his discourse, may perhaps be forgiven for rather misunderstanding its cause, and thinking that his almost-forgotten dream of stirring and touching a congregation's heart was near fulfilment. Many men, of a vast deal wider experience, had made not dissimilar mistakes with Desire.

The congregation no doubt found Desire rather interesting, but they would the rare advent of any stranger. She did not puzzle them as she would a more sophisticated gathering; in Twycross they hardly knew enough of the world to know she was of it; and the majority knew so little of the Grimstones, who were outside the life of the town, as to know and care little of or for their doings. The Harveys waited outside after chapel to say a few words to Mrs Grimstone, to ask after her husband, and to hear Desire's name. Otherwise no-one spoke to them until they had gone some little way up the sunny road, when Mr Williams caught up to them. He did so ostensibly to congratulate Mrs Grimstone on the news he had recently heard that Alexander and his wife were about to come and settle in Twycross.

To Mrs Grimstone this was hardly a matter of congratulation; in spite of her wish to see her granddaughter, she could not but feel that to have the household near under the present circumstances must be distressing. There was no possibility of reconciliation between father and son now, the time for that was past; indeed, Alexander had helped to make it so, for his father's present state was largely owing to him and his visit in the spring. Mrs Grimstone, though she never spoke of it, was aware of this, and aware, too, that it would not be consideration for his father's state or desire to make amends which brought Alexander to Twycross. Mr Williams, no doubt, thought it was; he also thought—and said—that she must be pleased for family breaches to be healed, and to have the support of her elder son's near neighbourhood. She answered him briefly, and with some little distress of manner; Desire wondered how the good man escaped perceiving it, but he did.

'They come at the end of the month, I've heard,' he said, 'to the River House? That is a long way from you, nearly two miles it must be; you could wish them nearer. But no doubt you are thankful to have them at all, to have them and their little children—there is a family, is there not?'

'One little girl,' Mrs Grimstone answered; 'there were two, the other one died in the spring, after whooping-cough.'

The subject was so tender a one with Mrs Grimstone and the good Mr Williams so unlikely, in Desire's opinion, to deal suitably with it, that she came to the rescue. Consequently the conversation soon reached the sermon, the bourne she was perfectly well aware the preacher had all along wanted it to reach. On that subject she talked with him till they reached the place where a road, by which he could return to his house, branched off from the one they must follow; and though the talk dispelled Mr Williams' momentary dream of the nature of his hearer and her interest, it still left him in a pleasant glow. When he parted from her, dismissed courteously but frankly and in a way unknown here, he had a feeling all over him as if he had drunk a glass of good wine, or stood in the warmth of a pleasant sun—an effect which he afterwards characterized, rightly, as "strange, very strange".

Desire and Mrs Grimstone went on up the hill alone; Mrs Grimstone went very slowly, she was a good deal upset by the mention of Alexander's coming and by the revived memory of the dead child she had never seen. Desire knew it and said nothing, only accommodated her pace to the older woman's.

'I'm afraid I'm a dreadful creep,' Mrs Grimstone apologized once, pausing for breath.

'So am I,' said Desire, 'especially in hot weather.'

She took off Mrs Grimstone's mantle and carried it the rest of the way.

'Not take it off?' she said, when the wearer protested. 'Why not, vain lady? Do you think you don't look so nice without it? Fancy sacrificing your feelings to your appearance! Besides, you look nice anyhow, and you know it. Oh, you don't think I ought to carry it? Is that it? Well, I'll promise not to drop it in the dust, and for the rest—what's the good of lusty young women like me if they are never to do anything for folks like you, who have spent all their lives doing for other people?'

So they went slowly on their way, and when the top of the hill was reached and they were on the lonely white road which ran past the house Mrs Grimstone began to talk of the dead child. And Desire listened, sympathetic, wholly pitiful, yet wondering if anywhere in her heart there could be dormant a similar feeling which similar circumstances, or any circumstances, could arouse.

Peter had spent the morning with his father—he frequently did so on Sundays. To Desire one of the strangest things in the household was the place the disabled man had in it. He was not thrust away and ignored, the attendance on him a necessary evil to be rendered and deplored, or heroically borne and not mentioned by those who must perform it; nor yet was he and his affliction an overwhelming, gloomy burden, darkening all life and always before all eyes. It was more like the place Death has in some of the finest Renaissance conceptions, just a fact. A solemn fact, perhaps, but not an extraordinary one; one having its share in life not morbidly insisted upon, nor morbidly hidden; neither obscuring life by its sorrow, nor obscured by life's joy. To Desire the attitude was new and somewhat beautiful too, so essentially sane and true. She searched for its origin and found it in Peter, and at first was surprised and afterwards not, it was completely unconscious and quite natural to him.

This Sunday at the Grimstones' was very unlike any Sundays Desire had previously known. It was a fast-day rather than a feast-day; so as to save the servants work; it was almost Puritanical in its aloofness from the rest of the week, yet she liked it. She thoroughly enjoyed the cold dinner with its absence of service; she wanted herself to clear the table afterwards, till it was explained to her that Mary, who had an etiquette of her own, would be offended thereby. So she turned her attention to selecting a suitable book for Mrs Grimstone to doze over in her husband's room, and then, as Robert was not back from chapel, went out to look at the oven fires.

Peter followed her, so did Paddy. The dog had established himself as a privileged inmate of the house during the past week. He had ventured in and out ever since Ezra's last illness, but somewhat surreptitiously. Since Desire's coming he had done it boldly, he had recognized her as an ally. When she went out to the ovens after dinner he looked wistfully from her to Peter, but when it was evident Peter was going too he was clearly satisfied.

Desire was not quite satisfied. 'Do you think I can't stoke?' she asked.

Peter was sure she could, and handed her the shovel. Whereupon she stoked with great vigour and satisfaction, and failed quite to fasten the oven door after.

Beyond the ovens there was a disused shed; an old bench stood there near the doorway, and on it were lying some papers. They were covered in the white dust which of necessity accumulated fast on everything; but Desire, passing out that way, saw that they were drawings, the design for some machine. She paused to examine them.

'What are these?' she said.

Peter had stayed to fasten the oven doors. 'Those?' he said. 'Only some designs, nothing. At least I'm afraid they are nothing.'

'Your designs?'

She took them up and examined them. 'I don't understand,' she said; 'is it a machine for doing something to plates? This looks like a press—but you don't use a press in plate making, at least you don't here.'

'No,' Peter said, 'nor anywhere else either. It never has been used. I just drew this to my own idea, I don't know that it would really work—theoretically it should. The idea has been in my head for months, grinding round slowly as things do, till it got evolved so far as this.'

'Tell me about it,' she said, and sat down on the bench.

'I'm afraid there isn't much to tell,' he answered, 'only that I saw, as anyone who looked at pottery remains and things in museums must see, that pressure has a great effect on clays. Such an effect that in some few cases, where the clays are suitable and the pressure suitable, it brings a shininess, almost like a glaze, to the surface.'

'And you have designed a machine to press plates to that extent, so that—I see, I see the idea—so that they as it were glaze themselves, and don't have to be dipped in a glaze preparation as they are now!'

'I don't know that I have exactly done that.' Peter never considered that he had done a thing which could be spoken of till it was an accomplished physical fact—at which stage of affairs, it must be admitted, it had rather a tendency to cease interesting him.

Desire, however, was different; in her own mind she was already applying the designed press. 'Surely,' she said, 'it is a thing much wanted! It would be a considerable saving. You'd do away with the dipping entirely. Would you do away with the firing, too?'

'Not the second firing, but perhaps the first.'

She asked him how. She had during the past week watched the process of manufacture with her usual enthusiastic attention, and she knew enough of the mechanical part now to follow an explanation roughly.

'Supposing,' he said, 'this were a real thing, and not just an idea, it would be like this—The clay would be mixed, but used dry, instead of wet as now. Oh yes, that can be done, I have tried it. Nearly every potter has a different way of mixing clay. I have tried lots, it is the only way to discover what is best; besides, it is interesting. I have found that it could be used dry if one could design a press suitable for pressing it into shape. And if one did that there would be no need for the first firing, the biscuit fire; the ware could be glazed and fired in the second firing, right away at once. I am practically certain this could be done; what I am not so sure about is the self-producing glaze.'

'But,' Desire exclaimed, 'surely that does not matter much. If you could do this, use the clay dry, I mean, and do without the first firing, the saving would be such that you need hardly bother about the other; why, time and cost, too, would be reduced almost by half? We could turn out plates and dishes as no-one else in the kingdom could! Cups and jugs could not be made that way, I suppose, they are the wrong shape; but that would not matter, we could make a speciality of plates—fortunately you already seem to do more in them than in anything else. We may make a fortune yet!'

Peter had not gone into the question of cost and saving; he was quite ready to admit the possibility of some of what she said, but dearly his own interest was in the other matter, the part she had set aside as of negligible importance. 'It ought to be possible,' he said, with thoughtful eyes on the design; 'it ought to be possible to mix the clay so that a glaze is self-formed in suitable circumstances. Possibly the addition of some glaze ingredients might do it. They should come to the surface on pressure, that is the line on which I have been working.'

He turned the drawings over, and Desire saw on the back his notes. She perceived also that he had gone much further into the subject than his words would lead one to suppose; but at the same time she perceived that his interest was more really in the speculative than the practical side. He had gone into it somewhat as he had written *The Dreamer.* Suddenly she began to understand. He had done both because an idea was in him, vague but strong, because it had gradually taken possession of him and had had to come out and be unravelled slowly. It was his way to do things so, and it was the doing that mattered, not the thing or the turning of it to pecuniary account; and his gift was the ability to work this way—it might as well be applied to one thing as another. He was not a novelist or an inventor really, he was a man who could see things clearly, and from a long way off puzzle his way to them in time, and then slowly build up a fabric to the vision-seen pattern. A constructor, as she herself had called him in careless speech; he did construct, and his powers, halted in one direction, had naturally and inevitably found themselves another.

'Will you tell me all about it?' she said, with a touch of humility.

'Does it interest you?' he asked.

And when she told him with unmistakable sincerity that it did, he explained what he could. He made clear to her, not only his experiments and the methods of his designs, but also what heretofore had not been so clear to himself, the possibility of the thing being used on a working scale.

'Why!' she exclaimed at last, 'don't you see, if you had the machine you could begin work with it tomorrow? You could turn out plates—loads of plates, crates of plates!'

Peter considered a moment. 'I almost think you are right,' he said.

'Almost!' She laughed at the uncertainty of his tone. 'You will not easily be foresworn, oh, Cautious One! If this thing is possible, practical, perfect on a small scale it is on a large!'

'I don't believe the idea of a large scale application had really come to me yet,' Peter confessed.

'No,' she returned; 'but it would in time, though it might have been a long time. That's your method. You're a builder up, a very slow builder, but one who builds rather remarkable things, whether they are novels or plate machines. It's odd, it never struck me you'd do these sort of things—though, after all, I suppose there is no real reason why genius shouldn't come out another way when its first way is stopped up.'

'Do you call this genius?' Peter laughed. 'Why, it's what any average foreman in a pottery could do; it's only seeing what any one might see and deducing from it, and doing it uncommonly slowly too.'

Desire nodded. 'Just so,' she said, 'seeing and producing or seeing and reproducing—all art's that, and most science, and most other things that are worth having. My friend, your inability to observe the common facts of life is as astonishing as your ability to arrive at much more wonderful things by some inside process of your own. But this is beside the point; let us, as Mr Williams would say, return to the fruitful subject of our present consideration, which is, or should be—the putting of ideas on a working scale, and in this, it would seem, the common brain is a useful asset. It's really rather a good thing you've got me. If we had that machine we could begin turning out plates tomorrow. If we had it next week or next month we could begin turning them out then. Clearly the thing to be done is to have the machine made as quickly as possible—made in pieces at different places, so that no-one gets the whole idea—two places, or at the most three, would do, I should think, and the pieces could be stuck together on the premises. You and I and a fat-headed local blacksmith ought to be able to get it together with the aid of the drawings, some bad language, and infinite patience. It will be a bother, but cheaper than patenting it and, I fancy, safer in our circumstances. The question is, where shall we get the bits made?'

'The question,' Peter corrected, 'is how can the bits be paid for? And the answer, I'm afraid, is—nohow.'

'The answer—make a grimace, you won't like it—' she made one for him—'is pearls!'

'It isn't anything of the sort, that is out of the question.'

'Why?'

'You have already spent—'

Desire laughed. 'Not all they fetched. Remember there were quite a good lot of them, and I drove a bargain, a hard bargain; they fetched more than five hundred pounds.'

'I don't know anything about their value,' Peter said, 'it isn't that I mean—you see, you—you have nothing—'

'Nothing?' Desire interrupted. 'Eight bracelets, three diamond stars, these earrings—' she took one of the pearls from her ears and held it up against the other, turning, so that he might see. "They match, do you see, match perfectly. They're worth a lot of money. There are some other things too, not to mention that "my face is my fortune"—"a poor thing, but my own"!'

'You know what I mean,' Peter said; 'you have already spent £500.'

'No, I haven't. I've invested it in Grimstones', and I'm going to invest some more.'

But with Peter this way of expressing it meant nothing. 'It's good of you to put it like that,' he said; 'like you. But it doesn't really make any difference to the thing.'

It did not, really. She knew suddenly that it was the feeling, not the fact, that Peter was talking about, and was conscious of it to the exclusion of everything else; phrasing did not matter much to one who was concerned with things as they are, not as they look. She felt half angry and half afraid—in a way discovered.

'Does it ever strike you,' she said, 'that you are a greedy beast? All the obligations must be on one side with you? You have always been putting me under obligations ever since I've known you, piling up the debt by first one service, then another, and now that there's a chance of my supplying a few pounds for a thing wanted by me as well as you—you won't accept it. It's just touchy vanity and gluttony!'

'I have already accepted—' Peter began, but she interrupted.

'No, you haven't, don't flatter yourself you did anything so gracious; that's an investment and made against your will. You could have got the money outside if you had tried, at a higher rate I dare say, because no outsider would have had such good security as I give myself. This is different, I own; it isn't an investment; it will pay me in the long run, of course, but that's not the reason why I want to do it, it has nothing to do with it. I want to—because I want to, because I believe in the thing and in you—because you are, you—'

She broke off, finding the explanation difficult. 'Won't you let me?' she asked, with a shy softening of the voice and a little appealing movement of the hands.

Peter's eyes darkened suddenly, then glowed. For an instant a feeling came upon Desire, a feeling that he would take the hand and kiss it—so strong was it that she almost felt the touch of his lips. But he did not, he grasped the drawings tight with his own hands and accepted her offer in a word or two words, she did not know which, then went out.

And she, left alone, stood a moment where she was, the colour ridiculously flushing her cheeks. She was glad he had not done it, glad he was still Peter of the-world-of-things-as-they-never-are; angry, too, that she had imagined it—at least—

Chapter XV

Mr Dodd of Grimstones' sat in the office. Mr Dodd was the traveller, the only one the firm possessed, but an exceedingly good one, too good for his work. A small, blithe person, possessed of one thing no-one else in the firm possessed—a great respect for Peter—not as a man of business but as a writer. Mr Dodd was a great admirer of the poets, especially the sentimental ones; Peter was not a poet, but as a fiction writer he ranked next in the little man's estimation, and so, business apart, he was seen in a sort of inky halo which at times helped to reconcile the seer to things otherwise unsatisfactory.

Mr Dodd had made formal acquaintance with Desire on one of his periodical visits to the works. He had been rather overwhelmed by her, and described her afterwards as 'a high stepper' and 'a regular toff'. He always addressed her as 'Miss', and obviously felt awkward and ill at ease in her too impressive company. This September morning he was making her further acquaintance, in his business capacity. He did not find it easy to talk business to her, he kept feeling she was on the wrong side of the counter somehow; the feeling was further complicated by the disconcerting way the shadows in her hair glowed and the manner in which her thick white neck curved—at least he found these things disconcerting, especially when his straying eye was caught by hers.

Desire herself felt the interview was not progressing as it ought. She did not understand Dodd, and thought him rather an odd little man, till, quite by chance, a sympathetic chord was struck. Then straightway she forgot all about his oddness, and he forgot the counter.

Dodd was referring to some incident. 'It was when I was down Pringdale way,' he said.

'Pringdale?' Desire said. 'I didn't know you worked so far down as that.'

Dodd turned red. 'I don't,' he confessed; 'not usually; it wasn't exactly in the way of business I went there; there are some dorgs I know—there was a match—'

He spoke awkwardly and apologetically, but he need not have apologized. Desire's eyes were alight. Sport, even this humble form, appealed to one of the man instincts in her nature. In less than five minutes they were talking like old friends. Dodd was telling about dogs, wonderful dogs; he was describing matches, giving the points of the competitors and, with veneration, the names of the owners. She was immensely interested, and soon there was between them the fraternity, which has nothing to do with equality, that sport alone can bring. She offered him a cigarette, and he smoked it unconcernedly in her presence as he spoke with authority of what he understood. When at last they returned to business he talked with a freedom and ease not before possible.

'It's a blackguard trick!' he said then. 'A dam dirty trick, but some one's doing it. There's an exact copy of our dinner ware being put on the market at a price under ours. I've seen some of the stuff, and I could hardly tell it from ours.'

'Who is doing it?' Desire' asked. 'Alexander Grimstone?'

Dodd shrugged his shoulders. 'He don't manufacture himself,' he said; 'still, he could get it made for him when once he'd got our patterns.'

Desire leaned out of the window and called Peter. 'Wait a minute,' she said to Dodd; 'Mr Grimstone had better hear this.'

'It sounds like Alexander,' she told Peter when he came. 'Go on, Mr Dodd, tell us all about it.' Dodd did as requested, at the end Desire looked across at Peter.

'If it is Alexander,' she said, 'he can't make much out of it; he would have to pay for the making, a good price, too, for a job of that sort—and then sell under our price.'

'Immediate profit is not necessarily his object,' Peter said.

And Desire, remembering the credit incident, was forced to admit it.

'Where did you see the things?' Peter asked Dodd, and, when he heard, he said thoughtfully, 'Old customers. He has a good memory; it is more than nine years since he left, but he has remembered the old people; he'll make a bid for the list of the newer names before long.'

Dodd breathed hard. 'I wish he'd make it to me, sir,' he said.

'I shouldn't be surprised if you had your wish,' Peter told him. 'Who are making for him, do you know? '

Dodd was not sure but fancied it was one of two firms.

'Can you find out? Do, if you can, and let me know.'

He could easily ascertain, Dodd said, and then began to speak of the damage already done and likely to be done, but Peter interrupted. 'We'll manufacture for him,' he said; 'get me the name of the makers, Dodd, and I'll offer to make for them under the price they are doing for him.'

But Dodd looked doubtful. 'Can't be done, anyhow to pay,' he said; 'you'd have to cut it too fine.'

'The hollow ware, yes,' Peter said; 'we'd have to lose on that, but we ought to be able to make up on the flat, plates and things.'

Desire fancied so, too; the pieces of the new machine which should make it possible were already on order. Dodd knew nothing of this and he was still doubtful.

'You'll have to cut a good bit under, sir,' he warned; 'they neither of 'em are the sort to give up a job of that kind unless the butter lies that side.'

'That'll be all right,' Desire said gaily; 'we'll do it. Mr Grimstone is Works Manager and I'm Business Manager, and we will manage, you'll see.'

'Oh,' Dodd said, with the look of one suddenly enlightened,

'you're Business Manager, miss? That's another pair of shoes. Of course it'll run through then, as easy as winking.'

Desire laughed, the utter sincerity of the tribute left her no alternative. 'You think I mostly run things through when I start?' she said. 'I believe I do; people find me such a nuisance otherwise. I do unless it is too long an effort—a monotonous strain—then Mr Grimstone comes to the rescue.'

Her voice dropped curiously at the last words, she was remembering the grey days at the Commercial College. To Dodd the drop was a new fascination, he forgot for the moment to explain that he meant no pottery or other man-managed institution would refuse her anything. Before he had recollected it she offered him a hand in farewell, a strong, warm hand, larger than his own, and with a grasp which he said 'made a fellow feel queer'. The curl above her neck, and the curve of the neck itself just below the ear—by Jove! a fellow would remember them a long time—they also might make him feel queer. Dodd, outside, straightened up and almost physically steadied himself as if he had had a long and very exciting drink. His opinion of Peter had gone up. 'A man who keeps his head with that at his elbow could keep it in a 'change panic', was the opinion he took to the railway station.

A little later that same day he met Alexander Grimstone; it was in the pottery town where Alexander's business lay. The meeting was a chance one, but apparently Alexander was glad of it, for he crossed the road to speak to Dodd.

'The man I want,' he said. 'I rather wanted a word with you. Got any time on your hands?' Dodd had, and as he expressed compliance they went into a quiet bar together.

It did not take Alexander long to come to his business. 'I was wondering if you knew of a man,' he said; 'I rather want one—or shall soon; a brisk fellow; who knows the trade and his way about, one who's in the business—someone like yourself'd do.'

Dodd acknowledged the compliment and mentioned one or two names.

None, however, met Alexander's requirements, he had something against each. 'Won't do,' he said; 'not good enough for my money. What about yourself, are you open to a job?'

'No, thanks,' Dodd replied; 'I'm still with the old firm.'

'I don't know that that's much credit to you,' Alexander observed dryly; 'still they're hanging on, I hear, that's something, seeing the old man's laid by.'

'They're likely to hang on my time,' was Dodd's opinion. 'Think so? So much the better for me some day.—Here's luck to 'em.' Alexander drank the toast. 'There were some queer rumours about them in the summer,' he said, 'but they've blown over, nothing in 'em, I suppose?'

'Nothing,' Dodd answered; he had very little knowledge, none at first hand, on the subject. He also knew few details of the disagreement between the Grimstone brothers, the justice of Peter's suspicions of Alexander, or the truth or otherwise of Alexander's insinuation that he would eventually have an interest in the old firm. But he knew on which side Miss Quebell was, and that is the sort of knowledge which experience shows us has a tendency to bias a man's judgment.

There was, however, only one bias Alexander Grimstone understood. 'It can't pay you; their work isn't up to your standard now.'

Dodd replied that it was well enough though he would not mind an improvement both in work and salary.' Alexander laughed. 'Won't get it there,' he said; 'better chuck it before it chucks you. It'll come to that sooner or later, you know, since the old man's been laid by things have gone. You don't think so! What? You believe in Peter?'

Dodd thought of the woman who had stood at Peter Grimstone's elbow, whose eyes had flashed and questioned and shone for him, the scent of whose clothing must always be in his nostrils, and he said, with emphatic conviction, 'I've a great opinion of him.'

Alexander laughed again but said he was glad to hear it. But the gladness did not prevent him from reiterating his advice as to leaving. 'You're too good for their work,' he said; 'a cheaper man would suit them as well, and a bigger job and bigger screw suit you a deal better; my advice is—chuck it.'

'And come to you?' Dodd asked.

'If you like,' Alexander answered carelessly, but he had the glasses refilled.

Dodd coughed, he was not much of an actor and he had some ado to hide his feelings.

'What'd you pay?' he asked.

'Oh, we wouldn't quarrel about that,' Alexander answered.

But Dodd wanted particulars and in time he got them, or as near to them as Alexander would go—and the magnitude of the offer almost broke down his self-control.

'That's for something more than my services, I suppose?' he said, with overdone slyness. Alexander shrugged his shoulders. 'What you remember, you remember,' he said; 'anything you remember—'

'In the way of connection and names, and so on?'

Alexander moved impatiently. 'You're not a fool, Dodd,' he said.

'No, nor a knave either,' Dodd burst out. 'You think I'm a blooming rat, Mr Alexander Grimstone, that's what you think, and Grimstones' is a sinking ship! Well, you're in error; I'm not a rat, and if I was I'd have more sense than to desert what's not sinking.'

But Alexander, who was by no means over-sensitive to such outbursts, merely laughed. 'Started a conscience?' he said.

'Looks as if it were young and pretty foolish, too.'

'You let my conscience alone and I'll let yours,' Dodd retorted, and muttered something about the latter not being difficult to do.

Alexander ignored it if he heard it. 'You think Grimstones' is a good going concern?' he said. 'And it'll pay you best to stay there?'

Dodd would not commit himself as to his reason. 'You're altogether wrong about them, that's what you are,' he said; 'right off the track. Things may have been rough, thanks to you as likely as not, but that's done with; there's another horse in that stable now and don't you forget it—Here, miss'—turning to the barmaid—'I'm paying for mine,' and tossing a coin he walked out, a proud man for all that he had saved Alexander the pain of paying for what he had not got.

He felt taller by several inches for this difference with Alexander Grimstone, and so particularly cheerful that when he reached home his half-blind old mother noticed it. The old lady's existence, by the way, made any other home and settlement out of the question for him on his present income; but it did not stand in the way of his being an honest man. 'It does a fellow good sometimes,' so he told her, 'to stand up and show he's a chap that can keep his hands clean—and smash the dirty face of anyone who doesn't!' And she, of course, quite agreed with him, even though she did not exactly understand what he was referring to, and certainly had neither the ability nor the wish to go into the nice question of motives—to decide how much of strict honesty Mr Dodd possessed, and how much he was swayed by that subtle sex influence which makes a man decline to act as 'she'd think caddish', even when he knows quite well the particular 'she' doesn't think about him anyway.

As for Alexander Grimstone—he, in the tortuous but mainly successful course of his life, had met with a certain amount of plain speech from offended fellow-men, and so his feelings were not sensitive to verbal insults. He put Dodd's words down to his account, of course, to be wiped off when opportunity offered; otherwise he troubled nothing about them beyond the information they conveyed—that Dodd was not going to sell his firm, and that firm, in his estimation at least, still stood as formerly.

The man himself believed in it else he would not stick to it, so Alexander reasoned—the question was, with what justice? Alexander was not sure on that point, but from sundry things he had heard he rather fancied there was more justice in the claim than he cared to admit. Dodd had spoken of 'another horse in the stable' and the saying gave Alexander food for reflection. Someone was backing Grimstones'; the difficulties he had arranged for them in the summer had been met, and profitably met; he had suspected a backer then, Dodd's words pointed emphatically to one now. There must be money somewhere, but in spite of all his efforts he could not find out where. There was no new blood in the firm, no visible outside interest; the old man would have been dead against such a thing as he was dead against any innovation; Peter was following on his lines in the main with the single trivial exception of the employment of a woman clerk.

Alexander had never regarded, and had never had reason to regard, women as anything but a less than negligible quantity in the only affairs that interested him; he certainly did not regard this woman as anything more; however, when he had failed in other directions it did occur to him he might learn something through her. From Peter, he knew from past experience, one never heard anything; whatever he could not do Peter could hold his tongue. But women all talked, especially when they got together; this woman would talk, he might get at information that way, at least, he would get at what she knew, and she must know something even if it was only a very little. This decision of Alexander's was come to a short time before the removal of his household from the old house near his business in the squalid pottery town to the more commodious River House in Twycross. The removal was an upheaval, conducted in the worst possible way and with the greatest possible amount of muddle and waste—that was inevitable in anything managed by Mrs Alexander Grimstone. She managed this unaided; Alexander, who had retained a room near his business, lived there during the period and left her to her own devices after having stipulated for the amount of money to be laid out. When, however, she had spent nearly a fortnight with workmen and charwomen, and pastry-cook meals on carpetless floors, he announced his intention of coming home for a Sunday. And Mrs Alexander, bemoaning herself, without ceasing, to anyone who would listen and some who did not, was compelled to get part of the new house habitable, for her fear of him was greater even than her general incompetency.

On Saturday night Alexander came, and on Sunday morning he and his wife—she against her will, though she knew better than to say so—went to chapel.

The congregation, no doubt, were much interested in the event; Alexander felt that he was recognized by a good many—many of whom he knew nothing. That probably was on account of his wife, who was an inveterate gossip, and could not live without neighbouring, and so had already made some acquaintances. When she came out of chapel one or two people spoke to her and asked after her cistern, or her lost hammer, or whatever tribulation had served as an introduction. Alexander paid small attention to any of them except the Harveys, who, as friends, after a sort, of his father, deserved a little more of his attention. He was speaking to Mr Harvey when Mrs Grimstone and Desire came out of the chapel. Mrs Grimstone's face was faintly flushed, otherwise she was as usual, more than usually self-possessed. Alexander came to meet her. 'Well, mother,' he said, 'how are you? Florence!'

Florence, in the midst of a cistern explanation, came and was presented to her mother-in-law, to whom she had never before spoken. Most of the congregation had gone by this time; Desire and Mrs Grimstone, according to their custom, had waited late before leaving the chapel. However, there were still a few people there and Mrs Grimstone could not, even if she had wished, do other than recognize her daughter-in-law. She did not, however, wish anything different, she received her in a simple matter-of-course fashion and began to ask after the child—she had forgotten about everything else.

'Gladys?' Mrs Alexander said, 'Oh, she's all right, at least I think so, I haven't seen her for some time. She is staying away, I packed her off, I couldn't do with her while we're moving: goodness knows there was enough without her—I have had a time—Willis's men—'

No doubt she would have gone on to confide some part of her troubles to Mrs Grimstone, but Alexander unceremoniously cut her short by asking after his father. Whereupon she, by no means resenting that to which she was completely used, turned to another hearer. 'I never saw such a place as this,' she complained to Desire, 'I was trying everywhere on Saturday to get a shade for a clock; Willis's men said they'd get it for me from town, but I'm sure they won't. It's a horrid old back number of a clock, it belonged to my mother—I'd put it in the attic, but Alexander will have it out, and now the shade's gone—'

And so on whenever Alexander did not want the attention of the person to whom she spoke; when he did she stopped in whatever she was saying and began afresh when there was a chance of bestowing her conversation on a listener. This till Alexander was ready to go, which he did without a word to her, she having to hasten after him, her last sentence unfinished. But she was quite used to such treatment and made no comment on it when she caught up with him. She made no comment either on her newly introduced mother-in-law except to say she looked quite a granny in that cloak and bonnet. Alexander did not answer, so she relapsed into silence except once when she complained about the state of the roads: he did not encourage conversation, in fact he so actively discouraged it that she had by now learnt the, to her, difficult lesson of keeping more or less quiet in his company. Even today, when she naturally had a great deal to say and to comment on, she was obliged to withhold it, no doubt saving it up for the first new acquaintance she should fall in with. But as it happened she did not have to save it all, for, to her surprise, after dinner that day he referred to the subject of his relations.

'You've got to go and see them,' he announced, to her great astonishment.

'Yes, you, do you understand? It's no good me going, just a waste of time, they don't want me. They think I'm responsible for the old man's last fit and other things—not but what I should go all the same if I wanted to, but I don't, it'd be a clear waste of my time.'

'But,' Mrs Alexander began, 'I can't go without you—' then seeing by his face that she both could and would if he decreed it she altered her protest. 'I can't go without an invitation—I'm sure I don't want to force myself where I'm not wanted.'

'You are wanted,' he said shortly, 'you and the kid; they'll ask you fast enough, and you've got to go, do you hear?'

Mrs Alexander by this time could recognize an order when she got it; she did not gainsay this one although she did not like it, she only feebly wondered why Alexander gave it.

And for once he told her more or less. 'You're to pal up with that woman who's there,' he said. 'You're a bit of a fool, but you're a chattering one and set others chattering; I want that woman set chattering, and when she chatters you'll have to remember what she says. She's in Grimstones' and she'll talk about the business, what she knows of it, I bet.'

Mrs Alexander stiffened a little. 'I suppose you refer to the person who was with your mother today. You want to know about her?'

Alexander did not; it was what she might be able to tell, not what she was, that interested him, he said so as he felt for his toothpick. But his wife for once did not heed him, she was on a subject where, with her kind, zeal sometimes outstrips discretion.

'She really isn't what I call respectable,' she said superiorly. 'Look at the feather in her hat today, it must have cost a guinea and a half if it cost a penny, that one alone! And her shoes too! It's a perfect disgrace! A typist indeed, with that hair and that voice! Why her voice gives her away, she has only to open her mouth for men to turn round! I should like to know where she gets her money!'

The virtuous indignation of the tone—a tone only to be achieved by a woman who has never had a chance of being anything but virtuous herself, was just waste so far as Alexander was concerned. He did not heed it nor the accusation either, the last words alone caught his attention and so saved Mrs Alexander from a discourteous silencing.

'Has she money?' he said sharply. 'Who says so? If she has what's she doing here?'

'That's what everyone wants to know,' Mrs Alexander said with meaning.

'Who?' her husband demanded, missing the meaning because it did not interest him.

'Oh, well'—Mrs Alexander was rather nonplussed by the

literalness of the question—'not everyone exactly; you see, so few people know your father and mother. It's perfectly extraordinary, that any one should have lived here, or near here, so long as they have, and yet know so few people; no-one really knows them or talks about them much. Still, of course, this Miss Quebell, or whatever her name is, is such a—well, I call her a showy sort of person—they can't help seeing her and talking about her a little—'

Alexander stopped her impatiently. 'I don't want your stupid gossip,' he said, 'you can keep that. What I'm trying to get at is—has she money or hasn't she? If you know, tell me; if you don't, for heaven's sake hold your tongue.'

'She must have money,' Mrs Alexander said decidedly, 'look at her clothes—' Alexander's contempt for such an argument was obvious, but his wife went on all the same—'I don't mean today only, but other times too. One of the Harvey girls told me she saw her on an evening in the summer—hot weather it was, Miss Harvey was coming home from somewhere, I forget where now, by the top road and she saw Miss Quebell and your brother come out of the house. She had her neck and arms bare, quite an evening dress, of most expensive silk, and really quite indecent, clinging so close, as if she had nothing on underneath, nothing but silk stockings—real silk, and you know they cost twelve and sixpence a pair. It was moonlight, that's how Miss Harvey saw; she, Miss Quebell, I mean, had come out to look at the moon with your brother—'

In spite of his impatience Alexander could not help laughing. The idea of any woman being considered dangerous because she went to look at the moon with Peter—Or any woman, dangerous or otherwise, doing such a thing at all except in the imagination of idle talkers was ludicrous to him.

'You'd better shut up,' he advised, 'if that's all you've got to say you'd better keep it for folks who swallow that sort of stuff. What are these? Willis's bills and the rest?'

He took them up and began to look at them. Mrs Alexander flushed. 'Oh well,' she said bridling a little in spite of the fact that her husband was not attending, 'your brother's not the only one, I can tell you. Mr Williams is mad about her, I've heard, she's been to tea there once if not twice, and the curate'—Mrs Alexander had leanings towards the Church as being more aristocratic than Dissent—'he knows her, someone saw them one Sunday evening in the lane; she was sitting on a gate and he was standing by and they were talking, so interested in what they were saying they never heard steps or anything. Of course they may have met by chance, I say they may, but—Well, at any rate no-one seems to know how she picked up with him, your relatives going to chapel as they do. But she picks up with anyone, one of the young Harveys saw her walking along with a quarryman one evening. She seems to be great friends with the quarrymen—he, young Harvey, you know, often takes his dog out before breakfast, and when he goes along that road he sometimes passes the quarrymen going to work. He says they, or at least some of them, always look up at a window in your father's house—her window, if you please—and if she looks out and smiles and says good-morning or anything, the one who sees calls to the others that the sun is shining this morning. Fancy having common working-men speaking of one like that! It shows what she is—'

Possibly Mrs Alexander would have gone on further, that is if at this early stage of her residence at Twycross she had further gossip to draw from—but her husband interrupted her to inquire about an item on one of the bills. It was linoleum, and as, to his thinking, a larger quantity than necessary had been used, Mrs Alexander had shortly enough affairs of her own to consider. When her husband left her she was on the verge of tears. He had told her she could pay for the excess linoleum out of her dress money. But tears were without effect on him, and he went to write some business letters in a perfectly equable frame of mind.

At the door he looked back. 'You'd better get the kid home this week,' he said, 'get her tomorrow or Tuesday; you can't start in with the old lady till you've got the kid, and the sooner you do start the better, d'you understand?'

And Mrs Alexander understood she had got to obey.

Chapter XVI

On a certain Thursday in October, a blacksmith from the hills came to Grimstones'; a silent man he was, a distant relative of Bolt's. Like him of the hill race, a different stock to the town people, darker, smaller, of greater enduring capacity, of slow intelligence and a curious aloofness of mind which made it hard for outsiders to penetrate through to the springs of action and emotion; a good staying stock, not easily shaken in an idea, and consequently loyal in like and dislike, though little given to manifesting either in words. This blacksmith worked an old forge on the now little used highway across the neck of the hills. Peter, who had known him to say a word to for many years, felt all along that he was the man when the time should come for the plate machine to be put together. Desire was of the same opinion when she had seen him and when she heard he was related to Bolt. So the job was offered to him—one did not tell the hill people to do things, one asked them if they would—and when the last piece of the machine had been delivered he came.

Bolt, under his direction, made a temporary forge in an outhouse, and throughout the whole operation, as he brought no assistant, acted as boy to him. No doubt he came in for the abuse appertaining to the post, but it was laconic and short-worded, and spoken in the dialect of the hills—a dialect which Desire, in spite of her linguistic skill, could not follow. She had little to do with the putting together of the machine; it was Peter's work, Peter and the man of few words and Bolt, who blew the bellows and eased a nut here and shifted a weight there to order. She had nothing to do but to stand back and look on, and she did that so completely that the men forgot she was there in their absorption in the matter in hand. Possibly, could the truth be known, those few women who have held men as well as charmed them have all understood that art of looking on, the difficult art of effacing themselves entirely at times.

But though Desire had no part in the work, she enjoyed it immensely. Skill and mastery, no matter in what displayed, always appealed to her. Peter's mastery over this thing, his sure grip, thrilled something in her curiously. She had known he had power of sorts, she had seen its mental result before now, but it pleased the primitive in her to see it physically. The sheer work, too, pleased her, the deft handling of unwieldy mass, the smithy work, the roar of the fire, and the cunning fashioning of metal to the accompaniment of ringing sound and curt, uncouth words. She felt as if she were back in the beginning of things, as if here and now were forces older and simpler than anything she had dealt with in her former half-forgotten life.

When at dinner-time she and Peter came out into the yard she spoke of one of the notions which had come to her.

'I believe,' she said, 'that I understand them now, Bolt and the other, and my friends of the quarries. They are a faraway people who have somehow got left behind into this time; they live close down to the earth and, being near, see things large and simple and without shades. Bolt is not troubled with any shades or grades, he has no complex motives. He hates Alexander, that is all. Every time he swings the sledge he thinks of it as coming down on Alexander, and every time he blows up the fire he thinks of it as heating for the burning of Alexander.'

Peter was not sure whether she was right. 'I don't know that Bolt feels quite like that,' he said, 'though certainly I own that Alexander has a rather remarkable gift for rousing people's antagonism. I don't know what he did to Bolt, possibly not so very much; Alexander has a way of doing small things so that they give great offence, and Bolt—I have noticed before with people like him, they have a different standard of things, especially offences.'

'That,' Desire said, 'is because they are a survival—a survival of the time when a money payment wiped off murder, and an unpleasant death was the natural retribution consequent upon taking a man's ox. We are late for dinner. I am not going upstairs to wash.'

There is a wonderful, some even say a dangerous, intimacy when two people plunge arms bare to the elbow in the same earthenware bowl and dry on the same towel; but if they are busy thinking of another matter, of great importance to them, they cannot think anything of this. Desire and Peter thought and talked of the machine and what it was going to do.

'Dodd sent another order this morning,' she said; 'just such a one as the last—large, but a lot under our usual price. Poor little man, he is in a great way about it, in spite of the fact that I told him we could take such and leave ourselves a fair profit—more than fair, though I didn't tell him that. Give me the dry end of the towel, this is wet.'

Peter turned the towel round for her. 'I wonder,' he said, 'whether Alexander has anything to do with those orders.'

'Why should he?' Desire asked.

'It's one way of helping a firm downhill; I mean, to advise buyers to go to them for certain things, but at prices which are practically impossible. You see, a man does not like to refuse an order, especially if it is a large one from a new or not regular customer. He is tempted to take it if he is having a fight to keep going; he persuades himself he can manage it somehow, or if it is impossible to squeeze a margin of profit, he will do it this once under cost for an advertisement and an introduction. And, of course, if he only takes enough of such orders and on such terms, the end is not hard to see, though it's possible he does not himself see it till too late.'

'How abominable!' Desire exclaimed. 'Do you know, I don't think I admire commercial fighting.'

'You must not judge it all by what you have seen here,' Peter told her. 'Of course, I may be wrong about this, though I can't help thinking it is being done; there have been rather a suspicious number of those orders lately.'

Desire laughed. 'Isn't it excellent?' she said. 'We couldn't have got many more if we had put another traveller on. Oh, Alexander, how beautifully you play into our hands! I congratulate you, Alexander; you have led plates, and plates is the suit we require!' She waved a hand in what she took to be the direction of the River House, then her gaiety dropped a little. 'Oh, bother!' she said, 'there's that woman coming this afternoon.'

The woman in question was Mrs Alexander Grimstone. She and her little daughter Gladys had been invited to come to tea.

As Alexander had foreseen, the grandmother's wish to see the child had overruled other feelings. Not very easily, not so easily as he imagined, nor without help from Desire. Mrs Grimstone wanted to see the child, but she wavered, remembering her husband and the objections he would have raised; the opinions and wishes the sick man used to hold were still considered and regarded in a way that, to Desire, was wonderful. However, on this occasion she combated them, pointing out to Mrs Grimstone that it could do no harm to ask the mother and child, and that it was impossible to decide what would have been done if Ezra had been himself, as these circumstances then were not likely to have arisen. So Mrs Grimstone decided to invite them.

'I should like to have asked them to dinner and to spend a long day,' she said doubtfully, 'but I don't know, I don't feel as if I knew her at all. She looks such a smart sort of person, with her bracelets and her charms and lace trimmings and all; I'm afraid she'd look down on our homely ways, she'd be used to grander things. You know, she had money of her own.'

'I know she's a bad manager,' Desire declared. 'Those thin-voiced, flat-chested women who frizzle their hair with tongs and trim their clothes with yards of wrong-coloured, machine-made trimming, never know how to order a dinner or speak to a servant. I wouldn't mind betting things don't often go right in her house. All the same, I don't think I would ask her to dinner to begin with; have her to tea and see how it goes, and see what the child is like.'

And Desire carried her point, and Mrs Alexander was invited to tea on that particular Thursday.

After dinner Desire helped Mrs Grimstone to get out and dust some of the best china. She liked helping the old lady, and she liked the orderly china closet where beautiful plates and bowls and several generations of tea sets, each with a history of its own, stood ranged on the shelves. But she grudged the time today. Bolt and the blacksmith were at work, and the wonderful machine was still being put together. She went out later to see what had been done, but she could not stay a great while, for Mrs Grimstone was particularly anxious she should help her receive the rather dreaded daughter-in-law. Particularly anxious, too, though she was too courteous to say it, that she should be dressed for the occasion. Desire guessed as much, so made a careful toilet and put her pearl earrings in her ears, and, in spite of her mourning, a pair of scarlet slippers on her feet.

Mrs Grimstone was sitting in the seldom-used drawing-room to receive her daughter-in-law. Desire had urged nothing against this, though she knew it would add formality. She thought it too much honour for that unattractive-looking person to be taken at the outset to the room where they principally lived. Mrs Grimstone started a little as Desire entered—she was clearly rather nervous.

'I thought perhaps they'd be here by now,' she said.

'They'll be late,' Desire assured her. 'I'm often late myself, but for a variety of reasons. That kind of woman is always late and always for the same reason—it can't get dressed in time.'

She went to a window and looked out to satisfy Mrs Grimstone; but only a short piece of the road to the town could be seen, and the visitors were not yet visible. She came back to the fireplace and stood, one arm on the mantelpiece, looking into the fire. Mrs Grimstone regarded her in silence for a few minutes, then she said, *a propos* of nothing but her own complete conviction—

'My dear, you are a very beautiful woman.'

Desire looked up. She was almost absurdly pleased with the tribute. 'Though,' so she declared, laughing a little, 'I believe it's my frock you mean; you don't often see me in my best clothes, you know.'

'No,' Mrs Grimstone answered simply, 'I wasn't thinking about that, I'm afraid I had forgotten to notice your dress, though certainly it is very nice—I was thinking I would like to see you, in just a white wrapper or anything, with a little baby cuddled to your breast.'

Desire flushed faintly, and for a moment her eyes grew misty, though she could not have told why. 'Should you, little mother?' she said. 'Perhaps I should too—if I could ever care for the man enough to care for the baby.'

'Oh, but you would—' Mrs Grimstone's voice had the curious softness and certainty of the mother-woman; but at that moment there came a ring at the bell and she stopped in what she was going to say.

Mrs Alexander came in with the rustling of silks, the scattering of scent, and the rattling of ornaments. The child,

Gladys, came in with the best imitation of her mother that eight years and grotesquely short skirts can give.

'Are we late?' Mrs Alexander said. 'It's such an awful way, I thought we'd never get here! We were late in starting, and we seem to have come miles and miles, and the roads are too awful! We are not fit to be seen for mud. I told Alexander what it would be, but he would not let me have a fly.'

Mrs Grimstone sympathized, but more with Gladys. 'Such a long way for such little legs,' she said, drawing the child to her. And the child, after offering a cool cheek to her grandmother, sat down, carefully spreading out her sash ends and arranging her bracelets.

Certainly Mrs Alexander could talk, her husband was not wrong there; she could and did talk in plenty and without much reserve. She spoke of private affairs, notably the shortcomings of Alexander, with a freedom positively shocking to Mrs Grimstone. He was so mean, he cut her off that and stopped this. He was so bad-tempered, she daren't for her life cross him, he snapped off her head if she did not at once understand. He was so sharp, he was one too many for this person and got even with that. He thought nothing of her and her opinion, treated her like a fool; but she took him in sometimes—her self-satisfaction was evident as she confided it—she did lots of things on the sly; it was the only way to manage men, they were all bullies and selfish brutes.

To all of which outpourings Desire listened with a stare which was not without ultimate effect on the talker, who eventually began to suspect that the tribute of surprise was not altogether flattering. Certainly Desire was surprised. This kind of woman was a novelty in her experience and one she did not admire. Mrs Grimstone did not admire it either; more, it distressed her and shocked her old-fashioned notions of seemly reserve. She did not realize that her daughter-in-law was less confiding domestic troubles to a comparative stranger than boasting of them as distinctions. Among Mrs Alexander's intimate friends every woman was in the habit of parading the things which discretion led old-fashioned ladies to wish to conceal, and to, if possible, out-talk and out-brag the others in doing it. They may or may not have cared for their husbands—Mrs Alexander certainly, not unreasonably, did not care for hers—but each and all seemed anxious to create the impression that they were matrimonial martyrs.

It was to Desire principally that Mrs Alexander addressed her conversation. Mrs Grimstone was devoting herself to the child; a not very satisfactory proceeding on the whole, for though Gladys was by no means shy, and answered with a readiness which bordered on the pert, Mrs Grimstone did not find it easy to get on with her. Almost any other kind of child would have been possible to the tender-hearted grandmother; but this mature grown-up, with her curled hair, and conscious clothes, and little superior smile, was very unapproachable. Once, before tea, Mrs Grimstone had a few more intimate words with her daughter-in-law. It was when she spoke, with the tentative gentleness of one fearing to probe a wound, of the child who had died. But she need not have feared hurting Mrs Alexander.

'Freda?' she said. 'Yes, she was always a weakly little thing, so peevish too, I never expected to rear her. I spent a perfect fortune on patent foods and so on for her at different times, but she never would take them. She was a fearful worry, no nurse I ever had could get on with her. Alexander said I gave way to her too much; he would have her turned out in all weathers and made to walk, and so on; he said I coddled her. I'm sure I didn't, I had no patience with her grizzling, neither had nurse; we were always sharp with her.'

Something suddenly stirred in Desire, it may have been the dormant motherhood she did not believe she possessed, it may have been only the large pity of the very strong. But at the vision of the sickly child and its prolonged, unnecessary suffering, there came a swelling in her throat, and an anger which nearly choked her lit her eyes fiercely. Fortunately, perhaps, she could not easily find words.

'Poor little wretch!' she said. That was all, but her voice, full and deep with feeling, struck almost like the note of a big bell, and for a moment brought the silence of surprise.

But Mrs Alexander was not easily impressed. 'It really was a mercy, her dying,' she said; 'she was so dreadfully delicate. I was delicate myself as a child, even now—'

Mrs Grimstone, with a little trembling of the lips, turned to Gladys and began to talk gently to her about her lost playmate. Gladys answered quite readily and without any trembling, her little high voice soon reaching Desire above the mother's talk of her own constitution.

'Yes,' she heard, 'and it was such a pity, it was the spring. We had to wear mourning in the summer, you see—fancy wearing black dresses instead of muslin ones! I had a silk dress with roses on put away—it will be too small for me next year.'

Desire was thankful for the advent of Peter and tea.

Peter did not stay long, he had much to do, but while he was there both mother and daughter gave their attention exclusively to him. The mother exhibited for him the kittenish manner she kept for mankind, in spite of the fact that he did not respond, indeed did not perceive it, but returned serious answers to her playful questions, missed all her giddy overtures, and gave a disconcertingly grave and courteous attention to what she said. The daughter imitated her mother to a certain extent, but not entirely. The shape of her forehead and the look of her eyes suggested that she had some of her father's characteristics, and already she showed signs of more brains than her mother. Her overtures to Peter were on the whole less foolish, but, to Desire, somehow more displeasing than the elder woman's. The child contrived to make Desire ashamed for her sex, a thing not easy to do. She also made her grateful for Peter's curious unconsciousness of such things, or at all events his apparent unconsciousness, and very thankful that he went back to work directly tea was over.

Mrs Grimstone went upstairs to her husband, and for a short time Desire was left alone with the visitors. Though this might be regarded as an opportunity to do her husband's bidding, Mrs Alexander evidently regretted Peter's going.

'But that's the way with the men,' she said; 'one really sees nothing of them except at feeding time. I'm sure when I have an evening I always say we might as well be without them for all we see of them. I remember once—I had a married girl staying with me then, a regular go-ahead, up to anything—the men were such a time smoking after food that she went and sneaked some cigarettes from her husband's pockets, and just before they came in we lighted up, and when they arrived there we were, all smoking—just to show that we could do it as well as they!'

Gladys tittered. She had heard this anecdote before, and it always created mirth. This time it did not. There was a palpable pause, the face of the tall woman to whom it was now told showed an expression new in the child's experience.

When she did speak, her voice again struck deep, though chilly.

'Did you?' was all she said.

Mrs Alexander was not displeased. 'I believe you're shocked,' she said.

'I believe I am.'

It seemed ridiculous in one who smoked as Desire did. She felt it herself, felt that it was almost hypocritical. But it was the literal truth, and at the moment she could not help saying it, though directly afterwards she tried to compensate by talking pleasantly of other things.

But Mrs Alexander was not in the least offended. To have shocked was almost as gratifying as to have amused—even more so in this case. She went on talking volubly of all manner of things.

'What a frumpy old place it is!' she said, glancing round. 'Look at those vases.' She pointed to two slender ornaments of glass, of graceful shape and beautiful gilding, in the fashion of fifty years ago. 'Did ever you see such back numbers? But everything's the same; doesn't it give you the jim-jams? It would me. I'd pretty soon alter it if I were here. They've got some nice things, too. I'd have them out—the china we had at tea, for instance.'

'They keep the tea things in the china closet.' So Desire said and again repented.

But there was no need, Mrs Alexander perceived no snub, only information.

'How ridiculous!' she said. 'They ought to be kept where they can be seen; they'd look perfectly sweet on the mantelpiece. You ought to see my mantelpiece—you must come one day—I have some lovely cups and two spiffing old plates; I'm cracked on those sort of things, aren't you?'

'I'm afraid I don't know much about them.'

Desire had dined off specimen Sèvres plates and old Nankin china, had taken tea many a time from Crown Derby and Worcester cups with pedigrees like prize bulldogs. But that did not occur to her now. She felt herself to be ignorant of the subject from Mrs Alexander's decorative point of view, also she was finding it difficult to be civil, more difficult than she had ever found it before.

Possibly Mrs Alexander found things a little difficult too. Not the talking—that was always easy and, she never doubted, always satisfactory to the other party—but the carrying out her husband's instructions. Miss Quebell did not talk, she said wonderfully little; certainly she said nothing whatever about Peter or the business. She made none of those accusing confidences that Mrs Alexander was used to hearing about husbands, brothers and fathers; or any of the other confidences about lovers, male employers and other men who were supposed to admire. As for business, it might never have existed; all she said, and that when she was asked point blank, was 'Yes, she worked in the office, typing and so on sometimes.'

'She is the most stuck-up, stand-offish creature I ever met,' she told her husband when she got home. 'She might have been a countess at least, instead of a—well, I don't know what. The way she shakes hands, the way she moves, the way she expects everyone to be quiet when she does condescend to speak.'—Mrs Alexander was here mistaking the effect for the cause. The fact of herself falling into silence, except under Alexander's orders, was so unusual that it is not surprising she thought someone must have emphatically expected if not enforced it.

Alexander was not in the least interested in his wife's opinion or her abuse. She abused all the people she knew in turn, even those with whom she was bosom friends. The thing which mattered to him was that the bosom friend phase had not here come on; he told her peremptorily that she had better look sharp and bring it about.

'But I can't,' she protested. 'I told you she is standoffish and stuck up.'

'Oh, rot!' Alexander retorted. 'You haven't cottoned to her, you mean. Ask her to tea, give her cakes and cream, and gossip. She'll give herself away, and Peter too, if she knows anything.'

'I hate her,' Gladys, who had been a silent listener, here announced.

'You go to bed,' her father said.

Gladys gathered her hat and gloves with a show of obedience and a lingering manner. She knew precisely how long to take. 'She has large hands,' she said, 'and eyes that you have to look at and look at, and Uncle Peter likes her—'

Alexander moved, and Gladys hastily withdrew, but her mother laughed. 'Even the child has found out the sort of person she is,' she said, 'though she's wrong about your brother; he doesn't pay the slightest attention to her.'

Alexander did not care if he did, that side of the question did not interest him; to have his orders obeyed was all that concerned him just now. 'Look here,' he said, 'I'll have no more bunkum. What if the woman is a damned sight better looking than you, and pays a pound or two more for her clothes? That's neither here nor there, it isn't business, and this is—do you understand?'

Mrs Alexander sniffed a little, but made no other reply except to mutter to herself something about 'owing it to the child to be particular, even if her own feelings were of no account', and 'she never could bear stuck-up people.'

And about the same time or a little later Desire was confessing to Peter—

'I never knew I was proud before; I never knew I had it in me to feel snobbishly that anyone "was not good enough". I am heartily and entirely ashamed of myself, but I believe, yes, I do, that if I have to see that woman again I shall do it again. I think almost I'd rather have to do with Alexander.'

'You don't know him,' Peter reminded her; 'though certainly,' he added, 'one knows more where one is with him. She—well she seemed rather a foolish sort of person to me. I believe, by the way, that was one of the reasons why my father objected to the marriage.'

'Your father was a wise man,' Desire said; 'a real fool is an awful and incurable thing; but he would have objected to that woman, anyhow—and your mother—It made me just sick to see her with your mother. As for the child, it was pitiful! I wanted to shake her and tell her to pretend a little, even if she couldn't feel decent.'

'I'm sorry,' Peter said.

'Sorry for your mother?' Desire asked. 'That's too small a word. The child is an awful pity; the woman of course does not matter. It doesn't matter to us if she is an inferior imitation of a poor artificiality, a thing without any inside, and somehow so vulgar. But no, I ought not to say that; I don't know her, no doubt she's better some other way round though I haven't got at it. She is—she's just a woman I can't do with.'

Chapter XVII

The Alexander Grimstones were at last really settled at Twycross. And when the delinquencies of the moving men and the difficulties with the cistern were forgotten in the excitement of being called upon and calling, Mrs Alexander was not ill satisfied. As well satisfied, in fact, as it is possible for one whose every domestic molehill is a mountain and whose general incompetency supplies plenty of small excrescences. Whether or no Alexander was satisfied did not appear. When it had seemed to him advisable to concede to his wife's often expressed wish to live away from the pottery town and his work, he had himself chosen Twycross as a place of residence. No doubt he had his reason. One, possibly, was a wish to appear on good terms with the parent family if not the parent firm—and in this he was fairly successful, for no-one knew the Grimstones intimately and everybody was ready to accept him at his own valuation. Another reason may have been a wish to annoy Peter by his proximity, and a third was certainly some notion of keeping an eye on Grimstones'.

In this last he did not entirely succeed. He learnt a certain amount about them it is true; but principally he learnt it in town and in pursuit of business, he did not at Twycross get any nearer the inner side of their life, and he knew quite well that it was the inner side that mattered to him. He had begun establishing some sort of intimacy between the household and his own through his mother and by means of Gladys. But somehow nothing came of it; it had had to be left to Florence and she of course muddled it; she had been invited once, but that was the beginning and end of the intercourse. Mrs Grimstone never came to the River House, she said it was too far and she could not leave her husband for so long; Alexander did not believe it, but he did not see how to alter it.

Desire Quebell did not come either, although, in pursuance of his orders, Florence invited her to tea. The invitation was refused by return of post and Florence was offended by the wording of the refusal, Alexander did not know or care why; the thing was quite plain, Florence had made a muddle of it. She had obviously made a muddle of her own first visit, too, for the invitation to her and Gladys was not repeated.

'You must have made a fool of yourself, a worse fool than usual,' he told her one evening towards the end of November; 'here's six weeks nearly gone and the old lady's shown no sign of wanting the kid again.'

Florence said something about Miss Quebell and spitefulness, but Alexander was contemptuous.

'It's no affair of hers, besides, if she can scratch I suppose you can too. You didn't expect they were all going to receive you with open arms, did you? I tell you what you've got to do, you've got to go again without an invitation since you can't get one to go with one. Go tomorrow and take the kid—'

'Oh, Alexander!' Mrs Alexander protested in some dismay. Indeed, she protested as much as she dared. The roads were very muddy, the afternoons were short and dark, she was invited out to tea that day. But Alexander was not moved, rather he was the more determined that she was to go tomorrow. Another day would do as well? Perhaps it might, but he wasn't going to wait for another day when it might rain or she might have an appointment with the dressmaker or some other faddle. He had said tomorrow and tomorrow she should go, he usually meant what he said, as she knew if she thought about it. She did know it very well indeed, so there was an end of the matter.

Now as it chanced some other day might have been better for Alexander's purpose, for the one chosen happened to be one of Ezra's bad days. The invalid's condition varied very little as a rule, but now and then there were times when there seemed a partial break in his lethargy and with it indications of a suffering the cause and cure of which were alike impossible to understand. At these times Mrs Grimstone never left his side and Mary did not hesitate to refuse her to any one if by rare chance she was asked for. When Mrs Alexander presented herself that November afternoon and asked for her mother-in-law she was promptly and plainly told she could not see her.

'Oh!' she said in some dismay. 'Can't I? Can't I really? I'm sure she'd see me.'

Mary was sure she would not and said so curtly.

'Oh dear!' Mrs Alexander exclaimed pettishly—'And it's such a way to come for nothing. I'm so tired!'

Mary held the door half to, she was never hospitably inclined and she would not have approved of this visitor at any time. However, Mrs Alexander was not to be refused, she said she must come in and rest, and in she came. Mary was for putting her in the chilly drawing-room, but in the hall she asked for Peter and then for Miss Quebell.

'They're in the office,' Mary answered; 'busy.'

'Don't disturb them,' Mrs Alexander said. Mary had shown no signs of being about to do so. 'I'll go and speak to them there,' and she pushed past the indignant old woman. She knew where the office was, she had asked on her previous visit, and now, before Mary had recovered herself, she, with Gladys following closely, made her way there.

'May I come in?' she said archly, popping her head round the door; but she came as she said it.

'We've come to hear how you all are,' she announced, 'and as we can't see Grannie today we persuaded Old Grumps to let us come in and rest, we're ready to drop.'

Desire looked up, there was both anger and astonishment in her face, it looked as if she resented this as an unwarrantable intrusion; she did not trouble to say anything at all.

Peter rose. 'Of course,' he said, 'you must be tired; please come into the dining-room and rest as long as you like.'

He held the door open, and before Mrs Alexander was fully aware what had happened he had taken them to the dining-room.

He drew chairs to the fire for them. 'You will like some tea,' he said; 'I will tell Mary.'

He went out as he spoke, and closed the door after him.

Mrs Alexander looked round, she wondered why he had not rung the bell and given the order; it did not occur to her that he had gone not to return. But he did not return; no-one came except, later, Mary with the tea. It dawned on Mrs Alexander very slowly, but at last it did dawn on her—no-one was coming. Mrs Grimstone was upstairs with her husband, Peter and 'the woman' were busy with work; they had supplied her with a chair and a cup of tea, but they were going to do no more, they were not going to leave their occupation on her account. It was abominable! It was an insult! It was precisely the sort of thing that made her more angry than anything else, far more angry than many greater and juster causes of offence and more real affronts. She almost choked over her tea in her anger at the realization of the fruitlessness of her coming.

She did not at once accept her humiliation, she even at one time had some thought of staying on and compelling Peter and Desire to see her—which, no doubt, they would have done when their work was finished, there being nothing personal in their proceedings. But she gave that up after a little, though she stuck to her position for a time. She dried her boots—totally inadequate ones for the occasion—she took the tea grudgingly provided by Mary, and waited for some while. But at last her dignity and her patience gave out, and she rang sharply.

'I can't wait any longer,' she said sarcastically to Mary. 'Tell Mr Peter and Miss Quebell that I'm sorry I couldn't spend the evening here. Tell them I'm glad they didn't disturb themselves on my account.'

Mary grunted, there was not the least chance of the message getting through in that form. But the giver did not know that; she walked to the door, with a haughty mien—sadly wasted on the old woman who was looking at the mud on the bottom of her skirt—and set out on her homeward way. The haughtiness was all gone before she reached home, and, as Gladys could have testified, only the temper remained and that had cooled to self-pity and a trace of complacency, too, before Alexander came home.

'I told you it would be no good,' she reminded him, after narrating the affair. 'I told you that the woman was a cat and that it was madness for us to go dragging up there with the roads a mass of mud and the days as short as can be.'

'You'd tell anyone it was madness for you to do anything you don't want to,' Alexander replied, 'and I could tell 'em it was madness to expect you to do anything at all; I might have known better by this time. You can't even make friends with a woman when you're wanted to, though you can be as thick as thieves with every cackling ninny when there's nothing in it but waste of time.'

Mrs Alexander sniffed a little. 'I'm sure I've tried to be friends,' she said superiorly; 'but she's not my sort. I may not be clever but I was brought up properly, and I'm not used to those sort of persons; I have nothing in common with them. And, anyhow—' dropping to a less assertive tone at the sight of Alexander's face—'anyhow, I'm sure she wouldn't have told me anything you want to know. I don't believe she knows it.'

'Then, as usual, you're wrong,' her husband retorted. 'I wouldn't mind betting a trifle she could tell one or two things I want to know; but she wouldn't, not to you, you're right there. Even some women have sense enough to know a fool when they see one, it seems.'

Mrs Alexander's already wounded dignity smarted, principally because she thought her husband implied an exaltation of Miss Quebell's intelligence above her own. This she felt was too much, and she relapsed into sulks, which did not matter to Alexander; on the whole it is possible he preferred her sulky, for she was quieter so. He paid no further attention to her that evening but gave himself up to his own concerns.

These concerns, as usual just now, had reference to Grimstones'. All his leisure, all his spare thoughts and extra energies, and some others besides, were centred round the old firm: it was never long absent from his mind. He meant to have it; he meant to do all he had promised himself, and threatened his father and, more recently, threatened Peter; partly because he could see that he might eventually profit largely, but partly also from motives of spite and sheer obstinacy. The spite had first been for his father, later, when Peter refused his overtures and definitely ranged himself on the other side, a share had been transferred to him—a pretty large share, not unmixed with angry contempt, for one so obviously inferior, who had the hardihood to oppose him. Of course the ultimate end was inevitable, that was plain at the time of Ezra's first stroke. It was made plainer and nearer, too, when the second stroke occurred. Alexander, though he would not, of course, have deliberately brought that catastrophe about, did not, after the first shock, regret that he had accidentally done so: it was too advantageous. He had not scrupled to take advantage of it immediately and fully, and of Peter's ignorance and the weak state of the firm; but someone had stepped in. Someone had come between Grimstones' and the difficulties he had arranged that summer; he had not been able to find out who. He had an account to settle with that some one: he had spoiled a good move. There were other moves, of course: Alexander was a man likely to know them; he had gone into the matter thoroughly and given time and trouble to it, and not spared some outlay; it was only natural he should succeed, for he also brought a not inconsiderable ability, and no scruples, to bear on the matter. For some while now he had been working, it was time, he felt, that, to a watchful connoisseur like himself, some small result should show. But so far there was none. Grimstones' apparently had swallowed the bait he spread, fallen into the traps he prepared, and yet held their own as well, better, rather, than ever. The watchful Alexander observed it and wondered, swearing. The end, of course, was inevitable, but it was beginning to look as if it might be longer coming than he had anticipated. With Peter on one side and himself on the other it would have come quickly enough; the delay could only mean one thing, there was someone else in it.

Alexander's jaw closed down as he sat thinking, while his wife, unnoticed by him, withdrew to bed in injured silence. Someone else! Dodd had hinted that there was some other interest in the old concern. He at least must have believed in it himself else he would have come to terms. Alexander cursed Dodd heartily; if he could have bought him it would have simplified matters and hastened them considerably. He cursed him again that evening, and also cursed the someone unknown. No suspicion of Desire as that person occurred to him, had it done so he would have been far less uneasy; women, even those with more sense than Florence, were always negligible factors. This one, in his opinion, was less than nothing; probably she was letting Peter keep her, respectably or otherwise, it didn't matter which, because she could not at the time find any one better to do it. Her sole importance to him was that no doubt she knew a little of what he wanted to know, and could probably supply the name of the someone and indicate the motive power which was holding Grimstones' together. Peter was sure to have been fool enough to tell her, and she was sure to have been induced to talk if Florence had been any good, as she wasn't.

'Twenty minutes in that office!' The idea came suddenly to Alexander; it would be better than all the talking in the world; it was doing the thing first hand, and there is nothing like it. Twenty minutes. One could learn everything; why, ten would do! Twenty minutes would give time to get some notion of the more recent customers, too!

For a moment Alexander turned the thought with appreciation, but it was hazardous. Peter, it is true, was slow to act, and had a distaste for publicity; he was not likely to prove awkwardly unpleasant even if any accident did reveal things to him. There was no particular danger, but Alexander had a preference for keeping the right side of the law; he knew very well what scoundrelism was the right side of that fine line, and what the wrong, and though he may have often approached the boundary, he never actually crossed it from choice.

'We'll try the other way first,' was his conclusion.

The other way was James.

James was a new importation at Grimstones'. He had lately been engaged to help with the extra work which in these days was coming to the old firm. Desire was opposed to his engagement; with gluttonous energy she seized upon anything and everything, and wanted to do it all; she resented having any taken from her. For a little Peter bowed to her wishes in the matter, but subsequently he changed his mind and insisted on James.

It was really owing to the American; Julian Lee; Desire considered that she owed it to him, and was proportionately displeased with him. Towards the end of October Peter had received a letter from him. It was forwarded by the publishers of *The Dreamer*, for Lee did not know his address or himself either. He wrote briefly to ask Peter, if he knew where Desire was, to send on an enclosed letter to her. There was no particular explanation of the request offered; Peter did not trouble to seek one, he simply handed the letter to Desire, saying 'Some one of the name of Lee asks me to let you have this if I know your address.'

Desire frowned. 'How tiresome people are!' she said. 'I suppose he thinks he has done something clever in hunting me out.'

He did, if the truth was known, for it had been a good deal of trouble. It had cost him the friendship of Lady Quebell to verify the chance aroused suspicion that Desire had, in a measure, disappeared; and there had been a considerable outlay in time, and some in money, in finding out the little he had about her. That was principally only that Peter Grimstone was the one friend of former times who had seen her between the coming of her trouble, whatever it was, and her leaving London for good and all.

Something of the state of his knowledge, or the want of it, was made plain in the letter to Desire, her brow smoothed, as, re-reading, she realized it. After all, it seemed he did not know much, and, anyway, it was nice of him to remember her. She had always a surprised pleasure in being remembered, which was rather odd in its perennial freshness, seeing how much and how many emotions she aroused. Lee wrote to say he had no idea when he said good-bye to her in June that it was for good and all. He ventured a reproof for not letting him or anyone else know. He suggested that she might at least have allowed some of them a chance of showing their sympathy with any trouble she might be in. He also asked that she would let him come and see her wherever she was, not to show a sympathy which, apparently, she did not want, but because he was tiring for a sight of her. He concluded with a postscript—

> 'I am still waiting for that answer, and I shall keep on waiting; though if you are not ready to give it yet, don't let that make any difference to your seeing me; that's for my good.'

A persistent person, Desire smiled as she folded his letter, a likeable person. Had the old life not melted and left her face to face with other things she might have ended by marrying him. Might have done worse than marry him if, as seemed probable, she must have married somebody sooner or later.

Robert came in at that moment—some question about an invoice. Desire threw the letter aside and produced the required paper. There were a lot of things on the desk, a lot of correspondence to be attended to; she went to work on it, and Lee's letter, having no special place, was speedily buried among other things and forgotten.

At the end of a fortnight Lee wrote again to Peter, and Peter appealed to Desire. 'That man, Lee,' he said, 'writes to ask if I sent you his letter.'

'Lee?' For a minute Desire looked mystified, trying to recall some customer with whom she was in correspondence.

'Julian Lee,' Peter said, and she remembered.

'Oh!' she exclaimed, 'I forgot all about it! I stuffed his letter away somewhere when I was busy and never gave it another thought. I wonder where it is now?'

It was then that Peter finally decided they must have more help. In vain Desire told him that she was not overworked, that this was not a case of crowding out, she was in the habit of forgetting things and people when she was interested in something else; the letter was not, as he imagined, important, it and its writer were totally unimportant, and quite suitably forgotten. Peter stuck to his point, and while she wrote, not quite so pleasantly as she ought, to Lee, he made arrangements for the engagement of James.

James was a nephew of Robert and Mary, a painstaking, timid, rather sanctimonious young man. A source of some astonishment at first to Desire, who, from plays and books—the only places where she had before met the qualities—had learned to associate them with hypocrisy, cunning and undesirable traits of that sort. James had none of these; he was, it appeared, as virtuous as he seemed, in fact, precisely what he seemed, except that experience eventually proved him to possess more ability than one would suspect, and more dogged loyalty than usually accompanies timidity. When Desire had got over her annoyance at his advent she found him very useful, for certainly it was true that there was great deal to do just now. There had been ever since the putting up of the plate machine. The machine, of course, saved labour enormously; but on the other hand it had induced them to accept orders of a quite unprecedented number and magnitude, and, owing to Alexander, such orders offered themselves. It was a wonderful time at Grimstones', the little old firm seemed to be waking to a species of new life: an inward sort of life, perhaps, of which, as of its other happenings, outsiders were slow to hear, and in which they did not share, but none the less real.

Desire thrilled with the feeling of it and rejoiced. She had cast in her lot here utterly and entirely; she had put her whole self, staked herself as it were, on success, she wanted it as she had never wanted anything before. In the main she was a good loser; in the past she had been able to accept failure fairly well on the few occasions when she had met with it; but in this she found the bare idea unthinkable. But they were succeeding; it was determined from the first. It was always 'they', she and Peter, indissolubly associated in the furtherance of a thing which was not really their own. They had an interest in it but no true possession, they worked together, not for each other; there was a freedom and equality in this partnership for carrying on Ezra Grimstone's business which may have been absurd—few things seemed absurd to Desire—but certainly was completely new to her.

There were other things, too, which were new to her experience, a new gift among them. Many men had offered her many things in the past, love and friendship, luxury and jewels, entertainments, dogs, amusements, homage—some she had accepted, some refused, but no man before had offered her work. Peter had offered her that, he had offered her a share of his—not noble or inspiring or fascinating work, just his work, what he had. He had offered it her, called her great energies into play, and set her to work beside himself in a furrow. And she was glad; for some reason she found it very good—so good that she asked nothing better—that, even, she was afraid to look it in the face for fear it should melt and reveal itself to be something different; that she told, almost grudgingly, the swift passing days—Shortening days, busy, crammed with work and interests; with thoughts and talks too, interludes not to be forgotten, every margin of time filled with things—not necessarily connected with pottery or buying and selling—Good, good days—days of wind and rain often and driving clouds that swept over the grey hills as the winter drew on, but always fine days to some. The wind is a great friend, men who have lived with it know it; and the rain—it has a thousand scents more living than the scent of flowers. And the clouds, and the tempests that howl intermittent, and the stripped hillsides, and the sudden sharp gleams of sun—they are friends a man's soul had in the time before ever he came to this habitation of flesh. Peter knew these things, he had had them always and shared them before with none. Desire had them now. And the grey world was very good.

But for all that they were not clear of difficulties; neither thought it. No-one at Grimstones' made the mistake of rejoicing prematurely over good fortune. They received her warily there and with reservations, as the folk of those parts receive sunshine in spring-time, knowing well that there are likely to be clouds below the horizon. Peter and Desire did not often talk of the clouds, it was not their way; as for Robert, the other speaking part of the firm, he summed up his opinion of the situation briefly. 'Alexander's not dead yet,' he said, and when he had said it evidently considered good fortune was qualified as much as need be.

Alexander was not dead and in early December they heard of him again. It was through James. One morning he informed Desire in the precise tones he was in the habit of using, that he had had a conversation with Mr Alexander Grimstone last night.

'Oh?' said Desire—she had not the business manner with any man. 'Did you enjoy it?'

James had the business manner, even Desire could not make him forget it; he said formally now, 'Mr Alexander seemed desirous of entering into negotiations with me.'

'What for?' Desire asked.

'Information principally, I think, miss.'

'Information?'

'Yes, he wants to know who is financing us, who is interested in the firm besides Mr Ezra and Mr Peter.'

'There isn't anyone interested but you and me,' Desire said. 'What did he ask that for?'

'I can't say, miss.'

There were a great number of things James 'could not say'; Desire had observed it before, she wondered if he had been in that position to Alexander. Promptly she asked 'Couldn't you say to him?'

'No, miss, I naturally could not speak of the affairs of the house to him, I told him so.'

Desire was a little puzzled, James's very mild manner had misled her.

'Do you mean,' she said, 'that he was trying to buy information from you, the names of our customers and that sort of thing?'

'There was no sum mentioned;' James replied, 'but he gave me to understand that if it was a question of price there need be no difficulty about it.'

Desire stared; James certainly was an astonishing person, he conveyed the most exciting intelligence and the most unexciting in the same colourless way.

'What a butler's lost in him!' she exclaimed afterwards to Peter. 'Nothing would surprise him, nothing make him forget what was due to his position and yours. He's just a wonderful person, and he is a person too, that's the wonderful part; he's something real, sterling-butler right through. I suppose Alexander made the mistake I did and thought that manner must cover something else. It must have been a painful interview for Alexander, almost as humiliating as trying to make a true-bred butler drink with you or flirt with you. It is humiliating to be put in your place.'

'I don't suppose Alexander was humiliated,' Peter said. 'I wonder what he will try next.'

'There's not much left,' Desire said; 'he's tried Dodd and now James, he'll hardly try you or Robert, and I don't count for much to him.'

'He'll try something,' Peter said with conviction, 'he must know I should have come to grief by this time, considering what he has done to help, if I had been really running this alone. He is looking for some substantial backer now; he probably does not reckon you as more than a clerk or a secretary, it would be a man he's looking for, a man with money and experience. I expect things have not gone quite as he anticipated and he wants to find out who is interfering. Lists of customers and so on are a mere blind, or at all events a by-product, it's the other he wants to know.'

'Then I don't much fancy he'll do it,' Desire said cheerfully; 'you and I are the only two people who could tell, and I don't think we shall. I wish he'd come and call on me and try; I haven't much taste for exchanging polite nothings with scoundrels, but just for once I wouldn't mind. I wish he'd come.'

As it happened he did come, but not in the way Desire meant. He did not come for the purpose of seeing her or, indeed, anyone else. That he found someone was an accident and not part of his plan, for failure in other quarters at length induced him to try the last resource.

Desire's room was in the front of the house. Usually she slept well, better than she had done in the London days, but now and again she had a restless night. One such befell in mid-December. For a while that night she smoked and read and tried the various plans by which she wooed sleep; then, finding none successful, she grew impatient and gave them up, put out her candle and lay on her back staring at the ceiling. The room was rather dark, though light enough for her to guess how light it would be on the other side of the house where the moon shone in. A big moon it would be, silvering the mist which always lay away beyond the canal, and revealing every detail near at hand, everything in the yard, the very brands on the packing-cases and the numbers of the crates if there were any. She began to wonder if there were any, or if they had been put under shelter as they should have been. Wondering anything is fatal to sleep; the more she did so the more wide awake she became. It really did not matter much about the crates either way, but in a while it seemed to matter a great deal; anything would have mattered, anything did. After a quarter-of-an-hour of lying still she at last gave way and, fully aware that she was weakly humouring herself, got up, slipped on a white wrapper and quietly left her room.

It was nearly three in the morning and the house was very quiet; she crossed the landing noiselessly, the old, well-seasoned timbers not creaking beneath her feet, and, lifting the curtain at the back window, looked out at the yard, all black and white in the moonlight. As she did so a sound caught her ear—someone moving below, a door—the office door surely—opening. She dropped the blind and listened. Someone speaking? She could not be sure, it was a quiet voice, if it was one, only audible because of the sleeping silence of the house. She went softly down the shorter flight of stairs. Peter's was the only voice with the quiet insistence, and Peter had no business to be in the office now. They had made a pact that neither should work very early or very late without the other's knowledge. They had made it for the sake of each other, each believing for everyone but himself the old adage about the unwisdom of burning the candle at both ends. If Peter was at work he had broken faith; and if he was not—and of course he was not—what was going on?

Desire paused at the head of the longer flight of stairs. She could not see the office nor be seen from there, the door was round the corner; but she could tell it was open by the light on the hall floor.

'Will you kindly tell me what you are doing?' It was Peter's voice, patient and polite, apparently repeating a question he had asked before. The answer came in Alexander's more rapid tones, offhand, a trifle contemptuous, not at all abashed.

'Paying you the visit I didn't think you'd care to receive in daylight.'

'In plain terms you have broken into the house to ransack my desk?'

The other laughed. His self-possession was evidently

restored—if it had ever been lost—by Peter's reception.

'Your desk don't hold what I want,' he said. 'You didn't think, did you, that I wanted your petty cash?'

'I think you had better go.'

There was the smallest hesitation over the last word.

Desire fancied it expressed more than it said, but she thought the suggestion inadequate. She did not know what she wanted, or what, indeed, was possible in the embarrassing circumstances of finding a blood relation in this situation, but she felt that for Alexander merely to go was poor.

He evidently did not entirely favour the suggestion himself.

'I'll go when I'm ready,' he said.

'I think that had better be now.'

'Oh, do you!' Peter's voice was still quiet. But Alexander must have felt a threat in it. 'Look here, Master Peter,' he said, 'you needn't play that to me; I've done nothing but what I'd do any day in daylight if you weren't such a cantankerous, suspicious brute there's no getting to you or your office on any excuse whatever. I've slipped in without permission now, it's true—what of that? It's my father's house, I've done no damage, I want nothing but a glance at some papers for the name of a fool. You can't do anything, so you needn't talk big; petty sessions wouldn't give you much of a remedy, even if it was in your line, which it isn't, so the best thing for you to do, my son, is to put a good face on it and be civil.'

Desire suddenly felt that the best thing for her to do was to come down; the presence of a third party, one with some knowledge of the world, might be an assistance. She descended the stairs quickly and, quietly crossing the dense shadow at the bottom, made for the doorway. There she paused, a startling figure, her glowing hair loosely plaited, the laces open about her throat, her splendid proportions but half concealed by the unshackling garments—a woman such as vikings fought for in the far time.

Alexander had seated himself carelessly by the desk. 'You're a cleverer man than I took you for,' he was saying; 'you seem to have got some money out of your lady friend—generally they squeeze us, but you've managed to squeeze her—' He looked up, and even his eyes lighted a little as they fell on the splendid figure in the doorway—'By Jove! There she is! Come to see why you don't come to bed—'

And then the end came. Without any warning, with the seeming suddenness which characterized some few of Peter's actions, it fell upon Alexander. He literally and really fell upon him, bore him down with irresistible force, the long pent-up feeling brought to a head and suddenly breaking bonds, bringing matters to the arbitrament that Peter understood.

Desire caught her breath, but she did not cry out or shrink back. Possibly she had in her something of the primal woman for whom the vikings fought. At all events, the only movement she made was to grip the dog, who apparently had followed Peter, and pull him back, stifling his angry bark.

Alexander recovered quickly from his surprise; he was breathing short, his face curiously grey, with blood on the lips and a light as of murder in the eyes, bad to see. But Peter, very quiet and white as he had gone at Alexander's last words, was by far the more terrible to Desire. She was not sure that he was aware of her presence until he spoke to her over his shoulder—

'Take the dog and go upstairs,' he said authoritatively.

And meekly she obeyed, closing the door after her.

She went upstairs and sat down at the top, clasping her hands round the dog's neck and ordering him to be quiet. He obeyed, only panting as if the effort were great; in the dark she heard him and sympathized, for she, too, was thrilling with excitement, her heart beating fast and the blood racing in her veins. She did not know what the two down below would do, she could only vaguely hear and did not know what the end would be. But she was not afraid—it was, after all, the simplest ending, the only ending. She leaned her head against the wall and gave a little shuddering laugh. It was horrible, of course, to come to blows; brutal. She had never found the brute in Peter before, it was not horrible to find it, she was not horrified, she was—yes, she was glad it was there. Ashamed that she was glad, perhaps, but not very. She never analyzed her emotions, she certainly did not now. She sat in the dark, thrilling as the dog thrilled, and waited.

A door across the landing opened softly, the door of the dressing-room leading from Ezra's room. Mrs Grimstone, who slept there now, looked out, candle in hand. Desire rose at the first sound. 'Lie still,' she said with low-voiced emphasis to Paddy, and leaving him she crossed the landing swiftly, keeping in the shadow and so coming close to the old lady before she was aware whence she had come or hardly that she was there.

'Were you disturbed by a noise?' she said, standing out of the candle-light. 'It's all right, it's only Peter turning somebody—some boy or some one—out of the yard.'

'Oh?' Mrs Grimstone said nervously. 'Hadn't we better call Robert? Don't you think Peter will be hurt? I thought it was someone in the house.'

Desire ignored the last, but repeated her assurance.

'Peter can manage best alone,' she said; 'he won't be hurt; it's nothing. Hadn't you better go back, because of Mr Grimstone?' And, reassured by Desire's manner, Mrs Grimstone was, after a few more words, persuaded to go in again.

Desire softly closed the door after her, then returned to her post on the stairhead. She sat there till she heard Peter coming up.

He came slowly, carrying no light.

'Well?' she said, rising out of the gloom as he approached.

She spoke softly, for fear of disturbing Mrs Grimstone again, but there was a thrill in her voice that surprised even her own ears.

Peter must have heard it, but he gave no verbal answer.

'Has he gone?' she asked.

'Yes.'

'Is he hurt?'

'He will remember.'

They ascended the second flight of stairs together. It was lighter here. Desire could see that Peter was fully dressed and carried a bundle of manuscript papers. He must have held them in the office, for she remembered now how sheets had fallen like leaves when he attacked Alexander.

'Are you hurt?' she asked softly.

There was a square patch of light at the top of the stairs, where the moonlight streamed in at a window. She paused in it, searching his face. For a moment their eyes met, and something leapt to life in his.

'No,' he said. Then he added suddenly, with a curious peremptoriness, 'Go to bed.'

He drew into the shadow as he spoke, and the manuscript he held crackled under the grip of his fingers.

Without a word Desire obeyed him. She did not run, yet she had a feeling of fleeing; her breath was coming fast when she reached her room, and her heart beating in big thumps. She climbed on to the bed in the dark, and sat there hugging herself, her blood racing, every nerve thrilling, half afraid, half ashamed, wholly glad. Night the wizard, passion and combat the primal, had done it; they had thrown back the trappings and covers and reserves, they had called to the original things, and showed them just man and woman. She knew and she shivered, laughing. She had been engaged once, and had been loved a good many more times than once, and always—as the much loved do—gone a little way towards reciprocating the emotion; but she had never really loved before. Never been foolish and mad and glad, gladder than anything in the world, and foolishly proud and foolishly shy at seeing the light spring in a man's eyes, and knowing that he had drawn back and bade her go for fear he should take her in his arms and kiss her.

She was also old enough to know that she would have forgiven him if he had.

Chapter XVIII

909 Brunswick Square, W C

My dear Desire,

Your father's lawyers have at last succeeded in getting me information as to your recent doings and present whereabouts. If while deploring the precipitousness of your proceedings, which I must characterize as somewhat ill-judged and unsuitable, I at the same time approve the independent spirit which led you to seek to maintain yourself even as a typist. I cannot, however, regard it as a proper course for your father's daughter. I do not forget—as presumably does Lady Quebell—that you are, in spite of the accident of your birth, Sir Joseph' s only child, and brought up by his wish in circumstances and surroundings suited to his legitimate daughter. I therefore write to offer you a home. I suggest that you terminate your present engagement and come to me as soon as possible. I propose to pay you, during the time that the arrangement proves satisfactory, two hundred pounds a year for your private expenses, and in consideration of various small services I may require. It would also be understood that I made suitable, though moderate, provision for you at my death.

I am,

Yours sincerely,
Phoebe Quebell

This was the letter Desire received at the end of December, and very pleased she was to receive it. Not that she had any idea of accepting the offer it contained, but because she was delighted with the remembrance of herself that it showed, with the old lady's generosity and also her spirit.

'Well done, Cousin Phoebe!' she said. 'The old dear has taken the field in style, and I'm not worth it a bit in the world. My hat! But she must have given the step-mother a bad quarter of an hour, a very bad one—and she means to give her more!'

She threw the letter over to Peter as she spoke. 'Read it,' she said.

He read it and returned it.

'I am glad—for you,' he said.

'I'm glad all round,' Desire returned, 'except of course for the step-mother. Cousin Phoebe's a brick. There was good stuff in my father's family—good stuff, but autocratic, they don't like being contradicted. I'm afraid she won't like being refused, though, if she would only realize it, it is no end of a let off for her.'

'You will refuse?' Peter asked.

'Why certainly,' Desire said. 'You don't think I'm going out of Grimstones', do you; just as it's commencing to pay and the fun's properly beginning?'

'It's never going to pay much,' Peter told her, 'and you know it; it may be, I think it will be, a living, but never much more. And anyhow—'

Desire stopped him. 'You needn't go on,' she said; 'I know all about that.'

But Peter did go on. 'It is not right you should refuse such an offer on that account,' he said. 'This is not the work or the life for you—'

'Yes, it is,' Desire interrupted, 'a good deal more so than being companion to Cousin Phoebe'

'It is not being companion only,' Peter said, 'it is really getting back to where you came from—'

'Brunswick Square?' Desire laughed. 'Do you know where Brunswick Square is?'

'It does not matter to you where the house is, you could have just as much of your old life as you liked wherever it was.'

'On two hundred a year? Dress and gamble on two hundred a year?'

'You can match expenditure and income if you want to, and as for dress—does it matter what you wear? You are always you.'

Desire quitted the position of argument. 'Well, I'm not going, anyhow,' she announced with finality.

'Will you tell me why?' Peter asked.

'Because I don't want to. By the way, do you want me to?'

'Yes.'

Desire looked him in the face. 'That,' she said, 'is the first lie I have heard you tell.'

'It is not a lie,' he retorted; 'I do want you to go, I think it would be the best, the right thing—'

'Oh,' said Desire, 'is that what you call wanting? When I say I want anything I mean I think I should find it personally agreeable, exciting, pleasant and altogether—or at least somehow—delicious. Now, though I'm frequently an awful nuisance to you, I flatter myself you wouldn't find it all that to be rid of me. When you say you want a thing it appears you mean you have a sense of duty that way. Well, as I never paid much attention to my own sense of duty it's not likely I'm going to begin paying any to yours.'

Peter, from previous experience, had some reason to think this likely to be the case; and his personal feelings—But he kept them severely in the background and took up the argument again.

'We never intended this should be anything but a temporary arrangement,' he said; 'It couldn't under any circumstances be permanent, we only meant it to last until we had something suitable and definite fixed. Affairs are in splendid going order now, principally thanks to you, you could not leave at a better time, and, since the chance has come, you ought to go. Here there is nothing; there there is everything. You see, there is the future to look to. You may marry—'

Desire's eyes flickered, she bent over some papers so he did not see. 'Yes, I may—,' she said quietly, 'but I shan't.'

It was nearly two weeks now since the night when Alexander came; the night when she had sat long on her bed with her new discovered secret; but Peter had never given either word or sign. She had almost begun to doubt if there had been that one, if she had seen that momentary flash of revelation. Peter was exactly the same as he had been before, curiously, singularly intimate with an intimacy she had never known before and a friendship which was the rarest of the rare, but nothing else. Perhaps—the idea was possible—it was only her own unbridled fancy, her own desire, which had in imagination seen what it was fain to see. But she did not really believe that, she was perfectly and inwardly sure of the reality. She could not understand. It did not enter into her scheme of things that a man, believing himself in every way her inferior, should not quickly understand that she cared for him that way; or that, remembering the converse mistake of other men, himself mistook for friendship what was something more. Certainly it did not enter into her scheme that such a man, even if he thought she had some passing fancy for him, would not ask her to tie herself to a narrow life burdened with poverty and failing parents. Such a solution of the mystery never occurred to Desire, who herself, even if she had been of the blood royal, would unhesitatingly have taken the road with a tinker had it happened to be a case of love and he could be induced to declare his passion. Consequently she was restless and perplexed, at times unhappy, though she did not want anything undone, and did not want to go back to things as they had been. Certainly she had no idea of leaving Twycross, that was not her notion of a solution. At no time during the past months was Miss Quebell's proposal likely to be accepted, there was not the least chance of it now.

'I'm not going,' so Desire announced finally, 'until we're done with Alexander.'

Peter had his back to her, yet somehow she felt that he was very glad, but all he said was, 'If you stay till then you'll stay a long while, for we shan't be done with him till we're dead, or he is.'

'Think not?' Desire said cheerfully. 'Well, you can't exactly work for the furtherance of that end even to achieve the getting rid of me. Alexander, in your place, might perhaps.'

Alexander's name had been very little mentioned between them since the night that he came unbidden to the office. Desire had not heard any details of what happened then. She knew on her own account that it was not accumulated offences against himself, his father and the firm, which finally broke down Peter's control that night and led him to strike, but the one insult to herself. No-one told her this, but she knew it quite well though she knew little besides. Peter had only explained that he had happened to be re-reading the manuscript of the unfinished novel that evening. He had meant to do so for some while, but never found the time; that night she herself had gone to bed early, so he had fetched the manuscript, and, becoming absorbed in it, sat late. Alexander must have approached the house from the back, and if he reconnoitred in front first, had not seen any light by reason of the shutters. The first indication Peter had of an intruder's presence was the uneasiness of Paddy, who was with him. The first indication Alexander had of any one still up in the house was Peter's appearance in the doorway. This Peter told; what happened after she left them at his bidding he did not tell her. She could see for herself that Peter had sustained comparatively little damage; and she could guess that Alexander had sustained a good deal, since it was reported about that time that he had met with some sort of accident. Mr Williams condoled with Mrs Grimstone on the subject the following Sunday, but he was so vague as to the nature of the accident, and the amount of the injuries, that Desire easily managed to allay the old lady's momentary uneasiness, and at the same time herself perceived that the true facts were being concealed, probably from Mrs Alexander as well as everyone else.

Mrs Grimstone never heard the truth; she accepted Desire's reassurances on Sunday as she had accepted the explanation she gave earlier. Indeed, the old lady was curiously content to accept without question, she seemed as if she were too tired to do anything else. Desire was impressed with it, and at the same time suddenly perceived that Mrs Grimstone was very tired; more, that she was failing.

With a startled feeling that was almost a pang Desire perceived it, and in the new light began to understand small signs she had hardly seen before. It was the not unfamiliar sight of the invalid life lingering on, and the unwatched life of the watcher burning quietly away. There had been a difference in Mrs Grimstone ever since she had seen her hungered-for grandchild. She seldom or never spoke of the child or of the mother; she never gave any indication of wishing to see them again, but since their first visit a little quiet sadness had settled on her; not diminishing her patient cheerfulness exactly, or coming between her and her many services, but making her silent and filling her eyes with the wistful resignation of a woman who has lost a young baby. It was as if she had transferred to the dead child the love which she had had for both, and which the living one wanted so little, as if she felt that the hungered-for child was dead. It was not this exactly which had aged her, but it had taken away one of the hopes and longings of her life, and when one is on in years one cannot well afford to lose them. Desire saw it, and it seemed to her pitiful, and she longed to supply the loss from her own superabundant zest for life. But it could not be done, any more than a transfer of her vitality could. She realized it, and began to realize, also, other things about Mrs Grimstone, small signs but not without meaning. Things were an effort now which had been no effort before, bravely borne and cheerfully made, but effort still. There was a tendency to doze over work, a dropping into cat-sleeps whenever the stimulus of necessity was removed, as if nature were worn. There were other small wearinesses and feeblenesses, indications all that Mrs Grimstone had, unnoticed by them, been gradually getting very frail.

On the day when Desire and Peter agreed about Miss Quebell's offer, there was an example of Mrs Grimstone's increasing feebleness and an indication that she herself was not unaware of it. At dinnertime Desire informed her that Peter was trying to get rid of her.

'He hasn't given me notice exactly,' she said, 'but he has indicated that the sooner I go the better.'

'Go!' Mrs Grimstone exclaimed in such dismay that they both looked at her. 'Oh, my dear, don't do it! I can't—I mean, I don't think I can spare you! Peter, must she go? Surely there is no reason why she should go?'

The last was a plea. True to her lifelong custom Mrs Grimstone would, after the first shock, bow to the dictates of the men of her house, no matter how they might press on her. 'Oh, Peter, must she?' she asked.

'Of course not,' Desire said. And they both hastened to reassure her, explaining that it was only a proposal from some relative who wanted Desire to live with her.

'But I'm not going,' Desire said decidedly. 'You're not going to get rid of me that way.'

'I am glad,' Mrs Grimstone said; 'I am glad!' again and again.

'Of course, if you ought to go,' she said tentatively after a little, 'I mean, if it is better for you, more suitable—'

'It isn't,' Desire assured her.

'Is it, Peter?' Mrs Grimstone asked.

'She says it isn't,' Peter answered; 'and anyhow she has made up her mind not to go, and you know what that means.'

Mrs Grimstone looked wistfully at Desire. 'Perhaps later on,' she said, 'after the winter—I've got so to depend on you now-a-days—'

Desire took her hand and kissed it. 'Flatterer!' she said. 'Nobody ever depended on me before—they all knew better.'

Afterwards, when she and Peter were alone, she said, 'Do you know, your mother's just been wearing out under our eyes and we never knew it.'

Peter nodded, and stood silent.

Desire smoked hard; she wanted to do something, she did not know what, but she wanted to do it at once for the woman who had become very dear to her.

'She isn't ill,' Peter said slowly, as if he were reviewing things, 'she is just tired. I think so tired that soon she will find it an effort to live.'

'A very little thing, a cough or a cold even, would make it too much effort,' Desire said shortly.

Again Peter nodded. 'And I never knew,' he said. 'I never knew. I took it as a matter of course that she should do things.'

There was remorse in his tone, Desire felt a share in it, but after a little she said, 'Do you know, I really think it was a matter of course. I believe if she could not serve she would not want to live. It's wonderful, isn't it? I never knew before, but there are people like that. It—it makes me ashamed.' She wiped her eyes openly.

'What can we do?' Peter asked.

'Nothing,' she answered; 'I believe just nothing. Save her

when we can, and take care of her without letting her see—but really nothing.'

And she was right. There was very little more they could do; for, as she had perceived, Mrs Grimstone was of that kind who would rather be doing and serving; who so long had never considered herself that she had little self left, and when the consideration for others was taken from her had small wish to live. So, in spite of what they saw, they largely had to let her follow her usual course and lead her usual life. They saved her where they could, unostentatiously, and without letting it appear; they gave her much thought and gentleness, and between them made the short winter days very happy for her. The last part of Mrs Grimstone's life was undoubtedly the happiest in spite of the condition of her husband, and the fact that she never ceased to feel it on his account. With Peter's home-coming the level grey years had, as it were, budded a little for her; little tentative shoots of pleasure had come, touches of consideration, unspoken sympathy, like gleams of sunshine. And in spite of the trouble which, within the first year, had fallen upon the household, the gleams grew and broadened. Ezra's disablement was the shaking of the pivot of Mrs Grimstone's existence, none the less, it gave her liberty and the opportunity to serve; and in Peter's company the shoots of happiness still budded. This until Desire came, when somehow it seemed they came to blossom. Gaiety and laughter and small joys sprang up like flowers in the genial warmth of Desire's large vitality. She was glad, and this grey world seemed glad because of her; she was strong, and burdens seemed small beside her; life had given to her abundantly, and she gave again, herself, her goods, her emotions, spending with both hands. She had brought the sunshine to the last year of Mrs Grimstone's life, though she had not the least idea of it until the end, when the old lady told her—told her with the simplicity which was part of her nature, and which gave a curious value to what she said.

'Ah, my dear,' she said, when Desire sat silent under her words, a choke in her throat at the sudden vision she had of the bareness of a life that could be thus brightened. 'It is a great gift you have, to make the world a brighter place by just being. It was like the sun coming into our house when you came—we don't have such a great deal of sun here, you know, the hills bring clouds, I think. You are very radiant.'

'I?' Desire said. 'No, oh no!'

'Yes,' Mrs Grimstone persisted, 'when you wish you are; you always wished to shine here, I think you knew we had not had much sunshine. You never thought of yourself and your troubles, only of us. You could shine in other grey places, too, if you liked. It is a great gift, my dear; many people try to make the world better, some do it, but not many can make it brighter by just being, by their smiles, by their voice, by little words and little deeds, by just living. Oh, my dear, take care of it, don't let the gift get dim!'

Desire could not answer, she was crying quietly but unreservedly.

Mrs Grimstone herself seemed to feel little regret at the approaching end, which she knew to be near; when once she was sure her place would be filled, she seemed quite content to go.

'I never thought to go before Ezra,' she said once, 'it's sad to leave him; but it would have been sadder to stay, and not to be able to do all he wants. Mary will take my place, she is a good woman, a good true woman, she never fails. Why, in the few days I have been lying here she has learnt to do for him better than I have of late! Think of that! It took me quite a long time to learn, but I never was clever.'

For the rest she seemed to have little regret. She was unfeignedly glad that her illness was short, that she would not be a trouble to anyone. It was vain that Desire told her it was no trouble, vain that her looks and words showed hers was a more than willing service. Mrs Grimstone had so long been the server she could not take to being served; she had so long spent all her energy doing for others, it made her uneasy to have another do for her, even though that other was Desire.

In these last days the office saw little of Desire. James did her work, and she became nurse, the woman in her suddenly come to the surface. The nurse and mother, which seems to lie dormant in most women, waked to life, and making her—herself still—but another, a gentler, a more tender, perhaps a truer woman too.

'My dear,' Mrs Grimstone whispered on the last day of all, 'you have been very good to me—not now only, but ever since you came. You and Peter—' she looked across at Peter, who was the other side of the bed.

'I have sometimes thought,' she said to him, 'since I have been lying here thinking of things, and of all Desire told me of London and your life. Sometimes I wondered if you did want to come home—if it was the best—'

'Yes,' Peter said, 'it was the best, I think the best work in my life, I know the best time.'

His voice had a curious depth as he spoke, and Desire knew he was speaking the truth, though to her there was something almost tragic in it; for the goodness he had found was the goodness of renunciation, and the hard-learnt lesson that work well done is better than work self-chosen, better than the success which may or may not crown it.

But Mrs Grimstone did not understand, and she was reassured and content. Her hand fluttered feebly, and Peter, divining what was in her mind, took it in his; in these late rare moments this expression of emotion was possible, though it never had been before in all their reserved lives. With Desire it was always possible, Mrs Grimstone's left hand had long lain in hers; now with her right she held Peter, and, so holding, happy in the presence of the two she loved, she fell into fitful sleep. So they sat there very quiet in the quiet room, a pause of peace to gather the thought harvest. So till the twilight fell, and the feeble fingers grew more feeble and relaxed, and gradually, in spite of the strong grasp of the younger hands, grew cold. The faint breath grew fainter, fluttered, and was gone, and Mrs Grimstone, tired with a long day's work, slipped from sleep to the longer rest.

Chapter XIX

The funeral was over, the few crape-bound cousins who had attended took their leave. Having parted with one who had to wait for a down train, the rest got into an up and settled themselves, the men taking off their black gloves, the women throwing back their veils and criticizing the funeral arrangements.

'I don't approve of innovations,' said the lady with the black currants in her bonnet—she was one who made it a point of duty to attend all the funerals she could—'I don't like the way things were done.'

A younger woman, by name Clara, did not like them either, and she said so, adding further, 'And whatever was right was no thanks to Peter Grimstone, I'm sure. I've not seen him since he was a little boy in knickerbockers until to-day, but he's not improved, anyone can see what he is.'

She sniffed just a little as she spoke, so it is plain whatever she saw Peter to be she did not admire it. She turned for corroboration to the head man of the party, an elderly gentleman, who last year had buried his wife with a funeral which had given complete satisfaction to everyone, including the undertakers. He had disapproved of several things to-day, though principally Peter. 'Peter Grimstone,' he said in a beard-muffled voice, 'a fool, a dreamer, wrote a book or something. Stand-offish ways too—doesn't know time and place—his mother's funeral not the time for that sort of thing.'

'What's-his-name-Alexander, was not there.'

A little man with a cheerful face, and gloves which had been inked at the tips, said this. He was somebody's husband, a south-country man, without a proper comprehension of family feuds. The rest of the party did comprehend, and with one accord they said, 'Of course Alexander was not!' One, it is true, afterwards added, and it was quite correct, 'He had influenza, I am told,' but another hastened to say, 'He wouldn't have come if he hadn't got it.'

'Why not?' the little man demanded, though he knew the answer. 'Because he happened to fall out years ago with a hard-headed old chap who is laid by now? Poof! If you were to ask me, I should say his mother's funeral wasn't the time to show off that sort of thing.'

They had not asked him, and perhaps it was as well that she of the black currants created a diversion by inquiring, in somewhat italic tones, 'What I should like to know is, who is the young woman?'

Somebody said, 'A companion,' and the irrepressible little man remarked, 'Queer kind for that job—Venus of what's-his-name, and all that sort of thing, don't you know. And manners too. She's the real thing!'

The lady with the black currants set her lips. 'If,' she said with severity, 'she is a companion, it would have been more becoming of her to have left the house by this time. Seeing that there is no-one there but servants—old servants, certainly, but still only servants—and a helpless invalid, she is virtually alone with a young man. She should have left directly after poor dear Susan's death; if she had had nice feelings she would have done so.'

She called Clara sniffed here, she did not expect the 'nice feelings', evidently. 'It's an extraordinary thing,' she said, 'that poor Susan should have left her china, even grandmother's tea-set, to her; such things ought to go to relatives.'

They were agreed on this point, as they had been on Peter's behaviour, and the two subjects, diluted by reference to recent funerals attended by the older woman, served them till they had to part company.

That Peter's behaviour fell short of what it should have been according to custom, was not very surprising, for he had no idea what was expected of him, or indeed, that anything particular was. And Desire, totally unacquainted with the rigid forms regarded here, was no help to him. Robert no doubt could have told him; but Peter's ignorance on the subject extended to not knowing there were thing he ought to know, so he did not ask, and Robert did not volunteer. The old man, as the cousins guessed, had to certain extent arranged things, at all events the things which pleased them. It was to him they practically owed their presence. Peter, left to himself, would certainly not have remembered them, and Desire would not have thought to ask if Mrs Grimstone had any relatives near or far off. Indeed, she rather objected to their presence; it seemed to her ridiculous, almost impertinent, that any one besides her and Peter should be there. They two alone had known and loved Mrs Grimstone; it was they she had loved, and they, with the helpless body which had so strangely survived her, formed her life and the centre of her existence. It was they surely who should alone follow her to the grave. The rest was mere convention, and Desire had small patience with convention when it interfered with or intruded upon her.

Peter, on the other hand, was indifferent to it; she felt that; and in the light of the feeling became more reconciled herself. It did not intrude with him, he was hardly aware of its existence. The cousins were there, of course, Robert had thought they should he, and James at his direction had bidden them, but they were nothing. Since they were there Peter was patiently polite to them, as he would have been to any one he found in the house or met on the road, but they did not count for anything, their presence was little more than the presence of flies on the window pane—they came, they buzzed, they went. He and Desire were alone in this, as formerly he had been alone in all things that mattered, and as they of late had been alone together. They had grown to be more and more alone together; he had not realized how much they were, nor how the original single solitude of his life had come to he shared, until the day his mother died. Then, when they sat in wordless sympathy and knew each the other's feeling without expression, he realized it; he knew then that, however material circumstances altered or what corporeal facts afterwards befell, they two would always have this time of oneness to look back upon. They had gradually come so close together in the past months of work and struggle, this sitting together in the death chamber, held by the feeble hands of the simple woman who had loved them, was as it were the consummation. What came after could not alter and could not take it. And certainly the trivial present, the mere presence or absence of women with crape veils and men with huskily subdued voices, was of no importance at all. It matters very little who comes for a while into one's house, seeing how perfectly impossible it is for anyone, blood-relation or bedfellow, to come unbidden into one's life, to understand and share the things that really count.

So the cousins came and went away, and their coming and their going was equally nothing to Peter; and, through him, not much more to Desire after the first. Though, after they had gone, she threw up the long windows to let out the smell of their crape and boots. Having done this she went to change her funeral dress, and Peter went up to his father's room, to tell the events of the day to the inanimate figure which he still believed might sometime hear and understand.

Desire, when she had changed her dress, went to the office; there were several letters she rather wanted to get off; moreover, she felt a restless need of doing something—something which would occupy her mind. She typed the letters, took copies, filed papers, gave all her attention to the business in hand. Yet between whiles, when she stopped for a fresh sheet of paper, when she folded a letter or fastened an envelope, other thoughts would intrude—one other thought—The end. It had come. The thing was ended, the thing as it had been, as it was, had come to an end, and she knew it. She had not heard the strictures of the lady with the black currants, and she would not have cared a snap of the fingers if she had. She would not have cared for better founded strictures passed by people of more importance, better able to form an opinion. She would not have had the slightest compunction about living on here on the present terms—but Peter, she knew, would not ask her to do it. More—for in her regal disregard of obstacles she might have got over that difficulty—he would not let her do it. The compromise of more or less continuing the present work and living somewhere in the town, she did not for one moment contemplate; it would have been a mere ridiculous evasion to both her and Peter. Conventions might have been satisfied by such a thing, but then neither of them thought of that, it was not a convention which dictated the end which was coming. She did not know how it would come, whether he would ask her to marry him. A shaking took possession of her at the thought, as if she had been the youngest girl; and as if she had been such a one she never pictured a point further than the question, which she somehow did not feel was likely to be asked. Or whether he would tell her that for some reason he could not marry her. It did not matter why, she had a large, tolerant incuriousness of such things, and the result, whatever the reason, would be the same. Or whether he would tell her she must go. This was the last thought, the ever-recurring one. This had no reason either and would ask none; she would, if this came, simply accept it and go. She had always kicked over barriers and stepped over obstacles, often without even recognizing them; she had not the slightest regard for any conventions which were hampering to her, but this time she would accept another's dictate, whatever it was.

But when, when would it be? Not that evening, it seemed, though they spent it together. They sat together after supper, they two alone; she noticed absurd little details that night, things which had occurred before but which in their intimacy struck her afresh. He carved, he knew precisely what she liked, he did not ask her, as if they had always lived together. She helped the sweets, Mary, who brought the plates, asked her some question, would she have this or that dish? as if she were the mistress of the house and had forgotten to give the order.

After supper he read prayers. When she first came she had found him carrying on this custom of the house, and somehow, though she could not tell why, she had been glad of it. She had known little of the Bible before, its splendid prose and vivid, many-sided humanity appealed strongly to her, and yet in some way seemed to fit with the life here.

She was glad that Peter read every night, as his father and grandfather and great-grandfather had before him, even though he, and probably they too, doubtless had a private interpretation of what was read. That night he read prayers. Robert and Mary at one end of the room, she and he at the other; the old Puritan custom of family worship, as if they two were the heads of the family.

After prayers they sat together by the fire. The earlier part of the evening Peter had felt compelled to spend in his father's room, and Desire had been alone. Now Mary was upstairs setting the invalid for the night, and they two were alone. They sat one on either side of the fire, the dog curled up between them. Desire was darning, she had learnt at last under Mrs Grimstone's tuition; it was one of the fine old pillow-cases she was at work upon. She felt Peter's eyes upon it and realized that here again was the same intimacy. In her previous life in her father's house such things had been impossible; any two persons might be there under any conditions, and even though they could outrage all the proprieties they could not come into this simple hearth-sharing relationship. In that hotel-like life it was the butler who knew one's tastes, the housekeeper who ordered the household, the sewing-maid who did the mending. That members of the family knew nothing of each other's wants, little of each other's sorrows, and not much of each other's joys; in that life it would have been possible to marry a man and, in most particulars, never really live with or know him properly. Here it was utterly and entirely different; here and now she and Peter were as she had never been with another man, never could be.

Suddenly she began to talk, about anything, the first thing that came to her tongue. Of course it was personal, in very short time it was bound to be; when you share work, and interest, and almost thoughts with one person every topic must be soon, but it is sometimes better to talk even thus than to be silent. So the evening passed, too fast, and yet not so fast but that she noted and remembered everything. At last it was bedtime, and she rose, folding her work neatly as Mrs Grimstone used to do.

Robert and Mary had already gone up when they came out into the hall, so Peter barred the front door.

'I believe we ought to get a new mat,' he said, as he caught his foot in a hanging thread. 'Do you know where they get them?'

'No,' Desire said almost sharply. 'Shall I put out the light?' she asked.

'Don't bother,' Peter answered. 'I'll do it.'

He came, but she had put it out before he got there, and holding her candle low, went down the hall. They went upstairs together and parted on the landing, after stopping to see if the staircase window was fastened. Peter examined the window, she held the light. Then they said 'good-night', and went each to their room. And then suddenly, as Desire shut the door, restraint dropped from her, the self-possession which in all her life, through all its happenings, in company and solitude, had always decently dropped her emotions, fell off, and the crude woman flashed out for a moment. 'I can't stand it! God in Heaven! I can't do it!' she said almost aloud. 'I can't sit at table with him, share the house with him, bar the door with him, play at wife with him, and no more!'

She turned with almost a fury of movement, like a wild animal, and like an animal flung herself across the room, hands clenched, eyes blazing, scarlet lips protesting in half audible outcry—'I can't, I can't!'

At the other end of the room there was a mirror, in the half dark a face looked out of it, a face unveiled and somehow terrible in its hunger and its passion and primitive unabashed emotion. Desire, seeing it, recoiled, then stood still. For a long minute she stood with averted eyes, and the dim face changed. The eyes grew tragic, almost fearing, and the mouth—it was hid in shadows—one only knew it twitched and worked. Her breath came heavily, as one who has struggled in deep waters. Then she threw up her head and though the mirrored face showed white, almost as if fingers had hardly pressed it, a trace of the old smile curved the wrung lips.

'Clearly,' she said to it, 'it is time I went.'

She put out the light and undressed in the dark. Her breath was coming evenly now, her pulse beating slow and regular; but she did not want to see herself again just yet.

The next day was Sunday, and in the afternoon she and Peter went up the hill together. It was a quiet, grey afternoon in early February, everything still, no sign of life, no promise even of the spring in this cold country. There was a sense of pause in the air, of waiting for something; it might be for storms and sleet, or it might be gentle rain and gleams of sunshine; there was nothing to tell; only the earth slept, brown beneath the grey sky, very silent. They went by the familiar way, by the path and past the landmarks now as well known to Desire as to Peter. She observed them particularly that day, each one as they came to it. When the top was reached she sat down on the dead heather; there had been no rain for some time, and the ground was moderately dry; dry enough, at all events, to satisfy her; and she drew herself out full length in the way she liked. Peter sat on a boulder near, his eyes on the spread landscape, and for a time there was complete silence.

At last Peter spoke. 'When you wrote to Miss Quebell, what did you say? Do you mind telling me?'

'I said that I was much obliged for her proposal; very grateful for it; thought it no end sporting, and all the rest; but I didn't see my way to accepting it—or words to that effect.'

Desire spoke carelessly, hut she rolled over as she spoke, and, elbows on the ground, chin propped on hands, watched Peter under her hat-brim.

'When she acknowledged your letter, was she angry?' he asked.

'Very,' Desire answered. 'The offer, apparently, was not pure philanthropy; there would seem to have been a teeny wee bit of an idea of scoring off Lady Quebell in it—or, at all events, of demonstrating a superior sense of duty and justice, and so on. Yes, she was annoyed, and she said so. There was, however, a postscript indicating that, owing to these or other reasons, the offer might still be open if I came to my senses—or, rather, her senses—at a future date.'

'I see,' Peter said, and there was another pause. Then he asked, 'Don't you think it would be wiser if you did go to her? It would be better, don't you think, than anything else?'

He turned to her as he spoke, and she raised her head to meet his eyes.

'Do you want me to go?' she asked.

'Yes.'

He did not explain, or apologize, or palliate it; he did not thank her for what she had done, or dwell on her gain in going, or his loss. He only answered the one word, and looked in her eyes as he spoke it. And Desire asked no more; it was enough; all else would have been superfluous, mere words. This was her order to go; and, for all her strength and persistence, for all her habit of overriding obstacles and gaily carrying her point, she accepted it. She was a woman to the core, and such, the most wayward as well as the most docile, the strongest sooner, perhaps, than the weakest, will take orders from the one man who can give them. So Desire took this order, and so the end came. She took it in silence; for one moment the immovable face and grey eyes which looked into hers held her silent, held her soul prisoned, as it were.

But she had learnt self-mastery in a good school, and practised it in private and in public—with one brief exception—most of her life, and it stood her in good stead now.

'All right,' she said; 'I'll write to-night.'

Then she looked away. She knew that, whatever his motive for sending her, it was not easy to him, and she was suddenly afraid of seeing it in his face. She tore up some heather roots and examined them carefully, entirely without seeing. A curlew cried once overhead; nothing else stirred, in the great silence. Peter looked straight before him; his face had grown grim and old; he had no word whatever to say, and she was glad of it. A word of any sort would have been so utterly inadequate, so false. She was glad, savagely glad, that his face was grim and old; and next moment she was ashamed, ashamed even of having seen what he wished hid. She sat up and felt for her cigarette case.

'Can you give me a light?' she said. He gave her one, and then rose, as if he thought it time they went.

They went home by the long way that day and they talked very little, talk seemed somewhat impossible. The path was a long and winding one, taking them some way among the hills before bringing them to the level of the road. At one point it passed a deserted chapel, a little grey building set on the hillside, built by some small austere sect since dead or scattered, deserted now except by one solitary member. He, an old bent man, a hill man by birth and at one time possibly a leading light among the lost community, still came. Regularly, in rain or sunshine or howling wind, he came; each Sunday afternoon he took the path, so little used now as to be rough and overgrown, and came to the chapel and alone he held a service there according to his lights. Desire and Peter had seen him sometimes when they passed that way; today when they neared the chapel they saw that the door stood wide. The light was failing fast and the old man, having no candle or lamp, had left the door open so that he might have the last of the daylight. The bare interior was all revealed, the walls stained with damp and disuse, the shadows in the corner, the kneeling figure. An old illiterate man, a bare place, deserted and forgotten in the lonely hills, and yet a temple sanctified by worship.

By common impulse Desire and Peter paused; then without speaking went quietly in and knelt down side by side among the shadows.

The old man prayed and preached. He preached aloud though for years there had been no congregation but the birds that sometimes, but rarely, looked in at the windows he had roughly mended. He prayed quietly, sometimes in silence, sometimes in a muttering voice for no earthly hearer. He was growing deaf, he did not hear the rare sounds without, would not have heard if quiet steps entered or left his little sanctuary. He was absorbed and did not feel the presence of human beings or guess that human hearts beat for a little in the shadows. For long he had been the only worshipper, he looked for no other, and that Sunday, as well as on all that had gone before, it was the same. There was no-one in the little building when he felt his way through the dusk to the doorway, no-one outside on the fast darkening path, no sight or sound of living soul. He turned to secure the door and on the cracked doorstone saw a tuft of dead heather lying. None grew within a mile of the place but he thought nothing of it, only picked it up and threw it away, and having fastened the door took his lonely way over the hills.

On the Thursday following Desire left Twycross. Preparations with her never took long making. She wrote to Miss Quebell, she received an answer; she bundled her belongings into trunks and boxes and, having arranged her papers and interviewed Dodd and James, she was practically ready to start.

The affairs of the firm were, largely thanks to her, in good order now. Peter, too, by slow learning and painful experience had at last got the grip of them; James was an able and methodical assistant; she knew that, however much they might miss her, they could do without her now. The manufacturing part was also in excellent condition—such condition as it had not been since the early days when small concerns and working masters were general. For this, too, she was partly responsible, for without her financial help the machine, to which the prosperity was owing, could hardly have been set up. Affairs were altogether in a condition to be left; such a condition, indeed, that Mr Dodd gave it as his opinion that it would have been a sheer waste of talent for her to remain.

Desire graciously accepted the somewhat laboured compliment he paid her on the subject, and thanked him for the manner in which he had worked with her and other things in a way which made him happy if embarrassed.

At the same time it emboldened him to ask if she would allow him to present her with a small souvenir, some local photographs a friend of his had taken, he would like to get them mounted for her if she would permit it. Of course she would—she was delighted and touched—it was easy to touch Desire—her heart warmed towards Dodd for thinking of the photographs. But it was not to him she made the one request she did make before leaving, but to Robert. She knew Robert, his surly sterling stuff, and his indissoluble connection with the firm and the household.

'Robert,' she said, 'I want you to promise to wire to me if at any time things go wrong, or there is a smash up of any kind, or anything particular happens.'

Robert hesitated; he was cautious in giving promises, being one of those who regard them as more binding than law or common sense, and always to be fulfilled to the letter. However, Desire had long ago won an ascendency over him and knew how to use it; before long he had promised what she wanted and she knew he would keep his word; probably without consulting Peter, who would naturally be allowed nothing to do with what was a matter of conscience.

Desire's farewells did not take long to make; she had no acquaintances in the town to call upon excepting the minister and his wife; on them she paid a real leave-taking call of great propriety. Notwithstanding it, however, Mr Williams came to the station to see her off, and gave her a little book as a farewell present. Several people gave her farewell presents, mostly of a somewhat unwieldy order. Her friends the quarrymen, to whom she had called good-bye from her bedroom window, left a market bunch of wallflowers and some fossils, found in their work, for her. A gipsy crone, with whom she had often smoked and chatted, gave her the wicker basket she was making by the roadside, when she heard that she was leaving. Robert presented her with a remarkable jug she had often contemplated with interest; the seven deadly sins were stencilled on it in shiny black. Mary gave a bottle of embrocation of her own compounding, and three mince-pies to be eaten on the journey. Dodd's photographs, which were mounted in a small but highly-ornamented album, were hardly ready in time. Indeed, he arrived by down train with them only just before she left the station in the up.

He came breathless over the bridge, and pushed his way through the little group about the carriage door. The porters, who were also Desire's friends, had gathered there to the annoyance of other passengers, who had rather to do without them that day.

'It wasn't done in time for me to send it;' Dodd explained, panting a little as he put his parcel into Desire's hand. Then he remembered the manners on which he prided himself, and asked her to do him the honour of accepting the trifle.

She accepted it with flushing face and softening eyes, just as if it were a great honour; as if he were a great man and it a great gift, something wonderful. To her it was wonderful, to be remembered and thought of by anyone; to have people like her, care that she left, was sweet and touching; it never lost its freshness or failed to surprise her, no matter how often it occurred. She always forgot the times which had gone before, and only remembered that she had done little to deserve it. She stood in the carriage doorway now; the seats within were littered with her coats and cloaks, and things which would not go anywhere else, and also with the unwieldy gifts. In her hands were the wallflowers, and now Dodd's little parcel. Her eyes filled with tears as she stood there—tears for Dodd and Mr Williams and the quarrymen and porters and everyone except Peter. It was all 'except Peter', that send off. Peter brought no farewell gift; Peter won no tearful smile, no parting admonition or ridiculous laughing comment which left a sunny memory. There was no last handshaking for

Peter, no farewells hurried by the starting of the train; they did not touch one another, they scarcely spoke. Only, when the quickening train passed under the bridge, it was on Peter that her eyes were—eyes whose memory he carried back to the lonely grey house.

Chapter XX

In September, some six months and more after leaving Twycross, Desire wrote the following letter. She did not post it, though why is not quite clear, for it certainly had the appearance of being written to Peter, and of being meant to be posted—

Vichy, September 15

This, O sole Working Representative of the Firm of Grimstone—this is a chronicle of small beer. I do not apologize, I write for my delectation, not yours. It is long since you have heard from me, so you ought to like it—or at least pretend that you do.

At present we take a cure, Cousin Phoebe and I; she does it for the good of her joints, also incidentally her physician; I do it for pleasures of experience. For long the nature of my disease has troubled the curists, I somehow don't look a desperate case; at last an embassy of two has approached me. In strict confidence I told them I was suffering from imaginitis—I am not sure if they have yet diagnosed it.

Before this, I mean before the cure, Miss Desire Quebell was the guest of Lord and Lady Dinfield, at Dinfield Towers, where a select house party was assembled all for to slay the little grouse bird. Miss Desire Quebell did not do any slaying, but she went out with the guns, which was decent enough; and gambled and talked, and went on much as usual in such circumstances in between whiles, which was rather dreary. Alas!—I do find such things a bit dreary at times—something has spoiled my taste for play, all sorts of play, gambling and fooling equally. It's sickening to lose a faculty, but it's what we all come to; old age and boredom are creeping upon me, in fact they have crept.

To tell the truth I am taking the cure because of the lost faculty—not as a remedy, mon ami, don't be obvious and say that—but because duty to an ailing relative is an excellent reason for not going to houses where you are bored. At two have I stayed, at two have I weekended since the 12th—no more, thank you, just yet.

Be satisfied: I have some pearls! I told you if ever I was in circumstances to want them I should have them, and I was right.—A short string, not a long one like my others, but better pearls. They are Cousin Phoebe's; I don't know what aged relative she got them from, but she has given me the use of them. She says she has given them to me to save probate at her death; but I tell her I will have the use of them only, and leave them behind when I flit. I have pointed out to her that, through no fault of my own, I seem to have a habit of 'softly and silently vanishing away' like the people who see a boojum.

Well, for the present I wear the pearls when I go out to parties and such. I went to many parties before I left town. Did I tell you when I wrote last that you were right about its not mattering where I lived in town? On the whole I prefer Brunswick Square, I think, there's more variety; I see as much as I want of the old lot—Not more, we're not on the telephone, also whenever I don't want to go anywhere I find it too far—so convenient. Cousin Phoebe is heroic, she puts up with my friends, and my vagaries, and my hours in a Spartan manner. I'm afraid she has her reasons, she and the step-mother had a row royal over me it seems; it also seems she has always hated Lady Quebell pretty considerably. I'm afraid my liberty and general encouragement to go forth and shine is part of a scheme of spite. I wish it wasn't, I hate that kind of thing, it seems somehow not in the least worthwhile. I met the step-mother of course several times; it appeared to be awkward to her, I was so sorry, it really need not have been, there's no earthly reason why we should not be as pleasant as anything. I fancy she gave up one or two parties for fear of meeting me again; then I gave up one or two for fear of embarrassing her by my presence—It is all very ridiculous.

One night at a big affair I met Edward Gore and his wife—she is his wife now. He has altered, altered tremendously—perhaps you will suggest, as I remember you did once before, that it may be I and my point of view that have altered. I don't know, I think it must be both, one alone could not account for that difference. Still, I was glad to see the Gores, especially her. It was so nice to see her with him in his proper position, recognized and all the sort of thing she wanted. When I caught sight of her I made for her right away, to tell her how awfully glad I was to see her. And do you know, she coloured a little and seemed almost afraid of me! And he looked as if he'd rather have met anyone else in the world; he was frigid, I believe, with embarrassment or fear or something. She and I talked weather-talk for five minutes, and then he hurried her away, though they had only just come. I fancy no-one but me knows anything really of this affair, I suppose they were afraid of something coming out through me. Or maybe it is that they themselves have buried it—folks do seem able to bury things and pretend they are not there—and my appearance was like a bit of resurrection. I don't know. It's extraordinary to me—As if it mattered, as if anything mattered—

That meeting with them led me to give up some other functions. I didn't mind meeting them, I should not have chosen to talk much to them of course, because they disappointed me, but there are always plenty of other people—but it was plain they did not want to meet me. So I abstained from several entertainments on their account, but I can't pretend it was pain and grief to me to do it. I'm afraid, these tiresome contretemps apart, I do not care for things as I used. I don't care, it's no good pretending I do. One outgrows it, or one loses touch, or something, I'm getting very old. Boys and girls are expected to outgrow marbles and dolls, and in middle-class life young men and women, the ones with stuff in them, are expected to outgrow games and dancing and generally playing—Why, I wonder, when one has more money, is one expected to have less sense? 'Le monde qui s'amuse' begins to strike me rather as a case of arrested development, doesn't it you? Well, my mother wasn't even middle-class, and my father was a man who worked, I suppose I don't belong, that's the truth of it.

The Brunswick Squarers—they mostly don't live in Brunswick Square, by the way—They say they are commonplace, at least they say each other are, and as they all say it it follows they all must be. But they are all quite different, and if they are all commonplace, then it's a fascinating quality. I should not like too much of them of course, but then I should not like too much of any one I fear—Oh, for a great great silence, a solitude you can feel, a silence you can hear!

I had it once while I was staying in Yorkshire last month. I got away on Sunday afternoon, out alone and up on to the moor, a big, big place where there were curlew. But a man who was staying in the house came after me—or perhaps met me, anyhow he turned up. He was Julian Lee, by the way, the man who wrote to you for my address. I'm afraid I was not very nice to him about the address, nor very nice to him that Sunday. After talking to him for about ten minutes, I just asked him if he'd mind going on or walking back, as I wanted to be alone. He went like a lamb, he really is a good sort; but of course the spell was broken, also I repented of my nastiness all the way home, which was uncomfortable. I knew by his face he didn't like it, and, as I say, he has been decent to me and never plagued me with silly questions.

I took the curate to the Tivoli before leaving London. I dined him first and took him there afterward, it rather took his breath away, I'm not sure that the dining didn't do it most, but I'm sure it was good for him. He has renounced the pomps and vanities of the wicked world without knowing anything about them—a Saint Francis sort of person—But I have told you about him before. He's Cousin Phoebe's curate, but my friend.

I have another friend, too, now, he is a draper's assistant—I have not mentioned this fact to Cousin Phoebe, nor have I mentioned the curate and the Tivoli. She has prejudices. We all have.

My draper is a socialist and a reformer, and all manner of sincere and uncomfortable things. Such an odd man, and so immensely real! I suppose he is what is called well-read, I've never met it before, it rather sticks out of him at times; but in spite of it I like him, he is so earnest and so really and simply spends himself for other people and the things in which he believes. He comes to the boys' club, fancy working in a shop—a draper's shop, where tiresome women worry—all day and then giving your evenings to a boys' club! It was at the club I met him; we did not get on at first, but now we are friends, and before I left town he used to come sometimes on early closing days and have tea with me in the minute sanctum which Cousin Phoebe has given me to be untidy in. St Francis turned up one day when he was there; they were as shy of each other as possible, though they knew each other quite well, it was so odd. Fortunately Julian Lee came also that afternoon, four's a much easier number than three, and he really is a comfortable person.

I invited the draper to do a theatre with me before I left town—a Shaw play and supper quietly after. But he wouldn't; I wish he had, I'm sure it would have been as good for him as the Tivoli was for St Francis, neither of them have any idea of recreating.

You remember the amiable Bamfield, who introduced you without knowing who you were? He has unexpectedly come into property; poor dear, it's quite embarrassing to him to know where to turn for a fiver, he's so long been unused to such affluence. He grew really sentimental when telling me, and spoke with feeling upon the loneliness of his big house. Whereupon I suggested he should invite the boys' club to do a fortnight's camping on his estate at his expense. And he did it too, like a brick.

The club flourishes. There is a new department added—Hooligans. It is mine own. One evening when I was out, 'when I didn't oughter be', I met a small band. One tried to bar my way, in fun solely, but I was furious for a moment. It was perfectly ridiculous, but I'm ashamed to say I felt my muscles all grow taut and myself sort of draw up for a felling blow; fortunately, however, the ludicrousness of it struck me in time, and I laughed aloud. They looked rather astonished, and the one with the stick rather sheepish; by the way, he had raised his stick on guard, so I suppose my first fury had shown in my face.

'You don't know much about fencing, if that's your notion of guard,' I said to him. 'Why, I could disarm you in a minute, I'll show you.'

I made him come out where there was room, and borrowed somebody else's stick and showed him. The others were frightfully pleased.

That was my first introduction; since then I have got to know them very well, and, as I say, have a sort of new department of the boys' club. No-one but me has much to do with them, St Francis can't get on with them very well, nor can the others; they say it is difficult work. It isn't, it doesn't strike me as work at all. Do you know, I sometimes think I shall really and truly take to it, I like it. I expect there are a good many of those sort of youths in the pottery towns—

The writer broke off here, suddenly becoming aware where her thoughts, or at least the expression of them, might seem to be trending.

'We will tear off this sheet,' she said. However, she did not tear it then, but left the letter, which had been written in sections during several days, unfinished.

Ever since her coming to town in February, Desire had written such letters when she felt inclined. She did not always post them, it is true; sometimes she was ashamed of their inordinate length, sometimes she decided that that incident was closed, and it would be kinder, more sensible and more dignified to leave it alone. At other times she posted them, this was most usually when she had lately heard from Peter. He had written occasionally since she had left Twycross, but not very often. When he wrote he answered her letters, told her what had happened, what was happening, sometimes what he thought, generally rather shortly but always exactly as if he had been speaking to her. When the letters came she did not think the incident closed, she did not think about it one way or the other.

There had not been a letter for a long time now, two months or more; and the lengthy epistle she wrote during the idle days at Vichy was hardly written really to Peter. It was more to amuse herself and for the sake of talking freely to somebody, even if it was merely a paper person. In spite of that it reflected her present life and her attitude towards it well. She had left Twycross more than six months, and with her joint faculty for adapting herself to circumstances and circumstances to herself, she was by now fitted into her present surroundings as well as she could be. It is true that where things rubbed at first they rubbed still, and where she, or they, originally fell short, they fell still, and seemed likely to. It is true also, as the long letter indicated, that a good deal that had before formed the greater part of her life, had lost its savour. But then there were other things to take the empty place, fresh interests, different people with different aims. Whatever she had lost, she had not lost her capacity for extracting enjoyment out of unexpected things, and momentarily losing herself in all manner of interests. She was usually in a cheerful frame of mind, her aptitude for fixing her attention on the lights was not diminished. At Vichy it was the same with her as elsewhere, and she contrived to enjoy herself. There were several people there who amused her, one or two she liked; Julian Lee, too, came for a day or two; he was passing through to somewhere, he said, where, did not appear, and she did not bother him to invent it. The fact that she had not heard from Peter for two months did not keep her awake at nights or interfere with her appetite; she put it out of her mind three-quarters of the time, the other quarter—that concerned nobody. One must be allowed to shut the door on one's self and one's feelings occasionally.

The long letter, which related Desire's most recent happenings, was broken off the day Lee came. It was left neglected for a day or two; indeed, until she chanced upon it when she was turning over her writing things for an address. The closely written sheets fell out then, and Lee picked them up as they fluttered to the grass.

'I didn't know you were such a correspondent,' he said.

'Didn't you?' she answered, folding them together. 'I'm really rather a remarkable one, a merciful one; I don't send it all when I spread myself on paper.'

And she tore off the last sheet as she spoke. 'I always let people down easily if I can,' she said. 'Ah, the post!' This as she sighted the postman. 'Let's hope somebody has done the same by me.'

There were several letters for her, but, so far as Lee could see, no-one excited her interest more than another. 'Have you got anything amusing to read?' she asked. 'I am sure to have, and then I'm dull company.'

She lighted a cigarette and proceeded to examine her correspondence leisurely; the letter she paid the compliment of keeping till the last was from her newest friend, the shop assistant. That, she was sure, would be interesting, though, he was only likely to have written to tell her of the welfare of some protegé she had commended to his notice. But when she opened it she experienced something of a shock; before she had more than half read it she gave an exclamation of dismay.

'Oh!' she said. 'What have I done?'

Lee looked up with anxious sympathy, but she did not heed him; she had returned to her letter and was scanning it hastily, distress growing in her face.

'What a dreadful thing!' she said. 'How can I have come to do it? How could I?'

'What is it?' Lee asked. 'Is anything the matter? Can I be of any help?'

She looked at him as if she were suddenly made aware of his forgotten presence. 'I've done a dreadful thing!' she said, as much to herself as him. 'It's my fault, of course. It is always more or less a woman's fault, isn't it, when, man asks her to marry him?'

Lee's face relaxed; he had never before seen Desire distressed, and he had, for the moment, feared it must be some great calamity to have moved her so. The relief showed in his face, also the surprise, he was far from understanding the woman who had bewitched him. 'Is that all?' he said.

'All!' she returned. 'Enough, too. You don't know the case. I wouldn't have had this happen for a good deal.'

Lee accepted the rebuke with meekness. 'I'm awfully sorry it's upset you,' he said sympathetically. 'I had no idea these things cut you up so.'

In spite of herself Desire laughed a little. 'They don't,' she confessed; 'not always, but this is exceptional. This man doesn't exactly belong, it was a difficult thing for him to do, clearly it was, nothing but desperation made him—and it's everything in the world to him, I mean it seems to matter so frightfully.'

She took up the letter with a little shiver. 'I'm not worth any one's caring like that,' she said. 'I shouldn't satisfy anyone really, certainly not one who doesn't really know me. It's awful to have people care when you are not worth it.'

Lee wisely refrained from any comment on the disjointed remarks, except an acquiescence he did not entirely feel. He watched covertly as she took up the forgotten cigarette and smoked hard in evident perturbation of mind.

'It'll be nasty to answer, that letter?' he suggested, after a little.

'Nasty? It'll be almost impossible! Whatever I say, however I put it, he is bound to believe I think him presumptuous, and don't think him good enough, and all that.'

'Well, I don't suppose he is,' the American remarked comfortably.

'He is,' Desire retorted, forgetting that she had excluded him from any knowledge of the writer's identity; 'besides, what does position and that matter? Good Lord!' her changing voice rang suddenly as with passion. 'If you loved anybody it wouldn't matter who they were or what they were, would it?'

Lee looked at her meditatively. 'No,' he answered; 'I should say not.' Fortunately she missed the personal allusion; she was turning over the letter.

'It's so humble and yet somehow so proud,' she said miserably. 'He states his prospects and his income quite frankly—says we could just do on it, and then talks about the gap between us! He says he never forgot it. Just as if I didn't know that, as if he wasn't making it plain all the time, making it gruesomely plain now in showing that it counts as anything to him. It wouldn't count a snap of the fingers to me if I cared!'

Lee looked up sharply, he suddenly guessed who the writer was. That is to say he got within range of the truth and decided he must be a man not in her original set, one of those with whom she had been doing philanthropic or other work. And in spite of his American birth he resented it, it was in his eyes presumptuous for such an one to address Desire. However, he had the sense not to say so, perceiving that she evidently considered that, when a man asked a woman to marry him, and offered her the best he had to give, he was paying her the greatest compliment in his power, and honouring her—no matter what his position might be, or hers either.

'Well,' he said, 'if, as he says, he didn't forget his position, and misunderstand your kindness, you can't blame yourself for what has happened.'

'But I do,' Desire said. 'My step-mother told me long ago that I misled men more than any woman she had ever met.'

'That's because they want to be misled,' Lee assured her.

She did not agree, but he maintained that it was so. 'It's like this,' he said, 'about every second man you meet falls more or less in love with you, if he has anything much to do with you. Don't feel compelled to modestly deny it, it's approximately true, though I may be a trifle out in the figures. A few of them think you care a bit for them, they mistake your way—and you have got a way of going headlong into a fellow's affairs that's flattering. But it isn't love and nobody in his senses thinks it is; only some few do think, "if she takes that interest in me I shall be able to bamboozle her into swallowing me whole". But most of them don't think much about it, they fall in love with you because they can't help it. It kind of makes a man's arm ache to keep it still all evening when he's sitting next to you. And to keep on hearing "friend talk" in your voice—well, it makes a man dream at nights—and not dream about friends. You can't help it, and we can't—don't—want to, but it always will be so. You'll never be able to be much with men, certainly not work with them, without that sort of thing being liable to happen. Some fellows may have the sense not to tell you, that's the main difference, the feeling is the same with most of them, however the sense may be.'

'Thank you,' Desire said; 'I'm immensely obliged to you for explaining it all so clearly; the only weak point is that you're judging the rest of the world by yourself and—isn't that a little hard on the world?'

Lee smiled but glanced towards the open letter. 'I guess there's a certain family resemblance between a good many of us where you're concerned,' he said.

Desire flushed a little, but next moment put a question.

'You don't think a man ever cared for my sou—for what I'm pleased to call my mind?' she asked. 'You don't think there ever was a man who liked the intangible part of me only, who—whose "arm didn't ache" when he was with me, who rather wanted to see a good lot of me but never wanted to touch me?'

Lee shook his head. 'No,' he said; 'can't be done.'

'You think not?' she smiled triumphantly. 'Then you're wrong, there is such an one.'

He shrugged his shoulders. 'Did he tell you so?' he asked with significance.

'No, but I know it,' she answered; 'I know his mind as he knows mine, you see. Oh, I don't suspect you of that sort of thing,'—her tone changed to lightness again—'you've expressed how you feel and judged the rest by yourself. Fortunately time'll soon cure all that. Old age approaches me and then even your gallantry won't suggest—'

> 'Time cannot change her,
> Nor custom stale her infinite variety,'

Lee quoted. 'It's no good; look your own experience fairly in the face and you'll see it. You are dangerous goods and you always will be.'

Desire declined to look at her experiences or anyone else's. 'Shall we talk about the weather?' she said. 'It'll be a more interesting subject.'

'There is no subject so interesting,' he assured her; 'you are the most fascinating subject I know, and the most dangerous—and you will be till you are safely married.'

She promptly and emphatically denied it.

But all the same his words struck a new note in her mind—the wisdom of marriage for other reasons besides worldly advancement, the safety and settlement in it and the comparative peace and satisfaction in its finality. Lady Quebell had always advocated marriage for Desire's own advantage. Lee, quickly perceiving the value of his opportunity, began to advocate it on every other plea and for every one else's advantage except her own. And Desire ridiculed everything—and listened.

'But,' she objected at last, 'supposing I were married—oh, we'll say to you, as it's the only person you will admit into the argument—do you suppose all the wonderful things you described would leave off happening? You think people would leave off falling in love?'

'They'd leave off telling you so,' Lee said, 'at least the more decent ones, the ones you care about hurting, would. And they'd all of them have less reason and less excuse for mistaking your meaning, and less opportunity generally for making fools of themselves. I really believe you'd be happier and more comfortable married, and I'm perfectly certain it'd be better for everyone else.'

'Including you? Oh, my poor man, little do you know what you're saying! I like you immensely, but I don't love you a scrap. I find you a most useful, a most comfortable person, but I should never dream of changing my spots for you or obeying you, or, on your account, going any way but my own, and that, do you know what that spells in matrimony for people like me?—destruction.'

'I'm open to risking it,' Lee said, 'and I rather believe you'd better. It'd be a heap better for a lot of fellows if you did. Oh, not the mind man, of course it wouldn't make any difference to him! Being mind he doesn't want to marry you, and you don't want to marry him, minds don't marry, they're like the angels. But matter does, and—well, why not take me for the mundane side of things and the good of your fellow-men?'

There were many reasons why not, Desire said; she stated them, mostly with a lightness which made it hard to tell how much she meant. He answered them, however, and though he did not apparently convince her, he believed that his cause was advanced.

He left her when she told him she must answer the distressing letter that day. He rather fancied that re-reading it and facing the difficulties of an answer would argue in his favour quite as strongly as he could himself. And no doubt he was right, she found refusing this proposal an extremely difficult and very distressing thing; she shrank from the thought of the pain she was giving, the false impression she was creating, and also from the idea that such a thing might occur again. She told herself the last was impossible, but past experience, honestly faced, did not bear that out. Painful things had befallen before, not the least painful the affair of her engagement to Gore and its ending. Painful things, as this unexpected passion of a man with whom she had only thought to work befell now. She was a little weary, more than a little weary, and perhaps a trifle afraid; since a certain Saturday night in February she had better understood the power of passion.

And Peter? She had acted lovers with him to serve her own purpose, she had worked with him to serve hers and his too; he had helped her in trouble and taken her help, he had shared home and life with her; but, as Lee said, he had no part nor lot in the matter. They had lived together in frank intimacy, they had sat together by the dying mother, they had knelt together in the lonely chapel in the hills, they knew each other intimately, but physically they did not touch. She had secretly wished that some man should forget her body and be drawn to her mind and soul. One had: that was all. It was an interlude, no more, a dream—and one does not live in dreams. It behoves one, rather, to live as little ill as one may, as little hurtfully in a world where there is no dream glamour, though still a good deal of ordinary sunshine for those who are wise enough to pick it out and not cry for the radiance of the gods' world in this place of men.

How much of this Lee guessed is not certain, he probably had some idea of the conclusions if not much knowledge of the way they were arrived at. At all events he knew enough of the trend of Desire's feelings to press his suit with discretion when favourable opportunity offered during the time he was at Vichy. When he left he carried with him a belief that, sooner or later, she would marry him. She had not said so; with a caution rather unusual in her she had not committed herself at all, but he believed that she would eventually do it if for the comfort and general sensibleness and peace of the arrangement.

It is possible other people thought so too, at all events Miss Quebell showed an unusual interest in Lee's going, and the possible time of his coming again.

'He returns in three days," Desire told her with a smile—she guessed the reason of her cousin's interest. 'He asks me then, if he thinks the moment good; to marry him; if he thinks the moment bad, he holds his peace. He is no fool, is our friend Julian, he seldom bores one inopportunely.'

'Are you going to marry him?' Miss Quebell asked in her definite tones. Hers was a definite mind, and a definite world, all blacks and whites and prearranged plans; not unnaturally Desire was somewhat beyond its radius.

'Am I going to marry him because he doesn't bore me?' Desire said. 'That's rather a good reason for marrying a man, I own—one of the best.'

'The best reason,' Miss Quebell returned rather severely, 'used to be considered because you loved him, and because he was in a proper position to marry you.'

'Oh, that!' Desire said, 'that's asking too much, you know. Love is unreason, it's glamour, romance; you can't expect to love a proper position and a goodly number of thousands a year; you like them, esteem them, admire and appreciate them—but love—why, it's a little naked thing; it hasn't anything to do with common sense.'

'You haven't much,' Miss Phoebe observed grimly. 'Then you don't love this man, is that what you mean?'

'Of course not,' Desire answered. 'Why, I'm approaching twenty-eight, also I have lived, yes, considerably; one can't expect romantic emotion at my age and experience. I like the man much, I know him, and he, more or less, knows me; we shouldn't have many unpleasant surprises for each other if we did marry; indeed, we should rather start where lover-people arrive after six months' mixed experience, so if we skipped the rapture, such as it is, we'd skip the descent to earth likewise. There are very decided advantages in marrying Julian Lee.'

Miss Quebell nodded; she thought so too. To marry Desire to a wealthy and eminently eligible husband, besides being a satisfactory settlement of Sir Joseph's daughter, would be an occasion for triumph over Lady Quebell, who had first failed in the attempt and afterwards cast out the subject of failure. Lee had a strong supporter in Miss Quebell, and one who knew the wisdom of not pressing his claim unduly.

'Well, well,' Desire conceded at last, 'I shouldn't wonder if I had to marry him in the end; it looks as if I should have to marry someone, and he really is a pleasant person.'

Miss Quebell, well satisfied, departed to her room. It was quite early, not much after eight o'clock, but part of her cure, also all her inclination, was to go to bed at astonishingly early hours.

She had been gone something more than half-an-hour, and was, no doubt, in her first sleep, when a telegram was brought to Desire. It had been sent, in the first instance, to Brunswick Square, and repeated on from there. It was for Desire herself, from Twycross; very brief.

'There is trouble.—Robert.'

So Desire read, and rose up as she read.

'I shall be leaving by the night train,' she said to the servant who had brought the telegram. 'See about a conveyance for me, will you please, and send one of the chambermaids to my room at once; Miss Quebell's maid is out. Yes, I shall have time—half-an-hour.'

Chapter XXI

Mrs Alexander Grimstone had a grievance; that, in itself was not uncommon, but this time it was founded on fact. Alexander had allowed her to accept an invitation for them both to go to Stoke, to go to the theatre with some friends, and afterwards stay the night, and now he said he could not get away. Mrs Alexander wept from pure disappointment, and said as much as she dared about the way Alexander put business before everything and cared nothing for her or for their friends' convenience or any one. All of which, though perfectly true, was not in the least likely to affect Alexander. He did not so much as trouble to contradict it, he merely reminded her, somewhat curtly, that he had not said she should not go to Stoke, only that he should not; that she certainly was to go, as he had no use for her here, in fact, he'd be glad to have her gone if she was in that frame of mind. Whereupon Mrs Alexander dried her eyes and wrote immediately to her friend, telling her to get some other man in place of Alexander, who could not come. This was eventually done, to the improvement of the party—Alexander was one of those people who decidedly improve a party by staying away from it.

So it befell that on a certain Tuesday late in September, Mrs Alexander, with her best blouse and all her bracelets packed in a dressing-bag, went to Stoke, and Alexander stayed late at his office. He was busy, of course, he always had plenty to do; but not so busy, apparently, as he had led his wife to suppose. Not too busy, at all events, to sit for a little with no other occupation than his toothpick and his thoughts. He was thinking of Grimstones', of course; the vertical line between his brows usually meant that he was thinking of the old firm and the way it had failed to do what he had expected, and the way he himself had failed in this matter. Here was September again, and almost a year since he had come to live at Twycross; almost eighteen months since Peter had been sole master at Grimstones', and still the old firm stood where it had done. No, it stood a good deal better than it had done for many years, it had prospered wonderfully in spite of all Alexander's efforts.

How and why? For a long time Alexander had not been able to find out, then at last he picked up a clue. Grimstones' took orders for certain shaped ware at a price lower than other people's; they took largish orders for that, but let other things go, and apparently, in spite of the price, made a good profit. They must have some trick or secret process for manufacturing these articles; a trick was not in Peter's line, but a secret process might be. Alexander knew something of the curious stupidity of inventors, he had profited by it before now. Peter, stupid as he judged him to be, might still have invented some good process. If he had he had not patented it, Alexander easily informed himself on that point; he was probably working it as a secret, a thing he could very easily do seeing the nature of the men who were still all he employed.

It was in July that Alexander had been finally convinced of this. And no sooner was he convinced than he at once set to going further into it. Nothing was to be learnt from the men he knew by past experience, so, without hesitation, he paid a second nocturnal visit to Grimstones'; this time it was to the yard, not the house. He remembered the old ways of the place perfectly well, it was not likely any one so conservative as Peter would have altered them. The gates used always to be locked, certainly, but nothing else was; one might easily come by way of the canal and effect an entrance pretty well anywhere—though, it is true, there never had been anything much worth the trouble of carrying away. Alexander had naturally no thought of carrying away, but a look round, he felt, would be very useful to him, a careful examination was likely to give him the clue to Peter's secret process. A few notes, a diagram if there was much machinery in it, would enable him to go home and probably work out something very similar. He had no inventive genius himself, but he had a great faculty for grasping another man's idea, and reconstructing it with just sufficient variation as to make a thing nominally different. He had done so more than once, to his own advantage, with inventions which had been submitted to him; he intended to do so with Peter's secret. And if it was not possible to arrive at something sufficiently different from Peter's process to pass, he could still 'invent' that, unknown to the original inventor, patent it; and leave Peter, the original inventor, the expensive business of fighting for his own idea, if he could. And whichever way the case went no-one, not even Peter, would be able to prove the coincidence of the identity of the two processes was other than accident.

Unfortunately for him, however, he was not able to carry out this plan when he made it in July. The night he went to the yard was hot, and Paddy, contrary to his usual custom, had chosen to sleep outside. The consequence of which was that he disturbed the dog, and the dog disturbed the household, and nothing was gained that night. He had, of course, taken vengeance on the dog as soon afterwards as he conveniently could; but Peter, in the meantime, got strong locks for all the outhouses, and even had bars fixed to the window of the one substantial shed, where it was easy to guess the secret process was carried on.

Thus things had been through the summer. But Alexander was not beaten; he had never been beaten except once—his face had a way of turning curiously greyish whenever he thought of that once. He was still bent on seeing what Peter did, and how he did it; but it was clear to him now that the thing he wanted was the loan of the key. He did not like taking other people into his plans, but needs must sometimes; it was the least risky thing, in fact, the only thing, for a man who wanted to get information quietly. There was one person in Grimstones' to whom he had not before made overtures—this because he believed him to be too stupid to be any use; but in the matter of the key he was the very man. Bolt, he remembered, was stupid, but he would be also cunning; he was surly and dull, but also entirely untouched by gratitude, loyalty, or any of the other unreasonable sentiments which occasionally sway men to their own disadvantage. Bolt was the man to borrow the key for a price; to leave it in some safe place where one who knew could find it, and to take it again from that place when it was done with, and before anyone else was the wiser. And Bolt was precisely the sort of person who need be no trouble after to Alexander, who was not one to be sold by an accomplice of any but extraordinary brilliancy, and not lightly even by such a one. Every man had his price, though, as Alexander had found out during the last year; it was not necessarily a money one. Bolt had his; it would be a money one.

So Alexander sat that September evening picking his teeth and thinking, but the thoughts were not altogether unpleasant ones; indeed, his face wore a look of some satisfaction when he put away his toothpick and returned to work.

It was very late when he left the office; there was no late train out to Twycross except the London mail which stopped there after two in the morning; usually, when Alexander was kept by work in the pottery town, he stayed the night at the rooms he had there. Tonight, however, he elected to come by the mail. People at Twycross retired early; they had all long been in bed when Alexander came out of the station road. There was absolutely no-one about; no-one saw him turn to the left when he reached the main road, instead of going downhill to the right and to the town. No-one saw him pass the few darkened houses that bordered it, and take the elm-edged lane which led steeply upward from the town and to the old high road. The road, white and winding, was quite empty; in the darkness one could still see it dimly far ahead; he followed it, and for some considerable way. Past the group of mountain ash, whose berried branches rustled in the wind; past the lonely grey house, where one lighted window told where Ezra Grimstone still lay helpless and unconscious of all that befell. The night was moist, yet breezy, with a fitful wind that shook the hidden gorse-bushes now and then; starless, too, and overcast with clouds that threatened rain before long. In spite of the dark, one could make out the whiteness of the road, and even the way it became rougher as it grew higher; make out, also, a loose stone wall that here bordered it, and at one point a solitary stone post standing. The gate originally affixed to this had long since fallen from it; the top, too, had at some time been knocked off, leaving a hollowed end on which a large stone was balanced. There was a gap under the stone—one could not see it tonight, but one could find it, if one knew where to feel. Apparently Alexander knew.

And Peter? What of Peter during the months that had elapsed since Desire went away? Principally he had worked; there was nothing else for him to do. There was plenty of that certainly, and he did plenty. He was very strong, a magnificent constitution entirely unabused; physically he was never tired, mentally he accepted life as it was and said nothing. Throughout the spring and early summer, in all his margins of time, in the hours he had before devoted to his mother or spent with Desire, he had returned to the long-abandoned novel. Slowly it had grown under his hand; slowly and with infinite difficulty taking shape and becoming informed with life. Not perhaps quite the life he had planned in the days of hope when he began it, or the one he had striven for in the later days when hard necessity was compelling him to abandon it, but still life. Writing it was not at all easy to him; writing never had been easy to him, at the best it was slow building, a feeling things out. Now the time for it was in scraps, and the hand that wrote was often stiff and tired; now the glamour was all off, past hope and past desperation alike gone, only patience and persistence remaining. So the book was written, resurrected in the dead after-time, to burn a wan taper in a lonely place. Feeble at times, a little unsteady, for the writer was not sure of himself; but for all that a great book, great at heart, great in patience and tolerance, and the wisdom that counts. But the author did not know it, and the publisher who undertook to produce it did not tell him so. Indeed, he was by no means sure of it himself, nor sure the book was going to have a public worth mentioning; in this doubt events afterwards justified him. Even when it was all set up and ready he held it back a while, waiting a favourable opportunity for publishing. Peter did not mind, he was in no hurry to see it in print; it was the making he cared about and missed, though it had been nearly all suffering. That, he felt, he could not replace, it seemed to him then that no further book would ever be possible to him, not so much as a thought of one stirred in his brain now.

But the business prospered. In the work he had set himself to do he had succeeded beyond all expectation or hope. The success did not cause elation, he accepted such goods cautiously at best, and now there was no-one else to care; his mother was dead, his father, in spite of the daily rehearsal of what took place, did not really know, and Desire was not. For himself it mattered nothing. It is good to do what you do as well as you can, but of that well or ill you alone are judge, outside accidents of failure or success, of praise or blame, fame or money, are not much. Peter did as well as he could, and for the rest very little sufficed him.

And of Alexander, to whom success or failure meant much, and the prosperity or reverse of the firm much more still, he heard nothing. He did not imagine Alexander had forgotten or grown tired, or that the personal encounter of the winter had done other than point his previous impersonal enmity to the firm with an additional personal enmity to himself. Alexander, he knew, was only waiting, or else making attempts of which he did not hear, either because they were not successful or, more likely, because he himself was not clever enough to discover them in their early stages. Once and once only did he feel Alexander's hand, in late July when Paddy died. Peter was not at first quite sure whether to associate the dog's furious barking at some real or fancier intruder with Alexander. Three days later he knew, for the dog died. He was ill twenty-four hours, but it did not need the testimony of the veterinary surgeon to tell that it was poison, and it did not need anyone to tell Peter that it was Alexander. Whether it was for spite, or vengeance, or to further his own ends did not matter, Peter did not ask himself; the thing was done, that was all that mattered, and the one living, loving thing left in his bare life was taken from him. He sat with the dead dog's head where it had fallen on his knee, and his heart very full and very cold within him. For the first time Alexander had got a blow truly home, a subsidiary blow possibly, a mere necessary clearing of the ground to him perhaps, but one that touched to the quick. The insult to Desire, which had roused Peter to blows, had been avenged by blows, punished if not wiped out; the attack on the firm's credit and on their commercial position, though dishonourable according to Peter's standard, were Alexander's usual methods and in a way impersonal. But this—

'He might have left me this!' Peter inly cried, protesting against fate, as men who in silence take the big things and in silence choose the hard part, sometimes do protest when some one thing, small to others, comes upon them. Though, perhaps, it is not altogether a small thing when the only eyes that brighten at your coming are closed, the only thing that runs to meet you is still, the safe, silent, sympathetic, dumb comrade of bad times and good is gone, and you are alone.

Peter took the dead dog up the narrow hill path. It was for the last time, and he found the once active body very heavy before he reached the spot he had mentally chosen, a lonely place a little off the path. There he buried him one still, grey afternoon. A curious, rather a childish thing to do, perhaps, but all that he had loved and all that he had suffered, all he had ever cared for seemed to belong up there, and it seemed natural to him to bury the dog there. Afterwards he came down again alone. Alone on the hill path for the first time since he had come home two years ago; perhaps really alone for the first time in his life, for in the far-off time, before he went to town, he had carried hopes and ambitions to the hills, no mean company when a man is young. But now he was alone; alone in his goings out and his comings in, a sober man leading a sober life.

Through August and through September nothing happened, nothing unusual that Peter was aware of. He had had the locks all seen to the day after Paddy disturbed them, and Robert had installed a young collie as watch-dog before the fox terrier was cold. Peter said he did not think it was much use as, no doubt, the dog would also die if it were in the way. But Robert would have it, so the collie lived in the yard, recognizing the old man as master, and showing an amiable toleration of Peter.

Peter met him in the yard when he went round one night in late September. He always went the rounds before he went to bed now, making sure that everything was secure and all the doors really locked, as they were supposed to be when work was done.

He met Robert as he came into the house again. 'Is it all right?' the old man asked.

'Yes,' Peter answered, then added, 'Why?'

'I don't like the looks of things,' Robert said.

Peter, who knew him and his usual outlook, was not disturbed. 'What things?' he asked without curiosity.

'Bolt,' Robert answered. 'You can believe me or not as you like, but it's true, James saw him and Alexander talking together three days ago.'

James, like many virtuous persons, had rather a faculty for seeing and reporting disquieting things, many of which came to nothing; this one Peter regarded as more surprising than dangerous.

'Is that so?' he said. 'I shouldn't think that would be much good to Alexander.'

'Why not?' Robert demanded. 'Bolt's a fool but Alexander isn't. I don't like the looks of it when a knave gets making up to a fool—there's such a thing as cat's paw.'

'Yes,' Peter allowed, 'but I don't think Bolt will be applying for that situation to Alexander.'

'And why not, pray?'

'Because he hates him,' Peter said. 'I don't know why, but he does.'

'He don't like him,' Robert allowed, 'same as a good many people don't; but what's that? Nothing. He don't like the old master, nor you, nor anybody else. He's got his own game to play, same as another.'

Peter shrugged his shoulders. 'Maybe,' he said, though he was not convinced. 'Anyhow, I don't think we need be uneasy, there's no harm he can do.' With that he turned to fasten the back door.

'Is Mary gone to bed yet?' he asked.

She was not, she was still with her master. Since Mrs Grimstone's death she had practically taken over care of the invalid; a young girl, a relation of hers, and likely, according to custom, to be affianced to James, being engaged to help her in the household. Peter relieved the old woman at times and spent most of his spare time in his father's room; much of the novel had been written there, the stricken man never showing any consciousness of his presence or occupation. He went upstairs now.

'Master's restless to-night,' Mary said, as he entered the room; 'he's not himself.'

Peter said he would leave the door between the rooms open when he went to bed. 'I'll stop awhile now, if you think it better,' he added; 'I'm not sleepy.'

The old woman made a show of hesitation, then acquiesced with that touch of condescension a nurse always has for one who takes her place and Mary had always had for Peter. 'You can call me, if he wants anything,' she said, putting some finishing touches to the room for the night.

Peter said he would, wished her good-night, and then sat down near the bed with a book.

The room, a large one, was for the most part in shadow, the only strong light was within the circle of the shaded lamp; but still one could see the outline of the inanimate figure. It was not quite inanimate, though, to-night; the fingers jerked feebly now and then, and there was an occasional spasmodic twitching of one leg; it was this which Mary had described as restlessness. Peter noted it, but he had seen it before, though he could not tell what it indicated or if it indicated anything at all.

For a while he read steadily, only now and then glancing towards the bed; but after a time he lost the thread of interest in what he read. For a little he sat looking at the still figure, seeing it and all it meant afresh and vividly, as men do occasionally re-see that to which they are completely used. Ezra Grimstone had lain thus for eighteen months now, alive, but to all intents and purposes dead; a strong man bound, locked in impregnable silence; a man who had not learnt to bend, broken. Peter was used to the sight; he had borne his part in Mrs Grimstone's pathetic play that the mind was not gone, and the man, as man, not dead; he had helped her to try and soften the blow to the thing which could no longer feel. But tonight it came home to him afresh and with grim tragicness. Such a fate for a man like Ezra Grimstone, who had never asked for more than to work and then die; who would have scornfully rejected leisured age or any half-gift of modified life. To live on in a world to which he was dead, to lie helpless where he had ruled, to know nothing where everything had been in his control—it was awful! But far more awful still if he did know, if the mind lived speechless in the dead body, and to living death was added the consciousness of death! God, in His goodness, forbid it!

But Peter was not sure—not unsure of the goodness of God; far down in the quiet places of his mind was a certainty of that, unshakable, inexpressible, a part of himself. But he was not sure whether his own reading of 'goodness' was aright. He could not be the sort of writer he was without being aware in himself that the creator's scheme of things must be vastly greater than the creature's view of it, and that it is idle for one who stands in the fog-bound midst to judge of one who holds the beginnings and ends. So he was not sure that the conscious mind was absolutely gone, and once again that night he leaned forward to the familiar face, grim still in overthrow, seeking the sign he did not wish to see. But there was no change; the eyes, half hid under the lowered lids, saw nothing and told nothing, lightened only when the lamp flickered, darkened only when an unseen shadow swayed.

Yet Peter did not feel inclined to leave him that night, but sat there reading awhile longer—indeed, until he dropped asleep over his book. It was an uneasy sleep, conscious of any sound and troubled by dreams. He dreamt he saw the sick man stir and move, and gradually, very slowly, rise upright; he was long doing it, and Peter himself seemed to have no part in the affair, he merely looked on as from a distance as his father slowly assumed his old position and his old authority. He would speak soon, Peter knew it subconsciously—he opened his mouth. Peter was not in the least surprised, he only wondered, with the same remote curiosity, what he was going to say. For a second no words came, the voice was rusty from want of use, then—Then Peter woke.

Instinctively he looked towards the bed; the inanimate figure lay as before, the silence of the room was intense, unbroken, except when the wind fingered the window pane—and yet he felt there was something. It could not be only the influence of the dream, it must be something else—there was, yes, there was some subtle, almost imperceptible, change. He rose quickly and came to the bedside—and the half-closed eyes followed him!

It was no trick of lamplight, no hallucination surviving from the dream; the eyes moved and saw, living eyes in the dead face that lay a wax-like mask on the pillow.

'Father!' Peter said.

There was no speech or sign in reply, only the eyes sought his with a burning eagerness, the quick imperiousness of one who has little time and much to say, the impotent impatience of one who fears his chance is slipping from him.

'What is it?' Peter asked, grasping suddenly that what was to be said must be said now, and what done done now and without delay. 'What is it? Who? My mother? Alexander?'

The pupils of the dark eyes contracted at the last word, and hatred, strong as a passion of strongest mankind, shot up in them. The answering chord was touched, they said so eloquently, somewhat awfully too, seeing what chord it was that had called the conscious soul back from the shadow.

'Yes, I understand,' Peter said; 'it is about Alexander. Something you want me to do or prevent him from doing? Try and tell me.'

He bent down, his shadow spreading black and large across the ceiling. The room was full of black shadows and of a grim silence that mocked at the speechless man. The muscles of the throat moved. It was like the dream, but worse—for now in the reality the body lay still and dead, only the soul lived and looked out fierce and staring through the eyes. The man swallowed as if he were getting ready to speak, words almost visibly came to the surface—and halted in utter silence. It was as if the rage which months before had smitten him down, choked him. Peter bent lower, he felt that by listening he must catch some whisper from the imprisoned soul; but there was no sound, only the rustle of the wind without. He put his hands on the numb hands and looked deep into the shadowy eyes. They looked back at him tragic in their futile eloquence, fierce with passion, burning with some warning to give, some fear to share. And Peter could not understand and they knew he could not. Under his gaze the passion grew, the fierce emotion welled up, till the sheer indomitable will of the man triumphed and for a moment mastered mortality. The mask face lifted three inches from the pillow, the straining throat moved convulsively, and a sound came from the dumb lips—a beast-like, meaningless, inarticulate sound, which broke despairingly and sank to silence.

Peter bent over the bed. 'Father!' he said.

But there was no response, no flicker of light in the eyes, the spirit which had informed them was gone; only the breath came feeble and fluttered, telling of a semblance of life that lingered.

The doctor who attended Ezra Grimstone always regarded him as an interesting case. He had given it as his opinion that the patient might die in convulsions, or he might have a return to incomplete consciousness and die an idiot, or—more likely—he might slip quietly away with no change from his comatose state. That there should be even a momentary return to reason was the one thing he believed unlikely; yet that, it seemed, was what happened. The doctor did not himself see it—he wished he had—but he did not doubt Peter Grimstone's word, nor did he ascribe the idea to fancy on his part. The Grimstones were not, in his opinion, people to fancy things, and Peter's bare and circumstantial account was good enough evidence to him.

'Temperament,' was his judgment; 'possibly it had as much to do with it as physique. He must have been a tough customer when he was set on anything, not often balked, till now. By Jove! A bit gruesome to die with your mouth shut, and something to be said stuck in your throat!'

This remark was made to Robert, as he led the way downstairs in the chilly dawn.

It was nearly five then, the doctor had been there three hours, useless hours so far as he or another could do anything, but he was keen on his profession, and he would willingly have waited another three hours for the chance of seeing the phenomenon of a momentary return of reason. He had not seen it, there had been no return, no awakening, no sign of pain; the mask of silence which Ezra Grimstone had often chosen to wear of himself, and which of late Another had set so tightly on him, fitted close down. Self-contained and dumb he passed out of the world in the chill of the dawn.

Robert let the doctor out without answering his comment. In his way he had cared for the dead master; he had worked with him all his working life, withstood him at times it is true, abused and contradicted him, a cross-grained man but a loyal. And even though it may have been Grimstones' that had been the central core of his affections, Ezra, impotent and set aside as he had been, still in the old man's mind stood largely for it. So he said nothing; rather, he resented the doctor's words as an intrusion; what the dead man had to say must have concerned Grimstones' and was no affair of a stranger's; to die silent were better than to die talking before such. Robert shut the heavy door after the doctor as if he were shutting the outside world from the silent house.

'It's Alexander that killed him,' he said to Peter as they stood together on the landing.

Peter knew better; he knew that big things, and some little things, usually derive their origin from wider sources than one man only, and seldom from sources entirely untouched by self. He did not say so, however.

'It was Alexander,' Robert repeated. 'You say yourself it was Alexander he tried to tell you about.'

Peter nodded. 'He had been restless all the evening,' he said; 'it was almost as if he had something on his mind, something which grew till at last the effort to tell it brought the end.'

Robert grunted. 'Well, it was about Alexander,' he persisted. 'A warning. It's my belief he knew what we don't, and saw what we can't, the dying do when the Lord wills—it's a warning.'

He went away strong in his conviction, and Peter crossed the landing and went downstairs. There was nothing to be done now, and it was useless to go to bed. It occurred to him that he would go out into the yard and look across the canal as he had looked in the spring dawn when he had waited for the barge. He drew the bolts of the back door and went out. The wind had dropped, and the small rain which had fallen earlier had ceased. It was all very still and grey without. The yard looked curiously deserted in the pale light; it should have been deserted at that hour, of course; no-one should have been there except the collie. He was not there, it is true, but Peter did not notice, he had forgotten the animal's existence. He shivered a little as he stepped out, not so much with cold as with the sense of the loneliness which hangs over the working—or the playing-places of men in the dawn. He passed the first shed and the heap of old saggars; beyond was the building where the machine had been set up, the door looked towards the canal, one did not see it till one stood on the canal bank. Peter did not see it till he was down there, close to where the white mist floated; then he saw. The door stood open, a dark space in the wall, and on the threshold, darker still, something was lying—so quiet, quiet as the creeping mist, so still. A man who was lying face downwards, his head within the building, his feet on the threshold without—one was doubled a little under him, one in a pool left by last night's rain, and he never moved it though it was wet, the boot soaked through. Peter started forward, then stopped and stood quite still. His eye travelled slowly over the figure from the feet upward to the head which was within the building. The man was Alexander.

Chapter XXII

The finding of Alexander Grimstone's body in one of the buildings of his father's yard caused a sensation in Twycross. For a while the name of Grimstone was on every tongue, and the affairs of the family, usually little thought or spoken of, were freely discussed. Everyone knew that there was a business feud between the Grimstones, although its origin and extent were alike unknown, every one also knew there was a family feud too; at least there had been between the brothers, though the women of the family, according to Mrs Alexander Grimstone, and as represented by herself, were ready to make peace. And now on the very morning that Ezra Grimstone died his son Alexander was found dead near the house, and found by Peter.

Ezra Grimstone's death would have called for little comment, it had been long coming, so long that by now it could make little difference to any one; its interest lay in its happening when Alexander, the still unforgiven, was so near, and at a time so shortly before he too had died suddenly, if not violently, on the spot forbidden him by the father. Alexander's death, however, was the real interest. How had he died? Who was responsible? Was anyone responsible? Was Peter implicated? Was it accident or murder? The last word was repeated more than once, and not without some natural relish—to the great indignation of Dodd of Grimstones', who was at Twycross at the time of the inquest.

The good men and true, who very willingly served as jury on the occasion of the inquest, viewed the body carefully. They had not liked Alexander in life—it was not very easy to find anyone who had—but they were very interested in him in death. They listened to the medical evidence with attention, examined the only wound to be seen, and asked questions pertinent and otherwise.

Some points about the death were perfectly clear. Alexander Grimstone had died about four o'clock on Wednesday morning, the doctor who saw the body not two hours later gave that as his opinion, and there was no reason against it. Death had been caused by a blow on the head; the doctor's opinion again was unimpeachable, also common observation bore it out. The question was, was the blow accident or design? Evidence was rather in favour of accident. There was a pulley with weights affixed to a beam just over the door of the building where the body had been found. Some part of the tackle had become loosened, and one of the weights, which Robert deposed to having been in its place when he locked the shed the previous evening, had fallen, striking Alexander on the head. Could such a thing have happened of itself? The question was put by the foreman. Was it not necessary for someone to have touched it, either accidentally or not understanding the mechanism, or maliciously and on purpose to endanger one standing as Alexander was?

Robert's answer was surly and non-committal as usual. It might have happened of itself or it might not. The thing had not been used for some time, he could not say what condition it was in or how far it was secure. As for Alexander touching it by accident, it wasn't likely he had been such a fool, he mostly knew what he was about. As for anyone doing it maliciously, they'd have had to stand close to him to do it, they would also have had to time it very exactly; it would have been a difficult thing to do with any man, very difficult with one as sharp as Alexander, who was likely to have been additionally on the alert on such an occasion.

After that information everyone looked again at the weight, the presumed cause of death. It was still dabbled with blood and hair as it had been when found. One man, he was the least important present, asked if these compromising signs could not have been put there after death had occurred.

'Supposing,' said he, 'the deed had been done with some other instrument—I think the medical evidence supports me in saying that the blow might have been struck with any blunt and heavy thing? Supposing, I say, that a fatal blow had been struck from behind with something unknown, could not the murderer have deliberately disarranged the pulley and stained the weight as we now see it?'

He could, of course, every one perceived that; but, on the other hand, no-one thought it likely—partly because the ingenious idea had not originated in the first instance with any of themselves, and partly because such an explanation presupposed a cold-blooded callousness in the perpetrator and the possession of a brutal enemy by the dead man. They investigated the possibility to satisfy the unimportant man, but without faith and without much result. Medical evidence did not help; the doctors pronounced it quite impossible to say if the blood which adhered to the weight had been deposited at the moment of death or immediately after; but they evidently inclined to the former and simpler explanation. So did most other people; but at the same time they felt there were some mysteries here. Had an ordinary workman, or other person with business to be on the place, been found under such circumstances the verdict would have been quickly given. But these circumstances were exceptional. Alexander Grimstone had no business there; he was in an unauthorized place at an unauthorized time, presumably for an unauthorized purpose. His death by accident in such circumstances was extraordinary; it partook rather of the nature of drastic poetic justice, and it seemed necessary to inquire into several things. For instance, was it possible to find out why he was in such a place at such a time?

It was, Peter knew, or at least could guess, and the jury learnt.

They were much interested, and, being all more or less mixed up in the pottery trade, not least in Peter's acknowledged possession of a secret process. This, by the way, he had already taken steps to patent, foreseeing that it must become known. They could not, however, whatever their wishes, ask him much about it; they asked instead, with some severity—although to a man they were personally convinced of Alexander's guilt—why Peter should suspect his brother of such an action.

Peter told them of the previous entry attempted by someone and frustrated by the dog.

They asked if there had been no barking this time, and why, under the circumstances, he should think it the same person.

Peter said that the dog who barked before had been poisoned two days after that attempt; and the collie who watched the yard now had been destroyed the night when Alexander entered.

The jury looked wise over this and suggested several theories as to how the collie died; then, brought back to the point, wanted to know if Peter had no other reason for suspecting his brother.

Peter, with a reluctance he concealed, told of Alexander's entrance into the house itself last year. The jury were profoundly interested by this; they were also impressed that the quarrel between the Grimstone brothers was of a much more acute order than they had ever known. Acute enough for almost anything to have happened, each man thought it, but could not on that account implicate Peter in the present business. Possibly, fortunately for him, his doings during Tuesday night and Wednesday morning could all be known, every hour accounted for. Owing to his father's death he was up all night, and not alone at all since midnight; up till which hour, indeed after it, Alexander was known to have been alive.

Peter, it was clear, could have had no hand in Alexander's not inconvenient death. Had anyone else?

There were footsteps about the door of the building where the body was found. But the ground was soft and had been for several days; there would be prints of Alexander's feet and of the men who had worked there during the previous day as well as the prints of any other who came after Alexander—if there were such a one; there was nothing to be learnt from the prints. There was one other line of inquiry and one other puzzle of considerable interest and possible importance—who knew that Alexander was in that place at that time? If murdered he had been, his murderer must have been in possession of that piece of information, he would not himself have come to that unlikely place by chance. Alexander was in the habit of keeping his affairs very much to himself; so far as it was possible to learn he had told no-one of his intention that Tuesday. His movements that night had been traced up to the time he left Twycross Station; from then on no-one seemed to have seen him. It was possible, of course, that he was followed from there to his father's yard, and there struck down for some reason unknown; but it was extremely unlikely, if for no other reason than that the chances were very largely in favour of his discovering his follower before that.

Someone, however, must have been aware that he was likely to go to the yard; someone, at all events, had supplied him with the key of the building where he met his death.

But all inquiries failed to reveal who. Robert had locked up as usual that evening, he swore to it, and the keys, on a string, had been put just inside the office. Peter had put them away some half-hour later; he had not counted them, the particular one might have been missing then, he did not know; when he went round at ten that night he did not use them, the doors were all fastened, he had no occasion to try the keys or to examine them minutely.

The next question was, who had been in the office between the time of Robert's placing the keys there and of Peter's putting them away?

Possibly any or all of the few people connected with the work, or even the household. The door leading to the house, though shut, was not fastened, and the door opening on to the yard stood open, Peter was not there and every one was about for a little. Robert had locked up in a peremptory manner before the rest were quite ready to go; he often did, he liked his own way in this as in other matters, and as he locked up when he thought fit he frequently had to wait to fasten the yard gate after the others. He did that evening, busying himself clearing up by the canal out of sight of the office, while he waited. The yard key? It was never put with the rest, but hung on a nail in the kitchen, as it always had hung the last fifty years, where it was always likely to hang so long as Robert lived. In point of time and opportunity any one of five people might have taken the key which somehow reached Alexander that night; the line of inquiry now pursued was, who could have conveyed it to him in the time? Not either of the two women of the household, their movements could all be accounted for. Nor Robert, he had not left the house or spoken to an outsider till he went after midnight to fetch the doctor to his old master. Not James, he went directly he left work to Shurthorpe with Dodd, who had been at Twycross that day. They travelled together to that small town where both lived, and then each went his separate way; Dodd spent the evening at a sing-song; James at a school of languages: both returned to their homes in good time. And, thanks to the railway, neither could have returned late to Twycross even had they wished, except by road, a somewhat difficult feat as James did not bicycle and Dodd had strained his knee and could not.

There remained only Bolt, and Bolt had spent the evening and night with his cousin, the hill blacksmith. He had fallen out with his grandmother that morning, and so, instead of going home to her after work, he went to the forge; spent the evening there, and slept there with the blacksmith who, like himself, preferred a sack among the warm ashes to any bed yet made. No, he had not sold Alexander the key. Alexander, it is true, had sounded him about it quite lately, only last week. He had likely sounded most of them some time; Bolt didn't know about the others, but for himself he had no fancy for Alexander, he didn't trust him and he wasn't for having any truck with him. Bolt's testimony could not be shaken any more than the others' could. James and Dodd had seen him start up the hill road when he left work, and when they took the road to the town. His cousin, the blacksmith, corroborated his statement of when he arrived at the forge, and how he spent the night there.

It was curious, it was mysterious even, and more than probable, though it could not be brought home, that someone was lying about the key, but it was fairly clear that no-one in Grimstones' could actually have given it to Alexander. And, however much one of them might have been morally responsible for his somehow getting it, it was shown impossible that that one, or any other of them, could have been near the place at the time of, or any way concerned in the death, which, after all, was the sole business of the inquest. The coroner, having reminded the jury of this, and also that they were expected to give a verdict on facts, not fancies, they, after a little deliberation, gave one of 'Accidental Death.'

Thus the inquest ended, and in time those concerned came out. They came in twos mostly, some stood a minute to talk, some, not important people, gave details to those who had had to be content with waiting outside during the proceedings. The four men belonging to Grimstones' went their ways with the stolid, impervious sort of look which they always seemed to have for the outside world. An old lawyer, looking after them with some admiration, speculated as to which among them had done the hard swearing and who had handled the affair of the key. But, he recognized it plainly, that was not a thing likely ever to be known.

But there he was wrong, someone did eventually know. But that someone was not a lawyer or a juryman considering evidence, but a woman who jumped to a conclusion by the light of her own intuitions. She was one, however, who had the advantage of understanding something about the hill people, their endurance in friendship and enmity, the primitiveness of their code of rights and wrongs, and of their clan feeling. One who not only knew Bolt, but who had also seen the taciturn hill blacksmith and judged him to be a man to be relied on at a pinch. Desire Quebell, when all that has been told was repeated to her, guessed the perjurer. But with singular reticence for her she kept the guess to herself; such a suspicion, when you don't want a prosecution, is not a thing to be lightly shared. And Desire guessed that the man who supplied Alexander Grimstone with the key did so to gratify a passion older than love of money; and that probably he did not, evidence to the contrary notwithstanding, spend the whole night among the warm ashes of the forge. There was one thing and one only that puzzled her, and on that she eventually got light, for she asked Bolt point-blank.

'Tell me,' she said to him, 'do you mind telling me, why you always disliked Mr Alexander Grimstone so much?'

'Cause 'e killed my rabbits,' was the answer.

'Your rabbits?'

'Yes, long ago, 'afore 'e fell out with t'ode maister. 'E 'ad a lurcher, yaller mongrel, and I 'ad two rabbits, wild uns, they were, but I'd made 'em tame. They lived down by t'cut; I'd a box for 'em but they come'd in an' out as they liked; they knew me, they did, they used ter run inter my coat. I took 'em 'ome ter bed sometimes.'

'And he killed them?'

'Set 'is dorg at 'em when I warn't there. One was dead when I corned, t'other t' brute was maulin'. I took it away, but I 'ad ter kill it myself. He laughed.'

The dull eyes lighted at the recollection, and Desire suddenly perceived that Alexander Grimstone, who had ruined some and injured many, died because ten years ago he had let his dog kill two rabbits. But she perceived also that it was because he had destroyed the one thing a dull nature had managed to care for, and in the place of the one feeble, gentle emotion had put a sense of injustice and impotent anger and helpless resentment. Plants nearly indigenous to the nature, and dangerous things in a slow, unforgiving mind, very ignorant, very unimaginative, without sense of proportion or capacity for remorse.

But this was not till some time later. On this cold, grey afternoon in late September no-one knew why and how Alexander Grimstone died—except, of course, so far as the coroner and jury had decided—and no-one would seem to have greatly cared, except as a matter of curiosity.

Mrs Alexander had the appearance of caring. That is to say, she was announced to be 'prostrated with shock', and unable to see any one, except a female cousin and the friend at whose house she had been staying when the news reached her, and who had kindly accompanied her home. These two and the husband of one of them saw Peter when he felt compelled by duty to ask for his brother's widow, though he had not the least idea what he should have said to her had she seen him. He was much relieved at being refused, and listened with patient courtesy to the extravagant descriptions of woe poured upon him. He believed them, and felt very sorry for Mrs Alexander, which was quite unnecessary, as, the shock once recovered from, she would find a morbid excitement and satisfaction in the interest of her situation, and would most thoroughly enjoy the importance and consideration which she would deem her due. Her supporters at the River House were appreciating the situation as it was. They were keeping each other up very sympathetically; they had whiskies-and-sodas and champagne at odd times, and very appetizing bits of food brought to them on trays in odd places. There was a general feeling of importance and 'anything might happen' in the darkened house, a good deal of running to and fro to 'the poor dear' upstairs, and a good deal of very friendly talk with the servants, who, thus encouraged, naturally collected any scrap of gossip there was. Peter's coming was, of course, what was to be looked for, and also enjoyed. The women gave him gushing details of 'poor Flo's' condition; the cousin told him how she had managed to persuade her to eat a few oysters and the wing of a chicken. The friend recounted how she had given way when she had received the carefully-worded telegram, how she herself had declared there was something awful behind, she had a premonition here—somewhere in the region of her lungs. The man, allowing proper time for these proper things, spoke aside to Peter of its being fortunate that the widow would be left well provided for.

'We have to consider these things, we men of business, and it makes a difference, a considerable difference; when she's got over it a bit it'll make a difference to her. Luckily they only took this house by the year—seems as if they felt something might happen to make them flit. She can get out of it before Christmas—she never liked the place—and come and settle down somewhere cheerful, somewhere near us perhaps. Em thinks it would be a comfort to her, don't you, Em?'

Em, the more voluble of the two ladies, corroborated and then turned to Peter with questions. There were a lot of things Peter could tell better than anyone else—the finding of the body, the details of the inquest, his own opinions and suspicions; of course he would want to talk as much as they to hear. The two women were expansively sympathetic, the man opened another bottle of champagne, all three proposed to be melancholily, somewhat ghoulishly, convivial. But Peter did not drink champagne at odd times, and he was not by nature either ghoulish or convivial, and certainly not expansive. His present company had the effect of entirely freezing him; he briefly answered their questions without satisfying their curiosity, unconsciously and politely rebuffing their morbid thirst for information, thereby earning a very unfavourable opinion. Then, as soon as he could, he took his leave and made his way home in the windy twilight, feeling intensely lonely. Extraordinarily lonely, seeing that by the two deaths which had so recently occurred he had lost little beyond a burden and an enemy. But when one has very little it is something perhaps to lose even those; they at least are something for which to think, if not to live.

Chapter XXIII

The trains which go to Twycross usually wait a long time at Stoke; the one by which Desire Quebell was travelling did. She did not look out of window or bestow any interest on her fellow-travellers, but sat, hands folded, body still, with the unnatural and abnormal patience of one whose impatience is far beyond expression, and who, mentally, is burning coals for the furnace, hurrying stragglers for the guard, almost dragging the train for the laggard engine. Her whole self was concentrated on getting on, her very limbs ached with it as if it was a physical thing. This was the one journey of her life when she had no thought or interest for fellow-travellers or humours of the way, nothing that was done, no face she passed, made any impression upon her. She saw them, she saw thousands of things—small things which she would normally have overlooked, not merely the people but the number of their buttons, too; not merely the advertisements but the separate letters that composed them, her nerves were preternaturally alive and her mind raced like a clock with the pendulum off. But nothing made an impression on her and nothing stayed; between the words she read, between any two impressions she received, came the recurrent question. What trouble? What trouble? Robert's laconic telegram had not told. It had given no hint of what had happened or when it had happened, it had not even summoned her. Not that that occurred to her, to read and to go were all one. She had travelled as fast as she could since getting it. She had caught the night-train at Vichy, reached Paris in the early morning, crossed by the day boat, and, late into town by reason of the delayed boat train, had had no time to do anything but drive straight from Charing Cross to Euston Station, and now, four-and-twenty hours after receiving the telegram, she was at Stoke—waiting at Stoke! Waiting for the engine to get water, or the engine driver to get dinner, or for leisurely passengers to saunter the length of that interminable platform and choose some carriage where they saw a friend!

At last the train began to move again. Just as it did so she glanced out of window. There was a bookstall close by with newspaper placards hanging upon it, halfpenny papers of more or less local circulation, with names little known in London. She scanned the sensational headlines, as she had scanned the advertisement boards and everything else she passed, with the rapidity and unimpressionability of dream consciousness. Suddenly one word broke through and reached her mind—'Grimstone'. She saw and understood the whole line—'THE GRIMSTONE TRAGEDY. INQUEST TO-DAY'—and the next line of the next paper—'THE TWYCROSS MYSTERY. IS IT MURDER?'

She sprang to her feet.

'A paper!' she called, leaning far out of the window and sending her full voice sounding down the platform, with a note in it which made the paper boys start.

'A shilling for one of those!' she waved towards the placards and leaned still further out. The train was going fast now and the boys had some way to run, but one reached her; she flung out the shilling and seized the flimsy sheets. Then she sat back in her corner, a strange sick dizziness, unlike anything she had ever felt in her life before, possessed her. For a moment she held the paper unopened, some vital thing in her dropped before the shock, as springs sink before an earthquake. Then she pulled herself together and, with hands clammy and cold for all her magnificent health, opened the paper.

Ah! here it was—'THE TWYCROSS MYSTERY'. Her heart thumped heavily once, then began to beat very fast as she read, while her breath, before difficult, came in quite audible gasps.

There were two men on the opposite side of the carriage; they looked at her curiously. They had looked curiously when she had sprung up and called for a paper in a voice they had before heard of normal proportions, now of such vibrating power. They looked almost anxiously now.

She lowered the paper suddenly, dropped it on her lap, and her hands on it, then she leaned back with a long-drawn breath, shaking suddenly, almost as if she had the ague.

'Excuse me,' the elder man said, 'but I'm afraid you're not well.'

She started, for the first time remembering their presence. 'Thank you,' she said; 'I'm quite well.' Her voice shook a little over the last word, but she did not trouble to explain, and was entirely unembarrassed. The rest of the world slips down and goes out before the stress of the great emotions: one is not embarrassed by it, one is oblivious. With Desire it did not count, it was nothing—not there. She sat quietly in her corner, her mind, springing back with sudden rebound, now more swiftly at work than ever. She was going over a list of names—well-known names they were of the most famous lawyers in England. Gore's name passed among greater ones, but was dismissed, not because of his onetime connection with herself, but because he was not big enough to conduct the defence—if defence there had to be.

The newspaper did not suggest that Peter Grimstone had murdered his brother, although, as the placard conveyed, it inclined towards the view of murder by someone as much more picturesque. It contained comparatively little real information beyond a *résumé* of what had been in a previous issue or issues, and the information that the inquest was to be to-day, the day of publication. Here, evidently, the news was old, it was startling no longer, no-one much spoke of it. Clearly Robert had not thought it necessary to telegraph to her directly after the happening—had he forgotten, been busy, or preoccupied? Or was it that he had thought there was no call upon his promise then, but something had since arisen to demand its fulfilment? Fear sprang up at the thought. For a moment there had been relief, an almost ferocious relief when it was revealed who was dead in the 'Twycross Mystery', which of the Grimstones had suffered in the 'tragedy'. Rut now fear came back, a thousand fierce anxieties crowding in. Supposing—

The train stopped again! Oh, Good Lord! Was it only the station after Stoke? They had been, it seemed, several hours doing that piece—and were they going to stay here all night? They were taking in milk-cans, milk enough for a whole province! Was the train never going on? A crazy idea of somehow bribing the officials to run right through to Twycross, without regard for signals or milk-cans or passengers or anything, occurred to Desire. But she did not try it, she had not given way to any of the frantic impulses which had once or twice possessed her during her journey. She sat still with an enduring patience which made her very feet ache while the train waited, while it went on again, out into the dark country, while it stopped at some other grimy station—it was scheduled slow beyond Stoke—how unutterably, indescribably, unendurably slow no-one else possibly ever knew.

But it was over at last; Twycross was reached. Desire was out of the train, out of the station, almost before another carriage door was open. They would know here about the inquest, they would tell her the verdict and the common talk if she asked. But she did not, she could not have stood it, she could not speak. She passed the ticket collector, who recognized her, without a word, sprang into a fly and told the man to drive as hard as he could—with a freedom of language which was entirely unwomanly and an immense relief. The road was indifferent, the vehicle old, the progress really not very great, but one felt it, one felt as if some efforts were being made. A small gusty breeze that whirled the dead leaves in eddies was blowing; Desire leaned forward and felt it on her face, and that cheated her into a feeling of pace. They were slowing down now, the hill—she would have liked to get out and push up behind if it would save time, only it would not. What a long hill; she did not remember it was so long, it never seemed so long when she used to walk up with Mrs Grimstone. Ah, there were the elms at last, dimly seen against the dark sky—the top, they used to call them. They weren't quite but one might reckon them so. The level high road at last and the hills!

Desire's pulses suddenly slowed as she saw the dark shoulders of the hills rising on the left against the cloud sky. Almost like a palpable thing the quietness and the solitude that was here fell upon her—reposeful, overwhelming, belittling to a man and his impatience. She grew suddenly afraid, not with the sick, inward fear of what she would find at the journey's end, but with a childish trembling at her boldness in coming. Peter had not bidden her come, it was not he who had telegraphed to her. No-one had really sent for her, no-one knew she was coming, maybe she would not be wanted. Out here in the silence, under the shadow of the great hills that were always the same, things were different, she herself was different, cooler, less sure, less impetuous, much smaller. She stopped the fly a little before the solitary grey house was reached.

'I will get out here,' she said, and even the driver noticed the curious quietness that had taken the place of her former hot impatience.

She paid him and told him to take the slender luggage which was all she had had time to bring, to the house. Then she herself went in at a side gate which was standing just ajar, as Robert had left it when he went out on some errand to the town. She found her way into the yard; the buildings showed dim black outlines on her right, a mound of clay and a pile of waste ghostly white near at hand. She crossed quietly, picking her way with silent, familiar feet, and from choice keeping close to the house wall. The office window looked that way. It was lighted and unshuttered, it cast a square yellow patch on the ground and illuminated a space around it; she avoided the light, but when she was near glanced up at the window. Peter was there, at the desk which used to be her desk. His face was quite clear to her, not very different from when she saw it first or saw it last, not different at all—or else she had known that it would be thus—or else she had always seen it every day and all day since she left, and so knew.

She passed quickly, he had not seen her in the darkness without, and came to the door. For half a moment she paused, hesitancy, to which she was a stranger, holding her, then without knocking she opened the door and walked in.

To the threshold, no further; her self-reliance, her decision, everything deserted her then; she stood in the doorway shy, shrinking, just a woman who had loved and who had come unbidden.

Peter turned for a second, his face went white as a man who sees a ghost.

'Desire!'

She put a hand on the door-frame, a deprecating hand, and she smiled rather feebly.

And then the end came, suddenly, overwhelmingly, without words; a swift step that was almost a pounce, a crushing grip that nearly hurt, a sense of yielding that was divine; a pressure that halted the breath in her body, and a kiss that was a wordless contract which never could be broken.

Mary, the taciturn, having set the supper, left it for ten minutes. At the end of that time, finding Peter had not come, she went to fetch him—she did not approve of unpunctuality nor yet of letting food get cold. She gave a perfunctory knock on the office door, opening it at the same time.

'Supper's ready,' she said.

She looked in as she spoke, and so saw Desire.

'Why!' she exclaimed, with something near welcome in her voice. 'You here, miss! I didn't know you'd come, I didn't hear you!'

'I came by the back way,' Desire explained. 'I left my luggage to come by the front; by the way, I suppose it has come?'

'Jane must have took it in,' Mary said; 'the little hussy don't half the time tell me what she does.'

'That's all right,' Desire said; 'that'll be all right.'

She turned to Peter. 'Let's go to supper,' she said hastily, as if to prevent further parley with Mary; 'it will be getting cold.'

Her eyes were bright and eager, but with fear. She had for a moment forgotten the grim shadow that was over the house; for that one brief, perfect moment she had forgotten everything. But now, with the coming of Mary there had also come remembrance; with the jerk of reaction all the fears which had possessed her before, and others born of more recent emotions, swept down on her.

'Peter,' she said, as he followed her to the other room, 'tell me about it, I can stand no more.'

But Peter hardly understood what it was she asked.

'Did you—,' she said desperately. 'How did Alexander die?'

'I don't know.'

'You don't know?' She looked at him for half a moment. 'You don't?'—then suddenly and without any warning she burst into tears.

Desire was not given to displays of this sort, such a thing had never occurred in her life before, but then other things which had never occurred in her life before had done so that day. She wept as only physically strong women whose emotions have suddenly got beyond control can weep, the weeping as primitive and complete in its abandonment as the kiss had been, a breaking up of the unsuspected deeps of her nature, a very tornado of tears, beyond control and beyond embarrassment.

And Peter wisely did not try to help or hinder her, perhaps he knew that the unprecedented upheaval was physical more than mental. At all events he left her to herself for a time, attempting neither soothing nor sympathy until the first passion had spent itself and she was recovering a little of her lost self-mastery.

'I am so sorry,' she gasped unsteadily at last. 'I've never made such a fool of myself before: I didn't know I could. I ought to have fled out of the room when I felt it coming on; I might have spared you this spectacle.'

'It seems to me it is I who might have spared you,' Peter said remorsefully. 'I didn't know it mattered so much to you.'

'I suppose it wouldn't matter to you if I were hung?' she returned, laughter hysterically catching up her tears. 'Oh, lend me your handkerchief; mine wants wringing out, and I've cried the dust of travel off my face in patches.'

'Peter,'—she looked up suddenly as she dried her eyes —'are you hurt at my not being sure you had no hand in this? You're not? Some men would have been, I suppose. Of course I didn't think you'd deliberately murdered Alexander, but accidents do happen, you know; one might have happened that night in the winter when you thrashed him. I didn't know in the least what had taken place, I only knew the long quarrel and the provocation you'd had, and just what the newspapers said, which, of course, is mostly nonsense. You see how it came about?'

Peter did. 'What would you have done if I had had a hand in it?' he asked.

'Got you off,' she answered promptly. 'I thought of it all the way from Stoke. I knew nothing about it till then, I decided Lawton was the man you would want; he is, too, supposing anything were to turn up, anything horrible was said. But, of course, it won't be now; they've had the inquest? And the verdict? I haven't heard it, you must remember.'

'Accidental death.'

She repeated the words after him, 'Accidental death'; then she nodded, but her lips twitched and her hands shook. Her relief was immense, but with it there came an exhaustion, sudden and temporary, but almost as great while it lasted as the strained emotion had been.

'Tell me about it, about everything—some other time,' she said weakly. 'Give me something to drink. I feel as if I should spread out flat. I didn't sleep much last night, and it was a vile crossing.'

Peter brought her some brandy; then he put the somewhat cooled food down to the fire to get hot again. It did not seem to him advisable to ring for Mary to take it out and reheat it. When he had done that he wheeled the sofa to the fire, and, without warning, carried Desire to it. She was a big woman and a heavy, but he lifted her easily.

'How strong you are!' she said. 'I believe you could hurt me if you tried. You did nearly hurt me; you crushed all the breath out of me when you—in the office—'

The sentence was not very explicit but Peter no doubt understood, for he asked, 'Did you think I might have had a hand in Alexander's death, then?'

'I didn't think,' she returned; 'I didn't think about anything. Besides, what did it matter?'

'It would not have mattered to you?'

'Of course not.' She leaned against the cushion he placed for her, her vitality coming back. 'You are you, whatever you do,' she said. 'It's what you are, not what you do, that matters; lots of doing is just accident and impulse, and, anyhow, I don't care, do you? You can't care for what I do, you must care in spite of it; I do such abominable things, things I'm heartily ashamed of. You do uninspired things, too, sometimes. You sent me away last February. Why did you do it?'

'Because I thought you ought to go. I wanted you to—I mean, I thought you ought to go back to your proper place—the reasonable part of me thinks it still.'

'The artificial part of you,' Desire said, 'the ridiculous, unnatural, conceited part.'

Later, when the food was hot and Peter had brought hers to the sofa and persuaded her to eat, she returned to the subject. 'Do you know what I think of that sending away?' she asked. 'I think it was the one untrue thing I have known you do. It was untrue if you—if you cared. You had no business to do it; it was divorce of soul, a wilful stinting and stunting of your life and mine for a conventional idea. It is a conventional idea purely that money to spend and nothing to do in the company of others similarly situated must necessarily be the best thing on earth, and the goal and hope of every one who has had it, and a good many who have not.'

But Peter only smiled, recognizing recovered energy in her tone. Then the smile went. 'The alternative here was not much,' he said gravely; 'it is not much, a poor life, narrow and small—and you are used to and fit for something better.'

'You might, before dismissing me, have passed the compliment of asking my opinion,' Desire observed.

'That was impossible,' he said; 'besides, if you had thought, most likely you would have seen it, too; it is only by not thinking that anything else could come about. We didn't think just now—I mean, I did not; I forgot everything but—you.'

Desire laughed softly. 'For once,' she said, 'no, for the second—third time—you acted on impulse. Peter, have you ever noticed that when you act so you always win?'

'Yes, I have noticed,' he answered; and her laughing eyes dropped shyly before his gaze.

'Do you know,' she said, after a pause, 'I used to want a man to care with his mind only for my mind only; at one time I thought you did.'

'I care for the whole of you with the whole of me—mind, body and soul, and it always will be so whatever you do or I do, in all circumstances and at all times, till life ends.'

She put a hand on his. 'Thank you,' she said softly, and after that they sat silent for some time.

By and by Mary came to clear the supper things, or rather she brought Jane to do that; she came herself to look after Desire, she considered Peter quite incapable of doing so.

'You'll be just tired out and wanting to go to bed,' she said.

'I'm just longing to wash my face,' Desire announced; 'you pottery people use the smokiest coal in the United Kingdom on your trains; one can't put one's nose out of window without getting a smut on it.'

She went upstairs with the old woman, to the room which used to be hers. But she did not go to bed, she had no intention of doing so for several hours. She unpacked what baggage she had; Mary, totally unused to such offices, assisting and talking the while—also a thing to which she was not usually given. But then Desire had found some way of thawing her; the old woman liked her and looked upon her as in a way part of the family and, since a woman, a member of the superior sex, and a capable one, in spite of some eccentricities. She answered all Desire's questions, gave her quite a lot of information, and altogether conversed so garrulously that when Desire went downstairs again she knew a good deal about what had occurred.

Before she went down she glanced in the glass and was not pleased with her own appearance; her face was pale and there were dark circles, caused by her recent uncontrolled weeping, around her eyes, her brilliancy was considerable dimmed.

'You do look tired, miss,' Mary said, observing her. 'You want a good night's rest.'

'I want a little rouge,' Desire corrected gaily. 'You haven't got that, I suppose? I thought not. Well, I don't expect Peter will mind how I look.'

Mary, scandalized at the idea of rouge, was yet more surprised at the reference to Peter; clearly it was absurd to her that anyone should imagine Peter had an opinion with regard to appearance, or that it mattered if he had.

And Desire laughed happily; she knew that it was nothing to Peter how she looked; it never had been, and never would be; he saw her through all her moods and variations, the becoming and unbecoming, the alluring and repellent were alike to him—nothing. He had seen to the core of her, and it was that he had taken and held.

Downstairs Peter was waiting for her, he evidently did not expect her to go to bed yet awhile. He had drawn the chairs to the fire just as they had been drawn that February evening when she had realized that she could not stay, and that the thing as it had been was at an end. She remembered it now as she sat down, but was too shy to refer to it.

She only said, with a little contented sigh, 'It's good to be back.'

She felt for her cigarette-case. 'Let us now,' she said, 'smoke the smoke of peace; I haven't smoked all day, merely wasted tobacco. When I'm worried I smoke, also when I'm not, and when I have things on my mind or nerves; but to-day—there's no word for to-day. It's a poor language, ours!'

'It's a poor fool that caused you all this,' Peter remarked.

But Desire only looked across at him and smiled. 'Give me a match,' she said, 'and let's talk sober business.'

And they talked it and talked till far on into the night; and mostly it was business, for there was a good deal to tell and to explain; and mostly it was sober enough, for shadows still hung about the firm of Grimstone, although with Desire's return, as with her first coming, they seemed suddenly to have lightened. It was not till after midnight that Desire allowed her own past concerns to come in for mention, then she said cheerfully—

'To-morrow I must write to cousin Phoebe, and tell her that, according to custom, I have "slippit awa". She doesn't know where I'm gone, or why. I just wired her from Paris, but I had no special information to give then, so I didn't give it. She won't be pleased when she hears; she will, I am persuaded, at once destroy her will and make another, cutting me off without the traditional shilling. Do you mind?'

'I should mind very much if you had money,' Peter said emphatically; 'at least,' he corrected himself, remembering her early surroundings, 'it's hard on you.'

Desire laughed. 'I have never been so happy in my life, as the six months I hadn't money. I shan't want any for a long time. I have most of my jewelry and stacks more clothes, enough to last me for years; and for the rest—you know how economical I can be.'

There was another letter Desire would have to write tomorrow—to Julian Lee, to apologize for misleading him, if she had misled him, and to tell him briefly that she was going to marry Peter. It should have been difficult to write, but it did not strike her that way; everything to her was quite simple and plain now, set in place by the one master emotion and master happening of her life; all else naturally fell into place beside that as inevitably as day following night.

She told Peter about Lee. 'You know,' she said, 'I had no business to abuse you for doing an untrue thing in sending me away, seeing that I was more than half thinking about doing a thing quite as untrue, more so, in fact. I guess I should have done it, too; it is quite likely I should have married him. Made him quite a tolerable wife maybe—he'd have given me no end of rope—and enjoyed life fairly well on the whole. It seems odd, doesn't it? I should have enjoyed the small things, not knowing—not knowing the big.' Her voice grew soft over the last words.

'And you'—she looked across at Peter. 'I suppose if I had done it you wouldn't have broken your heart; you'd have felt you'd done your duty in sending me away, that I had really gone back to my place, and you would have settled down in yours moderately content. It strikes me we are not heroic, for the heroic, missing Paradise, put up permanently in Hell—and we should have missed Paradise. What Paradise! Oh, Peter, if we missed it now it would be Hell!'

'We can't,' Peter said; 'no matter what happens now we shan't have missed it. That reminds me, when will you marry me?'

The question was put simply, it was the only thing approaching a proposal that Peter ever made; but Desire did not notice that; according to her somewhat unusual standards they were more than half married already.

'I don't know,' she said thoughtfully; 'when do you think?'

'I suppose it had better not be till after the funeral,' Peter said; 'it hardly seems respectful to my father.'

'No,' she agreed; 'no, I think not, we'll wait till after.'

'I wonder if you ought to stay here?' Peter said tentatively, as the idea suddenly occurred to him.

'Of course. I'm not going to begin bothering about that sort of thing at my time of life.' And they did not bother.

Of course there were those who said a marriage between Desire and Peter would not and could not answer, but that did not in the least prevent it from doing so. Neither of them had anyone with a title to be concerned in their doings—which, however, never prevents some disinterested people from having and giving an opinion. Mrs Alexander Grimstone was very emphatic in disapproval; she also decided that Desire was an improper person and not to be recognized; which was something of a relief, as Desire might otherwise have felt it her duty to try and be civil to the widow for the short time she remained in the neighbourhood. Of the rest of Twycross, neither Desire nor Peter had ever known much of the good folk there, and the opinion held among them, if one was held, never reached them. In the course of time Desire made some friends in the little town, in very various ranks of life—as she made some friends among the hill people, the hooligans of the pottery towns and in the great houses that scattered the county. And it must be confessed she made the top and bottom sort first, and the middle a long way last. From which it will be seen she remained always herself, flashing meteor-like on social horizons, accepted, in spite of every sane and sound reason to the contrary, wherever and whenever she chose, herself supremely unaware alike of success or singularity. But she did not choose very often, never unless Peter did, for her life was his, all else was accident, byproduct. All their real life was in the grey house by the hills, in the work they chose for themselves and the children that were born to them.

Desire's people, those to whom she used to belong, naturally did not approve of her marriage. Lee, it is to be feared, was not so angry as he ought to have been at her treatment of him; he was bitterly disappointed but at the same time not entirely surprised. He knew all along, whatever she promised, he was not sure of her until the ring was fairly on. So, with a generosity she admired, he forgave her—men did forgive Desire a good deal—and was friend still, to the great scandal of Lady Quebell and the entire satisfaction of Peter, who could as soon have been jealous of himself as Desire. Miss Quebell, as Desire foresaw, did not forgive her but left her money, and even the pearls, which Desire returned, elsewhere.

They had not much money, these two; Desire practically none, Peter, though his father's heir, not much. Then were his books, it is true, but they never sold largely; they brought in all told, perhaps, an average of £70 a year. They gradually grew in number, though there were never very many of them, for they were produced so slowly thought over and talked over and lived in, the work of scanty but loving leisure. Eventually they achieved some fame, in a way a curiously wide one, among rather a wide circle of people, but chiefly among those who do not talk much of what they read, especially when they feel it as the grip of friend's hand in a dark place. It was not literature or legacy which supplied Desire and Peter with their small income when it was small, or their growing one when it grew—it was Grimstones'. The work they did together, the improvements Peter made and the inventions he patented gradually did build them up a good sufficiency. In the end they were almost comfortably off as Desire's people count wealth, quite rich as the potters count it.

But what did it matter? Not much to them either way. As Desire said, 'It's a bore, of course, to be without money sometimes, but one can be very comfortable without much of it. One can't be more than happy, and we should be that, you know, if we made brown crocks with our own hands one month and took the road with them and peddled them ourselves the next. Oh, Peter, we should be happy if we did that!'

She held to that opinion to her dying day, probably correctly, and she announced it first on the Sunday before they were married—a Sunday when they went up the hill together to look at the fox terrier's grave.

On that Sunday they did another thing too, one which seemed like part of the marriage rite to them. They came home by the way they came six months ago when they last came down the hill—by the path that passes the deserted chapel. Now, as then, it was near twilight when they reached the little grey building; now, as then, they looked in and saw the old man kneeling at his service alone. With one accord they paused.

'Desire,' Peter said, and he bared his head as he spoke, 'shall we thank God together?' She put her hand in his, and they went in and knelt down side by side among the shadows.

When the darkness had all fallen the old man came out. He was alone, as he had been every Sunday these many years, as he always would be, for no-one to his knowledge ever shared his lonely orisons. On the doorstep something glimmered in the fading light—a gold coin and a woman's ring lying, placed side by side. He looked at them in wondering amazement; to him it was as if they had dropped from heaven, nearly a miracle.

But below him there were two who had that day paid their vows—two for whom the world also yet held miracles, for they walked together along a steep path on the grey hillside, a path that led to where lights gleaming through the gloom spoke of home.

THE END

Notes

BY KATE MACDONALD

Chapter I

yellow, or purple: Desire is referring to the cheap ephemeral fiction and very early 'true crime' stories published in 'yellowbacks', which specialised in melodrama, and, possibly, what we now call 'purple' prose: overwritten, showy writing aiming at sensation and effects on the emotions.

Apostles of the Ugly: Austin is referring to the Edwardian fashion for coteries of young men (occasionally admitting favoured, high-status women) with common interests in aesthetic and ideological ideals. The Cambridge Apostles were the most famous of these.

The great BP: the great British public.

Chapter II

supers: supernumerary parts, non-speaking parts on the popular stage.

toilet: toilette, hair, dress and make-up.

Chapter VIII

cut: canal

Chapter IX

palm bush: possibly gorse, or *planta genista*, the common broom.

Chapter X

congé: French term for notice or dismissal that moved through English etiquette terminology from the formal farewell made on leaving (*pour prendre congé*, to take one's leave, abbreviated to PPC on the visiting card left for this purpose by the departing person), to the dismissal of an inferior, or a rejected suitor. Here Lady Quebell is being dismissive.

Chapter XII

gauged yokes and val. insertion and bias fronts: technical aspects of dress-making and tailoring, suggesting that the home dress-making that these women are capable of is of a very high standard, and that Desire's ignorance of this particular skill—clearly common-place for women of her age at a different social level—reflects her lack of education or training.

Chapter XIII

chiffons: delicate fabric, here used by Desire to mean all dress fabrics, a subject she knows very little about.

Chapter XV

hollow ware: jugs, cups and bowls

'change panic: the chaos and desperate selling of stocks and shares that ensues if there is a panic at the Exchange, ie the bank, here used as a metaphor for the most alarming and unpredictable of times.

Chapter XVI

led plates: Desire is joking about the competition in making plates being a game of whist, in which one of the four suits of cards becomes the trump or winning suit, if it is 'led' first at the beginning of each game. Alexander has unwittingly made the manufacture of plates the winning suit, in which Peter and Desire have an advantage.

Chapter XVIII

A bad quarter of an hour: literal translation of the French idiom *un mauvais quart d'heure*, a synecdoche for a brief though intensely uncomfortable experience.

Chapter XIX

crape-bound: crape was the standard black fabric used for all mourning accoutrements, from hat-bands and armbands for men, to the decorations on the funeral hearse, to trimmings on ladies' hats and dresses to temporarily make them into mourning wear.

down train: on a single-track railway line trains would be instructed to wait for each other to pass, and the up train would be the one heading for the nearest large terminus. The down train would be the one leaving it, for less populated regions.

Venus of what's-his-name: Venus Anadyomene, Greek for Venus rising from the sea; a very popular theme in classically-derived paintings and sculpture in the nineteenth century, giving opportunities for the close scrutiny of the naked female body. The irrepressible little man is airing a slightly risqué subject for mixed company, and making plain his appreciation of Desire's physicality.

Chapter XX

Boojum: central but absent character in Lewis Carroll's 'The Hunting of the Snark' (1874–76). It is the object of the hunters' desires and fears, and when it attacks, its prey disappears.

Tivoli: named after the celebrated pleasure gardens in eighteenth-century Paris and nineteenth-century Copenhagen (still active), 'Tivoli' was a common name for British music halls and variety theatres. For Desire to take a man there as the hostess was breaking several important social codes for her class and sex for the period, and to take a curate there, as part of his education, was similarly scandalous, as prostitutes and drinking would not have been unknown there.

Time cannot change her, Nor custom stale her infinite variety: Lee misquotes Enobarbus' speech on Cleopatra from *Antony and Cleopatra*: 'Age cannot wither her, nor custom stale her infinite variety' (II, 2). Again, Desire is compared to a classical figure of irresistible allure.

Chapter XXI

saggars: ceramic protective boxes used for firing delicate or vulnerably-shaped pottery objects or vessels.